Gods
of
Ruin

J.S.B. MORSE

COPYLEFT ⊛ 2022

Gods of Ruin: A Political Thriller

www.GodsOfRuin.com

Published in the United States by New Classic Books, an imprint of Code Publishing.
For distribution opportunities, please contact publishing@code-interactive.com.

ISBN 1-60020-048-6
978 1-60020-048-9

First Edition

For lovers of liberty everywhere,
may the muse live on.

Gods of Ruin

PART 1:
THE RIOT ACT

One

"Rum or whiskey?" Com DeGroot asked himself as he let his eyes drift over a brochure. The well-dressed, lanky man sat slouched in a chocolate brown leather sofa in the dimly lit, air-conditioned living room of the Séjour Luxueux Grand Suite, ignoring the din of the television in front of him as well as the party in the adjacent room. His focus was on the small advertisement in his hand, which declared: "Starting your own micro-distillery is easy!" Com DeGroot believed it. If the slaphappy drunken fools in the brochure could do it, surely he could, too. Money wasn't an issue—he still had plenty of that. Plus, as the brochure stated, the whole process was easy. The only thing Com had to decide was what liquor he would produce at his very own microdistillery. "Rum or whiskey?" he softly asked himself.

Com let a smile creep over his stylishly gaunt face at the newfound dream of running a distillery. He would invent clever mixed drinks, meet new people every day, and help them get drunk. There would be no stress and no one telling him what to do. And there would be no chance for fail-ure either, not like with the two previous life goals he had set for himself. It would be the perfect existence. At the very least, he could join his cus-tomers in getting inebriated for the rest of his life. Com knew he couldn't fail at that.

"Let's talk about former professional basketball star, Com DeGroot," the glamorous television commentator Michelle Torres said, reminding Com of his first major life failure. Com winced. The mention of his previ-ous occupation brought more agony to the solitary viewer. Yes, he had played in the pros, but only for two seasons and only until an untimely rendezvous between his right knee and a sturdy power forward had ended his career. It was certainly not the career the player had envisioned when he had entered the league.

Com did have good memories from his stint as a professional basketball player though, including the two-week period he had led the league in scoring and the game in which he had nailed a buzzer-beater to finish a thrilling comeback victory and put his team in playoff contention. And even after the career-ending injury, his team had fulfilled Com's contract and filled his bank account, allowing him comfortable financial security for the rest of his life. But Com had gone from the best in the league to the best that could have been in a matter of seconds with his injury, and the taste of failure was impossible for Com to get past mentally.

Undaunted by Mr. DeGroot's self-deprecation, Michelle Torres continued her report on the room's fifty-two-inch illuminated glass panel. She was quickly able to remind Com of his second major failure and the reason why he was slouching comfortably in the Séjour Luxueux hotel that night, considering a career in intoxication. "Early exit polls show that incumbent Phil Dyer of Delaware will beat out challenger Com DeGroot and remain in his seat for another six years." Com was a candidate for U.S. Senator, and he was not going to win the election that night.

The candidate DeGroot briefly thought about his campaign but shuddered. He had it in the bag just weeks earlier, they had all said, but he blew it in the run-up to the election. All of his campaign promises to shake up the system and make a difference sounded pathetic, corny, and naïve to Com as he sat there in disillusionment.

Com nodded to himself and whispered, "Rum."

Michelle Torres persisted. "The popular DeGroot had a sizeable lead in his race, running on the platform of 'Security First,' until the challenger's infamous meltdown at a town hall debate last month." With that, an all-too-familiar video clip began to play on the wide screen in front of Com. It depicted a meek-looking man from the town hall audience posing a question: "Okay, a lot of us have not recovered from the economic depression over ten years ago. I personally have been out of work for over three years and I have a partner and a child to take care of—um,

4

not to mention my, uh, disrepaired back that keeps me from doing any manual occupation. I can't even, um, sit at a desk without being uncomfortable and I'm like on a two-year waiting list to see an orthopedic surgeon because *you* people in Washington won't properly fund the National Health Services! As senator, as it were, what are you going to do to help me and people like me get a job so I can get better health—"

"You know what?" An impatient Com DeGroot cut off the questioner in the video. "Just shut up. I've heard your type whine and whine ever since I entered this race, and I'm sick of it." There was a nervous murmur from the audience in the video. The questioner's eyes bulged out and Com continued. "No, look, it's not the role of government to take care of you like a little helpless baby. The role of government is to protect you from the evil people who want to kill you, period. No. I'm not going to lie to you like this guy over here." Com waved his arm toward his debate opponent. "I'm not going to tell you that I will fix your back and get you a job and better health care and then cut everyone's taxes at the same time. No, I'm going to actually tell you the truth. It can't be done. And it shouldn't. You need to stand up for yourself because our civilization cannot last if people like you continue to mooch off the rest of us. Whatever happened to John F. Kennedy's plea to 'Ask not what your country can do for you, ask what you can do for your country?' I'm sick of it. This country is full of worthless moochers now, including you, sir. Take, take, take. That's all you do and you don't care who you're taking it from. How about you *take* something else for a change? How about you *take* some responsibility for yourself?"

Com looked away but the questioner became excited. "How dare you—" The crowd exploded in disbelief.

"You won't just go away, huh? You're like a one-hundred-and-fifty-pound wad of chewing gum that someone left on the sidewalk and I just stepped in. Just shut up. Next."

Michelle Torres returned to the screen. "That was followed up with another outburst two weeks later." Com was shown again on the screen, this time at a press conference responding to another question. "I don't even know if I want to be Senator if idiots like you are going to be my constituents. Look, we need surveillance, ID cards, the works. If people aren't doing anything wrong, they shouldn't mind a little Big Brother watching over them."

Reclining in the plush sofa, Com covered his face with his hands to avoid watching the train wreck he had created. He dug his fingers into his tightly-cropped hair and scalp. Michelle Torres explained how those remarks had led to a sharp fall in the polls in the week preceding the election, then she turned to a political analyst in the studio. "Well, Sam, the only things that have been consistent in the DeGroot campaign are his unpredictable sound bites, and the early exit poll numbers show that they didn't help his cause. At this point, he's down by two points and it appears that Mr. DeGroot will not unseat incumbent Phil Dyer. In your opinion, does he have a chance?"

"Michelle, it really doesn't look like it," the scrawny voice emanated from the overweight analyst's face. "It's still too close to call, but he's lost so much momentum recently—he's really a loose cannon and I don't think the voters of Delaware, much less the population as a whole, are willing to put up with antics like his. It looks like the voters have finally come to their senses."

"Thank you, Sam. In other election news," Michelle Torres announced, "popular civil rights champion, Senator Duane D. Delano of Vermont, has won reelection easily. It looks like he can now get started on his self-proclaimed primary goal of taking down the failed charter city in Texas."

Sam added, "That's right, Michelle. It looks like the next stop on that Delano civil rights train is Ur, Texas, a shocking place where *corporations* dictate human rights."

Com slowly arched his neck back, as though to mentally block out the news on the screen, and let out a growl.

"It can't be all that bad." The soft voice came from a silhouette in the doorway between the living room and the boisterous party next door. Com jerked his head toward the voice and frowned. Com's visitor meandered toward the sofa and came into the light. It was Noni Alvarez, a twenty-three-year-old campaign staffer. Her brunette hair was perfectly curled, her skin was a flawless hazelnut complexion, and she owned a pair of light green eyes. But Com looked at the television monitor instead of at his alluring staffer. She sat down in a comfortable pose and draped her arm around Com's neck. Noni's voice was compassionate and serious. "Is it?"

Com looked at Noni, then returned to the brochure in his hand. "I'm going to start a micro-distillery."

Noni's eyes widened, as she had thought he wanted to be a legislator.

"What do you think? Rum?"

Noni puckered her lips and shrugged. "I don't know. Are you thirsty? Do you want me to fix you a drink?"

"Not yet. But I'm going to need a stiff one after they call the race."

Noni looked at her boss longingly.

"I'm such a numb nut!" He shook his head. "Anyone could have just kept their mouth shut and told them what they wanted to hear . . . I look like a fucking ass clown in those clips!" He spewed out.

The intern scrunched her face and reached for Com's head as if to embrace or do something more. "It's okay. You're still a great man." She moistened her raspberry-flavored lips. "Even if not enough voters realize that." It wasn't poetry, but Com appreciated Noni's sentiment. He could smell her sweet citrus perfume as she inched near him, but he concentrated on the television screen. Com's eyes dropped to Noni's heaving breast momentarily and then back to the news. Noni dropped her hand as she turned toward the television as well.

"Whoa, is this the champagne room in here?" Kevin Donovan yelled, announcing his presence.

"Shut the hell up, Kevin," Com responded dryly, implying that nothing inappropriate was going on.

Undeterred, Kevin walked over to Com's right side, opposite Noni, and patted the candidate on the shoulder. Even when they were sitting down, Kevin was noticeably shorter than Com, a characteristic Kevin made up for—in his mind—with extremely expensive clothes and a nice watch. Kevin was Com's campaign director, and he was energetic despite the gloomy mood in the suite's living room. Kevin unnecessarily pushed back his perfectly combed auburn hair and glanced at the television.

"Down two, Kevin," Com said as if to blame his campaign director.

"Look," Kevin assured Com, "it ain't over 'til the fat lady sings, right?"

"I lost, what, fifteen points to that bastard in the last two weeks? Fifteen points! I'm toast. My goose is cooked. No, my goose has been lit up with a fucking blowtorch and stamped out with an anvil. My goose is obliterated," was Com's reply.

"Well, we'll see," Kevin huffed, letting Com's mood affect him, then pointed to the television.

Com turned to him, "Don't you have some director duties to take care of or something?"

"Campaign's over, Com. I'm off until we're in Washington and I'm staffing a lot of slutty interns." Kevin realized his company, "No offense, Noni."

Noni blew the comment off. "Shut up, spuds."

Potatoes, Com thought to himself. "Maybe I should make vodka. Potato vodka."

Kevin scrunched his face and looked at Com with bewilderment, then shook off his confusion. "Oh yeah, Senator Thurston called about ten minutes ago to congratulate you."

"For what?"

"I don't know, a good campaign, I guess."

"Oh, yippity-freekin-doo-dah," Com said dejectedly. "I'm going to Disney World. I suck."

The three sat in a bearably uncomfortable silence for a half a minute until Michelle Torres returned to the screen.

"Okay," she said, pressing her finger to an invisible earpiece. "We're getting word—yes, we are going to call the Delaware senate race." The campaign party next door hushed. Com allowed a bit of adrenaline to run through his veins, perking him up. "And it's Senator Dyer." Michelle Torres paused briefly as the three viewers sunk into the couch. Com had known it was going to happen, but the shock of defeat still hit him like a brick. "*Losing*," Michelle Torres continued. "That's right, Mr. DeGroot, former basketball star, will take the state of Delaware for the Republicans in the Senate. In what appears to be the surprise upset of the evening after early exit polls indicated a convincing win for Dyer . . . ."

The crowd next door erupted, and Kevin Donovan jumped up from the couch and began beating his chest like Tarzan and screaming like a wild banshee. Noni grinned knowingly and squinted at Com as he sat upright on the sofa. His eyes were bulging and he looked around the room in shock. The candidate-turned-senator-elect gathered his bearings, then put the micro-distillery brochure into his jacket's breast pocket as a smile crept over his face. I knew it, he thought to himself.

On the television, Michelle Torres turned to the political analyst. "What do you think about that, Sam?"

"I definitely thought he could hold on to the slight lead that he took into the polls," the overweight man pronounced. "He really had it all along."

Noni gleamed at Com. She stood and extended her hand as if to escort her boss. "Mr. Senator, I believe you have an acceptance speech to give."

Two

Com DeGroot stepped into the elevator with Kevin Donovan and took a deep breath. Kevin sorted through files on his tablet computer while Com looked up at the ceiling.

"Don't need our concession speech," Kevin said in a celebratory tone and swiped the tablet monitor, getting rid of the document. "Here we go. This is a copy of your speech." Kevin handed the computer to Com. "It's pretty much the same stump speech you made every day of the campaign, but a little more meaningful, since you're going to actually be making good on these promises now."

Com looked at the speech then drew his eyes upward. "Oh my God," he said. "I'm going to be Senator."

Kevin turned to him with a stern look and an index finger pointed upward. "No . . . you are going to be fucking Senator of the United States of America!"

Com laughed.

"You da man!" Kevin yelled.

The elevator slowed to a stop and the doors opened to an empty service hallway in the bowels of the hotel. Kevin started walking toward the stage door one hundred yards from the elevator as Com reviewed his speech.

"You might want to mention the Internet security bill, too. That's a hot topic today," Kevin noted.

"Oh, yeah? What's that about?" Com wondered as he continued to peruse his speech.

"We want to link up every electronic device, every mobile, to a secure federal network so that we can track terrorists and other criminal punk asses."

"Right, control the whole thing so we can smoke 'em out where those bastards are festering," Com added.

"You got it, Com!" Kevin stopped walking and turned to his boss. Crowd noise from the victory banquet echoed through the service hall. "Look, the voters have spoken and they anointed you. They are calling on you to start making things happen. Now it's time to get some work done."

Com smiled and handed back the tablet computer. "Let's go to work, then," Com said before jumping up the stairs leading to the back stage.

* * *

"Politicians lie?" Com asked sarcastically adding fuel to the fire of excitement he had created in the crowd of supporters gathered in the victory banquet hall. The large, boisterous crowd seemed to be familiar with the question from the campaign because they all joined him in his enthusiastic response as he shook his head. "Not this guy!" A group of happy donors and campaign staffers congregated around the senator-elect on the stage, all laughing and clapping. "When I make a promise, I keep it."

Com had worked the crowd into a frenzy with his short acceptance speech and was wrapping it up in front of a crowd that wanted more. Each rowdy supporter in attendance in the packed hall was hanging on his every word. The stage lights shone down on the senator-elect, bringing back memories of the spotlight he had owned while playing professional basketball. Throughout his speech, Com was confident, irreverent, and he exuded authority. It was as if Com DeGroot was born for this moment—he was a star once again.

"And so, when I say that I promise all of you helping me celebrate and every American out there watching, that I will fight to restore a

11

government that is of the people, by the people, and for the people—a government that our Founding Fathers would be proud of instead of this ever-increasing nanny state that we have now. I will fight to restore a government that is truthful and transparent to its constituents, and one that follows the law of the land—that hallowed document we call the Constitution.

"To do that, I have to make one more promise. I promise that I will make this country more secure by the end of my first term in Congress. I am going to hunt down every terrorist out there until they're wiped off the face of the planet. And they won't be able to hide in the virtual world anymore either. I'm going after them on the Internet and on their mobile devices. We're going to create a network of communication that is safe and secure, not one that terrorists can manipulate in order to intimidate and bully the American public. This will not stand, my word is my bond. I'm going to make 2023 the year we secure this great country again."

Com looked out to the crowd. He quickly surveyed his audience and spotted some familiar faces. He recognized some young campaign volunteers. He noticed a mildly famous actor who had been supportive throughout the campaign and an old basketball teammate. After a brief hesitation, Com returned to the teleprompter to remind him where he was in his speech.

"The people elected me for a reason, to protect them, and I intend to make good on that. Now this campaign sure puts on a good party." Com surveyed the banquet hall. "But I have a suggestion. Let's take this party to Washington!" Com thrust his hand in the air and waited for an outburst of applause to die down. "Thank you! Thank you! God bless you all." He pumped his fist and then waved at the crowd as they erupted in cheer. Confetti and red, white, and blue balloons dropped from the ceiling while "We Are the Champions" played on a surround-sound system.

The senator-elect turned to find the stage exit when Kevin Donovan walked up behind him and slapped him on the back. "Com, I need you to shake some hands."

"Great, somebody else want to bow down to the next senator from the great state of Delaware?" Com said jokingly.

"Maybe not bow down," Kevin corrected.

Com looked at his chief and nodded, then Kevin directed the senator-elect to a group of major campaign donors. Mr. Donovan introduced an elderly lady, then a tall older man to Com. The shorter staffer then motioned to a man standing nearby and yelled over the noise into Com's ear. "You remember this guy, Hank 'fat wallet' Pierpont?"

Mr. Pierpont was a broad-shouldered man with a loud plaid sports jacket and a red tie. He was jovial, rotund, and had a cocktail in his hand.

"Hank!" Com yelled and reached for the donor's hand.

"You lucky son of a bitch, you pulled it out!" Hank gave a burly chuckle. "Congratulations."

"What are you talking about? I knew I had it all along. I was never going to let down my most important donor." Com flattered the man through a grin and continued the handshake, which Mr. Pierpont did not seem to want to let go.

Hank leaned into the senator-elect but still had to yell over the crowd noise and music. "Hey listen, I'm really glad to support you and be a part of this campaign. I want to continue to help, too, but, you know, there are obstacles in my way to being the most productive I can be; some regulatory obstacles, if you know what I mean." Pierpont leaned back a little to view Com's response.

"Hey," Com said with an earnest look, "I work for you. You just let me know what I can do, and I'll make it happen."

"That's my boy," Mr. Pierpont said and released the grip to slap Com on his shoulder. "Oh," the donor said, remembering his companion on the stage, "you know this guy, right?" Hank Pierpont shifted to his right to introduce a young, scrawny man. "This is Justin Timeus. He's the brains behind our online analytics products that basically made your campaign."

Justin was a straight-faced man in his early twenties and unfazed though his casual attire stood out from the surrounding cocktail attire. He looked at Com then looked down as he presented his hand. "Congratulations, Senator Com DeGroot."

"Yeah, I know this freakin' genius. We go way back." Com said and shook the young man's hand. "How's it going, Justin? You develop any killers apps to beat the stock market yet?" Com chuckled at the rhetorical question.

"It's going okay," Justin said in a robotic manner. "Today I asked my immediate supervisor if I could leave work because I wasn't doing anything of consequence at the office and he replied by saying that he needed me in the office even if I wasn't doing anything and that I should just go make copies of my ass in the copy room. He asked if my wanting to leave had anything to do with the coworker in a cubicle next to me who tends to smell of beef and cheese and I said that it wasn't because of him, though Barb, who is next to him, makes a lot of gratuitous office noises like stapling and closing of binders—"

Com laughed. "Wow, that's a lot more information than I was expecting." Hank had put his hands on Justin's shoulders and coughed to indicate that the young man was being inappropriate.

"Oh," Justin said. "Okay. But you were wrong, Senator Com DeGroot, when you said that I predicted your election correctly. Yours was one of two senate races that the application I wrote did not accurately predict. It was off by point zero-three-two percent."

"Well, after an election like that tonight, I think that's good enough!" Kevin said and looked around the stage to introduce Com to another, more socially acceptable group of people.

"Yeah, pretty damn close if you ask me," Com agreed.

"Yes, but I predicted a loss for you, not a win. And the other election predictions were a lot closer than yours. The analysis from the web bot attributes the discrepancy to a clandestine operation and perhaps voter fraud." Justin mentioned the significant assertion in an off-hand manner as if he were describing the weather.

Hank laughed, "Okay, Justin. That's enough. Thanks for your thoughts." He tried to move Justin away from the senator-elect, but Com was interested in what Justin was saying and stuck out his hand.

"Wait. Are you saying," Com thought about his words, "that my election was a bit . . . shady?"

"The evidence points to covert—perhaps fraudulent—behavior, yes. I believe that the word 'shady' is a suitable synonym," Justin stated.

Com's face became solemn. He looked at Hank and then at Kevin. They were all quiet, and then suddenly all three burst out laughing. Hank looked relieved that the senator-elect didn't blame him for his employee's inappropriate comment. Justin became morose and sought an escape from the conversation on the floor.

"Oh, that's a good one, mister," Kevin said between chuckles.

Com let out a boisterous laugh then looked at Kevin. "Can you imagine the type of jackass that would want me in the Senate that bad? No offense, Hank."

"Yeah, here's the most unconnected person in Washington," Kevin said, "Let's get him in there and then he can steal Capitol paper clips for us."

"Thanks for your concern, Justin." Com patted Justin on the shoulder. "Now if you'll excuse me." Com stretched his neck toward the stage exit.

Three

Com DeGroot walked toward the stage exit and Kevin Donovan followed, looking for important people to engage in conversation. Com looked out into the boisterous crowd and smiled. He gazed at the large banners that depicted his friendly, forward-looking visage. Below one of the banners, some fifty feet away from the stage, was a young woman who, to the senator-elect, stood out from the other attractive, well-dressed supporters. She wore a pleasant smile and, though she wasn't close, Com could tell that she was looking directly at him.

"You da man!" A young staffer yelled in Com's direction and raised his hand for a high-five.

Com looked at the man and grinned. "Yes, I am."

"You're going to change the world," the staffer said. "It was a pleasure to help you along the way, sir."

Com nodded then returned his eyes to the young woman. He recognized her but could not place from where. Jessica? He thought uncontrollably. No. Marie? That girl after the Lakers game? No. He couldn't quite remember who she was. He started walking toward the stairs at the end of the stage.

"Where are you going, Com?" Kevin screeched, turning the heads of some nearby celebrators.

Com placed his hand on Kevin's shoulder to put him at ease as well as to prevent Kevin from following him. "Uh, I see someone I know. I need to go say hi." The senator-elect walked down the stairs into the excited crowd.

"Com, the after-party. We have an after-party to attend."

Com got to the stairs and was confronted with a stocky security guard dressed in a black suit and accompanying sunglasses. The thick man shook his head at Com while putting his hand out to prevent Com from advancing. "Sir, we need you to go back onto the stage. The exit is behind the stage."

Com continued undaunted and maneuvered past the security guard, who quickly surveyed the immediate vicinity then apprehensively began to follow Com through the crowd. The senator-elect was instantly greeted with cheers, and he began shaking hands and bobbing his head to admiring guests. "Thanks for coming out. Thank you," he said.

"I love you, man!" a young man yelled as he opened his arms for a hug. Com patted the young man on the shoulder. "You're going to change everything. Finally a politician we can believe in!" said the young man as he grasped Com's torso, which was the extent of the height the young man could reach on the tall senator-elect.

"Thanks a lot, thank you," Com said, easing the supporter away from him. The security guard helped to gently pry the young man away from Com and trailed the senator-elect toward the back of the room. Excited partiers continued to greet Com as he walked slowly through the crowd. A young woman jumped on Com and confessed her undying love for the athlete-turned-politician. He thanked her and let her down easily.

Near the back of the hall, the crowd had thinned out and the guests that remained were not paying attention to the celebrity in their midst. There was an opening near the column that Com had his eye on during the speech. It was the right column, but no young lady awaited him there. She was gone. Com looked frustrated and jerked his head around before turning back to the stage. The security guard continued to survey the area and placed his index finger in his ear in order to communicate the senator-elect's position. Com looked back to the stage and saw Kevin staring at him with his arms in the air.

"Congratulations, Commodore." The crystalline voice floated over the noise of the crowd from behind Com, who peered into the air and searched his memory. Commodore was Com's full given name but he hadn't used it since he was a child. Since then, Com had told just one person what his real name was.

"Cate Heatherton," he said and turned around to a beaming relic from his past.

She was wearing a sophisticated and stylish sleeveless navy blue dress with a colorful silk fabric wrapped around the waist in place of a belt. One leg pointed toward Com and a slender arm folded up and allowed her index finger to rest thoughtfully on her chin. Cate's naked shoulders led to a thin but sturdy neck and a soft jaw line complemented by a fair complexion. Her eyes were wide and painted with a subtle shimmering light blue, and they were fixed on the taller senator-elect.

Com allowed a wide grin to creep over his face. "My God. What a surprise."

"Well, I was in the neighborhood. I had a case in D.C., and I couldn't miss this . . . Mr. Senator!" She stressed the last word. "I guess you're the man!"

"Well," Com said with a smile, "that's what they're saying. I really think I got lucky. Can you believe all this?" He waved his hand to the crowd and the stage.

Cate nodded and smiled. "Yes, I can. I always knew you would be a big shot someday."

Com laughed out loud. "What can I say? I had a great staff. So, I really can't believe you're here. How long has it been?" he asked, looking for the answer in Cate's eyes.

"Too long."

Com shook his head subtly. "You look amazing. I take it you're still playing tennis?"

"Yeah, I've tried to keep it up."

"So, where have you been all these years?" Com asked and looked for a ring on Cate's hand but found only a bejeweled representation of a flower on her right index finger.

"Well," she said, trying to recount the previous eight years, "I made it into Harvard Law, finished up there, and I've been working for a really great firm in D.C. The people are fabulous and we're doing some really great work."

"No help from daddy through all this?" Com grinned.

Cate shook her head in a proud denial. "Nope. No help from daddy."

Com paused for a moment while looking at Cate, then spoke, "You were right about him, you know?"

Cate squinted her eyes at Com's question, then smiled, "Yeah, I know."

There was a slightly uncomfortable silence between the two for a moment, which Com broke by changing the subject, "So you made it, huh? A lawyer?" Com looked impressed, then disappointed. "You're not here on business are you? I'm not going to get served, am I?"

Cate tilted her head down and smiled at Com's subtle joke. "No. You're not getting sued. But as a matter of fact, the firm did ask me to come here and speak with you. I was hoping we could meet at some point in the next few days and discuss—"

"The next few days? Nonsense, what are you doing right now?"

Cate looked surprised. "Uh, I'm free the rest of the evening, I think."

"You're going to join me at my celebration party. We can discuss whatever you'd like up there." Com looked back for the security guard. He was standing next to the couple and scanning the surroundings.

"Look, what's your name?"

The stocky security guard answered, "Reggie Williams, sir."

"What's your background—training?"

"Seventy-fifth Ranger Regiment through 2018, sir. I was Afghanistan, mainly," Reggie reported succinctly.

"Ranger, huh? Good man!" Com DeGroot exclaimed as he hit Reggie on the shoulder. Com's father was a drill sergeant in the Army and while that relationship fueled a sense of antiauthoritarianism in the young DeGroot, his exposure to the military helped him develop an appreciation for the servicemen and women and the security they provided. "You know any martial arts—defense techniques?"

"I'm a second-degree black belt in Jiu-Jitsu and a Dim Mak master."

"Wow, that is impressive. I don't know what you just said, but it sounds like you know your stuff. I have a request, Reggie Williams. Can you make absolutely sure this lovely woman makes it up to room five fifty-five?"

The security guard shook his head, "No can do, sir. I have to stick to you like white on rice. Captain's orders."

Com looked down at Reggie. "Captain, huh? Look, you know who your captain's captain is, right?" Com searched for the answer in Reggie's face. "That would be me. You do this and I'll make sure you are captain of this security detail by next week. Got me?"

The security guard widened his eyes and pressed his lips outward. "Sir, if you want me to do this, I will."

Com smiled and then turned back to Cate. "Reggie here is going to take you up. I'll see you in a few minutes, okay?"

Cate nodded skeptically. "Okay."

* * *

"I like your dress, by the way. So cute!" Noni Alvarez noted as she eyed Cate Heatherton's fashionable deep blue apparel. They were standing in a circle of campaign staffers enjoying a glass of wine or a mixed drink in the victory suite. The suite rooms were scattered with happy staffers and guests and filled with electronic lounge music.

"Oh, you're so nice," Cate replied with a tilt of her head. "You're very pretty. I love your hair."

"Aww, thank you," Noni said, wrinkling her brow. "I usually do it myself, but I figured tonight is going to be the biggest night of my life, so I went to a stylist. She's a friend of mine. She's fabulous and not too expensive."

Cate smiled. "I'll have to get her number while I'm in town."

"Oh, absolutely, you'll love her." Noni placed her hand on Cate's forearm.

Kevin Donovan, who was speaking with two other staffers, attempted to get the attention of the two young women. "So, what do you girls think of the Internet Security bill?"

"Um, it's okay, I think," Noni said softly.

Kevin nodded. "Brilliant input, there, Noni. How about you, mysterious friend from Com's past? Do you know anything about the bill?"

Cate nodded. "How about I answer your question with a question?"

"Oh, we have a philosopher, huh?" Kevin tilted his head back. "Go right ahead."

"What's wrong with the current system of self-regulation in the Internet industry?"

Kevin shook his head in exaggerated disappointment. "My dear, my dear. What's wrong with the current system? It's not secure. No one's securing it!"

"Aren't there dozens of private companies that produce security software for the Internet?"

"Yeah," Kevin agreed. "But you're telling me that you trust some fly-by-night computer software company over the federal government? Don't you want real security?"

Cate smiled. "So that some NSA agent can access the photos and calls on my cell phone and personal computer? Sounds great and all, but no thanks." She spoke in a light and carefree manner. She was not argumentative or hostile toward her accuser.

Kevin flinched but, before he could answer, Com DeGroot walked up to the circle and stood between Noni and Cate.

"Hey!" one of the young male staffers in the circle yelled. "The man of the hour!"

Kevin turned to Com. "How about the man of the century!"

Com smiled.

"Com, you didn't tell us your friend here was a flaming liberal," Kevin charged his boss.

Cate jutted out her head in amused confusion.

"Oh." Com smiled. "You must be mistaken. Not this friend."

"No, she is. Cate here doesn't like the Internet Security bill." Kevin turned to Cate. "I bet you don't like the security our military provides either, huh?"

Cate thought for a second before she elaborated. "I think you would find that this country would be quite all right without much of what the government provides in the form of *security* in seventy countries around the world."

"Oh, really?" Kevin said as if he were uncovering an ancient mystery. He then turned to Com. "I rest my case. Flaming." Then Kevin turned back to Cate. "I bet you'd rather go spend that hard-earned tax money on homeless waste-oids and drug addicts."

"Well, you would lose your bet, I'm afraid. I don't think the government should be spending hard-earned tax money on anything."

"Oh," another staffer said. "You're one of *them.*"

"One of who?" Noni asked.

"One of those crazy libertarians," Kevin answered.

"Libertines?" Noni hummed.

Com watched as Cate smiled in calm amusement. She turned to the circle of staffers. "Well, all comments of mental acuity aside, I have a question for you all since you seem to be happy with the current governmental system. What is one thing that government *can* do that private enterprise *cannot* do?"

Kevin had an immediate answer. "Uh, how about the roads, free public education, police the cities? To name a few."

"Okay," Cate thought aloud, "those are things that government *has* done, but so could private enterprise as well—in fact, they have done them. Private toll roads, parochial schools with scholarships, and private security companies. What is something that *only* government can do?"

Kevin was noticeably miffed and another staffer spoke up. "All right, what about putting a man on the moon, or building libraries, parks, or a sewer system? Well, maybe private organizations could do all that, but either they're too small or they don't want to."

"Well," Cate answered lightly, "the private space initiative saw dozens of companies sending people to space. It's conceivable that they could also get to the moon if it were worthwhile. The largest library in the world—the Internet—is a collection of private effort. Europe has private parks—and don't forget amusement parks. As for the sewer system, every building in the country has its own private sewer system; is it impossible to believe that some private enterprise could facilitate a sewer system for an entire city?"

"What about water? Private companies can't provide safe drinking water to the public. Would you trust a private company for your drinking water?" a staffer proclaimed.

Cate smiled. "Evidently you would." She nodded to the staffer's left hand, which carried a plastic bottle with a Dasani label wrapped around it. "You're very trusting with that bottle in your hand."

Com was amused. "So, what's the answer? What *can* government do that private companies cannot?"

Cate looked around the circle and, softly but certainly, said, "It can break the law."

Com thought about it but didn't say anything. The entire circle was quiet.

"It is illegal to forcefully take money from people . . . unless you're the government. It's illegal to take someone's liberty . . . unless you're the government. It's illegal to kill someone . . . unless you're the government. See, we grant government the authority to do anything in order to protect us from coercion, but *only* government has the authority *to* coerce people—though taxes, regulations, physical force, imprisonment, even murder. Private organizations can do everything that government can do except *legally* break the law—legally harm people."

Noni looked on, impressed.

23

"Oh, that's a load of crap!" Kevin yelled.

Noni frowned at the campaign manager. The other staffers in the circle threw their hands at Cate and scoffed at her.

"Com, what kind of Soviet spy did you bring in to your victory party?" Kevin whined.

Com shook his head. "Hey. I value you as a campaign manager and a friend, but Cate's absolutely right here. The only thing government can do that other people can't legally is push them around. It's a great point."

All the staffers besides Noni shook their heads.

Com turned to Cate. "You want to get some air?"

Cate smiled and nodded. "Sure." She turned to Kevin. "It was interesting talking to you, Kevin."

"Sure," he replied.

Com and Cate walked through the circle of staffers to the balcony doors. On the way out, Com raised his index finger to Kevin and spoke quietly but sternly. "Watch yourself, tough guy."

Kevin bulged his eyes and nodded.

Four

Cate Heatherton and Com DeGroot sauntered onto the balcony with full glasses of wine and peered over a small galaxy of lights from the city center. The progressing autumn offered a comfortable evening temperature and the couple enjoyed a light breeze.

Cate looked at her glass and gathered her thoughts. "So, what made you want to do this?"

"Do what?"

"Become a senator of all things?"

Com looked down at his guest, "I want to make a difference in the world and help America get back on its feet."

Cate bowed her head and grinned, "Okay, that's what the speechwriters want you to say. But really, how did all this happen?"

"Well," Com said agreeing with Cate, "I was asked to make an appearance at some basketball charity event a few years ago and after the dinner, some of us got into talking about politics—I don't even remember what we were talking about—security, I think. Anyway, I was getting really heated and completely dismantling some guy's argument and some big shots overheard me and told me I should consider running for office. I didn't really think much about it until a big donor offered to fund my exploratory committee."

"What big donor?"

"You heard of Hank Pierpont?"

Cate shook her head.

"I guess the Republicans have made a concerted effort to bring young, popular, fresh faces into the party and I fit their description, I guess."

"And the rest is history?"

"So they say."

The two reflected on the story silently until Cate turned to the senator-elect. "So, I'm sure you're dying to know why this flibbertigibbet from your past suddenly made an appearance after five years at your senatorial acceptance party."

Com laughed. "Actually, yeah."

"Well, as I mentioned before, my firm does a bit of pro bono work with government agencies and bureaucrats in the D.C. area and they asked me if I would provide some legal advice to you."

Com looked eagerly to his friend and inched closer. "Oh, really? Sounds . . . stimulating."

"Well, yes, but I think I want to just make a personal request to you and speak from the heart if you don't mind. It has to do with this new position."

Com moved his bottom lip upward and shrugged, then inched back away from Cate. He thought back to the couple's intense political debates at school and, though he didn't always agree with Cate's hardened views on politics, he always admired her courage to stand up for what she believed in and her ability to articulate it clearly and forcefully. The senator-elect looked at a nearby rooftop and spotted trash being blown around by the wind. "That's what I love about you, Cate. Most girls in college just went with the popular wind like a pathetic potato chip wrapper." He motioned toward the trash. "Not you. You always had ideas. You're no potato chip wrapper."

"Thanks. You sure know how to make a girl feel special." Cate nodded with amused gratitude.

"Like back in there. Those guys spend their entire life in politics and you just schooled them in a matter of minutes."

Cate smiled and was silent for a moment. Then she looked up at the senator-elect. "Com, the people have granted you a great deal of power and, while most people would ask you to use that power for good, I'd like to request that you *not* use your power at all."

Com was confused and didn't mind showing it. "What do you mean?"

"Just that—don't do anything. Don't try to fix the economy. Don't try to secure the country. Don't try to make people become moral. Just don't do anything."

Com laughed. "Excuse me for sounding like an idiot, Cate, but the people just elected me into the United States Senate. I'm thinking that they want me to actually do something when I get there."

Cate nodded and replied, "Yes, that is one of the major problems with the federal government today. People expect their representatives to do stuff, get results, make progress. They want Congress to create jobs, help people buy homes, or save some corporation from going bankrupt. But that's not the intended role of this government—at least not according to the Constitution. The intended role is to protect the unalienable rights of the citizens and that's it."

"I absolutely agree, Cate." Com took a large gulp of wine. "But I can't just do nothing. I can't get paid by the hard-working taxpayers and just sit on my keister over there in D.C. I need to get results for my constituents, right?"

"True. But there are always two ways to get to your results: the corrupt way and the just way. Instead of saying, 'I created jobs by taxing productive people to death and giving that money to less-deserving people,' you can say, 'I created jobs by clearing out the endless red tape that hinders entrepreneurs from starting businesses that create jobs.' Instead of eliminating the self-regulation in the mortgage industry, you can help people buy homes by getting government funds out of the market, which would keep prices at affordable levels. You can help good businesses by stopping the constant flow of bailout money into corrupt companies and letting them fail."

Com smiled. "Why didn't you ever run for office, you sexy little political junkie?"

"Very funny."

"I think I agree with all that, Cate. People just want to be left alone. They don't want a nanny constantly telling them what to do."

"Right."

"But what about security? I have to be proactive on security. See, I promised the people of Delaware that I was going to make this country secure, and you know that I don't make promises I don't keep."

"Yes, yes, I know. You're the *honest* politician."

Com looked at her, almost insulted that she didn't believe him.

Cate smiled at Com's earnestness. "No, I believe it, Com, and I really respect that. I really do."

"Anyway, in order to do that, we need to ramp up security in every arena. Security cameras on every street corner, stricter laws for repeat offenders. I'm going to get people to start taking responsibility for themselves. We've got a plan to create a type of world where people feel safe to let their kids walk to school . . . " Com caught himself giving one of his stump speeches.

"And by 'we' you mean the Republicans?" Cate asked.

"Of course. We're the only party in this country that is fighting for freedom—your unalienable rights—both here and abroad. And we're finally getting control back in both houses and the presidency, and we're going to do some things that will make this nation prosperous again." Com took another swig of wine.

Cate hesitated and then thought of the right words. "The government is going to 'make' the nation prosperous again? How?"

"Yeah." Com started to get excited. "We're going to finish the border fence and secure our borders; we're going to improve our infrastructure—create jobs by building our infrastructure; and we're going to finally finish off al-Qaeda, and if that means we have to march through the entire Middle East, then so be it."

Cate looked curious. "And how is that going to make our country prosperous?"

"Cate," Com said, incredulous at his guest's question, "once we stop giving Mexicans jobs and free healthcare, we can keep our resources within the border. And the roads will infinitely help improve commerce. And the war—well, war just makes countries more prosperous. Think about it. During World War II, we were probably the most productive we've ever been as a nation, and once we kicked ass in Europe and Japan, our economies took off. World War II got us out of the Great Depression. And think of all the military contractors that get paid when we're at war." Com was bored with their discussion. "Come on, Cate, can't we talk about something else?"

Cate pushed her lips to the side and squinted at Com. "And if we weren't at war, would that money not go to other, more productive things like schools and technology?"

"Well, we can't be productive as a country if we don't *exist* as a country, so we have to defend ourselves."

"That's certainly true." Cate nodded. "The only question left, then, would be is our existence really being threatened?"

"I don't know, Kevin has a really good argument for that." Com demurred and paused for a moment.

"I could never marry you," Com said, though they hadn't been talking about marriage. "You have an argument for everything."

Cate laughed out loud. "I am an attorney, after all."

The couple switched to small talk for a while, until a few of the party's guests interrupted them to offer their congratulations and say goodbye. Com inched closer to Cate with each change in the environment.

Cate hunched over the balcony railing, looking at the nearly invisible stars through the city's evening haze as Com said goodbye to a donor and his wife. The senator-elect downed a gulp of wine and turned back to Cate, then naturally wrapped his arm around her. He leaned his face into a stolid Cate Heatherton and kissed her on the cheek. Cate blushed and faintly smiled.

"How about we play a little one on one . . . upstairs?" Com posed to Cate. "I can teach you some . . . dribbling techniques."

Cate giggled. "You wish!"

"Awe come on, Cate, aren't you curious as to what a real pro baller can do?"

Cate smiled in peaceful contentedness. "No, not really. Actually, I think I might skip along home."

Com stood erect to mirror Cate. "Oh, come on, things are just getting good."

"I think that's the wine talking, not your noggin," Cate contested.

Com's eyelids drooped. "Come on, Cate."

Cate opened her mouth in exaggerated astonishment while looking around the city. "What on Earth could you possibly want right now?"

"Look at this face, Cate," Com said, pointing to his face with his free hand. "Look at my body. I'm a friggin' man-stud . . . and I'm a U.S. senator." Cate laughed and Com continued. "Don't try to tell me you really just came here to tell me all that stuff about the government."

Cate nodded in disagreement. "Actually, Com, I did."

"Any girl would kill to be where you are right now. You're hanging with one of the most important people on Earth, Com De friggin' Groot."

Cate's even face turned and she pushed her lips to the side. "But you don't want just any girl, do you? You want me."

A persistent Com inched closer to his prey and gently combed her hair back from her face with his hand. "I'm not saying you're just any girl. Look, Cate, I really feel something special between us. I always have."

Cate let a subtle smile sneak out. "Me, too."

"Cate, I could have anyone but right now, I want you."

Cate shook her head and whispered, almost to herself, "I wonder about you."

Com leaned in for another kiss on Cate's cheek.

She straightened her posture and inched away from the senator-elect. "Nice try, Commodore, but it's not going to happen."

Com's squinted eyes were glued on Cate's lips. "Hey! Cate, don't be such a freakin' prude."

"Okay!" Cate checked to make sure she had her purse and turned to open the door to the hotel room. "Thank you for a lovely evening, Com. Good night." Cate turned around and walked through the balcony door.

Com stood frozen and watched Cate leave the party. He took a deep breath and looked out to the city. Then he swirled the remaining sips of wine left in his glass and threw the glass across the balcony, shattering it and splattering the balcony wall with dark red liquid.

Five

"What is this happy horseshit?" Com complained to no one in particular and threw his hand up in disgust. The traffic was bad, even for District standards, and it looked worse up ahead. Com noticed that yet another lane was being coned off about one hundred yards in front of them, limiting a five-lane highway to just three during morning rush hour. "I'm going to be the first senator who completely misses his swearing-in ceremony."

Traffic on the highways around D.C. had gotten better briefly after the local transportation authority had restricted driving for individuals to specific days of the week. Each licensed car was allotted four days of the week to drive, and if a car was found driving on an unspecified day, the driver was fined. The plan resulted in reduced congestion for several months, but eventually, more and more drivers found ways to circumvent the regulation. There were the special exemptions to the law in which drivers with clean driving records and those with cars made by Government Sponsored Enterprises were allowed to drive whenever they wished. Those with enough money simply bought additional cars to be able to drive when they wished. And eventually, a black market of exempt licenses arose. Within a year of passing the regulation, District congestion was at an all-time high. Com and Kevin's driver had received his exempt permit from a cousin in the Transportation Authority. The driver rationalized that, since he needed to drive to make a living, the nepotism was okay.

The early winter sun was penetrating a hazy orange skyline and getting trapped by the closed windows of the car, making the interior warm and stuffy. The atmosphere was unconsciously irritating the bundled-up passengers, and Com was fidgeting and readjusting his legs to get comfortable.

"How much do you wanna bet they're sitting on their asses up there?" Com asked, referring to the construction workers who were to blame for the traffic.

"Yeah." Kevin tried to placate Com. "Those silly ass . . . ass-sitters."

Kevin turned a bit concerned. "You look tense, what's up?"

Com often became overtly and irreverently critical of someone when he was about to open up and make himself emotionally vulnerable. "Well, you know what you little mick bastard . . . "

"Mick bastard" was a favorite of Com's, but he often used "paddy," "paddy cakes," "piker," or "potato eater." Kevin was familiar with this type of sentiment. He never took offense and often returned the favor, usually referring to Com's Dutch heritage with terms like "dyke-jumper," "cheese-eater," or "cloggie." This time Kevin just let Com talk.

"I've already done this two, three times before—this acceptance shit." Com shook his head.

"What are you talking about?" Kevin asked, half-interested.

"Each new team, each new group of ballers. I was always the white guy trying to run with the brothers and I had to prove myself each time. But this is different. I don't know these people. I'm nothing to these politicians. Nothing."

Kevin had witnessed Com's political self-doubt before and it wasn't surprising to him. While Kevin had been entrenched in politics since he was a teenager, Com was a political novice. Sure, he followed the big stories in the news, but Com was an athlete first, a schmoozer second, and he wasn't very well-versed in political theory or the social requirements of being a politician at all.

"Well," Kevin said without compassion, "it's a little late to be reconsidering, don't you think?"

Com faked a smile and nodded.

"Look," Kevin reassured Com, "I got your back. I'll take care of all the particulars, you just need to focus on being likable."

"Oh, people are going to love me," Com replied with a phony sense of machismo. "I'm going to be the first senator with groupies. They're going to be throwing their bras up at me when I speak. They're going to be climbing the walls of the White House to get at me."

"Yeah, I hate to break it to you, Com, but you aren't going to be working or living in the White House," Kevin corrected.

"Whatever."

"Speaking of people loving you, have you thought about getting a wife?" Kevin asked earnestly. "People look for a good family man to lead them. A single guy just doesn't cut it in today's Senate."

"You've mentioned. Okay, I'll get a wife next week. I think they're having a sale at Russian bride dot com," Com said.

"Great, as long as it's not that flaming lib at the election night party."

"Who are you talking about?"

"You know, the real sophisticated broad you were drooling over the entire night. She looked wifely."

Com leaned his head back. "Ah, yes, Cate. You want to know something crazy? You know Zander Heatherton, the banking guy?" Kevin nodded. "That's his daughter."

"Getthefuckoutofhere that's his daughter," Kevin said, shifting his head back in disbelief.

"Serious."

"Well, that changes everything. You should hit that."

Com smiled. "You are a sick puppy, you know that?

"Yes, I am," Kevin agreed.

"Yeah, I don't know what happened. I don't think it's going to work out."

"Well, whatever. Probably for the best. She was too liberal for you anyway."

Brushing the idea off, Com turned to the driver. "Hey guy, how long has this construction been fouling up the works?"

"Man, it's always like this. But I tell you what, it got a lot slower after they stole them developers away for that construction site down in Texas."

Com and Kevin peered out the window to survey the construction. Com thought about using his upcoming power as a U.S. senator to fix stuff like this, to increase the transportation and infrastructure budgets across the board, but his self-doubt had crept back into his mind. Where would he start? Would he have enough power to make a dent in the bureaucratic mess that was the federal government? If it were even possible to fix traffic congestion, wouldn't one of the big shots in Washington already have done it by now? Wasn't traffic just something everyone had to deal with? Maybe everything was like that, Com thought. Maybe there was really nothing he could do to improve the country. A feeling of resentment for ever getting involved in politics came over Com. Why had he gotten involved again in this mess? He couldn't remember.

Com shrieked, "Four, five guys sitting around watching one asshole on a jackhammer!" He peered through his tinted window at the workers and mouthed "I hate you" with a sarcastic grin. One of the construction workers flipped Com off.

Kevin smiled to try to defuse the senator-elect, who was getting visibly impatient.

"Unbelievable!" Com muttered. "They're working for me and they pull that crap!"

The traffic appeared to be breaking up and Com asked the driver to step on the gas, which was followed up with "I'm trying." Com and Kevin returned to their files in preparation for a meeting after the swearing-in ceremony. A few moments later, Com noticed they were slowing down and looked up to see another traffic jam mounting ahead.

"Ugh! This is unbelievable!" Com let out. "Hey, driver, can you just drive on the shoulder?"

"Can't do it." the driver said, trying to empathize with Com's frustration.

"Look, just do it, I'll double your tip, all right?"

"Sorry, rules are rules and I can't afford to get a ticket," the driver said, shaking his head.

"Look, I'll pay for the ticket if you get it, which you won't. This is my oath of office we're talking about."

The driver looked angry, but acquiesced and worked his way through the traffic to get to the shoulder. Once there, the car was moving, leaving thousands of other cars in its dust. A moment later, Com heard an abrupt siren and looked back to see a motorcycle cop.

"Oh, for the love . . . " Com looked around for something to punch.

The driver slowed down and got the documents from the glove compartment. "You gonna get me a new exempt license, too?" the driver asked Com rhetorically.

After a moment of silent stillness, a police officer approached and the driver lowered his window, letting in a rush of brisk air. The officer asked for the driver's license and registration.

"What do you think you're doing, boy? Don't you know that the shoulder is designated for mechanical breakdowns and official business like . . . ticketing?" The officer said with a thick Southern drawl and smirked as he ended his sentence.

"I was just trying to get the senator here to his destination, officer." The driver threw up a thumb pointing to Com.

The motorcycle cop bent down to see what the driver was talking about. "Senator, huh? Who we got back there?" He saw Kevin then Com and looked surprised. "Well," he said with a chuckle, "if it ain't Mr. DeGroot." Com braced for the worst. "Well, hot damn. Why didn't you say so earlier, boy?" The cop looked at the driver. "Shouldn't you be in some sort of motorcade?"

Com smiled. "Yeah, they were fresh out of those this morning."

The cop offered, "Where you headin' to?"

Com responded, "Capitol."

The officer put away his notepad and smiled. "How'd you like to get there in about twenty minutes? Follow me." He walked back to his motorcycle and turned on his lights, pulled around the Lincoln and let his siren blare. The driver of the Lincoln followed the motorcycle along the shoulder of the highway.

Com breathed a sign of relief. "I think I might start to like this whole senator thing."

Six

"Will you call the names of the next group of senators?" the Vice President of the United States asked the Secretary of the Senate. Com DeGroot knew that he was up next, so he situated himself in the front of the three other senators to be called and Kevin Donovan followed him. They were at the entrance of the Senate Chamber in the U.S. Capitol Building and each senator was about to give the oath of office. Com looked up to the shallow domed ceiling of the grand room and was awestruck by the ornate gilded details. It was like something out of a European palace rather than a room for senators of a democratic republic.

Com spotted the beautiful wooden desks that were allotted for each senator in the chamber. The one hundred desks were split into two sections, each representing one of the major political parties. From his orientation tour of the Capitol the previous week, Com remembered that the oldest of the desks was almost two hundred years old. The Senate bought them in 1819 for thirty-four dollars each, but those originals were priceless today. The desk to which Com was assigned was one of the newer ones. He could tell by the freshness of the varnish and the lack of names etched on the interior of the desk drawer.

As Com found out on his tour, each desk drawer had a collection of names written or etched on. The occupant senators of each desk placed their names there at the beginning of each term and the result was usually a mess of graffiti that grade-schoolers might have been proud of. Com's desk, which was labeled "XCIX" hadn't had the chance to become as messy as other desks with only eleven names written on it. Other desk drawers had dozens of names tracing back to the beginning of the practice in the early twentieth century.

Pride engulfed Com as he prepared to take the oath of office, which, he thought, was the biggest accomplishment of his short life. Not only was he joining the great men and women who had their names etched in the drawers, he was becoming one of the youngest senators in U.S. history—just barely making the thirty-year cutoff by the day he was giving the oath of office. Com couldn't have imagined a better birthday present. Just being an elected official without any political background was impressive, but to be elected into the Senate was even more extraordinary. Compared with the House of Representatives, which met on the other side of the Capitol building, the Senate was by far the more prestigious of the houses of Congress. There were fewer senators—just one hundred compared with four hundred thirty-five seats in the House. And the terms were longer for senators—six years as opposed to just two for representatives. Senators also had the authority to consent to treaties and confirm cabinet secretaries, judicial appointments, and other federal officers.

All of a sudden, a thought hit the senator-elect with a sudden shock. I wasn't supposed to memorize the oath, was I? Com thought to himself. He turned to Kevin and whispered so that no one else could hear, "I'm not supposed to have it memorized, am I?"

"What?" was the whispered reply.

"The oath . . . "

The secretary then started with the names. "Mr. DeGroot of Delaware . . . Mrs. Derkins of North Carolina . . . Mr. Frank of Nevada . . . Mr. Grier of New Hampshire."

"Shit." Com hadn't memorized the oath and was about to make a fool of himself. The senators all positioned themselves at the chamber entrance with their significant others and their chiefs of staff, then walked down the royal blue carpeted aisle toward the podium, all the while Com was sweating from nervousness. Once situated, the vice president asked the senators to raise their right hands and all complied.

"Do you solemnly swear that you will support and defend the Constitution of the United States against all enemies, foreign and domestic . . . "

A rush of relief overwhelmed Com. He hadn't had to memorize the oath. He wasn't going to embarrass himself and everyone he knew.

" . . . that you will bear true faith and allegiance to the same . . . "

Ah, so what am I bearing true faith and allegiance to? Com thought. Did he say the Constitution? What an accomplishment, Com thought, shaking off his questions.

" . . . that you take this obligation freely, without any mental reservation or purpose of evasion; and that you will well and faithfully discharge the duties of the office on which you are about to enter . . . "

What an honor, Com thought.

"So help you God." The vice president finished.

Amen, Com thought.

The senators all declared "I do." Then the vice president congratulated them. A round of applause was heard and Com turned around to shake Kevin's hand and the hands of Elizabeth Derkins and the other fellow senators. He finally turned to Kevin and smiled. "Let's do this."

Seven

"So what do you think of your staff, senator?" Kevin Donovan asked his boss as they sat down for a brief meeting.

Com scrunched his face and nodded his head as if to a song, "Oh yeah, me likey."

"I have to admit, I'm pretty proud of myself." Kevin agreed. "Not only are they the hottest collection of women in any congressional office, they are actually fairly capable at what they do."

"Well, that's nice to know."

"So, who are you going to bang first?"

"Man, you don't have any scruples, do you?"

Kevin laughed. "Awe, come on Com. This is Washington, D.C., the only place in the country where hundreds of thousands of attractive girls geek out about a guy with legislative power. It's daddy's ship now. You steer the boat. So, who do you like?"

Com's staff was composed of a dozen full-time staffers including his legislative director, press secretary, office manager, "computer guy," state director, and constituent services director, of which all but the computer guy were gorgeous women in their mid-twenties. The staff also included twenty interns and staff assistants to help with the mail and constituent activities.

"My personal favorite is Maria," Kevin said of Com's press secretary without waiting for a response from the senator. "I don't know, there's something about those Russian girls. It's like she's white, but she's got a little Asian flavor."

Com nodded. "Yeah, very nice. I actually think Miss Owens is intriguing, to tell you the truth."

"Yeah, a real firecracker, that one," Kevin agreed.

"And the stuff she wears . . . ."

"What with the . . . " Kevin said and moved his hand up and down his chest indicating a blouse that revealed cleavage.

"Yeah, killer."

"What about Noni?" Kevin asked, referring to the intern who had worked on Com's campaign.

"Noni is a great girl."

"That's it?" Kevin smiled.

Com returned the smile and changed the subject. "So, some of the other senators are characters."

In his first week, Senator DeGroot had met the ranking senators on both sides of the aisle, Senator Roger Thurston from Montana and Senator Duane Delano of Vermont, without much fanfare. Com also met with the other freshmen senators, most of which were Republicans replacing Democrat seats. One freshman particularly caught Com's interest and respect, Senator Charles Wilson from Pennsylvania, the self-proclaimed "Afro-American," referring to his three-inch coiffure. "Damn straight I'm an *Afro*-American. I wear this shit with pride," he would say, framing his hair with his hands. Senator Wilson was happy to see Com in the Senate because, as Wilson claimed, he was "a brotha from anotha motha."

Senator Wilson was just one of the many freshman senators the popular newcomer DeGroot had met, and Com smiled at the thought of the immediate impression he was making on Capitol Hill. Everyone seemed to welcome him into his new role and, after just a few short days, Com was anxious to start turning popularity into power. His first goal, as his chief Kevin has made it abundantly clear, was to secure important committee assignments.

According to Kevin, it was in the committees where real legislation was written, power was brokered, and, as Com's chief said with a wink, it was in the committees where senators were able to bank on their position in what was known as earmarks. As Kevin had explained previously, a few days before a bill goes to committee, members in the corresponding committee get a call asking them to submit all of their amendments. In addition, they get a specific amount of appropriation money in the form of earmarks for each bill to designate to specific contractors or projects. Junior senators received less than senior senators, but, according to Kevin, Com could potentially appropriate hundreds of millions on each bill.

And because many of those contractors were run by friends of the senator, a share of stock in the company could easily be arranged for the senator after his official service concluded. It was something that every senator did and wasn't a big deal, or so Kevin had assured the neophyte.

The key to the earmark game was to get on a good committee, which meant more power because members of important committees could trade earmarks for votes and set the tone of much of the legislation that made it to the Senate floor. The only problem with committees for Com was that he was ignorant of the specifics about them and was not about to admit that to Kevin. "Well, it's obvious. I like Homeland Security . . . and the Defense Committee."

Kevin smirked. "Well, 'Defense' isn't a committee. There's an Armed Services Committee, however. That sounds great. Big appropriations and easy earmarks. No one questions Homeland earmarks. And that fits well with your whole security persona, too." Kevin marked the committees down on his notepad. "You might want to request a few other lesser committees, too, like Indian Affairs or Small Business, so that you have a better chance at getting on multiple committees." Com nodded. "Now, you're going to need to meet with the ranking Republican, Senator Roger Thurston of Montana."

"Yeah, I met him already. Kind of a chucko. I think I can take him out," Com said plainly, insinuating that he would win in a fight with Senator Thurston.

"Com, what the hell are you talking about? This isn't a freakin' basketball game. Look, I don't care what kind of guy he is, but you're going to have to suck it up and treat him with respect," Kevin suggested.

"Ah, you mean kiss his ass?"

"Whatever. You're going to need to get on the important committees if you want to do anything in this Congress, and you're going to need Thurston's help to get on any of those committees. I'll send him a bottle of whiskey and set up a meeting time. The sooner the better, really."

Com wasn't impressed. He thought that since the election was over, he was done selling himself. He wanted to start kicking ass, not kissing ass. All this talk about committees and sucking up seemed like *more* politics, and Com did not want to be a senator for the politics. He wanted to be a senator for the power.

Just then, Noni Alvarez buzzed the interoffice telecom. "Senator DeGroot, a Senator Freeman Jennings is here to see you."

Com looked a little surprised and noticed Kevin, who mouthed "Kiss his ass!" Com begrudgingly nodded, gave a sarcastic, oily look to Kevin, and pushed the intercom button. He asked his office staff assistant to send the senator in. Kevin knew Freeman Jennings to be the longest-running senator serving at the time, as well as President pro tempore of the Senate, the second-highest-ranking official in the Senate behind the Vice President of the United States. Senator Jennings was also from the other side of the aisle— a Democrat.

A moment later, the powerful Freemen Jennings stood in the doorway to Com's office looking anything but powerful. He was a fragile, antique man with white hair and eyebrows that seemed unnaturally lengthy. He wore a friendly smile—the type that only came with comfortable old age—and he carried a cane, more as a symbol of prestige than a walking tool. Com got up from his chair and walked toward the old senator, as did Kevin.

"Senator, it is a most sanctimonious honor," Com said with a saccharine smile, and then extended his hand to Kevin's chair. "Will you graciously have a seat?"

"Oh, no. I won't be long," Senator Jennings said in a warm tone. "I just wanted to stop in to congratulate you on your election and offer my help in getting acclimated."

"Well, that is so very nice of you," Com said as if talking to an old family member with dementia. "Actually, there is something that I do need some help with and a person of your eminence . . . ness would surely be able to help."

Jennings raised his eyebrows. "Mmm, yes?"

"Well, it is my earnest intention to be placed on the Homeland Security Committee and the . . . Armed Services Committee." Com showed he was learning. "Is there anything you can do in your infinite power and wisdom to help me in my quest?" Com's insincerity was becoming obvious.

Jennings looked down. "Well, my being a Democrat won't be able to help you in getting selected—you'll have to speak with, uh, Mr. Thurston, who is the ranking Republican. He'll be taking care of the committee assignments." Com was disappointed Senator Jennings couldn't provide him with new information but Jennings continued. "I can always put in a good word. Getting old has its drawbacks." Jennings lifted his cane. "But it also seems that people tend to respect my opinion more."

"That's very nice of you, Senator," Com said loudly, just now realizing that the Senator might be hard of hearing.

Jennings turned to leave. "Well, I should be off. Congratulations again, Senator."

"Absolutely, thank you so much for stopping by," Com said. He put his arm around the old senator and walked him to the front door as Kevin trailed.

"By the way, Senator," Jennings mustered, "you don't have to be so obsequious."

"I'm sorry? Ob-suck-what?" Com said with a friendly smile.

"Brownnose. You don't have to be such a brownnose, at least not to me," Jennings said, and Com looked back to Kevin with an I-told-you-so look of irritation. "You can save all that for Mr. Thurston, I think."

"Thank you, sir. For that." Com gave the old senator a knowing look and smile. "I'm still getting used to the whole politics thing."

Jennings patted Com on the shoulder. "That's all right, lad, you'll get the hang of it." Freeman Jennings then placed his cane on the floor and with a deep sigh, started the trek to his next destination.

* * *

It was well after midnight when Com DeGroot looked at his watch. He was the last person remaining after a meeting with various staffers in the north wing of the Capitol and it was time to get back home for rest. He shoved his papers and tablet computer into his briefcase and walked south toward the Rotunda. The building was quiet and dimly lit, but Com could see the Rotunda was illuminated.

A short, balding janitor mopped the marble floors leading into the Rotunda, and he smiled at the senator as he passed.

"How's it going?" Com asked, almost unconsciously.

"Well, I don't see getting out of this, so I might as well be happy!" the older janitor quipped.

Com smiled and walked into the Rotunda. He had the entire enclosure to himself and he paused to soak it all in. He looked up to the colonnades and the soaring dome above him, complete with a colorful work of art. Com breathed in and smiled.

On the ground level, the bronze statue of George Washington, which stood to the side of the Rotunda, caught Com's attention so he walked over to it and surveyed the work. The statue was not quite life-sized, but it rested on a marble base, lifting it well above Com's line of vision. Most of the bronze was covered with a dark brown from age, but the front of Washington's feet and the bottom of his cane were a golden yellow, polished by millions of visitors.

"You know why I like him the best?" The janitor was suddenly right behind Com and softly offered his question.

Com shook his head as he looked down to the janitor, who was resting his hand on his mop stick and gazing upward toward Washington's face.

"He didn't let no one tell him what to do. The French. The Brits. Congress. All his life, he did it his way. The right way. You know they wanted him to be king? But he said no, I'll just be president. For eight years. That's why I like Washington." The janitor nodded in self-agreement, grasped his mop handle, and continued to mop.

Com smiled at the old man and looked back up to the great figure.

Eight

"What up, my brotha from anotha motha?" Senator Wilson shouted down the hall so that everyone in it could hear.

"Yeah," Com replied as he pumped his fist. The two freshmen senators met right outside of Senator Thurston's office and gave each other a handshake and a "man hug" common between athletes and people who like to emulate athletes.

"When are we gonna play some ball?" Wilson asked. Senator Wilson hadn't played ball competitively since high school but recognized the honor of playing the former NBA player Com DeGroot. He also thought that it wasn't too much to risk for his forty-two-year-old frame, especially since Com would have to go a little easy due to his bad knee.

Senator Charles Wilson was part of a recent wave of black politicians recruited by the Republican party in order to wrest some of the "black vote" from the Democrats. And it had worked. While previous elections saw ninety-five percent of the black vote going to the Democrats, nearly eighty percent of the black vote went for Wilson in Pennsylvania, and a higher percentage went to other black Republicans in Representative races throughout the country.

Wilson was a mixed bag politically. He favored the exorbitantly pricey single-payer healthcare and Medicare programs that were in effect throughout the country, and the senator discouraged all military conflicts, both of which were typically Democratic issues. But Wilson was a churchman and consequently was pro-life and against forcing churches to recognize homosexual couples as married, typically Republican issues.

Wilson was also vehemently defensive of his ethnic ancestry. At a social event for the senators and their staffers, Senator Wilson was standing with Com and Kevin as they cracked jokes and flung the usual racist epithets at each other, Kevin calling Com "stupid cloggie" and Com returning the favor with "dumb potato eater." Wilson got into the act by calling Kevin a "little leprechaun" and everyone laughed, but when Kevin decided to retaliate by asking Wilson if he should be getting drinks for his "masters," Charles Wilson's smile vanished and he turned straight-faced. "I will cut you," Wilson said without humor. And despite Kevin's assurance that he was just kidding, he never made up for his out-of-bounds comment. Wilson's relationship with Kevin's boss Com, however, did not suffer, and the two senators grew closer because of the incident.

"We can ball once I get my court installed in my Senate office," Com joked.

Wilson chuckled. "Aight. Hey," he said, changing the subject, "you getting the hang of this senator thing?"

"Yeah, I think I'm gettin' it down," Com said confidently.

"Yeah, aight. That's good to hear. Me, I don't know what they hell they got me runnin' around doin'. Givin' me this bill to promote, that committee to join. I really was looking to get on the Ways and Means Committee, but they're trying to give me some ridiculous committees instead. I guess I'm just going to trust my staff. Where you heading?" Wilson asked and knowingly tipped his head to Thurston's office.

"Awe, I gotta go kiss some ass for a little bit," Com said in a matter of fact way.

"Mmm, yeah, you go get that ass." Wilson patted Com on his shoulder and began to walk off. "Don't bite it!" Com thanked him sarcastically and walked in to Senator Roger Thurston's front office.

Thurston's assistant knew who Com was, which made him smile, and asked that Com wait just one moment to see the senator, who was with an important constituent. Com surveyed Thurston's front office, which matched the exterior of the Hart Senate Building—cold, monotonous, and built in the 1970s. Com had told Kevin that buildings like the Hart

Building made him want to *vomit*. "If they're gonna make a building, why don't they just put a little effort into the design, instead of making something that looks like a calculator farted out a building," he complained. Luckily for Com, he was assigned to the first Senate office building, the Russell Building, which had been built in the early twentieth century with much more attention to detail and style.

The door to Senator Thurston's office opened and a tall, voluptuous, and slightly overweight woman with a conservative red dress walked out and did not acknowledge Com or the assistant before leaving the office. Com was confused and looked to the assistant, who raised her eyebrows, shrugged, and continued what she was doing. "Commie boy, get on in here, o-boy" came the call from Thurston's office.

"Senator Thurston, thank you so much for meeting me," Com said warily as he walked into the senator's office. He didn't like the fact that Thurston had just given him a nickname shared with a political movement to which he was diametrically opposed, but he wasn't going to complain because that might have offended the ranking senator. As Com entered Thurston's lair, he was shocked at how different the office was compared to the front office. The senator's office was covered wall-to-wall with rich woods—mahogany, cherry, walnut; expensive leather chairs; gigantic authentic oil paintings; and ornate lighting fixtures.

"Now this is what I call an office!" Com said, laughing.

"It's great, isn't it? I'll give you the name of my decorator. She's really cheap. Only cost the fine taxpayers forty-five." Thurston smiled.

"Dollars?" Com questioned naïvely.

Thurston laughed at the presumed joke. "Yes, God has been very good to me." He had a country drawl and a rasp to his voice that evidently came from smoking cigarettes, which would explain the stale smell Com noticed in his new surroundings. The ranking senator was tall—not as tall as Com, but within range—and wore a new but slightly out-of-style beige suit and a tie blotched with bright colors.

"Sounds good," Com said.

"Want a drink, Commie boy?" Thurston asked and, before Com had a chance to respond, added, "Yeah, me, too. We'll drink some of that nice bourbon you sent over. Nice goin' by the way."

"Yeah, you know, I thought it might be a nice gesture." Com hadn't known exactly what Kevin had sent over, but it turns out that it had been a good idea.

Thurston found the recently opened bottle of Pappy Van Winkle's twenty-year Family Reserve and opened it. He took a whiff and poured the golden brown liquid into two glasses and then handed one to Com. Thurston sipped the other in an obnoxious, noisy manner and let out a refreshed sigh.

"So, you probably want to talk about committees, huh?" Thurston raised his eyebrows.

"As a matter of fact, sir, yes." Com didn't want to appear too pushy.

"Well, you look like a nice young fellow. I'm sure you're going to do a lot of good work for the party, and I'm sure they will be able to accommodate you."

"That's all I want to do—help the party."

"That's good. What committees were you looking to get on?"

"The top two on my list were Homeland Security and Armed Services."

Thurston blurted out a surprised laugh. "Well, you are ambitious, aren't you?"

Com didn't know how to respond. "Yes, sir. I want to get crackin'! Do some good work for the party." He reiterated the party bit because it seemed to him that that was all Thurston was interested in.

"I get it, I get it. You're a young kid—fresh off the tit—and you want to get your ears wet. I appreciate that. But what you're asking is going to be a tall order." Com nodded disappointedly. Thurston added, "I tell you what. Since the Dems are still in control, they run the show, but the seats are tight and the Dems are going to need plenty of favors from me. I'd love for them to owe us one." Thurston pushed his top lip up in a breathy pause and then twitched a blink. "Okay, I think I have an idea to help you get on one of these committees." Thurston crunched an ice cube and swallowed. "We're planning on filibustering the Dem's first bill up in this Congress, and Delano has said they are one vote short of breaking it. You following?"

"Yeah, you're going to stop their bill from going to vote and they can push it through if they have, what, seventy votes?"

"It's actually sixty votes, and there are eight Republicans that are going to side with the Dems on the filibuster at this point. They need one more vote. So if you could vote to break the filibuster, that would help them out and they'll owe us—you—big time. That Senator Delano . . ." Thurston paused for a moment of reflection. "He's as queer as a three-dollar bill and I'm not too fond of the son of a bitch. But he is the Majority Leader and we need his help."

"Are you filibustering? Why don't you just vote against it?"

"Well I'm the Minority Leader and that's my role. I've got to lead. I can't break our own filibuster."

Com thought about it. "What's the bill on?"

"Ah. It's some eminent domain bill. Don't really know much about it—"

"Wait," Com said, realizing all of what Senator Thurston had just said, "you want me to break a filibuster that the *Republicans* are fronting to prevent a vote on some bill, whatever it's about?" Com was slightly insulted.

"Commie boy," Thurston began as if talking down to a grade-schooler, "bills come and go; some pass, some don't. It's not really relevant. By God, what's relevant is *compromise*. If you're willing to compromise, then you'll be able to actually get things done and people will remember that. You'll be known as someone who is willing to take the shots to actually make things happen. The Dems need a favor now, and watch, when you need a favor from them, it'll happen—just like that—because *you* can compromise. You're playing in the big leagues now, Commie boy. Do you think you can step up to the plate?"

Com felt a fury of righteous indignation stirring up inside him, but he subdued it and tried to keep his eye on the prize: the committees. "Compromise, huh?" Com asked skeptically and Thurston nodded. "If I vote to break this filibuster, you'll get me on those committees?" Com rationalized that if he could get on some important committees during his freshman Congress, it would be worth it to side with the Democrats this once.

"I'll take care of you. You scratch my back and I'll scratch yours. What d'ya say?" Thurston projected and put his hand out for a shake. Com put on a fake air of confidence and shook Thurston's hand.

"Let's get scratching," Com blinked and said with a phony smile.

Nine

The first major bill that was to be brought to vote by the Senate was called the Internet Privacy Act by its authors. Com's political advisor, Hailey Owens, and Kevin Donovan were describing the bill to Com in his office a day before the Senate was to vote on it. As Kevin described it, the bill's intent was to identify and weed out threats to privacy on the Internet, namely unsolicited emailers and Internet "hackers," and to protect critical government Internet functions from criminal threats. To do this, the bill's authors envisioned the federal government assuming control of all of the country's Internet Service Providers and thoroughly regulating the types of information that could be sent from user to user, veritably eliminating all potential security threats from the Internet whatsoever.

Com DeGroot was a longtime proponent of security in general, security on the border, national security when it came to terrorists, and security from violent crime. He was also interested in the idea of Internet security. Hailey and Kevin were feeding Com's desire for security and describing the Internet Privacy Act as a means to that end; the senator liked what he was hearing. To Kevin, and thus to Com, the bill was a way to secure an institution that had become as important and vital to national security as manufacturing or even agriculture. The Internet was the venue for about twenty percent of business in the United States and all other business was connected to the Internet in an integral way. Nearly twenty-five percent of the workforce in the country "telecommuted" via the Internet, and everyone else used email, mobile phones, and messaging that depended on the same technology. That wasn't to mention all the important funny email forwards that make office life bearable, Com noted. If someone or some entity was to target the Internet and shut it down, even temporarily, it would be catastrophic, Kevin and Com rationed.

"This is exactly what you were talking about in your campaign. This is security. The physical terrorists who use bombs are history. It's cyber terrorists we have to contend with now. And we can't just depend on those weak antivirus software programs to keep the entire Internet safe," Kevin said combatively.

"You're preachin' to the choir, big boy," Com hit back. "We need something stronger, faster, better. We need to open a can of Internet whoop-ass."

"You've heard all the statistics," Hailey said. "This bill should be a no-brainer."

"Yeah, the federal government is the only entity big enough to secure such an enormous enterprise," Kevin continued.

"Go!" Com yelled.

"There are some devious bastards out there just waiting to wreck havoc on the system," Kevin continued. "Are you willing to let that happen on your watch?"

"Hell, no. Don't hurt 'em!" Com screeched to pump up his chief.

"And we can crush child pornography while we're at it!" Kevin said, and Hailey looked at him.

"You know what," Com said to Kevin to slow things down, "you're probably the smartest of all the red-headed step-children in your family, huh?"

"Shut the hell up, you big dumb cloggie."

"Oh, yeah? Well, I think I'm gonna vote for this bill and then I'm going to introduce a bill where we invade Ireland. Just for you. What you think about that, you drunken mick bastard?"

"I think it's brilliant," Kevin said, keeping the humor alive. "Dyke-jumper."

Hailey widened her eyes and stood up. "You two have been working too hard." She was wearing a loose-fitting sheer dress that draped over her breasts and revealed the subtle details of those breasts, unhindered by a bra. The dress became tight under a belt positioned at her waist. As Hailey stood up, Com couldn't withhold the thought her bare body in front of him and his pulse quickened.

She leaned over and tapped the intercom button located on Com's desk. "Noni, could you come in here, please?" Hailey turned and collected a stack of papers, then walked to the door to Com's office and met Noni. "Could you be a dear and make ten copies of each study?" She handed Noni the stack of papers. Noni gave Hailey a bitter, sarcastic smile, then left the room. "Oh, and don't forget . . ." Hailey said and followed Com's staff assistant into the front office.

Kevin's lusting eyes followed Hailey then returned to Com after she left the room. But it had become apparent that Com had already shifted gears. The senator turned to Kevin with a sigh. "Do you really believe in the whole partisan thing between Republicans and Democrats?"

Kevin looked as if they had gone over this before and was tired of revisiting the idea. "Where is this coming from?" Kevin sighed.

"Do the parties really even stand for anything? I mean, it just seems like a whole lot of ass kissing and compromise. Like the 'S' twelve bill on eminent domain. The Republicans are going to filibuster, but Thurston wants me to break the filibuster as a favor to the Dems so that they 'owe us one.' It almost seems like Thurston devised the filibuster so that he could have leveraging power."

"Yeah, if it were up to me, I wouldn't even meet with the Dems. But you gotta pinch your nose and soldier on—keep your eyes on the prize," Kevin said excitedly.

"I don't know, I just didn't realize there would be so much smoke and mirrors at this level," Com admitted.

"Jesus!" Kevin screeched. "You sound like a little school girl. That's just how politics are. It's like that at every level, Com. It starts on the playground and doesn't stop until you're president of the United States of America. I know 'cause I've been at every level, and it's no different here."

Com was not impressed. "Yeah, I just thought that I'd be doing a lot more kicking Democratic ass than kissing Republican ass in the Senate. And I'm worried about committees. Why? They seem like just more bureaucratic mess."

"Look, Com," Kevin said. "Why do you think we got all that soft money during the election? Why do you think people like Hank Pierpont and Brian Kinney were behind you? It wasn't because of their high ideals, I can guarantee you that."

"So, they want me to take care of them?"

"Yeah, and the committees are where you get the money to take care of your constituents. An earmark here, a little legislative provision there, and all of a sudden, you have happy donors."

Com nodded. "And this is all legitimate?"

Kevin dipped his forehead as if he were scolding a child. "Come on. This is the rule of the roost. This is how things work."

"So, could I get an earmark to finally finish Highway One?"

"Com, you can do whatever you want. But you have to get on a committee to get your earmarks in the bills. Committees are where you cash out." Kevin took a souvenir basketball that was stationed on Com's desk and held it in his palm. "Just think of the power."

Ten

"This thing is amazing," Kevin Donovan said excitedly, holding his fingers on a small patch of his head right behind his ear. He was talking to Com as they walked toward the Senate Chamber. "I don't have to push any buttons, dial any numbers. I just say it and it calls. Literally, I just say the name of the person and it calls. Watch."

Kevin looked to the ground as they walked and pronounced, "Phone call Com." He waited for a moment. "Is it ringing?" Kevin asked and hit Com on his arm. "Is your phone ringing?"

Com looked at his handheld phone. "No."

"Hello?" Kevin said. "Mom? I'm sorry, ma. I was trying to call someone else."

Com looked at Kevin quizzically.

"No, mom, I gotta go. No, ma, I didn't get the Guinness braised beef recipe. Okay, I'll check again. Bye."

"Real great technology, Kevin."

"It was working earlier. Call Com," Kevin tried again. "No, not mom, Com! Call Com!"

Com shook his head as he felt a vibration in his pants' pocket. The senator looked slyly at Kevin and then to his handheld phone, which displayed a picture of Kevin. Com answered his phone and Kevin laughed. "Oh, this is unbelievable. Can you imagine what this means? The power of voice transferred into action. Pretty soon, we'll be able to open doors just by thinking about it or drive cars even. Awesome."

Com ended the call with his chief and shook his head. "Man, it's creepy. That's what it is."

"Oh, come on, it's the future," Kevin said with enthusiasm. "I love it."

"Nah. What if something goes wrong and your implant starts dialing sex lines in the middle of the night when you're sleeping or something?"

"Damn, Com. I'd love that. That's actually a good idea. I should write that down." Kevin challenged Com with a smile.

"You know what I mean. There are so many things that could go wrong."

"Ah, you're just a technophobe."

"Yeah, whatever, you're the one with a high-voltage death trap stuck in your ear."

"You're crazy. So, I take it you're not going to get one?"

"Hell, no. I would never allow them to stick one of those in my head."

"Wow, I didn't know you were such a big pussy!" Kevin said as he opened the door to the Senate Chamber.

"We'll see who laughs last, little man," Com said to Kevin and breathed in fully.

The Chamber was nearly full of senators and their staff discussing bills and less important topics. As Com walked down the aisle toward his desk, he smiled and soaked the ambiance in. "Today is going to be a good day, my little friend."

"Oh, yeah?" Kevin wondered.

"Yeah. We're going to finally get our first vote on a bill, and later today I'm going to get my payback for breaking up the filibuster on 'S' twelve. I'm gonna be announced as the newest member of the Senate Committee on Homeland Security and Armed Services, as well as a couple others for good measure."

"It's good to see you're keeping your expectations low," Kevin wryly threw at Com.

"Shit, it's time for Thurston to pay up. I done voted to break that filibuster for him."

Com and Kevin approached a group of people including an overweight man. He wore a black suit and a brown leather fedora with a white ribbon, and his face was unseasonably tanned and coated with a thin layer of perspiration.

"That's Majority Leader Duane Delano," Kevin explained to Com.

"Yeah, I've heard about him on the news. He's supposed to be some great civil rights guy."

Kevin let out a brief laugh. "Yeah, don't believe everything you see on the Interweb there, big guy. Delano's the one I've been telling you about. No morals. He's into some really bad shit, that guy."

Com looked skeptical. "Come on, now."

"No, really. It's just rumors, but I've heard he's got ties to the mob and I don't even know what. He's into some really nasty stuff. And it's funny because he's got such a good reputation for being a civil rights crusader, but he's about as racist as they come. He's also a very difficult person to work with, whether on coauthoring a bill or just setting a meeting time. If you ever have to work with him, good luck."

Com flinched and gave his chief a confident, "Hey, this is me you're talking about. Everyone loves me. I can work with anyone."

Kevin scrunched his face at Com's words, and they stepped into Delano's circle.

"Good morning, Senator."

"Who the hell are you?" was the lispy response. Delano turned to Com, tilted his head back, and tried to look down at a man who was over a foot taller than he. Delano peered at Com through a pair of foggy eyeglasses that were slipping down his nose.

"Why, I'm Com DeGroot, junior senator from Delaware." Com tried to subtly imitate Senator Delano's Northeastern accent.

Delano thought for a second. "Senator, huh? You don't look like a senator. You look like a monkey."

Com moved his head back in astonishment.

Delano continued. "Tell me Mr. Senator, what is section twenty-one of the Senate rules?"

Com swallowed and shook his head. "I—I'm not really sure."

"Huh, some senator." Delano turned away, but the young senator caught his attention again.

"I was the final vote to break the filibuster for you on 'S' twelve." Com thought that would jog Delano's memory and remind him that he owed him one.

"What? Do you think I owe you one or something?" Delano coughed.

Com frowned and changed his mind. "Not at all. I just wanted to give you a reference point."

"Good, 'cause the only person I owe anything to is my daddy, and he's dead. Anyway, that was Thurston's doing. He gets the credit for breaking the filibuster, not you."

"That's all right, Senator. I'll let you buy me dinner or something," Com joked and put up his hand for a high five.

Senator Delano rolled his eyes in embarrassment and slowly turned away from Com, ignoring his raised hand and blocking him from his circle.

Com looked at the backs of the senators and curled his lip. Kevin hit Com on the arm and walked around the circle of senators.

"Bastard," Com whispered inaudibly as he walked away. When they got to Com's desk, they heard Senator Thurston laughing his way into the Chamber, accompanied by a man who wore a plain suit with a clergy cincture draped around his neck and stretched down his chest. The cincture was black and bore a gold cross on each side. The two men approached the desk at the center of the room, and it appeared that everyone was preparing to get started with official business.

Kevin adjusted Com's tie and mocked a wife's voice. "Okay, honey, have a great day at work today. Go get 'em!"

"Shut up," Com said and shoved Kevin out of the way as he made his way to his row. Kevin left to go back to the office, and Com situated himself in his creaking wooden chair.

Most of the senators were at their desks when Senator Thurston, who was seated at the main desk in the center of the Chamber, called the Senate to order and asked the clerk to "Please read a communication to the Senate." The clerk then read a letter that appointed Senator Thurston to complete the duties of the chair and was signed by Senator Freeman Jennings, President pro tempore. With that, Thurston offered some opening remarks and then introduced his clerical friend who would be doing the opening invocation.

"Let us bow our heads," the cleric said. "Lord, in your grace, give these men and women of the Congress of the United States the wisdom to use their power to help those in need. Give them the strength to forge ahead with principles that ensure equality. And, Lord, we ask that you keep them safe as they work to protect the people of this great land. We pray in your Son's name. Amen."

Some 'Amen's were heard throughout the Chamber and Com nodded at the brief prayer.

After the invocation, Roger Thurston began what Kevin had previously called the "morning hour," which consisted of Senate Majority Leader Delano and Minority Leader Thurston offering their take on items in the news and the upcoming legislation. Thurston then called for the "Presentation of petitions and memorials," of which there were none. Finally, Senator Thurston opened up the floor for measures, which included the day's first and only bill to be voted on, Senate bill twenty-two regarding Internet privacy.

Senate bill twenty-two had already gone through much of the legislative process. It had been introduced by its sponsor, Senator Duggan of Rhode Island; sent to the Senate Committee on Commerce, Science, and Transportation, in which it passed by one vote; and then gone through the amendment process. It was ready for a vote. Thurston asked the legislative clerk to read the title and she complied. Then Senator Duggan came to the podium in front of the Senate desks and called for a vote. With no objections, the clerk began the roll call. At that point, each senator could select a "yea" or "nay" option on an electronic device at his or her desk. Com selected "yea" and began to look at his papers about the bill. It was customary to be able to change one's vote throughout the roll call and until the allotted time for that bill expired, after which the presiding officer would proclaim the final tally. But Com was confident in his vote and was not going to change it. Chatter in the Chamber began to pick up as the senators' names were called and those who had voted decided to stretch their legs.

"Commie boy," was yelled from about thirty feet behind Com. Com whispered that he hated that nickname under his breath before turning around to insincerely greet Senator Thurston. "How'd you vote?" Thurston asked.

"Yea all the way," Com said proudly.

"Good for you," Thurston complimented Com. "Say, by the way, I got the committee assignments."

Com's ears perked up. He knew that Thurston had put the lists together with other ranking Republicans but for some reason wanted to shirk the responsibility of owning the assignments himself, so he phrased it as if he had simply *gotten* them. Com looked eager to hear his new assignments to the high profile committees. "And?"

"I think you're going to be very happy," Thurston said as he looked at a small paper list in his hand. "So, it looks like you're on the . . . Energy and Natural Resources, and the Committee of Veterans' Affairs."

Com was stunned. "What the hell? Are you sure that's me?" Com turned to look at the paper in Thurston's hand.

"Yup, sure is," Thurston said and slapped Com on his shoulder. "You got on two. Congrats!"

"But I didn't even request those committees."

Thurston was unfazed. "Oh, I know, but there are only a few spots open on each committee, and I knew you wanted to be on a couple, so there you have it."

"And what about Homeland Security and Armed Services?"

"Well, Commie boy, those committees are very exclusive and there's a long line to get on them." Thurston knew Com would understand. "Just keep plugging away and you'll get there, son." Thurston patronized Com with a friendly punch on the shoulder.

Com was infuriated and suddenly thought of the filibuster deal he had made with Thurston, "Senator, do you remember promising me my committee assignments if I broke up the filibuster on 'S' twelve? Whatever happened to scratch my back and I'll scratch yours? 'Cause my back is itching like a motherfucker."

Thurston tried to sidestep the question, "Ah. Well, you're going to have to work a little harder than that, son. I said I'd take care of you, but I didn't promise anything in particular, now."

Com nodded his head yes but was in disbelief as Thurston moved on to talk to another senator. Com tore out of the Chamber and walked down the hall to the exit of the Capitol Building, ready to explode. Com punched his phone and waited impatiently until he heard Kevin on the other end. Com yelled, "That son of a bitch gave me Natural Energy and Veterans!" as he stormed out of the Capitol.

"What? Committees?" Kevin replied, confused.

"That's what I said."

"All right, look, we'll just have to work with it."

"I want to work my fist into Thurston's fat face, that's what I'm going to do."

"Now, calm down. You don't want to burn any bridges. Things like this happen. It's just a minor setback. You'll get your committee assignments eventually, you just need to play ball in the meantime."

"That's bullshit. There's got to be a way to go over his head. What can I do?"

"Com, Thurston is the Minority Leader. You can't really go over his head, unless . . . "

"Unless what?"

"No. It's not possible."

"Tell me, damn it."

Kevin hummed on the other line. "No, let me think."

"Look, you little asshole, do I need to remind you who you work for?"

Kevin's voice became deadpan. "Well, you could go to the dark side."

"Oh, come on—English, Yoda. What the hell are you talking about?"

"The dark side. That bastard you ran into today on the Senate floor. He's the Majority Leader—but, I'm telling you, you don't want to get involved with that smarmy bastard."

"Who, Delano?"

"Yeah, he's the most powerful senator and he chairs the Homeland Security Committee. I'm sure he could arrange something for you. Everyone listens to him, even Thurston."

Com huffed and looked around the dreary Washington landscape in front of him. "Are you telling me the only way to get onto a meaningful committee is to abandon my party?"

"Com, there's got to be a better way."

"That bastard lied to me," Com huffed. "I'm not going to let him get away with it."

Eleven

After Com hung up the phone with his chief, he spotted a dark suit topped with a leather fedora waddling down the Capitol's east staircase. It was Senator Delano, and he was leaving the Capitol. Com knew that he had no further business at the Capitol that day, so he briskly walked after Delano.

As Com walked a consistent hundred yards behind Delano, the young senator's shock and disappointment about his committee assignments fermented into a full-blown rage toward the responsible party, Senator Thurston. Com imagined that Thurston had played him on purpose in order to serve some devilish power trip. Thurston had lured Com into a deal, had received what he wanted, and completely shafted Com, he thought. "Who the hell does he think he is?" Com said silently to himself, then aloud. The more Com thought of it, the more he came to the conclusion that some sort of deal with Delano would give him leverage against Thurston.

Delano made it across Constitution Ave. without waiting and walked up the stairs to the Russell Senate Building. Com followed Delano into his building, produced a badge to pass through a security checkpoint with thirty people in line, and made his way to Senator Delano's office. As he approached the door, he noticed that Delano was inside, talking with his young male office assistant.

Senator Duane D. Delano was animatedly explaining something to the young man and inching too close for professional etiquette. Delano was noticeably perspiring from the walk and wiped his forehead before digging his index finger into his assistant's ribs. "And those fuckin' coolies think that they're on the same level as us?"

There was an odd smell of stale air and antique furniture hanging about the office. Com experienced a subtle sense of nausea as he stepped into the dim office. The newcomer felt as if he had interrupted something. Delano turned to the intruder and became accusatory. "Who the hell are you?"

A distinct sense of déjà vu hit Com, having received the same question just hours earlier. Com looked at Delano and replied with a disappointing tone, "I'm Com DeGroot, junior senator . . . from Delaware. I just met you at the Capitol this morning." Com said it slowly, and Delano glanced back to his assistant and waved at Com. There were only a hundred senators, Com thought.

"Yes, yes," Delano murmured. "There are a hundred senators." Delano flopped away from his assistant. "I can't be expected to memorize all of them. Especially those from useless states like . . . Delaware." Com had his second urge to physically assault a senior senator that day but restrained himself. Delano demanded, "What do you want?"

Com tore straight into it. "I want to make a deal. The Senate is very closely divided right now and I'm willing to give you my vote on crucial legislation like 'S' seventy-eight . . . " he trailed off.

Delano gave Com a disappointed look. "If?"

"I want on the Homeland Security Committee," Com blurted out.

Delano continued his disappointed look. "Oh, Senator, *I* can't do anything to help you in that regard." Delano let a sinister smile creep over his face, belying his words.

Com knew he was lying but decided to play Delano's game and attempted to get on his good side. "Now, Senator Delano, you mean to tell me that the Majority Leader of the United States Senate can't do anything to throw his weight around?" No pun intended, Com thought to himself, looking at Delano's girth.

"I believe the man you want to speak to is Senator Thurston of Montana, the *Minority* Leader."

"Suppose I wanted to deal with someone with more clout, someone more *powerful*?"

"Oh, you flatter me, sir. Well," Delano said, faking humility, "I suppose I could try to pull some strings. But why Homeland Security? What committees are you on now? I'm sure you were placed on some very important committees."

Com shook his head and smirked. "Uh, Veterans' Affairs and Natural Resources? It's kinda like they stuck the unwanted stepchild in the corner to play with a broken Slinky."

"Oh, nonsense," Delano said without losing his patronizing demeanor. "In fact, one of my very own bills is going to committee in Natural Resources tomorrow, 'S' six-sixty-four. Maybe you've heard of it? No? Resources is a fine committee."

"Well, that's fine. But I want Homeland."

"Well, Senator, it doesn't look like I will be able to help you."

"What if I voted for your bill in committee tomorrow?" Com asked, attempting to find an angle in Delano's game.

Delano opened his mouth as if to mirror Com's eureka moment. "Well, there may be a place for you on the Homeland Security Committee after all, but, then again, there might not be. It's hard to tell right now." He was obviously seeking more from Com.

"What, then? What do you want me to do?" Com was getting frustrated with Delano's game and he did not like having to beat around the bush. But he was so compelled to go over Thurston's head—to one-up him—that he endured.

Delano looked disappointed again and turned to his assistant, Terry, who spoke for him. "The senator's bill lacks a co-sponsor at this moment. Senate bills do not usually require co-sponsors, but the senator is looking for a universal . . . bipartisan appeal to this bill."

"You want me to co-sponsor the bill?" Com addressed his question to the assistant, then turned to Delano, who pretended not to have heard Com's question and slowly walked behind his assistant's desk.

Delano commented, almost to himself, "You know, I think there just may be an open spot on the Homeland Security Committee." He looked to Com. "You may be in luck."

"Okay, then," Com said and stepped back as if to move toward the door. "How do I go about doing that?"

Delano flopped his hand toward his assistant. "Terry will contact you about the details. That's all, Senator." Delano indicated that he was done and directed his attention to some papers on the desk in front of him.

"How do I know you're going to come through?" Com asked, looking skeptically at Delano.

"Oh, what do you want—a marriage contract?" Delano asked mockingly.

Com flinched, then stepped toward Senator Delano and reached out his hand for a shake. Delano snickered, shrugged, and held out his hand. Delano's hand was cold, clammy, and limp in Com's grip. Com felt uneasy and quickly retracted his hand.

"Thank you, Senator," Com said and walked toward the door.

"You may be a tall man, Mr. DeGroot, but your mind is like a peanut. You're going to have to improve your mental capacity if you want to work with me."

Com looked coldly at Delano then left the office.

Delano waited a moment to ensure Com had left, then picked up a secure phone sitting on his assistant's desk and punched a number into the dial. "Yeah, this is Delano." He paused as his assistant moved to a filing cabinet and pretended to be busy. "The big ape is on board. Yes, DeGroot."

Twelve

"To summarize," Senator Barruk of Arizona said of Senator Delano's Senate bill six-sixty-four, "this is the only way to bring justice to a remarkably unjust situation." Senator Barruk sat at the head of a long desk that bent at the ends to provide additional desk space. There were nineteen members of the Committee on Energy and Natural Resources stationed along the desk with their aids seated behind them and a nametag in front. Senator Barruk, a Democrat, was the chairman of the committee and had dominated the proceedings until that moment, including the nearly twenty minutes of argument in favor of the bill. On the side of the committee chamber opposite the senators was an area for the press, but it was mostly vacant for the first committee session of the new Congress.

Com was positioned at the end of the desk to the chairman's right, and his legislative director Hailey Owens and his press secretary Maria Virkusk sat behind him. Com was trying hard to not look bored. He had been hoping to debate about terrorists or security measures with trillion-dollar price tags during the Homeland Security Committee meeting that day, but instead was stuck discussing some insignificant jurisdiction in Texas that impacted no one and of which even fewer had heard. Still, Com saw this as an opportunity to get back at Thurston and show him that he wasn't the type to be messed with. As Com sat listening to the proceedings, he remembered a piece of advice his father had given him the night before transferring into a new high school when Com was a boy. His father, a former army lieutenant, had told the young DeGroot to pick a fight with the meanest looking kid in school and "whoop his ass." Then no one would mess with Com for the rest of the year. In high school, Com did just that and was immediately labeled the tough guy. He was planning on doing the same thing as senator in his first committee meeting. In Com's mind, Thurston had messed with him. Now it was payback time. By doing a favor for the Majority Leader, Com would receive a spot on the Homeland Security Committee and would now figuratively whoop Thurston's ass, partisanship be damned.

Barruk continued, "This is a bill to revoke the charter, Title nine-thirty-four 'A', which grants the special administrative zone of 'Ur' in the state of Texas privileged exempt status. As we've seen, the experiment that launched Ur has been an utter disaster and people are in danger. The charter city, as it's called, is putting an undue burden on the surrounding area and the rest of the country. The *foreign* partner—in this case an Indian corporation—has taken advantage of the American people and this government, and I've explained how the city-state of Ur is growing exponentially like a cancer and stripping away all of the resources from around it and from the rest of the country. It consumes one hundred trillion gallons of fresh water a day. Where do you think that comes from? That comes out of the reserves for you and me.

"And, since this special administrative zone is independent of federal labor laws, we see egregious violations of human rights within its borders. Who would have thought nearly two centuries after Lincoln's Emancipation Proclamation, that we would again be dealing with sweatshops within our borders?"

Senator Barruk paused for a moment to gather his thoughts. "Most important, however, are the problems caused by the nuclear disaster, which took place there just fifteen years ago. The greedy corporate monster in charge of the cleanup has failed to uphold its end of the bargain. It's time to right these wrongs and correct this unjust situation.

"You may be wondering why this bill was sent to our Committee on Energy and Natural Resources." Barruk acknowledged a few of the senators' thoughts with a fake laugh, then continued in a slow, metered tone. "Well, it goes back to the establishment of the special jurisdiction itself. You may recall that the original charter was based on the explicit agreement between the Department of Environmental Stability and The Green

Group of Hyderabad. It was agreed that Green would take responsibility for the cleanup of the waste caused by the meltdown that occurred on that site a decade ago and, in exchange, they would be granted the rights to the land under the special charter. Now, they have not held up their end of the bargain, and the only fair thing to do is to revoke Title nine-thirty-four 'A'. We must revoke Title nine-thirty-four 'A'."

Senator Freeman Jennings sat a couple seats to the chair's left and was listening intently. He decided to speak after it appeared Barruk had finished his summary. "If I may . . . ."

"Yes, Senator Jennings," Barruk responded tersely.

"I thank you for your summary," Freeman Jennings said warmly as he blinked his eyebrows. "I have just one question." The elderly gentleman gathered his thoughts for a moment, then spoke. "What does this bill cite as the foundation for its stipulation that the cleanup has been insufficient?"

Senator Barruk replied, "It is my understanding that a cleanup *has* happened, but that it was insufficient to meet federal standards. I believe the bill uses the EPA report from December."

"I see. But isn't The Green Group constructing living spaces in this . . . city?" Jennings pondered.

"Yes" was the reply.

"And isn't it the case that the executives of . . . The Green Group—they maintain residence within this jurisdiction, do they not? As we speak?"

Barruk looked back to one of his aides and returned to the front of the desk. "I am told that some executives are maintaining residences in Ur, yes."

"Well, if the cleanup isn't sufficient . . . " A small pause ensued. "If the lands are radioactive still, then why would those chief executives choose to live there?"

There was an outburst of chatter and Barruk thought for a second. "Well, I can't attest to the sanity of the CEO of Green Group, if that's what you're asking . . . " Some laughs were heard.

Jennings smiled but persisted. "Well, before we all get carried away with the whole rigmarole, I would like to call for a subcommittee to embark on an inspection with a third-party environmental agency to confirm the findings of the EPA report."

"Are you challenging the EPA report, Senator?" Barruk sounded almost offended.

Jennings tilted his head. "Well, I can certainly see where such a report could be misinterpreted."

"With all due respect, Senator, we hardly have the time to pull together an enterprise like that. We would have to get funding, we would need to find the third-party environmental group . . . ."

"Yes, yes," Jennings said knowingly. "It's funny, I probably have the least time left on Earth out of everyone on this committee," he said, reflecting on the ages of the senators, "but it appears that everyone else is less patient." There were a few quiet laughs. "There is far too much rushing going on in Congress these days. The Founders created a republican form of government to avoid quick irrational votes, and yet, that's all we seem to pass these days." Jennings nodded and thought quietly for a moment before turning back to the chair. "But if you must rush through, it looks like, with my help, the Republicans will be able to stop this bill. So, by all means, rush on!"

"Thank you, Senator. We will be sure to revisit the EPA report on the floor if the bill goes to vote," Barruk replied, as if he had satisfied Mr. Jennings' concerns instead of having just glossed over them. Barruk knew that wasn't the case, but thought it courteous to mention in the presence of the esteemed statesman Jennings.

The committee took several minutes to go through the amendment process and analyzed additions to the bill, accepting some and rejecting others. A large majority of the earmarks were approved, adding $2.3 billion to the cost of the bill. Com had submitted his requested earmarks the day before and was in line to receive $250 million for projects of his choosing. He smiled when his earmarks were passed with a large majority. After an hour of debate and discussion, the committee was ready to vote on whether to accept the bill and send it to the floor of the Senate, where the entire body would vote on it.

Barruk began the roll-call vote, and Com rubbed his forehead and looked at his phone nervously.

Just then, Hailey Owens, Com's legislative director, stood up and leaned over to whisper in Com's ear, "You must have some pretty powerful friends. Kevin just texted. He said that a spot just opened up on Homeland Security. The spot's yours."

Com looked at her with a slight skepticism but nodded confidently. "Thank you."

It appeared to Com that Delano had handled his end of the bargain. Now he had to handle his.

"Senator DeGroot?" the chair asked.

All eyes were on the senator as he looked down at an empty desk in front of him. The vote stood at nine to nine, and Com was the deciding vote. Hailey nudged him on his shoulder, but he just stared at the microphone in front of him.

"Yea," he said in a daze.

Thirteen

Com DeGroot was looking at a message on his phone right outside of the committee chamber just moments after the session was dismissed when he heard Roger Thurston call out, "Senator DeGroot!" like he was picking a fight. Com closed his eyes and breathed in, then turned around to face the senior senator.

Thurston was stern-looking as he sauntered up to DeGroot, and he pushed his bottom lip up subtly and began to shake his head. "I can't believe what you did, Senator," he said and crossed his arms. Then, abruptly, Thurston began to crack a smile. "You coy son of a bitch!" Thurston burst out laughing and slapped Com on the shoulder. Com joined in laughing, unsure of what Thurston's intentions were.

"I don't know what kind of deal you made, but all of the sudden you have some pretty important friends in high places, by God. You're playing the game, son. Congratulations." Thurston revealed a smoke-stained grin.

"So you're not mad?" Com asked naïvely.

"Mad? Why would I be mad? I taught you how to work the system, now you're doing it. And probably better and faster than any senator in the history of the Hill. You're on your way, Commie boy."

Com smiled. "I know."

"Hey, don't get too cocky. You should be careful who you deal with, especially on the other side of the aisle. You really don't know who can be trusted. They will stab you in the back like a wild boar on Thanksgiving."

Com stuck out his hand. "Thanks for the advice."

Thurston surveyed the younger senator. "Commie boy, I think it's time."

"For what?"

"You got plans tonight?" Thurston asked.

"Yeah, I was going to go to—"

"Break 'em."

* * *

Com stepped from the cold night air into the Hummer limousine and was greeted by two pairs of glittery high heels topped by four perfectly shaped legs. The legs reflected the neon pink and blue lights that emanated from organic, wave-shaped rows on the roof and an illuminated plastic floor. Com's eyes followed the silky shapes of the legs up to the knees and further to the miniskirts that produced them.

One of the girls had her arm wrapped around the other. She projected her free hand toward Com and yelled over the thumping hip-hop music, "Woo hoo! Fuck, yeah!"

"Well, hello," Com said as if surprised.

"Commie boy!" Senator Thurston said. He was sitting opposite the girls on a curvy leather bench. "Get in here!"

Com sat down next to Thurston and closed the door behind him. He maintained his gaze on the two girls across the limousine from him but shook the elder senator's hand as the Hummer started to move imperceptibly.

"This is Maia and Mackenzie." Thurston put his arm around Com and extended his hand toward the girl on the right, then the other. "They have been with my office for a few years now. They are very talented at what they do."

Com smiled. "Well, it's a pleasure."

Thurston raised his voice. "Girls, this is Senator Com DeGroot, former professional basketball player and now one of the most popular senators in Congress."

Maia looked Com up and down and licked the teeth and gums behind her lips.

"Come on," Senator Thurston yelled, "let's get you a drink." He shifted in the seat toward the bar. "Whiskey, right?" Thurston started pouring before Com answered in the affirmative and turned back to the younger senator to hand him the drink.

"Thank you, sir," Com said and lifted his glass to offer a toast.

Thurston followed suit and raised his glass, as did the girls. "To Com DeGroot," Thurston declared, "the newest god on the Hill and the only one that tall."

Thurston and Com clinked glasses with a chuckle, and Com leaned over to do the same with Maia and Mackenzie's glasses.

Mackenzie sang, "Yay! To tall, dark, and handsome senators!"

Com smiled. "Here's to sexy supermodels in limousines!"

The girls turned their faces to each other and laughed silently. "He's funny. I like him," Maia said.

Thurston patted the younger senator on the shoulder. "Commie boy, I want you to have a good time tonight. Cut loose. These girls are here for you to do whatever you want with. You deserve it." Both girls looked at Com seductively.

Com half turned his face toward Senator Thurston. "What, you're not interested?"

"Oh, I'm a married man, remember?" Thurston winked at Com before taking a sip of whiskey. "No, this party is for you, Commie boy. You're on your way, son. Hell, at this rate, you might get an invitation to the Turf Club soon."

"The Turf Club?" Com asked as he eyed Mackenzie seductively sip her drink.

Thurston chuckled, "You know when people always complain about backroom deals?" Com nodded and Thurston continued, "That's where the back room is." Thurston smiled as if he was letting Com in on a highly guarded secret. "It's very exclusive though. Only the elite of the elite get in. But you're on your way son!"

Mackenzie placed her foot between Com and Thurston's legs and pushed off from the sofa on her side. She turned around and sat half on Com's leg and half on the seat, moving Thurston out of the picture. Maia followed her friend and sat on the other side of Com.

"Wanna get fucked up?" Maia said as she pulled a small glass vial from her bosom and took off the cork top. She tapped a white powder onto her pinky finger and sniffed it.

Com raised his eyebrows and watched as Maia offered the same to her friend. Mackenzie sniffed off of Maia's small finger and wrapped her arm around Com's neck. She whispered into Com's ear, "Want a bump?"

Com grinned at Mackenzie. "Oh, naw. Not today." He tried to laugh off his aversion to the girl's offer. "I try to stick to horse tranquilizers and banana peels. Have any of those?" He put his arms around Mackenzie's naked shoulder.

"Horse tranquilizers?" Mackenzie yelled at the joke. "We don't have any of that!"

"Oh, okay. Bourbon's fine then."

"That's a good boy!" Thurston yelled. He turned away from the other three and bent over for a few seconds.

Maia nearly screamed, "Well, then let's get you fucking drunk!" She leaned in to Com, pressing her buoyant breasts onto him and kissed him on the cheek, leaving a smudge of red lipstick.

* * *

"Bye Senator Thurston!" Mackenzie yelled out the window in an inebriated outburst. "Give your wife a kiss for me!"

Senator Thurston turned back and waved, then shook his head as he stumbled up to his door.

Maia was fixing a drink for Com inside the warm limousine.

"I don't give a shit about politics," Maia she announced and flicked her shoulder-length hair back before handing the drink to Com

"What?" Com yelled as Mackenzie finished rolling up the window and put her arm around the senator. "What do you mean you don't give a shit about politics?"

Maia wiggled her spine. "I mean, I don't give a shit about politics. I mean, who really cares what dumb shit laws you're passing? I'm in appropriations for Senator Thurston and the word alone puts me to sleep. And don't get me started about C-SPAN. Have you ever tried watching that boring shit?"

Com laughed. "You don't care about how the Democrats are destroying our country?"

"I don't really care. Just give me my free health care and my free rent so I can spend my money on important things like tanning and waxing." Maia smiled at her irreverence.

"Oh, please do continue that!" Com smiled a drunken grin. "But let me ask you this, if you don't care about government, why the hell are you in D.C.?"

"Why else do you think? Washington is Hollywood for the ugly. I came here because I'm hotter than every other chick in this town."

"Excuse me." Mackenzie cleared her throat.

"I'm sorry, Kenzie, baby. Hotter than every other chick in D.C. except for you." Maia leaned toward Mackenzie and puckered her lips in a mock kiss. Mackenzie returned the favor by blowing a kiss toward her friend.

"I'm so drunk," Mackenzie whispered, turning back to Com.

"So, you're just here to score powerful men?" The senator asked, amused.

Maia puckered her lips and nodded. "Pretty much. I just didn't know I would be working for some ultraconservative d-bag."

"Who Thurston?" Com wondered aloud.

"Yeah. Well," Maia thought about it, "he gets us blow, so that's good. But don't give me that shit on your principles."

"Right," Com said with a drawn-out sarcastic tone. "There's way too much of that in this town."

Maia and Mackenzie laughed as the limo drove off in the cold night air.

Fourteen

"Thanks for seeing me on such short notice," Senator Freemen Jennings labored to say as he situated himself in the chair opposite Com's desk. "Nice lad. I understand you're a busy man what with all of your prestigious committee positions now."

Com looked down on Senator Jennings, smiled, and thought to himself how important he was becoming. After all, Com had been seen on the front page of *The Washington Post* and labeled as a "Potent Policymaker" by *Time* magazine, he reminded himself. It had been two weeks since his first Homeland Security Committee meeting, and he had been collecting what Kevin had called "political capital." Senator Thurston had realized that Com was someone to be reckoned with, and the Republican Minority Leader had taken Com under his wing and shown him the ins and outs of the Senate leadership. Com was brokering votes for certain bills in exchange for earmarks placed in the committees, and acquiescing votes on other bills in exchange for favors from other senators. He was "playing the game" as Thurston had said, and he was getting very good at it.

Com had officially co-sponsored Senate bill six-sixty-four and allowed his name to be associated with it. The bill had been renamed the Delano-DeGroot bill and was growing in bipartisan popularity. Com had already garnered a number of commitments to vote for the bill by giving various senators earmarks in Homeland Security bills—a subsidy here and a grant there—all in the name of good governance. He had also learned the talking points used to condemn the unique jurisdiction of Ur, Texas, the target of Senate bill six-sixty-four. Not only was it "getting away with murder," but businesses in Ur were draining the resources from the surrounding areas, most notably water; they were employing slave labor; and most contemptibly, the proprietors of Ur were covering up the nuclear radiation that was making everyone in the city sick without their knowledge. Com was playing such a major roll in getting the bill passed that Senator Delano had designated Com to be the voice of the cause on the major talk and news stations. He was even scheduled to appear on the widely popular news magazine show *Face the Facts* in a live debate about the bill a week later.

In the last few weeks, Com had also learned how to bargain deals with the "enemy" Democrats, which players in the Senate to trust, and which to ignore. Despite Senator Freeman Jennings's lengthy tenure in the Senate and his title as President pro tempore, Com had placed him in the "ignore" column thanks to advice from Thurston and others. Com was feeling charitable, however, and agreed to meet briefly with the old Senator.

"About this matter on Ur," Jennings began. "I've been approved to conduct an official Senate survey of the entire area down there, complete with an environmental analysis by another nice group of scientist folks. Now, all we need are two senators who are willing to go and be ambassadors." Jennings raised his eyebrows at Com and gave him a warm smile.

Com returned the smile. "Senator, are you asking me to go to that hellhole?"

"Well, it would be fitting because you are a co-sponsor and have done so much to paint an ugly picture of the place. I think it would be nice if you would make a little effort to investigate the place you're condemning."

"Look, Senator, I appreciate your gesture." Com searched for a reason to evade the request. "It seems like the whole situation stinks like my gym shorts after a ball game. Excuse my French. Even if your new environmental report came back clean, I don't know if it would change my mind. It looks like this *Ur* place is sucking us dry. I mean, they aren't taxed? Who thought that was a good idea?"

"You are referring to their exemption of federal income tax?"

"Right. Who thought up that ingenious idea?"

Jennings smiled. "Well, I believe the Founding Founders of the United States of America thought that was a good idea. And Congress agreed until 1913, when they rammed through the Sixteenth Amendment."

"You're trying to tell me there wasn't an income tax before 1913?" Com asked, unbelieving.

"That's right."

"Well, whatever, but I just got here to Washington. I can't be traipsing off to South Texas to investigate something I have no idea about."

Jennings was quiet and thoughtful though apparently disappointed. "I see. Well, I appreciate your point of view, Senator, but I wonder if you may be overlooking the importance of this bill. How do you feel about unalienable rights?" Jennings asked with a friendly smile.

Com shook his head, not really understanding. "I'm all for 'em, I think."

"And I assume that you would agree with me that the purpose of government is to secure those unalienable rights?" Com nodded. "Good, good. Well, what unalienable rights would we be protecting by passing this law?"

Com looked intently at the senior senator and thought about it. "Well, they're hurting us by taking all the natural resources from the area."

"Okay, well, are they taking any resources without compensation? Are they *stealing* resources?"

"Ah, well, no. They're just using a lot more than everyone else. But besides that, haven't you heard of the reports of slave labor?"

Jennings shrugged his lips. "I have. But those reports are full of conjecture and insinuation, not fact. I wouldn't be surprised if those folks they're calling slaves are just . . . volunteers."

Com looked doubtful. "Uh, and the nuclear waste? I guess there is no danger there? We don't need to protect people from that?"

Senator Jennings looked into Com's eyes confidently. "I think we'll find—if we look hard enough—that all the talk of nuclear disaster is a concerted effort by the oil lobby to dissuade people from supporting competitive technologies. I believe the cleanup was sufficient and, for Pete's sake, if the residents are there by their own volition, the government has no authority to dictate otherwise. Can I ask you, son, how would you feel if you were humming along and the government came along and just confiscated all of your property and squandered everything you've worked for? How would you feel if you were minding your own business and the government came along and tried to tell you how to live your life?"

Com widened his eyes and thought about the elder senator's words for a moment. "I'd hate it," he said pensively.

"Well, son, I think you'll find that's exactly what the government is trying to do there in Texas. This bill is the Riot Act all over again. It's making opposition to the state a crime."

Jennings smiled and spoke, sounding more like a polished speech-giver with a friendly, grandfatherly voice. "A long time ago, Thomas Jefferson said—and no, I wasn't there to hear it personally—I'm not *that* old. He said that everyone has a right to life, liberty, and the pursuit of happiness, and that applies to these nice folks in Texas just as much as you and me. They want a life that's free of government intrusion. They want what all of us are guaranteed by the Constitution." The old senator searched for the right words. "But the powers that be . . . they see this enterprise as just another corporation to nationalize and control, just like the car companies and the banks and the hospitals. And they rely on some flimsy doctored report from the EPA that no one will read and everyone will believe. The Delano bill—now your bill—is just another nail in the coffin of freedom in this country."

"Wow, Senator! I had no idea you had that in you!" Com was intrigued. None of Senator Jennings's ideas had been exposed at the committee meeting about the bill a few days earlier, and they piqued Com's interest. "Senator, I have to be honest, it really seems like you're the only one with this position. No one on either side of the aisle is going to like what you're saying."

Jennings smiled. "Well, if there's one thing I've learned, it's that in politics, if people on both sides of the aisle hate you, it's a good sign that you're doing the right thing." The senior senator chuckled.

Com smiled but was unsatisfied. "But, Mr. Jennings, you're a Democrat. Why aren't you in favor of this bill like the Majority Leader and all of the other Democrats? Where's the partisan fervor from you?"

Jennings nodded. "Yes, that's what people look for these days—partisan fervor. Today it's always Republican versus Democrat; conservative verses liberal; Left versus Right. But I've found that when people start talking about Right and Left, they stop talking about right and wrong. It's just an irrational tribal kerfuffle at that point.

"Let me tell you a little story, Senator. I've been in this office for almost sixty years. And over that time, the Democratic Party has gone from opposing civil rights to championing the cause. We've gone from a party of cutting taxes with Mr. Kennedy to raising taxes with Mr. Clinton. We've gone from a party of balanced budgets with Mr. Clinton to a party of mind-numbing deficits with Mr. Obama and our current president, Mr. Sullivan. And guess what? I can't keep up with all the changes. So, I just stick with what I know and believe in." Senator Jennings nodded as if comforted by his beliefs.

"And what's that? What do you believe in?" an entertained Com asked.

Jennings paused and collected his thoughts. "Freedom is good. For individuals and society as a whole. I believe in the people and their ability to make the right decision for themselves. I can't tell everyone in this country what to do. Heavens, I can't even tell my wife what to do! Much less an entire country. So, yes, I believe in these folks in South Texas to make their own decisions for themselves."

"And what if the EPA report was right and everyone there is going to be poisoned with—they're going to start growing a third eye?"

"Well, that's what I hope to find out with your trip there. I cannot go. I'm liable to not make it off the plane at my age." Jennings looked at

Com hopefully. "We need young whippersnappers like you to do the foot work."

"But I don't want radioactivity poisoning. Why should I go to risk my well-being for this crusade of yours?"

Senator Jennings shook his head. "Have you read the EPA report, senator? It showed such low levels of radiation that a two-day trip would not do more damage to you than staying out in the sun for a couple minutes."

"Sir, I hate to disappoint you. I really respect you as a statesman, but I've made this deal with Delano. I can't go back on my word. I shook the man's hand. It was torture, but I did it," Com said regretfully and Jennings nodded.

"I understand." Jennings hesitated to allow Com to change his mind if he wanted. "Well, this old senator needs to get moving. Could you help me up?"

Com rushed around his desk and helped Jennings up. "You have to understand," Com began an excuse, "I'm new in town and I have committees and constituents and meetings, and I have the media to consider. I have that big *Face the Facts* show . . . ."

"Yes, yes, well," Jennings said cheerfully as they reached the door to Com's office. "Please let me know if you run out of excuses." Com recognized the old man's wit and smiled as he helped him through the front office.

As Senator Jennings started his slow walk down the hall, Kevin Donovan hurried through the office's front door. Com's chief of staff looked back at Senator Jennings but did not question the meeting he had just had with Com. He hit Com on the arm. "Hey, let's get a drink. I know of a great spot in Georgetown with lots of, uh, stimulating minds." Noni, who was at her desk in the front office, rolled her eyes and continued to sort through papers.

Reggie, Com's security guard, was sitting in a chair at the front door. He stood up as if to follow Com and Kevin.

Com put his hand on his security guard's shoulder. "Reggie, you look like shit. Why don't you go home and get some sleep?"

Kevin shook his head. "I don't think that's a good idea."

Com shook off the concern. "Look, I can take care of myself. I don't need someone following me every second of my life."

Reggie stood erect and awaited a final decision.

Kevin nodded. "Come on, let's go. Reggie, see you tomorrow."

Fifteen

"Republican or Democrat?" The youthful, yet professional-looking woman asked Kevin Donovan with a seductively interrogative look. Her friend imitated her inquisitive manner and sipped a pink cosmopolitan through a straw. Com DeGroot was next to Kevin but faced toward the bar waiting for his and Kevin's drinks. He turned around to greet the two young ladies. Kevin put his hand out to introduce himself, but the women ignored his offer.

"Republican or Democrat?" The first woman repeated. She had long, wavy brown hair and matching freckles on her pronounced cheekbones. She appeared to have a combination of European and Asian physical features, a recipe that Kevin found ideal. Her lips glistened as she made a quick survey with her tongue, which stayed at the corner of her mouth, and she raised her eyebrows as if to say, "Well?"

Kevin had heard of this pickup line but had never used it and had never had it used on him. If Kevin gave the wrong answer, it would mean the end of the conversation; but if they were on the same page, it could mean a night of great conversation and perhaps more. Kevin looked at the young woman skeptically, as if examining an adversary in a boxing ring. She was attractive, and he didn't want to say the wrong thing. She was dressed in the next season's style, which said Democrat to Kevin, but she wore slightly ostentatious jewelry, which had Republican written all over it. Com looked on, trying to maintain his poker face. Kevin came to a decision and slowly but confidently said, "Republican."

At that, the two girls turned on their heels and began to walk away. Kevin grabbed the arm of his fleeing inquisitor and blurted, "Hey, wait . . . ."

The woman looked at Kevin's hand on her arm. "Oh, so you're an abusive Republican, too, is that it?" she asked, unforgiving.

"I was kidding! We're Green Party members," Kevin said, trying to reconcile. Com looked at Kevin and laughed.

"I see, so you're an abusive and lying Republican," the young woman charged. "Not good qualities."

"Okay, okay. I lied. You're very perceptive," Kevin offered.

The woman smiled a disingenuous smile. "I know. All of us Democrats are."

"I'm Kevin." He offered his hand again.

"And I'm unimpressed," the woman said.

"Nice to meet you, Unimpressed. And you are?" Kevin moved to the woman's friend.

"I'm Becki and this is Marta," Becki said warmly, bringing the group back together. Marta gave her friend a dismayed glance. "And who's your friend?" Becki asked, referring to Com.

"Hi, I'm Com," the senator said, surprised that the two young ladies hadn't recognized him. They were, after all, somewhat into politics. He gave Kevin a humorous glance.

Becki shook Com's hand, and Kevin took Marta's hand and kissed it. "It's a pleasure to make your acquaintance," Kevin offered.

Marta was blasé but pushed through. "So, who do you work for?"

"I work for Com," Kevin said, pointing to his boss.

"And who do you work for?" Becki asked Com with a friendly tone.

"Well, I work for you," Com said with a smile.

"You're too young," Marta said, disbelieving.

"Oh, you're a public official?" Becki asked excitedly.

"Yes, indeed," Com replied.

Kevin tossed it back to the young women. "So, who do *you* work for?"

"We work for Rep. Fuller." Becki said with subdued enthusiasm. Kevin had heard Fuller to be somewhat of a socialist, mainly concerned with advancing the completion of universal health care. He had introduced bills designed to replace all private health providers with government-sponsored enterprises. Fuller was also known to be extremely partisan and unwilling to work with "the other side."

"Fuller, huh?" Kevin asked as if he had just smelled something questionable. "Didn't he say, 'I will never vote for a bill that a Republican sponsors'?"

Marta jumped into the fray. "That's because bipartisanship is crap. Everyone runs around slapping each others' backs thinking they've done something important just because their bill is 'bipartisan,' but that usually just means *compromise*. And compromise means nothing gets done." The words reminded Com of Thurston's, and he raised an eyebrow.

A smile slowly crept over Kevin's face. "You're absolutely right. Bipartisanship is a joke. Like that energy bill last week. We wanted to drill off the coast to supply the country with homegrown energy, and you wanted to build those silly windmills. But the bipartisan bill did neither and we just agreed to purchase more oil from Saudi Arabia and OPEC."

"Exactly. You wanted to massacre the coastline and we wanted a clean, renewable alternative, yet the bipartisan crap made sure that no one got what they wanted," Marta replied.

"Except for the Saudis," Kevin said, and everyone chuckled.

Marta was amazed that she actually agreed with something a Republican said. She wanted to push it a little. "Okay, mister abusive, liar, Republican douche. Sex."

Kevin laughed and nodded eagerly. "M'okay."

Marta shook her head. "I'm not proposing, Mr. Conservative, I'm conducting a poll. Sex, with or without the television on?"

"Awkward!" Becki blurted out. Com was a little taken aback.

Without missing a beat, however, Kevin replied. "With Fox News in the background. Are you kidding? It can't get any better."

Marta let a smile creep in. "Okay, we're going to need to switch to CNN every other time."

Kevin laughed. "You're so hot."

Com looked at the two growing closer together. "You two are demented."

Kevin rearranged himself in the group of four so that he was next to Marta, and that left Becki and Com as an unintentional pair next to the bar. Marta continued to uncover Kevin mentally but Becki was more bashful and asked Com questions that did not involve sex. Com recognized that she was nice and pretty but was not attracted to Becki, and over the following few minutes, Com kept most of his responses to one or two words and often looked at the widescreen television hanging from the wall on the opposite side of the bar, which was showing national political news.

After a few minutes of half-hearted communication, Becki was answering a question about how she had gotten interested in politics when the television gripped Com's attention. It was a report on Senate bill six-sixty-four, the Delano bill, which had taken on Com's name as well. Com nudged Kevin and asked the bartender to turn the volume up. Becki frowned and looked toward the door of the bar.

"Ah! Can we go a half hour without being inundated with this?" Kevin complained unconvincingly.

Footage of a nuclear disaster zone was being shown, and when the bartender turned up the volume, it became evident that the report was about Ur. A British voice was heard on the television. "And there are even reports of slave labor coming out of the region." A tired man who had clearly been working hard in a field of some sort was shown and dejectedly stated to the reporter, "Wages? No, we don't get wages. There's no money in it for anyone here, just work." The reporter continued from a staged setting with a construction site behind him. "No one has been diagnosed with adverse symptoms of the ecological disaster that occurred here just years ago, but as Khale Henry of the EPA says, symptoms from radiation exposure take years, even decades to show."

"Those bastards!" Marta screamed. "I can't believe we're letting them get away with all of this."

Kevin tried to match Marta's attitude. "Those . . . terrorists . . . and what kind of anti-American name is *Ur* anyway? Well, you'll be happy to know that Com here is working to bring The Green Group to justice." He slapped Com on the arm and looked at Marta for a response.

Com was glued to the screen, partly to avoid the uninteresting conversation with Becki but also because he had become interested in the story about the legislation that he had worked on and that seemed to be very important to people like Senator Jennings. Com remembered the old Senator's comments about the bill and shook his head. How would you feel if the government tried to tell you what to do? Com reflected on Jennings' question. I'd hate it, Com repeated in his mind.

The news report blitzed through on the television. " . . . Counsel for The Green Group has claimed slander and vows to fight the charges . . . " The screen cut from a scene of a chemical waste dump to what Com presumed to be a press conference for The Green Group.

Com DeGroot was shocked by what he saw in the press conference. He recognized the attorney at the podium speaking on behalf of The Green Group. It was Cate Heatherton. She stood in front of a team of attorneys and worked off notes on the podium as flashes from press cameras lit up her surroundings. "The charges against The Green Group and Ur are slanderous and we plan on defending ourselves tooth and nail in the court of law. A countersuit is also in the works."

Com stared at the television, and the noise around him drowned into a murmur. When the screen showed the reporter again, Com lowered his head. He kept it lowered as Kevin and Marta threw their opinions at each other and Becki looked at her drink.

"You're senators?" Marta screeched after being educated about Com's position.

Kevin corrected her. "No, just Com." Becki and Marta looked stunned.

"And who are you? The designated pickup artist of the staff?"

"Uh, *you* picked *us* up, remember?" Kevin defended himself.

Marta smirked. "Yeah, I did, didn't I?"

After the news report ended, Com looked down and swallowed. He put his glass on the bar and walked out of the building into the brisk night.

Sixteen

Com sat in a cold apartment and rubbed his head. It was seven in the evening and Com's place was quiet except for the sound of his refrigerator buzzing in the room next to his. The senator was staring at his phone. After a shake of his head, he finally picked it up and called Cate Heatherton.

"Hello?"

"Cate, hi. This is Com. Com DeGroot."

The two hadn't spoken since election night. Cate sounded surprised and preoccupied, but they caught up in a business-like manner for a few minutes. It became evident to Com, however, that Cate wanted her caller to get to the point.

"So, I saw you were working for The Green Group," Com said.

"I am."

"You are probably aware of the Delano bill, then?"

"Uh, don't you mean the Delano-DeGroot bill?"

"Right."

"I am," Cate said, disapproving of the fact.

"Look, Cate, you have to believe me. I wasn't aware of what the bill was for. I was just trying to protect people." Com put a positive light on his actions but wanted to confess the whole truth. "And they gave me the Homeland seat for voting for it. I had to do it."

"Ah, so the truth comes out!" Cate shot back. "Com, is that the type of politician you want to be—achieving power by any means necessary? Even if it means making shady deals?"

Com tried to cut her off. "Look, Cate, I've changed my mind. I want to do the right thing, but I made a promise to Senator Delano, and I keep my promises. You know that."

Cate was silent for a moment. "What do you want me to do here, Com? Do you want me to say that it's okay that you are facilitating the demise of something so great? Do you want me to endorse your behavior in the Senate, just wheeling and dealing with the big wigs while the little people suffer? Sorry, Charlie."

"Look, I'm so sorry that I'm just trying to make a name for myself here in Washington. I'm an outsider, I need to build my political capital before I can really do any good."

"Okay, Com. You are free to do whatever you want," Cate said genuinely.

"Well, what would you want me to do?"

"Maybe not make deals with Duane Delano?"

"But Cate, he's the most powerful senator on the Hill. I made a very shrewd move, and I think it was smart." Both were quiet for a noticeable five seconds.

"Com, your bill is unconstitutional."

The senator thought about it for a moment. "And? We have the authority to pass legislation that we feel will help the country as a whole. I'm not the only senator who's involved, Cate."

"Well, if that's how you feel, I'm not going to try to change your mind."

"Okay."

"Com, let me ask you a question. Do you respect the Constitution?" Cate asked, exasperated.

"Sure, I'm American, I respect the Constitution. Right?"

"Com, I don't respect the Constitution because I'm American; I'm American because I respect the Constitution. It's the rule of law that this country was founded on. Because I believe in it, that's what makes me American."

"Cate, that's fine, but look, I made a promise to Delano. I have to keep it—you know that."

"A promise, huh? Well, let me ask you this," Cate said, utilizing her attorney skills to conjure up a closing argument, "do you remember your swearing-in ceremony?"

"Uh, yeah," He thought back and remembered the stressful day. "I almost didn't make it because of traffic, and I was so relieved that I didn't have to memorize anything. I was sweating bullets."

Perturbed that Com had misunderstood the question, Cate's voice became slightly annoyed. "The language. Do you remember the language of your oath of office?"

"Yeah, it was kinda like the Pledge of Allegiance . . . right?" Com asked, unsure of his answer.

Cate was getting frustrated. "Do you remember what you swore to defend?"

"My honor," Com replied instantly, then realized he was wrong.

"The Constitution, Com. You swore to defend the Constitution of the United States. You didn't swear to defend your constituents' happiness. You didn't swear to defend your party. And you certainly didn't swear to defend your unscrupulous political ties. You swore to defend the Constitution. You *promised* to defend the Constitution. I know because I watched it live on C-SPAN. I watched you swear to that oath. This bill—this Delano bill—is unconstitutional, and if you vote for it you will be breaking *that* promise. Com, I believe in Ur—I really do. I believe that it is exactly what the Founders intended and how life should be in a modern society. Your bill aims to do away with it." A quiver of emotion peaked through Cate's smooth, professional, feminine voice.

Com collapsed his posture and dropped his jaw. He tried to recall his oath of office and remembered reflecting on the Constitution. But he wasn't sure if he believed the Constitution. He wasn't even sure he had read the entire thing. All of a sudden, Com was humbled. He had sworn an oath to defend the Constitution but didn't have a clue what that meant. He decided to change the subject of conversation. "Where are you?"

"Don't change the subject, Com."

"Okay, you made your point. Where are you now?"

"I'm in Texas."

"Ur?"

"Yes. I'm staying here to work on the case." Cate decided to end the conversation. "Com, I have to go."

"Cate, just tell me . . . " Com said and Cate sighed.

"Tell you what?"

"Tell me that I'm doing the right thing."

She hesitated. "Tell me that you'll vote against the bill."

"Cate, I can't do that. Delano would have my cojones in a sling if I voted against that bill. And there are so many things working against Ur right now. You've heard the claims—resource hogging, slave labor. For the last few weeks I've been working on senators to vote *for* the bill. I can't just flip-flop like a damn pancake. And I promised Delano."

"And you promised everyone else that you were going to defend the Constitution. Com, it looks like you have a decision to make." She paused then continued. "Eventually, you're going to have to decide between the power elites in Washington or simple common sense. Excuses aren't going to help you when you're face to face with a lawless country."

Com breathed in deeply and let out a yell of frustration. "Why do you have to make this so difficult?"

Unexpectedly, Cate burst out laughing. "Awe, come on, Commodore. You know what the right thing is here."

Com nodded silently then agreed. "Yeah."

"Well, thanks for calling. Keep me posted on your adventures."

Com pushed air out through his nose. "Okay. Will do."

"Take care."

"Bye."

The phone went dead and Com looked down. He took a few deep breaths and shook his head, then looked out a nearby window.

Com looked back at his phone and pushed a couple numbers.

"Hey, Kevin. I want you to get in touch with Senator Jennings' people."

"Why?" was Kevin's reply.

Com breathed in and out and shook his head. "Because we're going to Texas."

Gods
of
Ruin

PART 2:
VULNERO NEMO

Seventeen

Cate Heatherton had been studying when she captured the attention of Com DeGroot in the main library on the campus of the University of Delaware. He was rushing toward the exit when he saw her and was compelled to make a detour by her table to get a better look. Once he was in her vicinity, he had noticed that she was buried in her book and unaware of any potential romantic interests walking around the library. Com took the open seat across the table from Cate and picked up a nearby magazine, then started flipping through it.

Cate had looked up from her notes on twentieth-century American history and smiled at the eager newcomer. She looked at his magazine. "You know," Cate said before Com turned his ear toward her and lifted his eyebrows, "those things usually work better the right side up." Cate made a counter-clockwise circle with her finger.

Com looked down with an exaggerated stare and saw that his magazine was upside down. He threw the magazine up in the air and woke up a student at the table behind him. "I'm not dyslexic! Mums will be so happy!" He extended his hand. "I'm Com DeGroot."

Cate subtly nodded. "I know. I've seen your jump shot. Not bad. Though you could work on your defense a bit." She shook his hand. "Cate."

"Pleasure to meet you, Cate. You know something? You are so attractive, I actually walked all the way over here from that aisle over there to say hi to you." He waved his hand at the main aisle twenty feet away.

She looked and smiled. "Really? From way over there? I'm such a lucky girl."

"You're lucky and ridiculously attractive. Do you mind if I ask you something personal?"

She shook her head.

"What do you call a crazy North Pole resident?"

Cate leaned her chin out toward Com, and squinted her eyes. "Is that a personal question?"

"Well, it's personal to me. I have a lot of crazy North Pole residents in my family. So, what do you call them?"

"Um, I don't know."

"A bi-polar bear." Com let out an exaggerated laugh, annoying some studiers nearby, to whom he looked to help him enjoy his pun.

Cate smiled at the bad joke. "Did you just make that up?"

"Yeah." Com grinned and shook his head. "So, I'd love to hang out more, but I have a really important meeting to get to and you look like you're busy with all your right-side-up words and stuff—"

"Oh? What's your really important meeting?"

"Ah, well, I'm meeting with this big cheese, owner of a pro team. You know the new team, the Czars? Me and the owner are going to have a little powwow."

Cate looked intrigued. "Oh, really?"

"Yeah. Actually, I really hate the guy. He's a real asshole, but he could be my boss in a few months, so I have to suck up a little, I guess."

Cate leaned forward. "Really? Tell me, how is he an 'A' hole?"

"Well, the guy's a banker or something by trade and he's not a basketball guy at all. I don't know why he's even in the league. He doesn't know a thing about the game really. The Czars were an instant contender until he bought the team and now they're completely pathetic. He's just awful, but I guess that's what happens when you don't really care about the game and you're only concerned with money."

"And you have a problem with money?" Cate asked.

"No, not at all. Money's fine for what it can get you. But I don't understand people who sell their souls for money, like this owner I'm meeting.

I would never give up my passion for green. I would take half the money to play for an owner that is actually passionate about the sport."

"Like you are?"

Com nodded.

"Well, I have to agree with you. The owner, Mr. Heatherton, can be very money-driven and self-centered."

Com scrunched his face. "Hey, I didn't tell you his name. How did you know his name?"

"Actually, because I'm having dinner with him tonight. He's my father."

Com shaped an 'O' with his mouth and then smiled. "Get out of town he's your father."

"I'm serious."

Com then scrunched his face and leaned toward Cate. "Wait, you're *that* Cate? The Heatherton heiress Cate—you?" She smiled and nodded. "I heard she was going here. Oh, shit, I feel like a real jerk. I'm sorry." He turned the right corner of his mouth down and looked around. "Well, at least I'm honest." Com smiled.

"Right. I wonder if you would have told me all of that if you knew who I was."

Com nodded. "Sure would have. I'm an open book. I never lie."

"Never?"

"Never."

Cate smiled. "Well that's a very appealing quality to have, honesty. And, as it turns out, I completely agree with you about my father. His only passion, it seems, is money."

Com winced and half-smiled. "Wow, you're Cate Heatherton?"

She raised her eyebrows. "The one and only."

A grin overcame Com's stoic face, and he nodded. "I'll see you around." He knew that he would.

Cate's eyes followed Com as he left the room.

Com DeGroot's twin-engine Citation X landed in pitch darkness at a small airport in Raymondville, Texas, which was four miles outside the roughly one-thousand-square-mile city limits of Ur. The senator and his chief of staff, Kevin Donovan, were in a late-night mental fog as they deplaned and found their luggage. A driver dressed in a simple black suit and black tie met them just outside the security gates on the tarmac and asked them to follow him to the car.

"This is it?" Kevin asked the driver. "No security?" The driver shook his head no, and Kevin looked at Com with a concerned hesitance as they walked. "I still don't like that you left your entire security detail in D.C. It's not wise for a person in your position to go anywhere unprotected."

"I'll be fine, Kevin," Com said assuredly.

Com took the front passenger seat, Kevin opened a backseat door, and the driver, who had introduced himself as Gregory, got into the driver's seat. Gregory looked at the passengers slyly. "You ready for an experience of a lifetime?" The driver gave Com and Kevin a wide grin and wrinkled his forehead.

Kevin looked out the window. "Nothin' like a little hyperbole to start off a diplomatic mission."

"It's not hyperbole, my friend. Ur is unlike anything you've ever seen." Gregory pulled away from the airport parking lot and drove two hundred yards to an unmanned checkpoint. In front of the car was a pitch-black road with brilliantly lighted road markers. Gregory handed Com and Kevin each a thin plastic tablet computer with a single line of text displayed on the monitor. "Everyone who enters Ur is required to sign a formal agreement," he explained.

The tablet monitor read, "I agree to respect the unalienable rights of all human beings and to harm no one."

Com frowned and tilted his head backward, then signed the tablet with the attached stylus. After selecting 'OK' on the computer, an outline of a hand was displayed. Gregory noticed some confusion on Com's face and he explained, "You need to give them your handprint for the biometric readout. It's fine." Com placed his hand on the tablet, and the tablet scanned the hand and produced a signal of approval. Com then handed the computer back to Gregory.

Kevin followed suit and asked Gregory, "So, what's so special about this Ur place?"

Gregory stored the tablet computers and fastened his seat belt. "What do you know about foam, Mr. Donovan?"

Without response, Gregory hit the gas and drove through a checkpoint. Once they merged onto the main highway, Gregory pointed to the road in front of them. "You see this road we're on?" The two passengers looked, then nodded. "That's not asphalt, that's foam. It's durable; it's safe; it's quick to repair; and it makes for a hell of a ride." Gregory looked for confirmation from his passengers before continuing. "It also happens to be illegal to use anywhere outside of Ur, Texas."

"Oh, yeah? Why's that?" Com asked curiously.

"Because the contractors' union and the asphalt association have connections in Washington and got the foam listed as an environmental hazard. But that's absolutely ridiculous. This foam is as clean as anything you've seen. But have you seen how asphalt is produced? It's a hot, smelly environmental wreck, but their associations have people in powerful places who can okay asphalt and outlaw foam roads, which don't have the powerful lobbyists."

After a brief silence, Gregory called out, "Ana, drive to North Park, Ur." A sultry woman's voice emanating from the car's speaker system affirmed the driver's command, and the lights on the dashboard dimmed. Gregory let go of the steering wheel and sat back in his seat.

Com was alarmed that the driver had released the steering wheel and looked around for an answer—no one was driving the car. Kevin yelled an obscenity from the back seat. Gregory jumped back to the wheel. "I'm sorry, I forgot to mention," he calmly said. "This car is equipped with an autonomous driving feature—it's called Ana V., Autonomous

Navigational Vehicle. It uses GPS, video cues, and radar to determine where you are and how to get you where you want to go."

Kevin was incredulous. "Impossible. Why haven't I seen anything like this on the market?"

The driver thought about it. He had again taken his hands off the steering wheel to let the autonomous car do the driving. "Well, I'm pretty sure this feature is illegal on the outside, too. See, I couldn't activate Ana V. until I got within the Ur borders. Not *safe* enough. The U.S. Auto Conglomerate made sure of that because they knew the technology competition would have crushed them." He finished with a mocking tone.

"What kind of car is this?" Com asked, intrigued.

"This, my friends, is a Tesla Model T 800 with a 120-volt AC induction air-cooled electric motor with variable frequency drive."

"Tesla, huh?" Kevin said skeptically. "Didn't they go out of business?"

Gregory nodded. "As far as the outside is concerned, yes."

Com squinted and subtly shook his head. "Well, it looks like they haven't sold many of these here in Texas either." He noted the absence of other cars on the three-lane highway. "You got a real nice foam highway, but no cars to drive on it."

The driver nodded at the critique. "Well, actually, during the day, there are more cars per mile on this highway than any other three-lane highway in the country. But it's always moving—there's no congestion. No insane traffic delays or construction that takes three years longer to complete than it was supposed to. That's the difference."

Kevin leaned up between the two front seats. "What do you mean there's no congestion? Because the cars are all automated or something?"

"Well, not all the cars here are, though that is part of it," the driver said. "Really, the engineers were just smart when they built this road—like for instance, you know how they have those traffic lights to limit cars piling on the highways in other cities?" He waited for a nod from Com.

"Well, the point of those is to keep traffic flowing, but the lights make cars come to a complete stop right before getting on the highway. And those cars can't speed up to highway velocity before they have to merge and they end up *slowing* down people already on the highway and eventually cause *more* traffic! Well, duh!" Gregory was visibly getting excited. "The people who designed this puppy got rid of the stop lights right before the highway and helped cars get to speed by starting on-ramps uphill, like over there." Gregory pointed to such an on-ramp. The ramp made a bridge over the highway, and each on-ramp began nearly twenty feet above the road. "So instead of using physics against traffic, they're using physics to prevent it here. Like I said, you haven't seen anything like Ur."

Almost to himself, Kevin muttered, "Yeah, that's nice for preplanned highways, but not every road can be built like this."

Gregory did not hear Kevin. "And each lane has a designated speed." He pointed at the road ahead. "See how this lane says '65'? That's the designated speed. The next lane is seventy, and the far lane is the passing lane. That way, there's none of this ninety-year-old granny driving thirty-five miles an hour in the fast lane."

Com recognized that the idea was smart but shrugged it off. "So, how does the government pay for all this? Do they get state money? I know they don't get federal money here ' cause they're not paying any federal taxes, right?"

"What government?" the driver asked earnestly. "This is a private road."

Com was unbelieving. "What?"

"Yeah, in fact we've gone through two tolls so far to pay for it." The driver patted a small box on the dashboard that displayed '11.64.'

"Is that how much it's cost?" Kevin interrogated the driver.

"Yeah. It'll be about a hundred five dollars to get you to North Park where your hotel is."

"That's outrageous. What kind of toll road charges a hundred bucks?" Kevin squeaked.

"Well, roads aren't cheap, even foam ones, and that's what it takes to pay for it. And if it's too expensive for someone, they always have the option to just not drive on it. That way they would never have to pay for it. It's not like that everywhere else. In the rest of the country, you have to pay for roads whether you use them or not . . . or even when no one uses them. Remember the bridge to nowhere?" Gregory chuckled but Com and Kevin weren't in the mood to laugh. Gregory's passengers weren't combative, just tired. "That's all right, Senator," the driver assured. "Ur takes a little getting used to, but I think you'll be very impressed if you give it a shot."

At that moment, the autonomously driven car followed the road as it descended for what appeared to be a hundred feet into a well-lighted tunnel that seemed to go on forever. Com looked ahead in astonishment at the long tunnel.

"What is *this*?" Com asked.

The driver nodded. "This? This is why the toll costs so much." Com and Kevin listened for more. "So, I told you that this highway was privately funded, right? Well, the company that built the highway couldn't secure the rights to build it through all the development above, so everyone involved agreed that a tunnel under the city would suit everyone's needs. You've heard of the Big Dig they did back in the day in Boston? Well, this is like a Big Dig on steroids."

Com remembered the Big Dig. They had taken an entire Boston freeway and put it underground to make room for parks and walkways. It was an enormous project and extremely controversial. He remembered that it had been projected to cost two billion dollars and ended up costing nearly twelve times as much. He also remembered the instability of the construction. At one point, a section of the roof caved in and killed a woman in her car. Com looked up at the roof of the tunnel he was riding through and shuddered.

"How much did this cost? It can't be worth it," Kevin challenged.

The driver nodded. "Just under ten billion. Of course, these guys didn't have to deal with all the bureaucrats and unions. Those guys make it impossible to get anything done under budget." He looked at Com. "No offense. You know, it's amazing what can be built when you get all the leeches out of the way —people that don't contribute, they just *manage*." Kevin said something about slave labor under his breath.

Com cut off the driver's rambling. "Look, I don't think the Big Dig was justified. How can *this* be justified?"

"Well," the driver said thoughtfully, "that's the point. It doesn't have to be justified. No one forced anyone to pay for this road. No land was confiscated. Only people who want to use it have to pay for it. On the other hand, people riding their bikes in California had to pay for the Big Dig in Boston through their federal tax dollars. That doesn't make much sense, does it?"

"That isn't true, Kevin interjected. "The highway fund gets money from gasoline taxes and car registration. If you don't have a car, you're not paying for bridges to nowhere."

"Well, that's the theory," Gregory quickly responded, "but you should know that's not how it works in practice. Actually only about a third of those taxes and fees go to roads and highways. The rest goes to unrelated stuff and, when there's a big project like the Big Dig, money comes from the General Fund. It's not a direct transfer of money by any means."

Something didn't sound quite right for Kevin. He leaned forward a little. "But don't people have the right to travel wherever they want? Shouldn't people have access to roads for free?"

"That assumes that things government does are free, which is incorrect," the driver replied, as if he had argued this point before. "But sure, people can go wherever they want as long as they're not trespassing. And people *do* go wherever they want in Ur. The only difference is that they can't take money and property away from others to build a road to go wherever they want and they can't ask some government authority to take money or property for them to do it. Like in the twenties and forties and fifties in New York City where they wiped out whole communities and taxed the bejeezus out of people to build a cross-town freeway that no one wanted in the first place." Com shook his head, partly in astonishment at the driver's knowledge and partly at his argument.

"Look, guy, they had good intentions," Kevin threw out.

"Yeah, that reminds me of another famous road paved with those," the driver responded quickly.

The rest of the trip to Com and Kevin's hotel was quiet, as Com was exhausted and Kevin was waiting for the driver to say something so that he could criticize it. After about ten minutes in the tunnel, the car autonomously changed lanes and exited the main thoroughfare to the right. Ana V. announced that they had arrived at their destination.

The car pulled up to the underground entrance to the hotel, and a night manager greeted the senator and his chief of staff. Kevin asked if they needed to tip the driver, and he replied that everything had been taken care of. The night manager showed Com and Kevin to their rooms, which were spacious and detailed with a modern classic style. The hotel was nice, but Com was unimpressed. He had seen nice hotels—the nicest—during his stint as a professional ball player.

Com laid himself down on the bed, turned on the television, and briefly thought about the potential that he was receiving radioactivity poisoning. He then promptly fell into a deep, much-needed sleep.

Eighteen

Com woke up to a call from Kevin Donovan. Once Com answered, Kevin explained that Com had thirty minutes to be ready to meet with the so-called "archon"—the mayor—of the city, Santiago Garza. He was scheduled to give Com and Kevin a personal tour of the city of Ur. Com jumped into action, showered, and threw on a nicely pressed suit then met Kevin in the hotel lobby. They walked through an underground tunnel to arrive at the basement entrance of the archon's building.

As Com and Kevin passed through a security gate, Com noticed gilded letters emblazoned on the building above the entrance: VULNERO NEMO. The words had an austere, profound look, which complimented the clean, modern building. Com mouthed the words, "Vulnero nemo."

Once inside, Com and his chief saw a number of people in an open expanse of the building's lobby.

"Senator! It is a distinct pleasure! My name is Santiago Garza." The Latin-accented call found Com DeGroot like a friendly beacon as he walked into the lobby of the archon's building. The voice came from a finely dressed man who stood out from a small group of people, including Senator Elizabeth Derkins and Senate staffers. Santiago Garza, the archon of Ur, was tall, handsome, and he exuded an aura of good-natured confidence. His accent, which had been shaped in a coastal city in Venezuela, added to the charming presence of the thirty-five-year-old gentleman.

Garza had first come to the United States in his early twenties for medical school and was set to return to Venezuela when his parents informed the young student that the Venezuelan government, run by Horatio Martinez, had confiscated the family's oil refinery business. In one swift despotic act by the Venezuelan president, the Garzas descended from the heights of wealth in Venezuela to the depths of dependent poverty and eventually required government benefits in order to support themselves. Santiago ignored the guilt he felt when his visa lapsed and secured a job working illegally as a physician in a homeless shelter in the San Diego area. Garza justified his illegal presence by rejecting any welfare he could have obtained while he was in the United States. He did not pay income taxes, and so he did not take advantage of the social safety net for which most of those taxes paid. In his mind, Santiago was not a drain on his adopted society, he was a boon. He was technically breaking the law before the amnesty, yes, but he was not doing anything *wrong*.

Years later, Garza took advantage of the amnesty that U.S. President Robert Burke had granted to all undocumented workers within the borders of the United States and became a full U.S. citizen. At that time, Santiago felt he was no longer a refugee from political corruption in his home country—he finally had a home.

The Venezuelan and his family were not strangers to political refugee status. Before Santiago fled Venezuela to escape Martinez's despotic ways, his grandparents had fled Spain during the Civil War of 1936 to avoid the dictates of Francisco Franco. Earlier descendents of Garza's had even moved around the Basque region in Spain to avoid domination by the Spanish government during pre-modern unrest.

But Garza was no longer under the shadow of a totalitarian regime in Venezuela. In fact, the archon of Ur had lived a charmed life ever since his arrival in the United States, and he was constantly aware of that detail. He was grateful for his prominent position in a place with such a high standard of living, and he made his gratitude known by maintaining a subtle smile on his consistently placid face.

Santiago shook Com's hand with both of his hands and welcomed him warmly. "I must say that I was disappointed when I heard you were not going to support this wonderful place. But I am too happy to see that you are here to learn too much about it."

Com returned the smile. "Thank you, Mr. Garza. I look forward to learning more about this place."

"Very good, señor!" Santiago said and turned to Kevin for a firm handshake. He then addressed the entire group. "Okay, then, now that we're all here, I'd like to lead you to the showing room where we have a wonderful presentation about this land of Ur. After that, I will be glad to address any questions you have about Ur and then I'd like to take you on a wonderful tour of the city-state itself."

Santiago Garza led the group to a room adjacent to the main lobby. As they made their way over to the theater, Senator Derkins addressed Com sarcastically. "Nice of you to join us, Senator."

"Senator." Com nodded.

"What do you think of this guy?" Mrs. Derkins asked, indicating her question referred to Santiago. "Do you think he uses the word 'wonderful' enough? He's like a life insurance salesman."

"Well, I just met him, but I think he's genuine enough."

Mrs. Derkins' face did not change.

The group made their way into a dim theater composed of twenty comfortable seats facing a projection glass in the front of the room. Com sat down in the middle of the theater but regretted his decision after Senator Derkins took the seat next to him. The backlit room darkened as soon as everyone was seated, and Santiago yelled out, "Enjoy!"

Suddenly the projection glass became illuminated in a brilliant display of color and energy. The display showed a dark blue field of color spotted with light yellow specs. The yellow specs formed to give the visual impression of the continents of the Earth. A voiceover began to speak. "The Earth at night. Ninety-six percent of the surface is dark. The light regions represent electric light. In other words, technology, civilization, industry." The image on the screen zoomed in to China. "The brightest spot in China is Hong Kong, a free-market enclave established by Great Britain on the edge of communist China. With the same resources and people as mainland China, Hong Kong grew to be the epicenter of economic activity in Asia and now enjoys its place as the sixth largest economy in the world. How did Hong Kong become so successful?" The narrator paused for dramatic effect. "Freedom."

"Imagine . . . " The video showed a panoramic aerial flyover of the wide expanse of a farm. "A place here in the United States where people are free to produce. Imagine a place where people have the liberty to live their own lifestyle." The video cut to a group of friends enjoying a drink in a tavern. "Imagine a place where people take responsibility for themselves and hold compassion for others." The video depicted a friendly woman helping a young man in a wheel chair. "Imagine the city of Ur."

A detailed three-dimensional animation of ancient Iraq was shown on the screen and the voiceover continued. "Named after the birthplace of civilization in the Fertile Crescent, Ur, Texas, located in the Southern United States, promises a rebirth of civilization, today, in the twenty-first century." The graphic display switched to an oil painting of the Founding Fathers signing the Declaration of Independence, which came to life in a natural three-dimensional representation. "Two-hundred-and-fifty years ago, the Founding Fathers of the United States set forth a vision of the ideal society. It was based on one principle: that people should be able to do whatever they wished as long as they did not restrict that right of others. This principle proclaimed that our creator granted unalienable rights—to life, liberty, and the pursuit of happiness among others—to everyone and that no government had the authority to take away those rights.

"But early struggles prevented the United States from completely fulfilling the vision of that principle." Clips of protests and marches were displayed. "It took nearly two hundred years and consistent effort for that vision to be extended to every human being, regardless of sex or race." A photo of Susan B. Anthony was shown followed by a slow-motion film clip of Dr. Martin Luther King, Jr. A flawless artificial representation of King, Anthony, and Thomas Jefferson walking forward together appeared onscreen.

"But while some in the United States have been able to pull themselves out of slavery, everyone has been drawn back into another, more comprehensive, insidious type of thralldom, serfs in a corporatist-socialist state of existence." Views of military personnel and riot police were shown on the projection glass fighting with scruffy-looking rebels. "In fact, since the beginning of the twentieth century, nearly every facet of American life has been overrun by government control." Scenes of lines outside a government medical center were shown, followed by images of a needle being injected into an unhappy youth. Images of stock market charts depicting declining values were displayed over video of frantic traders on the floor of a stock market. "The Founding Fathers never envisioned the government in control of medical services, banking, transportation, or any of the thousands of industries in which the federal government has become entrenched. Yet, today we find ourselves confronting a federal government that controls over half of the economy of the United States and tells us what to drive, what we must inject into our bodies, and when we must risk our lives in war." Video of a young soldier marching was shown. "And the government pays for this massive coercion by taxing over fifty percent of the remaining activity that it doesn't have direct control over."

Senator Derkins leaned toward Com and whispered, "Do you believe this crap?" Com looked at her and raised his eyebrows but said nothing.

"Ten years ago," the narrator continued, "like the Founding Fathers, a new visionary came to America to change all of that. Arun Kula, originally from Hyderabad, Andhra Pradesh, India set out to turn a disaster area into the rebirth of civilization." Video of a scarred landscape growing plant life in a time-lapse video was shown. "Using cutting edge technology, Kula's team of scientists converted the radioactive area leftover from a nuclear meltdown into an ecologically safe and naturally robust landscape." A well-dressed and sophisticated-looking East Indian man was shown in a visionary posture overseeing a construction site. "In exchange for the cleanup efforts, Kula was granted the rights to a charter city with independent status within the borders of the United States. As with its predecessor Hong Kong and other special administrative zones, this meant that the people within Ur had no obligation to follow U.S. regulations or pay federal taxes. Additionally, the district would receive no federal funding for social welfare, infrastructure, or other benefits. The city was to be completely independent of the federal government."

Another time-lapse video showed the construction of a building. "But Kula did not establish Ur in order to develop the next greatest shopping mall—he had much bigger plans for the area. It was to become a model of liberty for the rest of the world, the Hong Kong of the West, an enclave of freedom. Many charter cities have been introduced recently with different or fewer laws than their host country, but the people of Ur were to live under just one law: Vulnero nemo—harm no one. In exchange for unprecedented freedom, every citizen of Ur must make this one vow to harm no one, whether it be physically, mentally, or environmentally. An elegantly simple structure of self-regulation and a robust voluntary judicial system maintains that rule of law."

A flyover of the growing metropolis of Ur was shown accompanied by soaring symphonic music. "Today, Ur stands as a magnet of creative and productive liberty-minded people. Thousands of companies have moved their headquarters to Ur to enjoy the tax-free environment. Inventors have come to Ur in droves to escape restrictive regulation. And people of all demographics have flooded the city to live their lives as *they* see fit." Images of happy people bustling in an open city forum were shown.

"And it has worked. Hundreds of vital inventions have been developed in Ur already, including nanotechnology liver reconstruction, magnetic resonance tissue regeneration, and the well-known foam highway complete with autonomous vehicles. In addition, per capita GDP in Ur is over twice that of surrounding areas and nearly three times as much as the U.S. as a whole."

Video of a doctor bouncing a baby on her knee was shown. "The result is the healthiest, happiest, and most productive population on Earth." The video showed a family in a park, businesspeople, and then panned to the sky. "Welcome to wealth. Welcome to peace. Welcome to justice. Welcome to Ur."

Nineteen

As the viewers filed out of the theater, Senator Elizabeth Derkins disregarded the content of the film. Instead she turned to Com DeGroot and thanked him for the bipartisan nature of his co-sponsorship of Senate bill six-sixty-four. "We Democrats have the majority in both houses, but we need progressively-minded people like you to ensure important bills like this make it through."

Com nodded and smiled. "Yeah, I'm pretty important."

Mrs. Derkins feigned a pleasant surprise at Com's audacity.

Santiago Garza gathered everyone together. "Well, I hope you all enjoyed our program. Did you see me in the film? I was in the background when they showed Mr. Kula. No? Oh well, next time look for me," Santiago said in a friendly tone. "Are there any questions that I can perhaps answer for you? Any observations?"

"I thought it was a nice little show, but clearly propagandistic," Mrs. Derkins said in a nasal tone.

"Ah, I see. Was there anything in particular that you felt was misleading or untrue?" the archon inquired.

Derkins curled the left side of her lips and squinted. "Yes, just about the entire presentation was misleading. Your figures about GDP are debatable, and how can you claim to have the happiest people on Earth? Who knows that?"

Garza smiled. "Sí, there have been scientific studies that compare the wealth and happiness of the citizens of Ur compared to other places around the globe. The figures are all in the materials your staff was given."

"But doesn't that depend on how you define happiness? If money makes you happy, I guess this is the place for you."

Garza became conciliatory. "Yes, of course. This is true." Santiago's accent was thick on the word 'this' as looked for someone else to speak. "Are there any specific questions I can address?"

One of Mrs. Derkins' staffers straightened his back and spoke. "Why do they call you 'archon'?"

"Ah, yes. 'Archon' is an old Greek term meaning 'ruler.' It is what they used in ancient Athens. But, of course, that word is a little misleading. There's no much *ruling* going on here in Ur. At least not in the traditional sense of a king or president telling all his subjects what to do or even a mayor or governor dictating what goes on in his jurisdiction." He thought for a second and asked the entire party, "Tell me, have you all been briefed on the overall structure of the society here?" Garza received blank stares and hesitant looks. "Well then, shall I go over the structure again so that everyone is, how you say, on the same page?"

Garza accepted everyone's nods and began to describe the governmental structure of Ur. "As you all know, Ur is a sovereign city-state within the borders of the wonderful state of Texas and within the United States of America, much like the independent Indian nations or special administrative zones in various countries around the world. We are no beholden to any of the laws or rules of the surrounding governments. Of course, if a fugitive of justice somehow was able to enter the borders of Ur, the appropriate outside authorities have the right to extract this man.

"Believe it or not, the film you just saw was correct. There is but one law of the land for the entire place of Ur and that is 'harm no one.' You all have signed an agreement to this law when you entered the borders. It is illegal to harm someone's person, his or her property, or his or her environment. You may say, well, Santiago, these is pretty vague and you will not be surprised that many people have tried to push the limits of this law, but the enforcement of this law is where the—how do you say—magic comes in." Santiago raised his eyebrows as if he were reading a book to a class of children. "Everyone in Ur is responsible for the protection of everyone else, thus we have numerous security agencies and consumer protection advocates—all are independent and voluntary. If someone feels that they are harmed in any way, they can go through the appropriate private channels to resolve the issue. Everything is reported through the various advocate agencies, and companies or people who have caused harm are rated poorly with those agencies."

"Kinda like eBay," a staffer said.

Santiago smiled. "Sí. Kind of like eBay."

Senator Derkins cleared her throat and protested, "Well, that's great for small yard-sale transactions, but what about large multi-million dollar fraud or extortion?"

"Those are handled in the same way. If a business is defrauded of millions of dollars, the criminal party and the others involved are recorded by hundreds of auditors and business advocate groups, and their respective business ratings reflect such fraud. And each person in those companies is held accountable, too. Here in Ur, transparency is real, not just a campaign promise."

Com was curious. "But the criminals don't get punished? Where's the justice? Where's the security?"

Santiago nodded. "Oh, but they do get punished. After such an act, the criminals do not get business after this time. What's more, they are subject to moral judgment of the population as a whole, not just one judge or small jury."

"But what about the millions of dollars they stole? What happens to that?" Kevin questioned.

"The associated banks have the authority to rescind any illegal transactions. Some of the banks around here are known for that and do better business because of it. They offer protection for the little guy. For example, it's much the way credit cards operate on a large scale. When there is a fraudulent purchase made on your credit card, you have certain protections in place. Your credit card will cover the activity once it is investigated. Justice is served. It's the same with illegal transactions with banks here."

"And what about physical harm? What if some thug beats up an innocent bystander?" a staffer squeaked.

"That would be tragic if it ever happened, and, unfortunately, I'm sure it will at some point," Santiago said compassionately. "But here in Ur, every building owner, every shopping mall proprietor, every park manager is responsible for the security within their establishment. It is up to them to accept or deny whomever they wish. As you will see, Ur is one of the most secure places in the country."

Com subtly shook his head. Without an authoritative police force? It can't be secure, he thought.

Senator Derkins spoke out. "Mr. Garza, a few years ago a young girl went running at a park in one of my districts and a criminal deviant sexually assaulted her and brutally killed her." Senator Derkins' voice quivered. "As a result, I put forth legislation to increase police patrols in parks and recreational areas and to restrict the times that those parks are available. But now you're telling me that a police force isn't necessary to prevent sickening crimes like that?"

Santiago's face became solemn. "Senator, I am deeply moved by such accounts. That is truly the worst thing that could happen to a community. But, may I remind you that this crime happened in one of *your* districts, not in Ur. I don't know if a society can completely prevent crime from happening, but they can do the next best thing and that is to enable everyone to fight crime, not just to rely on a designated police force."

Mrs. Derkins' face did not change. "Don't you think you need more regulation and more than just one law to stop criminals like that?"

"My dear friend," Santiago said warmly, "was there not a law on the book already to prevent that? Additional laws would not help. It's true, more laws create more criminals, but not necessarily more justice."

Senator Derkins looked away.

"Of course," Santiago continued, "we have an official and robust judicial system, called the *dikasteria*, made up of well over ten thousand members—whomever wishes to be included. If you believe someone has wronged you or justice has not been served, you can bring your complaint to the *thesmothetea*, or city council, of which the archon—me—presides. We then assign a judge randomly from the list of volunteers in the *dikasteria* who have offered their services for this purpose. The defendant is asked to appear before the court and the trial is heard. The judge decides the case and, if there is no appeal, provides the penalty. If there is an appeal, the process is repeated with three randomly selected judges." Santiago grinned.

A curious Senator Derkins spoke up. "And if that judgment is challenged? What if there's another appeal?"

"The process repeats, but this time with nine judges. And if there is another appeal, seventeen judges are used, and so on up until all available judges in the *dikasteria* are called to decide the case based on the information previously submitted. This judgment is final."

"It's like ancient Greece," Kevin said softly.

"Indeed, sí. Much like ancient Athens, in name as well as form," Garza agreed. "No institution on Earth is more democratic."

"Or more ridiculous," Senator Derkins jabbed.

Santiago stared at Senator Derkins momentarily before replying. "My dear Senator, is it any more ridiculous than the maze of bureaucratic nonsense that has enveloped the federal government of the United States?" Garza continued, speaking to the rest of the group. "At any rate, no case has ever gotten as far as the entire *dikasteria*. In fact, most cases are resolved in the initial stage of the judicial system if not by self-regulation."

"And the enforcement of the judges' decisions?" Com inquired. "How is that handled?"

"Well, we haven't had a trial where the losing case has failed to agree to the terms. People here want to be contributing members of society, and they realize that they must abide by the law of the land. If that were to happen, the judges may ask the appropriate banking institutions to withdraw funds from the guilty party's account."

"It's anarchy!" Senator Derkins practically yelled.

Santiago nodded. "*Autarchy*, señora. Not anarchy. While anarchy implies no ruler, we here in Ur are *self*-ruled. Anarchy is a lack of the rule of law. As you will see, the rule of law is present here, perhaps more than anywhere else, including—or especially—Washington, D.C. It's a funny paradox about government—the more laws there are, the harder it is for everyone to comply."

Senator Derkins was skeptical. "Well, that can be debated. So, who pays for all of your simplistic . . . rule of law here?" She let her eyes wander around the sophisticated lobby.

Santiago acknowledged that her question was a good one. "Yes, sometimes the judge requires the losing case to provide the fees associated, including attorney fees, and other times non-profit legal organizations pay the necessary funds. When the damages are considerable, the defendant may be required to work to pay off the settlement."

Com interjected. "This seems so haphazard. Why doesn't the city council pay for the justice system?"

"And where would the council—the *thesmothetea*—get the monies for this system?" Santiago asked, knowing what the answer would be.

"From . . . taxes, of course," Com replied.

Santiago smiled as if he had caught a bear in a trap and was leaning down to let him out. "But Senator, what is taxation but the forceful confiscation of monies by the government? If the *thesmothetea* taxed its citizens, it would be guilty of breaking the one law of the land: to harm no one. Voluntary donations are gladly accepted, like at any other private non-profit, but as soon as they take money against the people's will, they are breaking the law."

Kevin and some of the others rolled their eyes. "But isn't that the authority of the city council or the state government or the federal government? To tax for the general welfare?"

"Why should the makers of the law be exempt from the laws that they make? And doesn't that ideology inevitably lead to tyranny, as it has done in my home country of Venezuela? Isn't that popular concept of a hypocritical government what has led to the all the revolutions throughout history?"

"But what if everyone in the Ur here agrees to pay taxes for the judicial system?" Com asked. "Wouldn't that be okay?"

"But they are, through voluntary effort and charities. Everyone knows that if they fail to support the system, it will fail them. Here, my friends, everyone shares the responsibility of justice, not just the judges."

Com and Senator Derkins were silent, but Kevin peered at Santiago through squinted eyes. "It can't work."

"What is it they say, Señor Donovan? 'Those who say it can't be done are usually interrupted by someone doing it'? It *can* work, and it is working! I will show you. Come, let us begin our tour." Archon Garza waved the collection of people toward the elevator as he jumped out to the lead.

Twenty

The group of politicians and staffers led by Santiago Garza ascended in the elevator and walked through the main lobby to exit the building. The sun was intense as it beamed down on the perfectly manicured office park to which the archon's building belonged. The park was covered by billowing jacaranda trees that were just starting to reveal their lavender flowers as an indication of the arrival of spring. Businesspeople were scattered about, casually taking breaks from their workday. The atmosphere was quiet except for the occasional birdsong, and the air smelled fresh and clean and the temperature was warm but not uncomfortable.

As they walked, Santiago Garza gave each group member a hand-sized black electronic device and explained that it would be needed for the tour. Com thought it might have been a sort of radio that would provide an audio description of the city. He noticed a small amount of static emanating from the devices, but it was barely noticeable compared with the atmospheric sounds of trees blowing in the wind.

Santiago Garza pointed out some of the major international companies that had relocated their headquarters to the ever-growing Ur: UBS financial firm, Exxon Mobile, McDonald's, Coca-Cola, Google. They were all taking advantage of the city's tax-free environment to maximize profits and expand their enterprises, Santiago explained. The companies had brought over fifty thousand employees to the jurisdiction and more than doubled the population of the city within the previous five years.

While Garza spoke, however, most of the group members were preoccupied with either their standard handheld cell phones or the implant versions, which were invisible to a bystander but elicited similar inconsiderate chatter. Com, on the other hand, was attentive. In a friendly tone, Com addressed the archon. "Santiago—can I call you that?" Santiago nodded. "Santiago, there are a number of high-level concerns regarding this city and not one of them involves the businesses that have moved here. Are we going to address those concerns today?"

"Sí, sí," Santiago said, nodding. "You refer to the claims of resource-hogging and perhaps radiation cover-up?"

"Yes. That's right."

"Sí, señor. We shall address every concern you have today. Please bear with us." Santiago lifted his voice to make sure everyone else could hear as he shifted the focus of conversation. "Ur is divided into forty-seven townships, which have evolved very distinct personalities, if you will." The group walked through the office park and climbed a set of stairs to an elevated tram station. "We will visit the least attractive of them all first. This is the manufacturing-heavy Rand Industrial Sector."

Santiago paid for everyone's tram fare at an automated ticket teller and instructed each group member to place his or her hand on a biometric scanner near the entrance to the tram. Each guest held a hand to the scanner and entered the tramcar, which held about thirty passengers comfortably. Kevin Donovan took a look around and posed a question to Santiago. "Why all the trams and trains? What's wrong with roads?"

Santiago acknowledged the good question. "Sí, we do have a lot of trams here. The truth is that they are much more efficient and practical than bulky and inefficient roadways."

Mrs. Derkins overheard the exchange and interjected. "I actually agree with you on this, Mr. Garza—I'm a huge proponent of mass transit. But you make it sound so easy. It's really not; you have to force it down people's throats. If the tram system is so efficient and practical, why doesn't it just catch on everywhere, like in D.C. or Los Angeles?"

"Well, if I had to answer that question, I would guess it has something to do with the corporatist system in place right now in those cities."

Mrs. Derkins peered at her interlocutor. "What corporatist system?"

"Señora, surely you are aware that six of the ten largest corporations in America are gas or automobile companies?" Santiago raised an eyebrow.

"These companies have done extremely well in the current transportation environment. Exxon Mobile and Valero lobby the federal government for more highways and more construction, which the government happily provides because the people want to see something done with their tax dollars. They want to see new roads. But these new roads just push development further away from other development in what I think they call 'suburban sprawl.' And the oil companies are happy pumping more and more gas into the cars of the commuters to get them around the sprawl. And their money is sent back to Washington to support more roads and more distant commutes.

"But none of this would be possible if the government didn't have the authority to take people's money to build the roads that the oil companies want. You take away government roads and you will see efficient and ecologically sound tram systems in every city in the country."

Senator Derkins was skeptical but said nothing and just lifted her eyebrows.

The tram shuttled the tour group, along with a dozen other passengers, to a factory-like building within a couple minutes. The squat building, with numerous pipes projecting out from all angles, was a clean and stark inside. The tour guide explained that the facility—a desalination plant—converted seawater into potable water.

The tour group's host described the place as they walked into the building. "You may have heard that Ur is 'stealing' resources from around the country, including fresh water. But I assure you that all of our water is *created* right here. We do not take any fresh water from any other source, In fact, water is fast becoming a major export from here." Once inside, the group inspected the plant and saw how enormous turbines and filters transformed millions of gallons of water from the nearby Laguna Madre into drinking water and other useful derivatives, like sea salt, every hour.

"So where do they get the claims that Ur is stealing water?" Com asked.

"Ah, it is one of the old standbys of the modern media conglomerate—they made it up. Obviously, water is a very important resource and a hot topic today. So those who wish to antagonize Ur will use those types of issues to win support to their side."

From the desalination plant, the archon-turned-tour-guide shuffled the group to another tram station. This tram was different from the first. It consisted of small cars suspended from above on a track, much like a rollercoaster. Each tramcar was meant for individual passengers and had room for baggage below the seating compartment. Again, Santiago paid for the group and each member took a car before it swiftly moved out of the station. After a few minutes of the exhilarating ride, the tour members exited their cars onto the destination platform. Mrs. Derkins laughed, saying she had never had more fun than on that ride. Others in the group shared a wide grin with her.

After the group took a moment to refocus, Santiago Garza pointed around their new location and described the area.

"This, my friends, is Amaurot. An ardent socialist purchased this nineteen-square-mile plot of land after The Green Group had put it up for sale. Since then, he has welcomed everyone who wants to come and participate in a great communal living experience. Throughout this district, there is no money and no property. Everyone here works to his own ability and gives to others according to their need. It's really a marvelous experiment."

One of Senator Derkins' staffers scrunched his face. "Mr. Garza, I thought you were strictly opposed to communism, as in Venezuela."

"Well, señor, there is nothing inherently wrong with socialism as you see here. People can get along quite well under socialism. The problem is when you *force* socialism on a people, as they have in my home country."

The tour guests peered past the tram station where they were and looked out to a small shantytown and a collection of lush vegetable and produce fields. Santiago continued. "You may have heard reports of slave labor here in Ur, and they usually point to these citizens. The citizens in Amaurot make no money, per se, but there is no money to be made. Of course, this type of existence would be illegal outside of Ur because these workers would be taxed on their production even though they had no money to pay for these taxes."

Senator Derkins' mouth was open in astonishment. A staffer mouthed the word "wow."

After his description, Santiago led the group back on the tramcars and away to the next stop.

The tramcars flew to a neighborhood called Jefferson Heights, just miles away from the shantytown. It was full of new buildings modeled after the European style of a bottom story dedicated to retail and dining and the top two or three stories dedicated to residential living. There were very few roads for cars, but everything was connected with well-manicured walkways. The area was bustling with activity. Children were running around a small playground in a center courtyard, customers were bobbing in and out of fashionable stores, and young couples were enjoying an early lunch at various cafés. Com thought he might see Cate at one of the cafés, but his halfhearted search came up empty.

The group walked through the shopping district and down what seemed to be an alleyway for pedestrians only. They came upon a tree-shaded trail that followed along a large pond. The trail was full of bikers and joggers. A mom was pushing her infant in a stroller, and a kid weaved in and out of traffic on his skateboard. Santiago explained that they had just left Jefferson Heights and were entering Parc Jefferson, the Central Park of Ur, a twenty-square-mile expanse of open fields, small wooded areas, and lakes and streams.

After walking a short way into the park, Santiago asked everyone to look around. The heavenly scene combined rolling hills, ponds, fountains, and various forms of wildlife in a picturesque landscape.

"We are presently standing over the very site of the nuclear power plant, which failed over ten years ago," Santiago said clearly.

Immediately, there was an uncomfortable shift in everyone's stature. Senator Derkins began to look around nervously, and Com looked straight at a completely comfortable Santiago Garza.

"Oh, I get it," Mrs. Derkins said. "So you put a park over the melt-down and you think everything's fine? You think that just because it doesn't look like a problem, it'll be okay?"

"Yeah," Com agreed skeptically and pointed to a nearby pond. "You got any three-eyed fish swimming around in there?"

Santiago reached out his hand and patted Senator Derkins on the shoulder. "I assure you that this environment is as clean as it gets."

No one was convinced. A staffer responded, "Yeah, I assure you."

Santiago offered to explain the cleanup process that The Green Group had undergone to eliminate the radioactive isotopes from the surrounding land using state-of-the-art potassium iodide solution spray and injection, but Senator Derkins rejected the offer, saying that they had hired scientists to do all the number crunching. Instead, Santiago addressed the entire group. "Well, let's see. You all remember that I gave you a black device this morning outside of my office?" Everyone acknowledged that he had, and some got their devices out of purses or pockets. "These devices are Geiger counters." Santiago stressed the word 'Geiger.' "They are used to evaluate the radioactivity in any given area. If you notice, there is a subtle crackling sound coming out of it." The group collectively listened to the devices' crackling. Com noticed a small display on is device that read "0.025 µSv/h."

"Each crackle represents a radio particle—an alpha, beta, or gamma ray—entering your Geiger counter. Now, you will notice that this reading has not changed dramatically throughout this tour. The noise you hear now reflects background radiation from space or the Earth itself. It is the same as if you were in Kansas or Alaska or the middle of Venezuela. Please, you are welcome to take them home with you and compare the radiation reading there to here. You are standing on the original site of the nuclear accident at this very moment, yet there is no harmful additional radiation. My friends, Ur is spotless."

Twenty-One

The afternoon swelter had escaped from Ur and was replaced with a comfortably warm air that befitted the setting sun. Exotic green jays fluttered around the Arun Kula Museum of Art, which sat on a small hill surrounded by native jacaranda trees that mingled with the imported date palms in the warm breeze. A sweet smell of wildflowers wafted through the air and was accompanied by the sounds of cicadas in the distance.

Com DeGroot, who wore a fashionable Giorgio Armani cocktail suit, walked up the plant-lined travertine stairs to the museum entrance with Kevin Donovan, who wore a suit by a new French designer, Le Grange. They had accepted Santiago Garza's invitation to this reception just after the tour of the city and were eager to relax and enjoy the evening.

At the top of the stairs, a beautiful young woman in a black dress acknowledged Com and Kevin by name and accompanied them to a small elderly lady sitting behind a clothed table who checked a list in front of her. The beautiful young woman invited them to follow a walkway to her right that was lighted by scattered spherical paper lanterns resembling enlarged stars. Com thanked her, and Kevin smiled and winked at her.

As Com and Kevin made their way along the path, the sounds of steel drums and a bass guitar became clearer, as did the picturesque setting of the museum grounds. Multiple off-white travertine buildings intermingled with lush flora. The senator and his chief turned a corner of one of the museum buildings, and the reception party presented itself. Well-dressed groups chatted at standing tables with cocktails under a canvas of lanterns. An island band that consisted of two gentlemen in colorful flowered shirts with khaki pants played warm uplifting music. Their audible elixir had lured a few of the guests on to the dance floor and made everyone else drunk with subconscious joy. The setting sun cast an orange glow through the plants that surrounded the patio and contributed a surreal poetry to the ambiance. Com thought the atmosphere was perfect, but there was something missing—a feeling that he could not pinpoint.

Com looked around for someone he knew, but found no one until his survey of the crowd came to a thin young man dressed in jeans and a T-shirt standing against a row of bushes. Com laughed to himself and tapped Kevin on his arm. "Come on, let's say hi to this guy."

"What guy?" Kevin asked as he followed Com over to the young man.

Justin Timeus looked down as Com and his chief of staff approached. He took a step and a half to his left then retracted and stepped back to his original position. He glanced up at his new company but returned his gaze to the ground.

"Well, if it isn't the computer genius, Mr. Timeus," Com declared.

"Hello, Senator Com DeGroot," Justin said robotically.

"What are you doing here?" Com wondered. Kevin looked around the party and ignored Justin's response.

"I was given an invitation by Veronica Smith earlier today," Justin said while his eyes darted around. "Veronica Smith said that there were extra invitations available because fourteen employees had declined their invitations. I asked her why those employees had declined and she told me that she didn't know personal information like that and then she smiled at me. Veronica Smith has perfectly aligned teeth. I like it when Veronica Smith smiles at me."

Com laughed out loud. "Justin, you are a trip!"

"What's a trip? Why am I a trip?" Justin inquired tersely.

"You're just funny. So, I take it you're not working for Hank Pierpont anymore?"

"That is correct. My immediate supervisor let me go because of budget constraints."

"So now you're here in Ur?"

"Yes," Justin confirmed. "I am researching the intrinsic hypertextuality of the universal nature of humanoid communication for the Alpha Corporation."

"That's great, Justin!" Kevin blurted out. "Hey, question—what in the world does that mean?"

The humor was lost on Justin and he ignored Kevin's question. "I have come across information that may be of interest to you, Senator Com DeGroot. I ran an algorithm involving certain parameters over the last forty thousand days and was able to derive unique but verifiable data showing a statistically significant elevation in ICD-nine categories 'E' eight hundred to 'E' nine-forty-nine among Class-A employees as defined in the federal code. I even used statistical interference."

Com lifted his upper lip. "Uh, sorry there, bud. I don't speak Klingon. Can you give me a little English?"

"My friend Ahmed always says I need to speak to people like they are in grade school, so I was describing the information to you as if you were a third-grader," Justin said without humor. "I will try to rephrase my statement. The empirical data show that Class-A federal employees, or public officials, have a higher rate of 'E' eight hundred to 'E' nine-forty-nine category deaths, which are accidental deaths. This is despite the fact that most public officials have a higher standard of living and are more well-protected than other citizens."

Kevin smirked at the young man and shook his head in disbelief but Com scrunched his face and peered at Justin. "Yeah? What do you mean by accidental death?"

"The list of causes of accidental death includes but is not limited to death by machinery, medical and surgical complications, poisoning by gases, poisoning by liquids, automobile and airplane accidents, falling."

"Okay, so what's your point?" Com looked at Justin with a scrunched face.

"Public officials accidentally die more often than other people. Public officials accidentally die more often than other people by a large margin—beyond any standard of statistical significance. I don't have any information that would explain that data rationally."

"What? Are you talking about me? *I* have a higher chance of accidental death?"

"That is correct, Senator Com DeGroot," Justin said flatly.

"Loony," Kevin hummed then turned to look around the party.

"Man, you're just full of cheerful news, Justin," Com said with a laugh. "Talk about a buzz kill."

"I'm currently looking in to cross-referencing the cause of death data with data from public officials' voting records. It is the next logical step."

Com smiled and shook his head. "That's great, bud. Let me know how that goes."

"Gentlemen!" the warm, exaggerated voice of Santiago Garza proclaimed from ten feet behind Com DeGroot. "I'm so glad you could make it." Com turned around at the sound of Garza's voice, and the Venezuelan-American shook hands with the tall senator and his chief of staff. Justin Timeus took the opportunity to dart away quietly.

Santiago provided a brief survey of the party and pointed out that Senator Elizabeth Derkins had already arrived and that other guests of honor were interspersed throughout the crowd. There was Peter Westings, a British immigrant who studied and taught history. Also present was George Aboyami, a Nigerian chemical engineer who had helped develop a much-heralded cure for bone cancer. World-renowned German violinist Mika Danube graced their presence as well.

Santiago led Com and Kevin to the bar and each ordered a drink. "I wanted to thank you for a fantastic tour today, Santiago," Com said enthusiastically.

"Sí, you liked?" Garza responded. "I suppose if this archon thing doesn't work out, I have a backup in the tour guide industry." Garza chuckled.

As Com waited for his whiskey sour, he looked toward the patio entrance and couldn't help but notice one of the party guests—a stunning living painting of a woman in a dress the color of the sun. Her hair was held up by ribbon, but strands of it found their way to the curve between her neck and shoulder. Her arms were folded but one hand ventured out toward her discussion partner, aiding her thoughts. She was smiling and warmly laughing.

"Ah! Señorita Heatherton." Santiago informed Com after noticing the trance he had fallen into. There were many other women at the party and quite a few in the area of Cate Heatherton, but all eyes were naturally drawn to her. "She is a wonderful, marvelous woman."

Com nodded. "Yes, she is."

Santiago continued. "You would not be surprised but I've asked to court her. Alas, I believe she loves another."

Com looked at Santiago with a raised eyebrow and let his words drip into his mind as he stared at Cate from across the patio. Loves another, he thought. Could it be me?

"Hey, it's your flaming Liberal friend from election night," Kevin blurted out as he attempted to hand Com his drink.

Com ignored his chief of staff and, as if drawn by an irresistible pull, slowly started walking toward Cate. He maneuvered his way through the crowd and found himself interrupting Cate's conversation with two other gentlemen.

With a smile at Com's tactless entrance, Cate welcomed him. "Hello, Senator."

"You look absolutely stunning." Com said, staring into her eyes.

She dipped her head a bit and thanked him, then turned to her company. "These are my colleagues, Hugo and Brian." Com tried to earnestly greet the two but couldn't help return his gaze to Cate.

"It's really good to see you," Com let out.

Cate acknowledged Com's sentiment but tried to keep her colleagues included in the conversation, "This is Senator Com DeGroot, an old friend." She then turned back to Com. "We were just discussing the role of the church in the arts."

Com raised his eyebrows. "Wow, that sounds really . . . boring," he said in an attempt to be funny.

Cate did not take it personally and instead laughed at Com's irreverence. "Stop it. No, Brian says that the arts have benefited heavily from the church, but Hugo thinks that the arts would have been much better off if the artistic geniuses hadn't been monopolized by the church for so long."

Com wanted to talk to Cate alone and he didn't really feel like talking about church or the arts, but he let the topic sink in. Brian spoke up before Com could say anything. "Let's be honest, if it weren't for the church, there wouldn't be the Sistine Chapel, or Montmartre, or any of Bach's music."

"Right," Hugo replied, "but there might have been *more* beautiful works of art in their stead if it weren't for the church dictating what they should produce. Michelangelo and Bach would still have been artistic geniuses if the church hadn't been there, they just would have directed their talents to other, more meaningful causes."

Cate shook her head. "I don't think there could be a more meaningful cause than God, Hugo."

Brian agreed. "Right, just compare Saint Peter's Basilica in Rome with the crap buildings that secularists are constructing today."

Com suddenly found something he could add. "Yes! I know exactly what you're talking about. There are three Senate buildings and the most recent one is hideous, like a big white box with slits on it where the prisoners can look out. What's the point of building something like that?"

Brian nodded. "Well, that's what you get when you replace God with the state as your muse. And when the *government* starts dictating what good art is, look out. That's when you start getting elephant dung on a canvas and people calling it art."

"Well," Hugo said, "I'd rather the government that we all vote on dictate what art is produced rather than some collection of guys with funny hats pushing some phony-baloney tooth fairy. But there are other muses than God and government. I mean, think of all the great plays and music since the Enlightenment that were dedicated to love or higher ethics, not just some dogmatic religion."

Cate thought for a second then spoke. "Absolutely. Love is a great muse. But that's not to say that religion and love are opposed to each other. Have you ever heard the phrase 'God is love'?"

Hugo was on a roll and ignored Cate's question. "And religion actually prevents the spread of good art. Like have you heard of the story of *Miserere*?"

Cate nodded. "Yes, yes." She looked to Com, who was clearly unaware of the story, and sought to explain. "So an Italian Renaissance composer, I think it was Allegri, wrote the most beautiful piece of music ever heard for Easter Mass. Believe me, Com, if you heard this piece, you would convert right there and then. It takes your soul and squeezes every last drop of emotion out of it and fills you with a warm, peaceful appreciation for life. "

Com was captivated. "Wow. I think I can hear it already."

"Oh, you would love it, Com. I wish the church here would perform it for us. They are absolutely phenomenal." Cate smiled at Com.

"Oh?"

"Yes. Com, you have to come with me tomorrow."

"What, church? Uh . . . "

"Anyway, you were saying . . . " Hugo interrupted.

"So, anyway," Cate continued. "*Miserere* was so beautiful, that the Pope wanted it only to be performed at the Vatican, so he prohibited anyone from performing it outside of the Sistine Chapel and even threatened excommunication for anyone who tried to copy the sheet music." Her eyes widened as she became excited about the story. "An interesting side note is that after a century of keeping the masterpiece under lock and key, a twelve-year-old Wolfgang Mozart visited the Vatican on Easter and heard the renowned performance of *Miserere*. That night at his lodging, he wrote out the entire piece from memory."

Com was interested. "Wow, so then Mozart introduced the world to this masterpiece?"

"It's not clear," Cate explained, "but I think Mozart's father sold the piece to an Englishman who then published it for the world."

"Right," Hugo said, "but the point is that the church tried to monopolize art. That's not right. People have a right to that music."

Brian squinted his eyes at Hugo. "And I guess now you're going to tell us that the government should ensure the arts? That we need Senator DeGroot here to tell us what's beautiful?"

"Well, he can't tell us what's beautiful, but the government should definitely play a role in inspiring the artists. A vibrant cultural life is vital to a healthy society." And almost just to perpetuate the divisive nature of the conversation, Hugo added, "And government is the only institution that can genuinely encourage the arts."

Cate was skeptical. "God have mercy on us when government is the only inspiration for the arts."

"Not the only inspiration, just one of them." Hugo amended his statement.

Cate smiled. "Hugo, surely you see the difference between a work of art inspired by sacred love as opposed to a production inspired by the false gods of the state? I'm sure you can hum any number of Bach melodies, but how many dictator theme songs do you know? *Ode to Stalin*?"

"What? No one's talking about Stalin. I'm just saying government should fund the arts. I mean, what kind of arts would we have if it were left to the devices of the corporations?"

"What about the Getty Museum in Los Angeles?" Brian scoffed. "It's one of the premier art museums in America and it was built solely on private funds. Oil money, I might add. And . . . " Brian thought for a second, "it appears that Mr. Kula is doing quite well in that department, too." Brian tilted his head backward to indicate the museum behind him. "He had no subsidy from the government, no taxpayer grant, and has amassed a wealth of quintessential art and encouraged the creation of more works through his development programs."

"So, this Arun Kula guy—do any of you know him?" Com wondered.

Cate smiled, but Brian took the question. "Uh, he's a little busy to be spending time with the likes of us. He is the one that made all this happen." Brian twirled his index finger in the air, indicating that he was referring to the surroundings. "And not just the museum. He is the president of The Green Group and the architect of Ur itself. He's the most prominent man in Ur."

Com was mildly impressed. "Great. When do I get to meet him?"

Brian smiled and Hugo laughed.

Hugo tilted his head. "Arun Kula is the only son of Rajesh Kula, founder and president of Universal Steel Company. He attended Oxford in England when he was sixteen and graduated in three years. He has three doctorates and is a concert pianist. When he's not inventing miraculous feats of engineering, he's starting new forms of currency or devising brilliant investment strategies. So, no, I don't think that he has time to meet with you, Mr. DeGroot."

"What? Is he too good to meet with a senator of the United States?" Com stressed the last part of his question, slightly miffed.

"Yes. He is too good," Hugo replied straight-faced

Cate saw that Com did not like Hugo's presumption. It appeared that he felt instantly competitive for the power of a man he had never met. Cate tried to deflect Hugo's statement. "It's not that he's too good, just very busy. But I think you'd like him, Com. He's a sportsman like you."

Com released his stare at Hugo, turned his head to Cate, and smiled. "Oh? Does he play ball?"

"Tennis. And cricket, mainly. But he loves the challenge of good competition in a mental and physical contest."

Com nodded. "That sounds about right."

"And he has excellent taste. You should see the collection of art in there."

"Okay. Speaking of which, is the museum open for guests?"

Cate nodded. "Yes, I believe so. Shall we?" She was looking only at Com.

Hugo did not catch Cate and Com's subtle attempt to escape the circle and added, "Sounds good. I haven't seen the museum either." Hugo started walking toward the entrance and turned to find Cate and Com begrudgingly going along with him. Brian followed the three into the museum.

Twenty-Two

Upon entering the museum's main wing, it was evident that the curator, Arun Kula, had an affinity for works from the Art Nouveau period of the late nineteenth century. The entire first floor of the wing was disproportionately dedicated to European painting from 1890 to 1900. The paintings and sculptures predominantly consisted of women, dressed in light clothing or no clothing at all, lounging around classical settings with nature creeping in on man-made structures of marble.

"Ah, yes," Hugo said after taking stock of the masterpieces he was surrounded by. "The Pre-Raphaelites." He said it as if he wanted Com to appreciate his vast knowledge.

"You know the works?" Com asked.

"Oh, yes. This is one of my favorite periods. It was one of the freest times for art—the late nineteenth century. None of the nonsensical iconography from the church." Hugo pointed to an illustration of a woman floating in front of an organic design of circles and diamonds. The subject's hair was dancing in the presumed wind as her pink covering clung to her breasts and hips. The title card read: "*Dance*, Alphonse Mucha".

"They say that the sexual revolution happened in the 1960s, but just look at these paintings. Pure sensuality. This is where it all started."

Cate scrunched her face at Hugo. "This is when they invented sex, huh?" Hugo ignored Cate's sarcasm.

A painting from across the gallery caught Com's eye and he walked over to it. The painting depicted one woman sitting on a fur carpet teasing another woman with a dress pin. The other woman was reclined on a marble bench and had her arms sprawled out. Both women wore see-through fabrics tied at the waste with ribbons. The soft flesh of the women contrasted the hard, cold marble walls and bench and matched the fur. *Mischief and Repose*, Com read the title card to himself. He was amazed at the attention to detail and turned to tell Cate about the painting but found her looking at another painting with her colleagues. The senator looked at the beautiful paintings and sculptures in the gallery and then at Cate. He wondered if there was a difference.

Com rejoined the others, and the group walked into a different gallery. Hugo asked Com something about his senator experience, and Brian mentioned something to Cate and the two turned around and slowly walked to a different gallery. Com disappointedly pushed his lips to the left side of his face as he watched Cate walk away. "Oh, I almost forgot I was a senator," Com said jokingly. "I've just been so caught up with this place and . . . your colleague." Com tossed his head backward to indicate he was referring to Cate.

"Ah yes, *Hylas and the Nymphs*," Hugo said in a pretentious tone. "I remember hearing about this sale to The Green Group for over eighty million dollars and was shocked. I mean, what was he thinking? The subject matter is fine, but there's no abstraction. It's so safe. There's no real . . . " Hugo let the thought trail out as Com tried to ignore him.

The senator looked at the painting and was impressed again with the beauty of the piece. The painting consisted of a number of nude girls with varying shades of dark hair floating in a pond. The girls' fair skin contrasted the dark natural surroundings as they lured their target, a young man in a blue robe, toward them. It was stunning and erotic and brilliant. "Amazing," Com whispered as Hugo spouted off a complaint about the brushwork of the painting.

Hugo continued rambling about the lack of artistry as Com turned his head and slowly drifted away from the critic. He spotted Cate walking across an open doorway to another gallery and walked in her direction.

"What do you see in that guy?" Brian asked Cate with a nasal tone as they walked through a gallery. "He's just an uncultured egomaniac . . . for me."

Cate thought for a second then replied, "Yes, I can see how you could get that. But he's not really like that."

"Oh, not a cocky control freak?"

"Believe it or not, Com has very good heart. He's really a very kind, thoughtful person."

"Thoughtful about himself, maybe." Brian rejected his colleague's assessment.

"And he's honest. You always know where you stand with him because he will tell you the absolute truth."

"Sure that wasn't just a campaign promise?"

"No, I know him. That is who he is."

Brian lifted his eyebrow. "Well, you can convince yourself of that if you'd like." He spotted a bronze sculpture of a young girl holding a piece of cloth in the shape of a crescent moon. "Ah, this is a beautiful piece."

Cate felt a tug on her hand from behind her. It was Com. He tilted his head as if to direct Cate to follow him. She smiled and eased away from Brian, who paid no attention. Once Com led Cate away from her colleague, their hands barely connected, they quickly walked out of the gallery and ran through another one, which was empty, then slowed down to walk side-by-side. Cate allowed a giggle to escape, and Com smiled. "I thought I'd never get away from those guys."

Com's hand touched the small of Cate's back, not for support or protection but simply to remain connected with her feminine presence. Her raspberry-glistened lips formed a smile. "Yeah, that Hugo can be quite the contrarian."

The two entered a new gallery and turned in front of a large canvas covered mainly in a gold paint. It was composed of a vertical male figure draped in abstract square shapes holding a soft female figure folded over in conflicted sensual pleasure and fear. She wanted the masculine presence that was embracing her, but she was not willing to give herself completely to him. Her arms were wrapped around the male, but her face was turned away from his lips.

After a glance at the canvas, Com looked at Cate. He wanted to take her right there just like the subjects of the painting. He wanted to consume her lips, her pink cheeks, her eyes that were gazing up to his, longing him to be closer to her. His hand, which was still on the small of her back, grasped her and he pulled her figure toward his. He leaned his head to the side and inched closer to Cate's. A wave of adrenaline and various other stimulating hormones rushed through Com's body as he felt like he was going to fall into his beautiful possession and become one with her.

"I can't," Cate said and pushed Com away with a weak gesture. "I'm sorry."

Com was in a daze. He was confused but didn't feel necessarily rejected. He was a breath away from sampling ecstasy, but still held her and was still in the aura that Cate exuded. He looked at his friend warmly but said nothing. She slowly shook her head as she stared into Com's eyes.

"Let me go . . . please." She said it as if she meant the opposite. Com released her.

"Sorry. I was just inspired," he said and motioned toward the canvas in front of them, pretending that the embrace didn't mean much.

Eager to discuss something new, Cate looked at the painting. "I love Klimt. It's visual poetry," she gasped, thinking about her embrace.

Com breathed in noisily and folded his arms in an effort to shake off his excitement. He remembered what Garza had said about Cate earlier and looked at her. "Santiago said that you love someone. Is that it?" He was not confrontational, but his words did not come across the way he wanted them to.

Cate looked at Com but did not answer. Instead, she asked in a light tone, "Com, do you remember what we talked about on election night?"

Com looked confused. "Uh, sure."

Cate smiled. "You know, your role in government."

"Right." Com nodded. "You wanted me to do . . . nothing as senator."

Cate laughed. "That's right! Com, I studied Constitutional Law. If I'm going to be with someone, he's going to have to appreciate that document as much as I do."

"I appreciate the Constitution," Com defended himself.

Cate let out a burst of laughter. "I've looked at your voting record, Com, and it doesn't reflect someone who understands the Constitution."

Com frowned and looked up.

"Have you even read it?"

"Parts."

"Com, if our elected officials don't pay attention to the rule of law, why should anyone else?" Cate asked, sternly looking into Com's eyes.

A gallery guard approached the couple and softly explained that the museum was closing and that the guests were welcome to continue their night on the patio outside. Com frowned and turned to Cate, who gave him an accepting look. The two left the gallery and strolled back to the patio.

Twenty-Three

"That's why we're all here, madam," proclaimed Peter Westings, a plump, mustachioed man with a slightly pompous British accent. He was directing his ideas to Senator Elizabeth Derkins of North Carolina, who was apparently miffed. Kevin Donovan and Santiago Garza stood in the same circle, as did the biologist George Aboyami. "We want to produce things and we want to keep the fruits of that production. Unfortunately that has become impossible in the outside world, where it is accepted that a certain population of political elites can *forcefully* take wealth from people and give it to another demographic under the pretense of social justice."

"No one is forcibly taking money from you, I assure you," Mrs. Derkins responded condescendingly.

The round man held up his cocktail. "The government doesn't *forcefully* take money from people?"

Senator Derkins shook her head. "No, the government doesn't forcibly take money."

The round man tossed his head back. "Can the citizens or businesses choose to *not* pay their taxes?"

Senator Derkins thought for a second. "Well, no. But I don't like how you use the word 'force.' It doesn't really fit what the government does."

"Well, what would you like to call it? The government requires people to pay taxes. What would happen if someone didn't pay his taxes?"

Derkins jumped on the man's question with righteous indignation. "They would get thrown in jail! That's what."

"So, if I may." The round man wanted to see if he understood the senator's position. "Certain authorities can take away a man's liberty by tossing him in jail because he didn't voluntarily forfeit his property—or money—to the government? Is that not *force*?"

Senator Derkins looked toward the darkened sky for an escape from the barrage of unkind thoughts being thrown at her by a man who obviously lacked social grace. At that moment, Com and Cate joined the forum and looked eager to jump into the debate. Senator Derkins turned to Com and filled him in. She pinpointed Peter, the British man, as the irrational one, though Santiago and the other men agreed with the round man. "Finally another person on the side of good governance." Senator Derkins looked at Com and held out her arm toward Peter. "This man thinks that the government *forces* people to give up their liberty and property."

Kevin, supporting Senator Derkins' position, turned to the round man with mental artillery ready to be launched. "Look, I appreciate your right to exist here in Ur as you see fit. But what you're saying about government is wrong. The government is a voice of the people; it can do anything it wants because it is what is best for the people. If you don't like it, then you can vote in another government. That's what makes our system legitimate compared to the Taliban or the commies."

Santiago, Com, and Cate all looked on with interest, but another man spoke up. He was tall, wore glasses, and was dressed in a Hawaiian shirt and ten-year-old brown corduroy pants. He spoke with a thick Nigerian accent. "That's a good point, sir. But let me ask you a question. It's not okay for Peter here," he said as he pointed to the round man, "to forcefully take money from your wallet, Mr. Donovan, right? That's called stealing, right?" Everyone agreed. "Now then, is it acceptable for Peter to tell someone else, say Santiago here, to take money from your wallet?" Kevin was a little confused with the question, as were the others. The tall man reworded his question. "Should Peter be able to pay Santiago to steal money from you?"

Phrased like that, Kevin understood. "No, of course not. That would still be stealing also."

The tall man continued. "Well, then. If someone doesn't have the right to take money from you, he can't simply grant the right to someone else now, can he? Stealing by proxy is still stealing. If it's unjust for Peter to take money from you, it's still unjust for him to tell Santiago to do it instead, right?"

Kevin understood where the tall man was going with his train of thought. If it was wrong for Peter to tell Santiago to steal, it was wrong for Peter to tell the government to take his money. But Kevin rejected the idea. "You're saying that it's wrong for people to tell government to tax people, but that's not the case. If everyone accepts that there is a need for certain public projects like common defense, or the roads, then it's okay to ask everyone to contribute to that progress. Otherwise we wouldn't have security to live. It would be anarchy. Mass hysteria!"

"But *does* everyone accept that there is a need for certain government projects?" Santiago interjected.

Peter, the round man, added, "I, for one, do not."

"Well, if there is a majority, that's what matters," Senator Derkins replied. "This is democracy, not a tyranny."

The round man returned Derkins' proposition. "To be sure, the United States of America is a *republic*, not a democracy."

"Senator Derkins," Cate interjected, "your point is well-presented and it's a popular one, for sure. But let me ask you this, if a majority anywhere wanted a law, would you say that that law would be acceptable, then?"

Senator Derkins replied, "Yes, that's what this country was founded on, majority rules."

Cate inched forward to speak. "Okay, so if a majority wanted, let's say, to *enslave* the minority, would that be okay?"

Senator Derkins gave Cate a snide look. "No, of course not. That would be preposterous."

"I agree," Cate said. "The problem is that a majority might not always have everyone's best interest in mind. Another question: what's the difference between a fascist government forcing its people to do something against their will and a republic forcing its people to do something against their will? The result is still injustice, no?"

"The laws that the majority enact have to make some sense." Kevin nearly yelled his response, then whispered to Com to help out a little.

The round man interjected. "Make sense to whom?" He let the end of his question reverberate.

"To the . . . majority, I guess," Kevin replied, searching.

The round man looked straight at Kevin as if he was indicting him for murder. "That's exactly what the Nazis thought about the Jews. A majority thought it was right to *eliminate* a minority. No, sir! Some things are unjust, no matter how big of a majority believes in it."

"No one's talking about eliminating minorities here. We're talking about roads and hospitals and police," Kevin said, shrugging off Peter's indictment.

Cate smiled. "True, government does a lot of good things, but it never does them well."

"And in order to produce those goods, they must take money from people against their will to pay for them. Is that okay?" the tall man asked earnestly through his thick accent.

"But everyone pays taxes," Senator Derkins blurted out. "It's just something you need to do."

"Not so," the round man replied. "On a federal level, only people who work and produce things of value must pay taxes. The people who produce the most must also pay the most. And those who do not work are the beneficiaries of those taxes. It's completely converse to a rational system of economics. We live in a society in which the majority of non-producers and non-workers have enslaved the minority of workers. All for the sake of a misnomer called democracy. No ma'am! I believe in the rule of law, not the rule of the majority. That is why, my friends, I live here in Ur. And that is why I will defend unto death our right to exist here without government intrusion and coercion."

"Unto death?" Mrs. Derkins inquired. "You should be careful what you wish for."

A cool breeze came down onto the group as they reflected on their conversation. Santiago tried to ease the tension. "Well, if there's something that we can all agree on, it is that, while we may disagree, we should all be able to express our viewpoints!"

Peter, the stocky man, kept his stare on Senator Derkins. "Mrs. Derkins, are you voting for the Delano-DeGroot bill?"

"I most certainly am," Senator Derkins said confidently.

Santiago was saddened. "So the tour today did nothing to change your mind?"

Senator Derkins shook her head. "No. Sorry."

"Why are you voting for the Delano-DeGroot bill, may I ask?" Peter questioned.

"This place is harmful to its citizens and to the country as a whole. It is a clear example of the problems that arise due to lack of regulation," Senator Derkins replied.

Cate looked around at the beautiful landscape and reflected on her tour of the museum and the peaceful evening. "You're right, Senator. It is a great example of what happens without regulation."

"Not here. Look at what's happening out there." Mrs. Derkins pointed in an easterly direction. "All the fat cats here are having their cake and eating it, too, while everyone on the outside is hurting. We saw today that all the corporations are moving here so that they can get out of their tax obligations, yet the everyday working middle class must struggle to get by in the real world. Struggle with crime, poverty, unemployment. Goodness, we're still climbing out of the depression out there!"

"Then perhaps the problem is not here, but out there?" Peter quipped.

Santiago Garza turned to Com. "And I suppose we weren't able to change your mind either, señor?"

Com looked at the group and smiled. "No, I think you did an excellent job of dispelling some of the myths surrounding this place."

"But you will still vote for your own bill?" the tall Nigerian asked.

Cate looked on stoically as Com hesitated, then opened his mouth. He looked around at the small group of people staring at him. They all expected him to follow suit with Senator Derkins. After all, he had co-sponsored the legislation and it was being called the Delano-DeGroot bill. Com enjoyed the brief silence as everyone awaited his words, then he spoke. "I'm going to vote against the bill." Com chuckled. "I'm going to vote against my own bill."

The circle of people erupted in laughter, and Com smiled. Peter produced a rich guffaw. "Oh, that's rich."

"What?" Senator Derkins screeched, incredulous. Kevin peered at Com, half surprised, half concerned.

Com nodded. "The bill is garbage. All of the issues that people have about this place are misguided. Santiago showed us that in a couple hours today." Com smiled at his host, who returned the gesture.

"But you can't," Senator Derkins said. "This place is sapping the economy of the rest of the country. It's weakening the government, your employer!" She lifted her arm to Santiago and Peter. "They will take all of our resources away from us. They will suck us dry. You can't possibly . . . " She showed nervousness.

"Perhaps you can tell us how you really feel, Senator," Peter said to Senator Derkins calmly, happy with what Com was saying.

Senator Derkins composed herself then turned to Santiago. "Thank you, Mr. Garza, for a lovely evening. I must excuse myself." The senator turned to find her staffers and walked toward the exit. Kevin looked a little startled and his eyes followed Mrs. Derkins.

After Senator Derkins had left, a cheer went up from Peter, Santiago, and the tall man, directed toward Com. "Glad to have you on board, Senator!" "Nicely done!" "Hooray!" The gentlemen congratulated Com, and Cate smiled at the confident senator. The group drifted into separate conversations as Kevin directed Com away from the others.

"Hey, this might be good for the party," Kevin said, "but I'm worried about Delano. He's not going to let this fly."

Com deflected the concern. "Thanks, Kevin, but I can take care of myself. I'm a big boy."

Kevin shook his head. "Yeah, but I don't think Delano is the type of guy you want to cross."

Com looked up as if to shake off Kevin's warning. "Look, I'm going to try to enjoy the rest of the night here. We can talk about the bill in the morning."

Twenty-Four

Cate Heatherton awaited the tennis ball with her knees bent and her arms slightly extended toward her hitting partner, the assistant coach for the University of Delaware women's tennis team. Cate wore a powder blue athletic skirt that allowed her slender legs increased mobility, and a fitted white tank top. After a pop from her partner's racquet on the other side of the court, the ball came whizzing over the net. Cate shifted naturally to a sideways stance and brought her right arm backward. She dipped her racquet and swung in a fluid motion, connecting with the ball and sending it back toward her partner. The pair exchanged several ground-strokes, and at one point during the rally Cate stepped toward the net and crushed a ball toward the opposite side of the court.

The ball zipped past the assistant coach and he yelled, "Great! Did you see how you set that up? Excellent."

Cate smiled and tucked a few strands of hair that had slipped out of her ponytail behind her ear. "Yeah, that felt really good."

"See, you don't need to rush it. Just let it come naturally. Let's try it again."

Cate selected another ball from a nearby hopper but hesitated before striking the ball as she heard someone calling her name.

"Cate!" The college senior Com DeGroot was walking toward the court. He wore basketball warm-ups and a worried look.

Cate gave him a regretful smile, then nodded at her coach. "Danny, is it okay if we take a short break?"

The assistant pursed his lips and looked at Com, then nodded. "Okay."

Cate walked over to the court's waist-level side fence where Com was standing and said, "Hi."

"What is this?" Com asked humbly as he waved a piece of paper in the air.

"Sorry, I had to write it all down. I never can remember what I want to say when I want to say it."

Com shook his head. "So, you're over it? You don't want to see me anymore?"

Cate frowned. "Com, you know this isn't heading in the right direction. I have certain things I want in a relationship—certain qualities—and you definitely have some of them, but I really thought you were someone else when we started seeing each other."

"What do you mean 'someone else'?"

Cate looked down. "Well, I just thought you wanted the same things as I do. And now it seems like you're getting swept up in this whole *pro-baller* lifestyle—and that's great, Com, it's exciting, I'm sure—but I just don't see us being together."

Com nodded. "It's the parties, then? You can't handle me going to all the parties?"

Cate moved her lips to the side of her mouth before speaking. "Com, when I met you I thought you were an honest, principled guy—a little brash, but principled. I grew up around a man who wasn't principled at all, and you were refreshing. But it looks like things have changed with you. I mean, what happened to never playing for someone like my father—someone without a passion for the game?"

"Cate, is that what this is about? Your father?"

"That, and you broke the contract with San Antonio. Did the legal contract you signed not mean anything to you?"

"Cate, your dad offered me two and a half mil more than San Antonio. I had to take it."

"Even after you had signed with San Antonio?"

"Yes."

"Right, and now you know your price—that's what it costs for you to give up on your principles?"

"I didn't give up my principles. The Czars are going to be good this year—playoff contenders. That's what I wanted, a good team that I can play my heart out for."

Cate nodded. "I know, and I'm happy for you. I really am. But I just . . . I'm just looking for something more from the man I'm going to be with."

Com looked around the tennis court. He spotted the assistant coach stretching, then turned back to Cate. "So that's it, then? We're done for good?"

"I don't know about that, Com. People grow. They change. Maybe in another life we will find each other again and be perfect together."

Com's smile was tinged with disappointment. "I just . . . I'm stunned. I guess I'll see you in another life, then."

Cate took a step back toward the court and swung her racquet in the air. "Bye, Com."

Com turned to leave and then looked back at the slender figure of Cate Heatherton bouncing toward the baseline to warm up again. He lowered his head and walked away from the court.

* * *

Com was wrapped in the Egyptian cotton sheets of one of Ur's finest hotel suite and to a sweet voice whispering for him to get up. He smiled as he imagined the beautiful face that had accompanied the voice. "Cate."

"Wake up," she said again. But Com's euphoria quickly turned into confusion. He did not recognize the sultry voice that was pleading for him to greet the day. He slowly turned toward it and was startled to find a round plastic head with a dark shiny mask hovering over his head.

Com immediately yelled and jerked his arm up, smacking the head of a bipedal humanoid machine that was leaning over his bed.

The head of the machine cranked backward, and the entire figure slowly started tipping over. It let out a deliberate, "Oh, no!" and fell to the ground.

Com sat up in his bed and looked at the humanoid on the ground. "What the hell? Okay, that's creepy."

The robot was moving its legs and arms and let out, "Warning! I've fallen and can't get up."

Com looked at the robot and threw up his hands. "Ah! What do you want me to do?" Com touched the base of the robot, which consisted of a plastic-and-rubber tread on wheels. Once he gripped the tread, however, the wheels started moving and threw off his hand. Com tried to grab a moving arm to pull the machine upright but was given an electrical shock. "Ow." He grabbed a bunch of blankets from the bed and threw them on the moving machine. At that, a small rolling robot came from behind him and rammed into his foot. "Shit!" Com yelled.

The rolling robot announced, "Foreign object on the ground. Foreign object on the ground." The robot then rammed into Com's foot again.

"What are you doing, you little robotic jackass?" Com yelled, then moved so that the rolling robot could get to its presumed destination, the fallen android, which it bumped into repeatedly.

Com chuckled and shook his head. "Great wakeup call, dickheads." He remembered that he had indeed asked for a wakeup call the previous night. He had made an appointment with Santiago Garza to go over the science behind the cleanup procedure that The Green Group had provided in Ur. Com wanted to see for himself how they had pulled off the astounding feat.

Com showered, dressed, and left his room to the sound of a moaning and wiggling android on the floor. As he descended in the elevator, he looked at his handheld computer and navigated to images from the reception the previous night. He shuffled through numerous photos and came to one with a posed Santiago Garza, Cate Heatherton, Kevin Donovan, George Aboyami, and himself. He zoomed in on Cate and stared until he was alerted to his arrival on the lobby floor. Com shook his head with a perplexed grin as he walked through the lobby and to the archon's building.

When Com arrived, he saw Santiago approaching him from the opposite side of the large hall. They greeted each other and walked to a small conference room off to the side of the building. In the middle of the dimly lit room stood a glass table with a small semi-sphere resting on the surface. Santiago tapped the semi-sphere, and a strong beam of light emanated from it, projecting a monitor.

From what Com could surmise, the monitor was nothing more than light reflecting off thin air, but the picture was clear, and the luminosity was brilliant. Com shook his head at the machine.

"It's amazing, isn't it?" Santiago asked as he pinched the top right corner of the monitor and dragged it a couple inches away from the table. As he did so, the size of the monitor expanded. "This is a patented helio-projection monitor." Santiago stuck his hand through the lighted panel and caused shadows from his fingers to flicker on the monitor. "It's one of the most advanced products we have."

"Wow," Com said.

The monitor showed documents being sorted through but it looked to Com as if the computer was working on its own. He looked at Santiago. "How are you controlling this?"

Santiago smiled, "Ah, sí," he said, pointing to his right eye. "I am using a state of the art contact lens equipped with video capture and Bluetooth capabilities. Also very advanced."

Com shook his head. "Are you serious?"

"Sí, it is a very wonderful product. The company that makes them cannot sell them on the outside, however, until the FDA reviews their case. Right now, they're on a two-year wait list. I will have a pair shipped to you, though, if you'd like."

Com nodded, "Yeah, that'd be great."

Santiago agreed with a dip of his head then began sorting through scientific documents on the computer. He and Com browsed data that revealed the thorough cleanup process used to remove the toxic radiation that had saturated the area after the nuclear meltdown years before. According to the reports, seven hundred and twenty petabecquerels of radioactive xenon were released in the meltdown, but, as Santiago explained, radioactive xenon was relatively harmless because of its extremely short half-life—about two days. However, nearly twelve tera-becquerels of harmful radioactive strontium—with a half-life of twenty-nine years—were also released, causing major fallout around the melt-down site.

The Green Group had used innovative decontamination techniques, including a potassium iodide solution spray and injection to cover the entire fallout area and render the radiation inert. The Green Group had also deconstructed the unusable power plant and secured the materials miles underground.

"But of course," Santiago said after going over the electronic and paper reports in front of him, "the proof—how do you say—is in the pudding. Since the cleanup was officially considered complete by The Green Group ten years ago, there have been no cases of thyroid cancer, the typical ailment following exposure to this kind of radiation. Zero. To compare, it is estimated that the Chernobyl accident in the former Soviet Union caused over fifty thousand cases of thyroid cancer."

"Well, all of this is very convincing," Com said thoughtfully. "It almost seems like our independent researchers out there today aren't necessary."

"No," Santiago challenged Com. "If there is anything that I've learned since being here in Ur, it is that redundancy is boring and inefficient, but it is a necessary path to the truth."

"One thing I don't get." Com thought about his words. "Delano's using the radiation as the reason to revoke the charter, but there is no radiation. Did they just fabricate the numbers? Why is everyone up in arms?"

Santiago raised his eyebrows. "My friend, the entire bill is a smoke-screen." An idea came to the archon. "Here, let me show you." He typed on a keyboard and brought up a document on the monitor. "This is the

EPA report that your bill is based on." Santiago scrolled through the dense document, then typed in a search query. The search brought the document to a specific spot and highlighted a few words. "See here. This is the reported concentration of radioactive iodine found in the inspection—four hundred millirem. New York City has this much radiation a year. My friend, the EPA report tells the truth, but the senators have spun that truth so that it tells them exactly what they want to hear. Certain senators want a government takeover of Ur, and they're using any means necessary to do it."

Com's mouth was open. "And why would they want to take over Ur?"

"My friend, we are competition for the government. Ur provides a shining example of how self-rule can work, and the more that people see that freedom works and that the current governmental model of modern serfdom is just that, serfdom, then the more they will reject that coercive power; more people will ask for free charter cities; and more people will invoke the Constitution in defense of their natural rights and nullify the federal government. When enough people see that freedom works, we will have a revolt of sorts and overthrow the current power structure. Those who are in power now cannot stand to lose their iron grip of control in this country and the world. That's what they're trying everything they can to defeat us."

Com smiled and looked back at the EPA report. "You're a convincing man, Santiago. Want to come back to Washington with me to help convince the rest of the country?"

Santiago smiled but waved Com off. "Oh, no. I cannot leave my post here. Plus, I'm not sure that the climate of Washington will suit me."

"In more ways than one, Santiago, more ways than one." Com slapped Santiago on the shoulder. "Look, Santiago, you've explained every critique about this place that they brought up in six-sixty-four, but aside from all this mess," Com motioned toward the monitor showing the EPA report, "there is one thing that I cannot come to grips with about Ur."

"Sí. What would that be?" Santiago inquired.

"Security," Com said with a gloomy look. "I just don't see Ur being secure enough without a central police force or an intelligence service. I mean, what if some organized crime unit wanted to come in here and take over the place?"

"Organized crime, hmmm, like the federal government?" Santiago said with a grin.

Com couldn't hold back a smile. "Well, apart from the federal government. What if the mafia wanted to take over? And they could rough up whoever they wanted because there's no police force to stop them."

Santiago nodded. "Goodness knows, we wouldn't be able to survive if something like that happened. But let me show you something." Santiago pulled up an Intranet browser on a nearby computer and navigated to a private website. He rubbed his thumb over the biometric scanner on the monitor, and the website displayed a number of links. Mr. Garza touched the screen over one link, which led to another and still another. Eventually he brought up a surveillance video of the area just outside the archon's office lobby.

"This video takes place right before you and Kevin came here yesterday morning. See, there you are." Santiago pointed to the video depicting the senator and his chief walking through automatic doors. "Now watch very carefully."

The video showed a burly figure dressed in a black trench coat charge toward the door behind Com and Kevin. The figure made it to the door but the door slammed shut on the figure, and an electric shock was seen incapacitating the man. Several security officers were seen rushing to apprehend the man.

"What the hell?" Com cried. "That happened right behind us?"

"Sí, señor," Santiago said in a subdued tone. Then he clicked on another link and brought up a profile of the man. "Biometrics gave us this information. He is a drifter, a scoundrel, and he was on the do-not-enter list for this building. It appeared that he was attempting some form of attack, perhaps on you, though he had no weapons to speak of. We gave him the choice of going to a wonderful rehabilitation center here in Ur or being moved out of the city-state. He chose to be removed from the area."

Com looked impressed.

"You see, señor, most every district in Ur is monitored and secured in similar fashion—no, every square foot in Ur is monitored in a similar fashion. We are responsible for who enters this building, another company is responsible for who enters those tunnels you took to get here, and the road companies are responsible for the people they allow on the roads. In Ur, there is always a responsible party. There isn't a square foot of Ur that doesn't have some sort of security. It's a complex and redundant network of biometrics and surveillance. Even the tugurios we saw yesterday has a minor security check."

"Tugurios?"

"The socialist neighborhood. I call it tugurios or slums. Even they have some sort of security. You have to check in and out of the area. And so, Ur has become the most secure place I have ever lived."

Com nodded. "Very impressive. So, what about this guy with the taser stuck in his neck?" Com asked, pointing to the video showing security guards addressing the man stuck in the door. "Is he going to sue?"

"Of course," Santiago said, "he has that right. But he was clearly in the wrong—he was trying to do harm—and has no case. He knows that, so he will not be successful."

"How often does stuff like this happen?" Com wondered aloud.

"Not as often as on the outside, Senator, I assure you. Like I said, this is the most secure place I've ever been. I think one factor that people forget when discussing the topic of crime is that, in a truly free society, there is very little incentive to perpetrate a crime. Everyone here has what they deserve—no one is allowed to take another's property, whether illegally or legally. So there is a natural disinclination toward harming others in this society. When it happens, there are usually outside influences acting on the criminal."

Com nodded and let the concept sink in. "Well, I hope you're right, Santiago. For your sake and mine. If I back you guys up, this place better not fall to pieces on me."

The two wrapped up their meeting and headed out of the conference room. Santiago allowed Com to leave first.

"So," Santiago said with a smile, "did you enjoy yourself last night at the reception?"

"It was perfect, Santiago. Thanks for having me."

"Oh, you're welcome! And I noticed some—how do you say it?—enamoramiento between you señorita Heatherton last night. Should I be reserving the date any time soon?"

Com produced a half-hearted smile. "Santiago, you're an observant guy. But, unfortunately not observant enough. She turned me down last night. You were right. She loves someone, but it's not me."

Santiago patted Com on the back. "Join the club, right, Senator?"

"Sure, I'll join. I just wish the membership wasn't so painful."

"Are you going to Mass with us?"

Com looked at Santiago. "Who, you and Cate?"

"Sí, I am meeting her right now."

Com pushed his bottom lip up. "Okay. I have a little time to kill."

Twenty-Five

Com DeGroot and Santiago Garza took the tram over to Jefferson Heights, where they were to meet Cate Heatherton at a small church for the Sunday service. The sun had warmed the atmosphere to nearly eighty degrees by the time Com arrived at eleven-thirty.

"Oh, you came," Cate sang, pleasantly surprised.

Cate was wearing a stark white summer dress with rounded straps that covered most of her shoulders, an empire waste, and an eyelet pattern near the hem. She was slightly blushed from the heat, and the vivid white of the dress made her fair skin appear darker than it was.

Com and Santiago alternated embraces with the young woman and turned toward the front entrance to the church. The building was a new, Spanish mission-styled building with white stucco topped by a red clay tile roof.

Com DeGroot and Cate Heatherton walked up the front steps to the church's entrance with Santiago Garza close behind. Com was grinned skeptically at Cate. "That's something I don't get, Cate. You're such a free spirit and you think that everyone should be able to do whatever they want, but you don't seem to mind the church telling people what to do."

"Well . . . "

"You know me. I went to church when I was a kid, but I can't stand authority. I hate it when people try to tell me what to do. And it doesn't really help if they're wearing funny hats and gowns," Com said, trying to make a joke.

Cate smiled. "Funny gowns and hats, huh? Very clever, Commodore. Actually, it may shock you, but I would say that liberty is the foundation of the church, not coercion."

"Oh, yeah? That sounds a little backward to me."

"Well, maybe this service will shed some light on that. I've heard some really good things about the priest here at the church."

The interior of the building was impossible to ignore—a perfectly designed mission-style church with white walls and dark brown wooden support beams. To compliment the architecture, hundreds of colorful people shuffled in and filled the wooden pews as a pipe organ played background music, filling the atmosphere with light, airy notes. Com noticed Asians and Latinos, Africans and American Indians. He figured the church was a tourist destination of some sort. There were people here from all around the world, it seemed.

"You're in for a treat," Cate said to Com in a matter-of-fact manner as they took a seat near the middle of the nave. "The choir for this Mass is unparalleled. They really are one of the best in the world." She lifted her thumb to indicate the choir loft behind them and above the entrance. Com looked back and nodded in acceptance of her claim.

"Yeah, this is what you were talking about last night?" Com asked.

Cate nodded. "Hey," she said, "how long has it been since you've gone to Mass?"

"Uh, it's been a while," Com replied.

"Okay, so when you go up during Communion, just cross your arms like this." Cate folded her arms into an 'X' over her chest. "And they will give you a blessing. I love the blessing. I almost want to go to two Masses to get Communion and a blessing."

Com blinked his eyes at Cate. "You're funny."

The choir leader announced the start of the Mass, and everyone stood as the choir began to perform. The music was a slow but soaring piece in some foreign language and gradually picked up tempo over time. The sound was rich and beautiful, and, though Com did not understand the lyrics, he thought he understood the meaning.

However, he did not understand the meaning in most of what followed. The priest walked to the front of the church and, once there, spoke. Everyone sang, the priest spoke again, and everyone sang again.

The priest prayed and then everyone sat down. Someone in the front row stood and walked to a podium before reading a passage from the Bible, which Com did not follow, and the reader sat down.

The organ began to emit music again and a shrill woman's voice began to sing another song. It was awful and made Com cringe. He looked at Cate and winced. "Yeah," she whispered, "she's not the best."

After the song, another reader got up and read another passage from the Bible, which Com did not follow again, and the reader sat down. At that point, music started and everyone stood up again. A well-dressed man held a large book with a red cover and golden trim and walked toward the podium. The song ended, and the well-dressed man read another passage, this time from the Gospel. Com analyzed the stained glass around the basilica, the rafters, and the people in front of him. He started to let out a yawn and tried to stifle it. He remembered from his church-going experience in college that some churches provided doughnuts after the service. Com wanted a doughnut.

Everyone sat down after the reading, and Com turned to Cate with a look of disappointment. "I forgot about all these Catholic *calisthenics*." Cate half-smiled and looked toward the front of the church, where the priest had moved around the altar, closer to the congregation. He looked around, then down to his feet, and began talking.

"In today's first reading, God tells Noah that He's going to wipe out mankind with a flood, and that Noah needs to make an ark to save some of the species. Now, the story may be parable. It may be a divinely inspired fable. But it makes me wonder about how that situation would play out in today's world. I think they even made a movie about that exact scenario, but I only gave it three stars." Some laughs were heard in the congregation. "This is more how I would see the story taking place today: God says to modern-day Noah, 'Noah, in one year, I'm going to make it rain very hard, and that rain will flood the world. But I want you to save the righteous people and two of every kind of animal on God's green Earth—well, that's Me—*My* green Earth. So, I'm commanding you to build an ark. What? You don't know what an ark is? Right. It's a big boat. Yes, and you have to do it within one year. Got me? I'll email you the instructions for the boat tomorrow. And if it doesn't go through, check your spam folder.'" More of the congregation chuckled.

"Exactly one year later, clouds began to form all over the Earth, and God came down and saw Noah sitting on his front lawn, crying. In a deep voice, God asked Noah, 'Noah, where's the ark I told you to build?' And Noah turned up to heaven and pleaded, "Lord, forgive me. I tried to do what you wanted, but there were major problems. First, I had to get a permit for construction, and your plans did not meet the building codes. I had to hire an engineering firm and redraw the plans. Then I got into a legal battle with OSHA over whether or not the ark needed a sprinkler system and approved flotation devices. Then, my neighbor objected, claiming I was violating zoning ordinances by building the ark in my front yard, so I had to get a variance from the city planning commission.'" Laughs were heard throughout the congregation as the priest continued.

"'Then, I had problems getting enough wood for the ark, because there was a ban on cutting trees to protect the Spotted Owl. I finally convinced the U.S. Forest Service that I really needed the wood to *save* the owls. However, the Fish and Wildlife Service wouldn't let me take the two owls 'cause they would want to eat the last surviving bass. The carpenters formed a union and went on strike. I had to negotiate a settlement with the National Labor Relations Board before anyone would pick up a saw or a hammer. They sent over a group of lawyers, so now I have sixteen lawyers on the ark but still no owls. Then the Army Corps of Engineers demanded a map of the proposed flood plain. I sent them a globe. Yes, one of those twirly ones. Right now, I am trying to resolve a complaint filed with the Equal Employment Opportunity Commission that says I am practicing discrimination by not taking atheists aboard. The IRS has seized my assets, claiming that I'm building the ark to flee the country to avoid paying taxes. I just got a notice from the state that I owe them some kind of user tax and failed to register the ark as a 'recreational water craft.' I told them this wasn't Carnival Cruise Lines. And finally, the ACLU got the courts to issue an injunction against further construction of the ark, saying that since God is flooding the earth, it's a religious event and, therefore, unconstitutional. I really don't think I can finish the ark for another five or six years, if at all. We're doomed!'

"Noah waited. The sky began to clear, the sun began to shine, and the seas calmed down. A rainbow arched across the sky. Noah looked up hopefully. 'You mean you're *not* going to destroy the Earth, Lord?' 'No,' He said sadly. 'I don't have to. The government already has.'" At that, the entire congregation erupted in laughter.

The priest continued. "You know, since the beginning of this country, there have been those who would eradicate religion from not only government, but from the entire public realm. One hears 'separation of church and state,' 'separation of church and state,' ad nauseam. But what really needs to happen is a separation of state and everything else. We don't need to get the church out of the state, we need to get the state out of everything—the schools, the hospitals, and yes, the church. Believe it or not, when this country was founded, the government wasn't involved in any of those facets of daily life.

"The Founders had it right when they rejected a state-mandated religion, because one simply cannot *force* morality. In fact, the opposite of force—freedom—is requisite for a truly moral society. People cannot be moral unless they *choose* to do the right thing—unless they have the freedom to do the right thing. Forcing morality just doesn't make sense, and the Founding Fathers knew this. Of course, the converse is also true. A sound morality is necessary for a truly free society, but that's a topic for another sermon. My point *here* is that one cannot force the types of ideas and experiences we hope to encourage through the church's teachings. And the same applies to every aspect of life. One cannot force another person to be healthy. One cannot force another person to work hard or innovate. And one cannot force people to love their neighbors.

"But that never stopped a government bureaucrat from trying to force those things through the regulation of food labels, publicly-funded schools, or welfare. And when government tries to *force* health, innovation, and love, everything just goes awry. Because it's clear as day—overregulation, corruption, and waste permeate government, and when government oversteps its constitutional bounds, everyone suffers. It's ironic in that way. It seems that by attempting to force the cardinal virtues—love, hope, charity—government actually ends up proliferating the deadly sins—greed, sloth, and pride.

"One might quote Jesus' passage and claim it is right to give to Caesar what is Caesar's and give to God what is God's, and I would agree, that statement is right. But are half of your wages really Caesar's? Is your intellect Caesar's? Are your medical records Caesar's? The religious beliefs you hold dear—are those Caesar's? In the last few decades, Caesar—at least in this country—has become an ever-growing embodiment of intrusion and coercion, and that simply is *not* just."

'Amen's were heard from various parishioners.

"In today's Gospel, we see Jesus confronting the Pharisees, who chastised Jesus because his disciples hadn't washed their hands before they ate. Jesus calls the Pharisees hypocrites and tells them to stop worrying about the rules of the elders. The Pharisees were so caught up in the exact wording of their regulations, see, that they completely forgot about the *purpose* of those regulations. The purpose wasn't to patronize the washrooms; it was to be clean, for one, and to be respectful and grateful for their bounty. Likewise, today's federal government is so caught up in the *specifics* of their laws that they have utterly lost track of the *purpose* of those laws—and, in fact, the purpose of government itself. The purpose of government isn't to make sure that General Motors exists so that thirty thousand people can keep their jobs; the purpose of government isn't to make sure you don't eat French fries every day; the purpose of government isn't to make sure everyone feels good about themselves. The purpose of government *is* to protect life and liberty. That's it. Anything beyond that, and government acts like the hypocrites that chastised Jesus. And when government goes further and starts to actually endanger life and liberty, government moves beyond the hypocrites in the Gospel; it behaves like those who nailed Jesus to the cross itself."

Com stared at the priest, wide-eyed and unbelieving. He looked around, and many of the parishioners were similarly taken aback. The priest walked around the altar and said, "Let us stand and profess our faith."

Twenty-Six

Com stood up with the rest of the congregation and looked around as everyone else recited a prayer. He noticed that a man sitting in the pew in front of him was struggling to stand up using two metal braces. The man finally stood and joined the rest of the parishioners in prayer. Com wondered why no one around him had helped him to stand up. A sense of pity for the man crashed over Com, but he quickly brushed it off and looked elsewhere. The prayer ended, the priest spoke again, and then everyone sat down.

The choir began to sing an upbeat melody that sounded almost childlike—happy and light. Ushers walked through the aisles and collected money while the liturgical staff moved about in the chancel at the front of the church. Cate looked through her purse and found a fifty-dollar bill, which she gave to Com with a slight grin, tilting her head to indicate that he should place the money in the collection basket. Com smiled at the unnecessary transfer of money and placed the bill in the basket as it came through.

After the choir had stopped singing, the priest raised his hands, and everyone stood up and recited another prayer. Com tried to pay attention to this one but couldn't follow along. Over the next few minutes, the priest and the congregation traded words, all of which were lost to Com. He tried to mumble something along with everyone else, but kept very quiet so as not to announce his ignorance to his neighbors.

The choir struck up once again and filled the small church with the most emphatic, heartfelt music Com had ever heard. It ended with a couple of sopranos reaching high notes that Com wasn't sure had existed before. Everyone kneeled when the song ended, but Com wasn't sure whether they knelt out of tradition or because of the overwhelming emotion in the heavenly harmonies that had come from the choir loft above them. The senator knelt, too, and was reminded of a pop song lyric that went, "If you want to kiss the sky, better learn how to kneel." So he did.

The priest went over some material about breaking bread and something to do with wine that was again lost on Com. He was looking forward to the next song from the choir. When it came, it came like a tsunami over his body. Three simple chords knocked Com over emotionally and then subsided. The priest spoke some more and then raised up a wafer and a chalice and sang a brief song. Then the choir began the same three-chord song as before but sang just "Amen." It was impossibly beautiful, Com thought.

Everyone stood, and Com felt the springtime warmth in the air as he rose. The temperature was permeating the atmosphere, and Com felt as if it was connecting the entire group of people surrounding him.

The priest invited everyone to another prayer, which Com eventually recognized and began to say along with everyone else. "Our father, who art in heaven, hallowed be Thy name; Thy kingdom come, Thy will be done, on earth as it is in heaven. Give us this day our daily bread, and forgive us our trespasses, as we forgive those who trespass against us; and lead us not into temptation, but deliver us from evil. Amen." The priest spoke again and asked everyone to offer each other a sign of peace. At that, the entire congregation came alive as each person turned to a neighbor and gave a hug or shook a hand. Com turned to Cate and offered her his hand. She pushed it out of the way and hugged him.

"Peace be with you," she said, and he returned the gesture.

She then turned to the others around her and shook their hands, saying the same thing to them. Com shook Santiago's hand and looked over to the man with the braces. He was shaking his neighbors' hands with one hand while supporting himself with the other. The man looked over to Com and smiled. He was too far away to shake Com's hand, but he waved and mouthed, "Peace be with you." Com smiled a genuine smile and turned to the front of the church. He thought about the man with the walking braces and wondered how someone in such a state could be so happy. Sure, Com had had bad injuries, but nothing like what it appeared this poor guy had undergone. Was it ever valid for Com to feel self-pity when a guy like that was out there being happy? Com wondered.

The next few moments were a blur to Com. He kneeled again, along with the congregation, and perceived the most angelic song floating down from the choir loft. It sounded like a chant from the medieval ages but was so complex and intricate that Com thought it must be modern. He got up to follow the congregation to the front of the church in a slow, methodical pace and, when he got to the minister standing before them, he remembered to cross his arms in front of his chest. The minister blessed him with the sign of the cross, and Com returned to his pew and knelt again. He saw the man with the braces holding himself up with his arms on the pew in front of him and letting his invalid legs hang below.

The music built slowly and softly with a few warm voices and then exploded into a thunderous culmination of polyphony tinted with the lightest of tones floating above it all. The harmonies hit Com at the base of his spine and moved up his back to his neck and then burst into his head. An unfamiliar tingling sensation crept over his face and accumulated near his eyes. He couldn't believe the sensation and tried to swallow back his feeling. He hadn't cried since he was a child, and there was no reason for him to do so now, he thought.

Com felt a stinging in his watering eyes and his throat. He coolly wiped his face as if he were tired and tried to swallow back his emotion. The air, the music, the communion were all wrapped up in his mind, which was overflowing with stimulation. His heart was beating rapidly, and he was sweating profusely in a rush of adrenaline and serotonin. Com folded his hands and bowed his head in prayer. Cate looked at him and smiled.

When Com regained his senses moments later, he noticed that everyone was leaving their pews. He was still kneeling, and Cate was sitting next to him. Com wanted to see the man with the braces, but he was gone.

"Wow, what a way to end my trip! And you people do this every week?" Com said jokingly. Cate smiled. "I don't think I want to do that again."

"No?" Cate asked calmly.

"I almost lost it," Com said warily.

Cate nodded and smiled. "I think that's the point."

Twenty-Seven

Com DeGroot rushed down the hallway toward the office of Duane D. Delano in the Russell Senate Building. He looked down and spoke into his handheld phone. "Any news?" Com asked his chief of staff.

Kevin Donovan answered on the other line. "Sure do. We got some good news on six-sixty-four. Senator Freeman is going to put a game plan together sometime next week for the *nays*. His office says that we have forty-four nays and there are forty-six solid yeas. The rest are undecided. Jennings is preparing a case for each of the undecideds. I'm pretty sure we can cut deals to get them on board, but we're going to have to be like freakin' Geppetto pulling strings to get it done. He's organized a town hall discussion with you, Delano, and Thurston to break down the evidence on the bill."

Com nodded. "Where would we be without that guy? When's this town hall meeting?"

"It's in one week. It'll be televised. Should be entertaining," Kevin commented.

"You gotta love that old fart Jennings."

"Yeah, Jennings is throwing everything he's got into this one. You going to talk to Delano?"

"Yeah, I'm on my way to his office now. Hey—"

Com looked behind him before turning into Delano's office and accidentally collided with a large rock of a human being in the entrance. "Whoops, I'm sorry," Com said as a reflex as he tried to assess what had happened.

The thick, bald man who had run into Com did not speak or offer any conciliatory gestures. He simply stood in the doorway and looked at Com blankly. He was dressed in a fashionable suit that contradicted a stern, cold look. Com's eyes drifted toward the man's forehead on which an incomplete tattoo of barbed wire was etched.

The man firmly pushed Com out of the way and stomped away from the door and down the hall.

"What the hell?" Com asked himself aloud.

"What? What's going on?" Kevin asked through the phone.

"No, nothing. Look, I have to run. I'm at Delano's."

Com walked into the front office of Duane Delano and found the senator standing with his office assistant, Terry.

"I see you made the acquaintance of my latest charity case?" Delano chomped at Com. "A political refugee from the former Soviet Union. His English isn't very good, but I think he will be helpful to us."

"Oh?" Com wondered aloud.

"You wanted to talk?" Delano asked. "Well, get in here. I don't have all day." Delano turned around and walked into his office.

Com looked at the rounded senator and twitched his upper lip, then followed him into his office.

Com and Delano both took a seat. After a moment's silence, Senator Delano jutted his head toward Com and gave him a stunned look. "Well? My time is precious. Why the hell did you want to meet?"

"Well, sir, about your bill. I just got back from Texas, and I didn't see anything wrong with that charter city. Every criticism about the place turned out to be absolutely false. I don't know why they aren't reporting it—"

Delano cut Com off with a raised hand. "Excuse me, but did I hear you just try to come up with an idea? Are you presuming to think for yourself right now? That isn't your job, Senator."

Com squinted his eyes. "How do you mean?"

"Look, no one asked you to go to this Ur place in the middle of a legislative session, and no one as sure as hell has asked you to form your own opinion of the place. You do what I say on this matter."

"Excuse me?" Com said, stunned. "Are you trying to tell me what I should think?"

Delano took a deep breath and reset his thoughts. "Ur is a leech on the rest of the country, Senator. It's a venomous, contemptible leech that is ripping us off, and it needs to be exterminated. Now you know this . . . " Delano scrunched his face as if he had tasted something bitter. "I don't need to tell you how important this bill is to us . . . to you."

Com nodded and swallowed. "I know, I know. We made a deal for this bill. But I'm telling you this bill is crap. There's no legitimate need to revoke the charter."

"Wait a second, Senator, you're saying that you have played cop, judge, and jury in this case based on your brief visit there?" Delano asked, assuming the answer.

"Yeah, well it's pretty obvious that the basis for the bill is bullshit. The EPA report shows radiation levels that are comparable to those in your backyard in Washington, D.C. People are not in danger down there. There's no safety issue, and we have no right to go in there and play third-world dictator."

Delano looked amused. "And where did your naïve little mind get all of this information?"

Com thought for a second. "Well, from the mayor there."

"The mayor of Ur," Delano said and lowered his head while keeping his gaze on Com. "Do you not, perchance, think that the mayor of Ur has an inordinate motivation to lie to you?"

Com looked around Delano's office. Did Santiago lie to me? he asked himself. "No he didn't lie to me! I mean, he just showed me the same EPA report that the committee cited in the bill."

Delano looked down to gather his thoughts. "My friend, my little-minded friend. You simply do not understand the nuances of this bill. Those people in Texas will stop at nothing to make sure this bill fails. And we, in turn, must do our part to make sure that this bill passes."

"Why? This bill is unconstitutional," Com blurted out.

Duane Delano laughed out loud. "Oh, that's just like your adolescent little mind to bring up *that*." Delano said the last word with disdain. "It appears you are not sophisticated enough to understand, Senator. Let's just say that some very powerful people have a stake in this bill. If you attempt to defeat it, those parties will not be particularly happy."

"Oh, really?" Com asked, intrigued. "Who?"

"Let's just say some very powerful people."

"What, more powerful than you? So you're just taking orders? You're their little lackey?" Com joked.

"No!" Delano snapped and slammed his fist on his desk. "I do what I want, when I want. This is my bill. I'm in charge."

Com pushed his head back in astonishment. "Okay, fine. It's your bill."

Delano breathed in a few times and looked down, trying to compose himself. His upper lip twitched. "It's not just the powers that be who have a stake in this. *You* have a lot riding on this bill, too, Senator."

Com persisted. "Yeah, I know. But, surely, you can alter the bill a little? You can change the bill to something that makes a little sense, right?"

"No!" Delano appeared to be getting impatient. "The bill's already gone through the committee. It's already been approved. Must I remind you that you made a deal. You agreed to support this bill, and I agreed to get you on the Homeland Security Committee. Now, one of us has kept his half of the bargain."

"Actually, I only agreed to co-sponsor the bill, not to vote for it," Com corrected Delano.

"Oh, cut the crap, Senator. Whether it suits your erratic whim or not, you made a deal. I plan to hold you to it."

Com pushed out his chin in thought. "I also made a deal with the American people."

"Look, Senator, we're done here. Having a conversation with you is like talking to an orangutan. No, listen. You had better get your pretty little head straightened out soon. No one needs to see your philosophizing and pondering tomorrow in front of millions of people. You do realize how big this *Facts* show is, right?"

Com shrugged. "Yeah, it's like the number one program on television." Com was unimpressed.

"It's not 'like' the number one television show, it *is* the number one show on television. It has been for five years. Sixty-five million households watch every Sunday. It is the number one source of news for most of those morons. Do you get the picture?"

"Look, Mr. Delano," Com said with a smirk, "I played professional basketball in front of millions of people. You think that bothers me?"

"I don't give a fuck if it bothers you, Senator. I give a fuck that you do what you're told about my bill."

"Maybe we can delay the vote? You don't want the environmental study to come back clean and be stuck with a bill—"

"Look, Senator, we're not delaying the vote. Now, you're going to vote for this bill and you're going to push for it tomorrow night on that fucking show. Do we have that clear?"

Com gnashed his teeth and stared at Duane Delano. The last sentence struck Com. It reminded him of his drill sergeant father, who would regularly ask him, "Is that clear?" when his authoritarian mentality carried over into his relationship with his son. But Com never reacted well to his father's totalitarian personality, and over time, a total disrespect for authority blossomed. Mr. Delano did not look, sound, or smell like Com's father, but the senior senator from Vermont was telling Com what to do, and all Com could think of was his father.

Delano pressed Com. "I want you to clearly understand that I'm not to be fucked with on this."

"And if you are fucked with?"

"Then I will take you down," Delano said coldly. "I will ruin you."

Com inhaled and exhaled in order to cool his thoughts. He stood up without a response.

Delano began sorting the papers on his desk and addressed Com in a nonchalant manner. "You have a big opportunity on the show tomorrow night to ensure your current position."

Without a word, Com turned to the door and slowly walked out.

Twenty-Eight

Com placed his right hand over his eyes and tilted his head back in frustration. "How long does it take to fill a pothole?" he nearly yelled to no one. He was in the back seat of his staff Lincoln Town Car, and he was becoming impatient.

His driver, a young man in a weathered suit, said nothing. He was paid to drive Com's car, not to comment on the condition of the traffic. The traffic was bad, as usual, on the Beltway, and it looked like construction that day had made it worse.

Com looked out the tinted backseat windows to an exhaust pipe spewing puffs of chemicals into the air. The senator then turned back to the driver. "You got any news in this puppy?"

The driver turned on the radio and selected the National News Coalition radio station from the preset options.

The commentator on the radio presented a level voice in an interview question. "The GAO recently reported that upwards of five point three trillion dollars of the Pentagon budget are unaccounted for—there's absolutely no record of the funds. Now, if a private corporation suffered that sort of accounting mishap, there would be outrage. It happened with Enron and Goldman. Now, how do you, as the public representative, respond to that?"

Another voice projected from the car's speakers. "Well, the Pentagon isn't a private corporation."

"Of course," the interviewer responded.

"If you want a private corporation running your defense department, then I wish you luck with that," the interviewee struck back.

"Yes, well, no matter who is running the defense department, there should be accountability—"

The interviewer was cut off. "Look, the Pentagon provides the essential security for this country. If you want to just give up on national security—if you want to leave the safety of your children and grandchildren up to Ace Rent-a-Cop, then by all means, call your congressman and ask him to end the Department of Defense."

Com looked out the window again into the gray clouds that hovered three thousand feet off the ground as his car inched along the congested highway. He stared for minutes while the radio talk faded into the background.

The radio program switched to another commentator, who caught Com's attention. "Yesterday evening," a grumbly radio voice reported, "Senators Derkins of North Carolina and DeGroot of Delaware returned from their inspection trip to the failed charter city of Ur, Texas to little fanfare. Senator Derkins gave a statement after they landed."

The voice of Senator Derkins projected through the car speakers. "We are faced with a growing threat in South Texas—a threat to our freedom, our environment, our way of life. The corporate cronyism that pervades the city of Ur has been allowed to run rampant without regulation, and the dangers of such anarchy are beginning to show. The city is a black hole for resources and wealth and is draining the rest of this country dry by the minute. Why are your water prices skyrocketing? You can blame Ur. Why are there no construction crews for your highways? You can blame Ur. Why are your wages going down? You can blame Ur. I've been there. I know."

The deep voice of the radio commentator was heard again. "Senator DeGroot did not speak upon his return but issued this statement: 'While I respect what they are trying to do in Ur, agreements have been broken, and we must hold the responsible parties accountable. We must act immediately to pass the Delano-DeGroot bill in order for justice to be served."

Com jumped in his seat. "What? I never said that!"

"I never said that!" Com yelled as he tore through the door of his press secretary's office in the Russell Senate Building. "I didn't say that!"

Maria Virkusk sat wide-eyed in shock. "What are you talking about?"

Kevin Donovan was seated at a chair next to Maria's desk but remained silent. Kevin had been in the process of flattering the Ukrainian-American press secretary before asking her out for dinner and drinks, but Com's intrusion put his plans on a temporary hiatus.

Com looked at a television monitor that was positioned in the corner of the office, then flung his hand in the direction of Maria's keyboard. "Can you bring up the news?"

Maria started typing on her keyboard and brought up a news channel on the television. A video began to play, but it wasn't what Com was looking for.

"Search my name," Com instructed.

Maria typed "Com DeGroot" into a search field, and a list of recent news clips were displayed on the monitor.

"That one," Com said and pointed to the top clip.

Maria selected the clip with her mouse, and it began playing on the monitor. In the video, Michelle Torres was seen sitting at an anchor's desk. "Last night," she reported, "Senators Derkins and DeGroot returned from their inspection trip to the much maligned charter city of Ur, Texas to little fanfare." A video sequence showed the senators departing the plane on the tarmac of Reagan Washington airport. "Senator Derkins spoke to the press after they landed."

The video showed Senator Derkins giving her statement in front of a group of press members. It was the same statement Com had heard in the car. Michelle Torres then repeated the statement about Com. "Senator DeGroot also issued this statement: 'While I respect what they are trying to do in Ur, agreements have been broken, and we must hold the responsible parties accountable. We must act immediately on the Delano-

DeGroot bill to see that justice is served." While Michelle Torres read the statement, a picture of a friendly-looking Com DeGroot was shown on the video.

Com threw up his hands and focused on Maria Virkusk. "It's everywhere."

Maria Virkusk and Kevin Donovan were staring at the screen, unbelieving.

Michelle Torres continued her report. "Senator DeGroot of Delaware has co-sponsored Senate bill six-sixty-four, which aims to revoke special privileges granted to the breakaway district of Ur in South Texas after the nuclear meltdown ten years ago."

Com punched the power button on the television and returned a stare to his staffers. "I didn't say that."

Maria stood and spoke up. "Com, I don't know where they got that. We have issued no release concerning your trip, per your instructions. You were going to wait until the *Face the Facts* show—"

"Where did it come from?" Com asked, pointing to a blank television screen.

Kevin was looking up in the air, pondering the question before Com had asked it. "What is in this bill that is so important . . . " he muttered, then let his question trail off.

"Delano?" Com asked in disgust.

Kevin's eyes widened. "Well, I wouldn't put it past him."

"That's not what I said," Com repeated.

Maria spoke up. "Senator, you know that doesn't matter. The truth doesn't exist until the public knows about it."

"Delano's hedging his bets. He wanted to get to the press before you had a chance to. He knows your poll numbers are killer and anything you put out there means a lot more than something he says," Kevin surmised.

"Can he do this? Send out press releases in other senators' names? Isn't that libel or something?"

"Well, I'm sure he didn't deliver the press release in person," Kevin said sarcastically. "But I bet it was his idea. What better way to force your hand? Get the people to believe you're still in support of the bill. And if you contradict your own press release, then you're just crazy."

"So let me get this straight. Neither of you had anything to do with this?" Com asked, shifting his flattened hand toward Kevin and Maria.

"No." Kevin laughed, amazed. He and Maria both shook their heads. "Com, we would never do something like this. Go over your head?"

"Well, can we find out where the release came from?" Com asked impatiently.

"Yes," Maria said confidently. "I'll follow up on that immediately."

The senator breathed in deeply and looked at the ground. "Okay, we'll need to canvas the news organizations. Explain to them that this press release wasn't authorized." Maria nodded empathetically and Com continued. "I want a retraction everywhere that this story is running." He raised his hand to help him think of a name. "And get this, uh, Michelle Torres on the phone. I want to speak with her personally."

Kevin looked disappointed. "Com, you know this isn't going to go anywhere. They already got the headline they wanted. 'Senators come back from Texas and confirm the horror stories.' No one's going to pay attention to your retraction. No one ever does."

"I don't care. I want you to get the word out to every news organization. I didn't say that!" Com was nearly yelling. He pursed his lips and walked out of the office.

* * *

Com woke the next morning and made his way to his computer terminal. He navigated the National News Coalition website and scanned the headlines. There was no mention of a retraction of the previous news story concerning Senator DeGroot in the front page. He searched his name in news headlines and saw a number of stories reflecting his support for Senate bill six-sixty-four. After navigating through a number of pages he found a link to a news article entitled "Correction: Senator Denies Support of S.664." He clicked on the link to find an error page. There were no other mentions of Com's authentic press release concerning Ur.

Com spoke into his handheld phone. "Maria Virkusk."

After a moment, a voice came through from the other end of the line. "Hi, yes, Com."

"Hi, Maria. Any word from Michelle Torres?"

"Her office said that they have bigger fish to fry and to, I quote, call back when you have a real story."

"You're kidding me."

"That's what they said."

"Unbelievable. All right, thanks, Maria."

Twenty-Nine

Com DeGroot sat in his car with Kevin Donovan in a National News Coalition television studio parking garage. His left hand was pressed to his forehead, pushing his skin up. Com shook his head in tight angles and let out a frustrated sigh.

"Didn't I tell you not to mess with Delano?" Kevin scolded Com. "Working with that guy is like trying to juggle a cactus."

"Yeah, you told me. So what are my options?"

"Well, I have no reason to believe Delano's bluffing. If you go against him, he will probably set out to crush you, and I have no doubt he can."

"Yeah, he said he's going to ruin me. What does that mean?" Com scrunched his face and looked at Kevin.

"Delano's got connections in Congress, and he can get you kicked off the committees. He's got connections in the justice system, and God only knows where that will lead. The guy's got connections everywhere."

"Fat bastard."

"And what's more is that, in the public eye, you support the bill. If you go back on that, voters are going to lose faith in you. They're going to see you as inconsistent, a liability."

"Everything I've worked for—"

"Could be flushed down the drain," Kevin finished Com's thought. "The committees, the political capital, the popularity. Everything."

Com shook his head and wiped his face around his mouth. He looked at his phone, which was resting in his right hand. The display on the handheld device illuminated with a text message from Cate Heatherton. It read: "I'm in D.C. for your show. Good luck. Can we talk after?" Com tilted his head back in surprise, and a smile slowly crept over his face.

"What?" Kevin was curious. "Who is it?"

Com looked up to Kevin and smiled. "A friend." Com took a deep breath and reached for the door handle. "Are we ready?"

* * *

"Jesus, where have you been? You were supposed to be in makeup a half hour ago!" the studio assistant screeched. "Christ, you look like hell. What have you been doing?" She didn't wait for an answer from the serene senator. A black headset adorned the assistant's head, and she moved her clipboard from one hand to the other to take Com by the arm and direct him down a white hallway. "This is Thornhill fucking Brooks and the most popular television show in the world we're talking about. We can't push you back," she gasped. "This is a catastrophe." The assistant spoke into her headset. "We're going to need makeup on the deck, pronto." Com watched the frantic girl in amusement.

The assistant shoved a group of stapled papers into Com's hand. She spoke loudly and clearly. "Here's what Mr. Brooks will be asking and what your responses are going to be. We need you to stick to the script, got it?" Com did not reply. Seconds later, another black-clad young brunette flew around Com and began patting his face with foundation.

"Let's walk," the studio assistant commanded.

The three entered a dark studio and passed bleacher stands full of the enthralled studio audience watching the live filming of *Face the Facts*. Com and the studio assistants quietly walked up to a group of people standing around enormous camera equipment watching the esteemed news anchor, Thornhill Brooks. He was presenting commentary about a small civil war in Africa. Com DeGroot stared in the direction of the anchor for a while and then briefly looked around the studio.

He glanced at the observers to his right and saw Cate Heatherton standing opposite two studio technicians. Com's pulse quickened. He moved the makeup artist away from his body with a gentle extension of his arm. The makeup artist huffed and threw up her arms in complaint toward the studio assistant. Com quietly walked over and positioned himself so that he was right behind Cate. He gently touched her back with his left hand. She turned around and smiled, letting out a surprised "Hi. How's it going?"

The studio assistant turned to Cate and moved her hand across her throat to indicate that they should be quiet.

Cate gave Com an embarrassed look and glanced to the stage to see that they were filming live.

"Cate, they're coming down on me. Delano threatened to ruin me if I voted against him," Com said too loudly.

With that, the studio assistant turned to Com and stared him down with enlarged eyes and gritted teeth.

The senator then leaned into Cate and whispered into her ear, "But it was all lies. I didn't say any of it." He pulled back to see her response.

Cate looked confused. "Any of what?"

Com leaned back into Cate. "The press release. I didn't do that. They're trying to set me up."

"Right, I saw the release. Who's trying to set you up? What do you mean?"

"It's Delano, or someone else. He threatened to ruin me."

Cate gasped. "Com what's going on? I'm worried." Her look was of genuine fear and concern.

Com bowed his head. "They want me to do exactly what they say, or my career is probably finished."

"Com, are you in danger? Just get out. Leave. Quit the Senate," she whispered back in Com's ear.

Com shook his head and looked for solace in Cate's worried eyes. "I can't just quit." He paused, then whispered again in Cate's ear. "I'm sorry if I let you down."

On the stage, Thornhill Brooks spoke into the camera. "After this short break, we'll speak with Senator Com DeGroot, who is leading the charge against the crimes of Ur." Music came up, and the studio lights dimmed. Com reluctantly let the studio assistant pull him away from Cate, but the two never broke their intense stare until the senator was stumbling onto the stage.

Com strode to the center of the stage and greeted the outreached arm of Thornhill Brooks. They shook hands, and Brooks' soft, puffy hand collapsed under Com's rough grip.

"Well, well, well, Mr. Senator. Didn't get to makeup on time? You're going to look like hell on the camera," Brooks said with a grin and a wink. The makeup artist frantically attempted to straighten Com's suit. She tucked in his shirt, which had been hanging out, and pulled down his suit sleeves.

Brooks sat down and extended his hand for Com to do the same. "Well, now. I'm sure you've been briefed on the line of questions I'm going to ask here?"

Com nodded.

"Great. If you can just stick to the script, that would be great. We need to set the tone, you know, so that the general public can understand the situation." Brooks winked again, then carefully adjusted a few strands of greased hair on the side of his head.

Com browsed the script in his hand. He immediately spotted his lines. "There are various points of contention that I have about Ur. First, the resource monopolization . . . " The senator looked back at Brooks.

"If you ever get caught," Brooks added as he pointed to an angled glass panel just off the stage, "just read it off the teleprompter. You don't have to worry about what to say."

Com solemnly nodded. The makeup artist made some finishing touches on Com's face, then huffed before walking off.

Com heard, "Five . . . four . . . three . . . "

Music came up and studio lights glowed brighter as the program returned from commercial break. Suddenly, the environment had entirely changed. White-hot theater lights blared onto the stage, and Com had trouble focusing. He looked out beyond the stage but could see nothing but a sea of blackness. He looked over to Brooks, who was smiling and leaning toward Com, then back to the pitch-black abyss.

"Welcome back, ladies and gentlemen. Joining me for our next segment is the remarkably popular freshman senator from Delaware, Mr. Com DeGroot." Brooks' cadence was measured and certain.

The audience applauded, and Thornhill Brooks leaned into Com. "Now, Mr. DeGroot, it seems you've been a very busy man recently. You've only been in office for a few months now, and you are already making a name for yourself. On the Homeland Security Committee, you have spearheaded many major bills aimed at making this country more secure, and you co-sponsored the bipartisan Delano-DeGroot bill to alleviate the injustices going on in South Texas, in the little town called Ur." Brooks turned to the cameras. "For the viewers at home who are unaware, the charter city of Ur was where the nuclear meltdown occurred ten years ago. The foreign investment corporation, The Green Group, purported to have cleaned up the area and have since built an entire city at the heart of this radioactive mess. They have stripped resources from neighboring communities, most importantly, water, which we are all well aware of as a result of the recent water shortages. And without minimum wage regulation, The Green Group has employees working for as little as a dollar a day."

Com heard gasps from the audience.

Brooks then returned his attention to Com. "Now, you have even risked your life to go to this wasteland, this land of corporatist greed, to see what it was like for yourself. I, for one, am honored to have civil servants working for me who are willing to put their country first and stick out their neck to make sure that the rest of us can sleep safely at night."

Com was nodding but did not wear a smile that would typically be expected in an interview of this nature. He did not speak when Mr. Brooks paused to briefly the senator to accept his compliment.

Brooks continued. "So, give us your impression. What was it like to be there?"

Com leaned in toward his interviewer and immediately sat back up in his chair. He glanced at the teleprompter that displayed his line, which he recited word-for-word. "It was very eye-opening."

"I bet," Brooks said, eager to get the juicy details out to his audience. "I bet you could feel the reckless greed that just permeated the place. Tell us about it."

Com breathed in deeply and looked at Brooks without amusement, then read off his cue, "There are various points of contention that I have with Ur. First, the resource monopolization. The city of Ur uses hundreds of millions of gallons of water a day—"

"Stealing—" Brooks cut Com off, and some members of the studio audience murmured. "They are stealing fresh water from surrounding communities."

Com did not refute the interviewer. "Second, there are people working in fields for less than a dollar a day."

"Slave labor . . . on our continent! It's unconscionable!" Brooks gasped. "At an age when the rest of the industrialized world is making great strides to maintain dignity in their labor force . . . ." The interviewer let his idea trail off.

"And then there's the nuclear cleanup," Com said, nonchalantly reading off the teleprompter. He waved his hand in the air.

"Yes," Thornhill Brooks said. "An absolute debacle."

"If you say so," Com said over a breathy sigh.

"Well, I say, Senator DeGroot, it was a very shrewd political move to align yourself with Senator Delano of Vermont on this one. That man is a brilliant statesman, and once that train gets moving, look out!" Brooks said and peered to the audience for a positive response. "You just can't stop that Delano train. Nothing you can do but jump on board." Brooks chuckled.

Com looked at Brooks' wrinkled half-smile and his perfectly gelled hair. Brooks was leaning into Com, looking for agreement about Senator Delano. Nothing you can do, Com repeated silently to himself.

Com DeGroot looked out into the crowd and saw nothing beyond the lights. He raised his arm to cover the white beams and peered over to where Cate was standing. He made out a dim figure but could not see her clearly. Com dropped his arm.

Thornhill Brooks proclaimed, "Duane D. Delano is a fighter, a champion of the Constitution." Com squinted at his interlocutor, but Brooks continued, "And it is people like Senator Delano, people who fight against lawlessness in places like Texas, who keep the Constitution alive and well."

Com pulled the corners of his mouth downward. "What the hell do you know about the law, Mr. Brooks?"

Mr. Brooks' eyes bulged. "Excuse me?"

"And Duane Delano wouldn't know the Constitution if it slapped him in his face."

A murmur spread across the live studio audience, and Thornhill Brooks put on a fake smile to display control of the situation.

Com continued. "The only people who are actually following the Constitution are in Ur. They want more justice, more freedom, and they want the government out of their business—exactly as the Framers intended."

Thornhill Brooks tried to talk over Com. "I think you're mistaken, Senator."

"Ur isn't the problem." Com's thoughts shifted to Santiago Garza and his tour of the unique charter city. "Ur is spotless."

Brooks' grin turned into a frown. "How—how do you mean?"

"I mean it's spotless. They make their own fresh water out of seawater. They're not stealing it from us. The people there working for less than a dollar a day are doing so of their own free will—they don't believe in money, they're socialists! And there is no abnormal radioactivity anywhere in the area. I saw it with my own Geiger counter. Mr. Brooks—Thornhill—Ur is spotless!" Com said, exasperated.

Brooks was caught off guard and stumbled to recover as the studio audience murmured. "I, I'm not—is that on the teleprompter?" Brooks laughed and turned to see the script. "Don't you mean that Ur is *worse* than we've all—"

"No, you arrogant asswipe," Com said firmly, and the studio audience gasped. "There's nothing wrong with Ur, except for the fact that the government is trying to take over the property of individuals there with absolutely no just cause. This bill is unconstitutional. Everything we're doing is unconstitutional. And your government—my employer—is trying to stamp out the last bit of freedom left in this country. You should be pissed." Com waved his hand toward the crowd. "You should all be infuriated at this."

The audience was buzzing with excitement.

Brooks put his hand to his ear. "Uh, I believe we're having technical difficulties . . . " He looked for confirmation from the sound booth. "Yes, well, we will try to correct them, and we'll be right back."

"Yeah, the technical difficulties are that I'm not going to play ball with these corrupt politicians anymore," Com yelled in the direction of the cameras. "You hear me, Delano? You can threaten me all you want, but I'm not going to play along with you anymore."

The stage lights dimmed, and the studio exploded with commotion while the audience spewed jeers and loud chatter. Brooks turned to Com. "What the fuck are you trying to pull here, Senator?" Com just looked at him with amusement. Brooks realized that Com wasn't going to cooperate, so he waved him off the stage. "You're finished. Get off my stage."

Com stood up and smiled at Brooks. "Don't you want to hear what it was like in the land of debauchery from a brave civil servant?"

The senator walked off the stage and spotted Cate. The room was spinning for Com as he approached the woman and put his arms around her. They embraced and held each other tightly. Com released his hold and inched back to view Cate's face. A suggestion of fruit and flower scents engulfed Com's mind as he surveyed her fair skin.

"I think I just pissed off some really powerful people," Com said with a half-smile.

Cate looked admiringly into Com's eyes. "You're really going to do it, then?"

"I don't know what I'm going to do exactly, but yes, I am."

Cate beamed at Com but said nothing.

"You're a genius, Com, you big dumb cloggie!" Kevin Donovan yelled as he approached the couple from the hallway leading to the studio.

"Oh yeah?" Com wondered aloud.

"Instant reaction polls show you up five points after the interview. Ratings are off the charts for the show. People are lovin' it!"

The corners of Com's mouth moved down in astonishment. "Really?"

Kevin nodded while placing his finger on his ear. "Yeah, people across the board. They say they want to see more. You're a hit."

Com produced a wide grin and looked at Cate. "Come on. Let's get out of here." Com held Cate's hand and led her out of the commotion of the studio, through the staging hall, and out of the building into the early evening light.

* * *

"What? Yeah, I saw it," Duane D. Delano barked into his handheld phone. His room was dark except for the flicker of light from the television.

"I know, I know." Delano paused to listen to the voice on his phone. "Look, I'm already working on it. I'm going to yank that overgrown monkey back into line . . . let's just say he might run into a little trouble with the law."

Delano looked around his room and listened to his phone.

"Well, I'm not worried too much about the bill. But if he starts pushing too hard and people start asking questions, we're going to have to shut him down . . . yes, it would be a pity, wouldn't it? A national tragedy." Delano chuckled and ended the call.

Gods
of
Ruin

PART 3:

CODE

Thirty

"Watch your head," Com DeGroot advised as he navigated a labyrinth of white iron girders and stairs in the dim light.

"Wow, I had no idea this would be such a workout," Cate said, exasperated.

"What? Are you getting soft on me in your old age?" Com joked as he proceeded up the curving stairs.

"Whatever!" Cate yelled. "I'll kick your butt. I don't even care that you're a cripple." She turned around and tapped Com's knee with her toe.

"You still couldn't beat me in thumb wrestling."

"Whatever, cheater. Race you to the top!" Cate yelled and took off up the cramped stairwell.

Com started after her. "How can you see?" he yelled.

Seconds later, Cate burst through the gate to the open dusk air. She slowly stepped to the marble railing and soaked in the view of Washington, D.C. from hundreds of feet above the ground. Cate breathed in the brisk air and held herself before Com stomped onto the balcony.

"This is absolutely beautiful, Com. I can't believe I've never done this." She was staring at the constellation of warm city lights covering a deep blue sea of buildings and budding trees.

The Capitol Reflecting Pool, hundreds of feet below the couple, mirrored the dimming orange sky above. Beyond the pool, the National Mall stretched for a mile to the soaring Washington Monument obelisk. From the top of the Capitol Building, it appeared that the two were above everything in the city.

"It's pretty amazing, huh?" Com huffed.

Cate nodded slowly as she kept her gaze on the Washington Monument. A light breeze from the west greeted her face, and she almost couldn't hear the sounds of a honking horn and a faint siren. "It's like we're above all the politics and the back-stabbing and the greed and corruption that goes on down there. It's so calm and peaceful up here."

"Yeah, it's refreshing up here." Com thought about it for a moment. "Everyone down there either bores me to tears or is so depraved and power-hungry it makes me sick."

Cate raised her eyebrows in agreement. "You're not depraved or power-hungry though, huh?" She smiled.

Com pursed his lips and shook his head. "Not anymore. I feel like a new man. Like I just shook off all that corrupt nonsense down there."

Cate looked at Com and smiled.

"Come here, I'll point out where I work," the senator announced. He put his hand on Cate's back as the two walked around the balcony atop the U.S. Capitol dome. Com pointed down to the nearby Russell Senate Building, which stood directly to the northeast of the Capitol.

Cate saw the Russell Building briefly but scanned the horizon. "Oh, is that the Basilica?" she asked excitedly and pointed to a distant building with an illuminated tower and dome.

"Not sure," Com admitted.

"It's beautiful." Cate smiled. "Did you know that tower at the Basilica is the tallest structure in D.C. besides the Washington Monument?" Cate asked with a hint of pride.

"I thought this was the tallest building," Com said of the U.S. Capitol.

"Actually, the Capitol is the fourth tallest behind the Basilica, the Old Post Office Building, and the National Cathedral."

Com looked down at Cate. "Look at you. You're just full of useless knowledge, aren't you?"

Cate nodded happily.

"Okay, I got one for you. What's the name of the statue on top of the Capitol?" Com asked while pointing up.

"It is . . . " She thought about it. "The Statue of Freedom by Crawford, I believe."

"Very impressive. You're right."

Cate started lightly humming and slowly walked away from Com.

"They will see us waving from such . . . great heights . . . " Cate sang.

She stepped around the balcony to the southwest. Com followed her and walked up behind the slender figure. He wrapped his left arm around Cate's waist and whispered, "This side is boring to look at."

There was no response at first as Cate just stared into the air. After a moment of silence, she turned around and looked into Com's eyes. "What are you going to do?"

"What do you mean?"

Cate took her worried look downward. "I mean, what are you going to do?"

"I'm going to fight this bill. I'm going to fight *every* bill. You were right, Cate. Government's role is to protect its people, and we're not doing that right now. We're doing the exact opposite. And this Delano bill is a perfect example of what's wrong with this system."

"And what about Delano? Aren't you afraid of what he can do if you fight this?"

Com looked down and thought about it for a moment. "When I was a kid, I used to wake up in the middle of the night in a cold sweat, yelling. It was always the same nightmare. I wasn't being chased. No one was attacking me or anything. My nightmare was being buried alive. I remember the dream—I was in a confined wooden box under feet of dirt with worms crawling through the cracks in the coffin. I couldn't move; I couldn't breath; it was hell."

Cate frowned in sympathy, and Com continued. "When people try to tell me what to do—it may sound weird—but I start to feel like they're burying me alive. I can't stand it. I'm not really afraid of getting hurt or anything. I just hate when people like Delano try to control me by telling me how to vote or threatening to take away my committees. I guess that's why I feel kind of relieved now. I feel free—like someone unshackled me."

"Wow, that sounds like fun."

Com smiled. "Yeah, I feel like Braveheart." He backed away from Cate a bit and began to yell in a pseudo-Scottish accent, "They can take me committees, but they can never take . . . my freedom!"

Cate laughed. "You're crazy."

"It's fun. Try it," Com said.

Cate shook her head no.

"Come on." Com faced the open sky. "Freedom!" he yelled, letting the word ring in the air.

"Freedom!" Cate yelled.

"Freedom!" Com yelled again.

A faint voice from a passerby in front of the U.S. Capitol was heard in response. "Shut up!"

Cate and Com looked at each other and laughed.

Com yelled back, again in a pseudo-Scottish accent, "No! You shut up!"

Cate laughed hysterically and gazed into Com's eyes.

The couple watched the sun set on the capital and turned back inside.

Com and Cate slowly walked down the dimly lighted staircase underneath the Capitol dome. They came upon a doorway to the highest interior level and walked in to view the Rotunda.

Above the couple was an enormous fresco with colorful depictions of men and women draped in Romanesque robes and flowing gowns. The subjects were all floating in clouds. Com walked to the marble railing and leaned over to view the floor a hundred feet below him. Cate followed and looked down.

Without looking at Cate, Com began to speak. "My knee is fine."

Cate looked at Com with confusion. "Okay."

"No, I mean, my knee was never that bad. It definitely wasn't bad enough to end my career."

"Not sure if I catch your drift. What are you getting at?"

"So, it was right before the playoffs my second year, and I had my injury—I ran into Del Strong and twisted my knee. The doctor told me it was a second-degree sprain and that I could get back on the court in a couple weeks."

Cate nodded, unsure where the story was going, and Com continued. "But as I was sitting there on the doctor's table, my agent came in to the operating room with an attorney for the league. They laid it all out for me right there. They said that I was one of the best in the league and that I had a very bright future—that I was going to get endorsements and championships and MVP awards. They said they could ensure all that, but I had to do something for them."

Cate looked on with a scrunched face. "What do you mean 'do something'?"

Com looked down to the Rotunda floor and explained. "They told me that I had to play hard, give the fans a show, and . . . " Com paused. "I had to lose when they wanted me to."

Cate squinted at Com in confusion.

"They told me that my team was going to win their first series in the playoffs and then lose the second. And they needed me to cooperate if the plan wasn't working out as expected."

"I don't get it."

"They wanted me to lose on purpose—to throw the series when I was healthy enough to play. And they said that they would want me to intentionally lose regular season games, too—to help ratings, to ensure big market teams' success, whatever. Eventually, they told me, if I played by their little rules, they would help me become one of the greatest players of all time."

"Unbelievable. Did my father have anything to do with this?"

Com nodded slowly.

"Com, I'm sorry. I knew he was shady, but I had no idea."

"How could you? This was way after you had stopped talking to him. And you warned me. You told me to stick to my principles and, instead, I chose the money over what I believed."

Cate deflected the credit, "So they wanted you to fold in exchange for greatness?"

"Right, but this is me you're talking about. I was pretty sure I was destined for greatness with or without these chumps, right? And I knew the league was supposed to be just entertainment, but they were asking me to lie—to commit fraud. So I asked them what would happen if I declined. They told me that the refs would call every little ticky-tack foul I made, they'd let other players pummel me and would pretty much make my basketball career a living hell."

"But you didn't do either?"

"The league attorney said there was a third option. I could opt out of the entire thing. They could declare my injury a career-ender, and I could sit out the rest of my contract on the sidelines."

"They told you you could opt out?"

"Right. You ever wonder why great players just up and retire out of the blue? Or when healthy players through college get to the pros and their all of a sudden riddled with injuries?" Com looked for acknowledgement from Cate. "They opted out too, they just took different paths."

Cate tilted her head back and let out a concerned, "So that's what you chose to do?"

"Right. There was no way I was going out there to lose on purpose, and I really didn't want to get beat up night after night. It felt like they were burying me alive."

"Ah." Cate sighed.

Com let out a groan. "What rational person would want to be controlled like that? I can't stand the thought of people trying to dictate every little detail of my life."

Cate laughed, and Com wondered what was funny. "I just think it's amusing that such a strong anti-authoritarian like you ended up with so much power. The apostate in an Armani suit."

"Yeah, that's me." Com raised his eyebrows in amusement and smiled. The couple stood there in silence for a moment.

Cate stood up from resting on the railing. She started singing again. "But everything looks perfect from far away, come down now, but we'll stay." She dragged her index finger across Com's shoulder and smiled as she slowly walked away toward the stairs.

* * *

Cate held Com's arm and leaned into his tall figure as they strolled slowly down the hallway to Cate's hotel room. Neither spoke, but both shared a comfortable silence. At the end of the hallway, Cate pointed to a door.

"This is me." They turned to face each other. "I had a wonderful time with you, Com."

The senator smiled and bent his head down to kiss Cate on her forehead, but Cate tilted her head up, expecting something more intimate. Com stared into Cate's eyes for a moment, then smiled at her naturally glistening lips and kissed them. For a minute, Com was lost in a tender dance with the soft beauty before him. When she gently pulled away, Com was frozen in euphoria.

"Kissing you could be my favorite thing ever," Cate said, looking at Com's mouth. He smiled but said nothing.

The young woman turned and used her keycard to unlock the door to her room. She opened the door and stepped in, not inviting her company to follow.

Com stepped closer but stayed outside the room. "Stay in D.C."

Cate raised a corner of her mouth. "I can't."

"I know."

"We both have work to do."

"I know." He leaned in and pressed his lips to hers once again. "Good night, Cate."

"Good night, Com."

Thirty-One

The next morning, Com DeGroot walked into his office in the Russell Senate Building to a deluge of questions and comments from his entire staff, all of whom were waiting for him in the front office.

"Where have you been?"

"The phones have been ringing off the hook!"

"Thurston is looking for you."

Com walked toward his office, and several staffers followed. The senator pointed at his press secretary, Maria Virkusk, and calmly said, "Go."

Maria began. "The press are going berserk. They want to know why you changed your mind on the Delano bill. There have been accusations that you were bought off by The Green Group. Michelle Torres wants an interview."

Com nodded. "Right, we should have expected them to try and turn it against us. All right, thanks." He turned to Kevin, then back to Maria. "Tell Miss Torres that she can forget the interview."

Com sat down at his desk. "Kevin, what you got for me?"

"Poll numbers are steady, you're up five percent. The people seem to agree with the move. You're at an all-time high."

"That sounds great. And about the bill? How we doin'?"

"We got a few undecideds to turn nay after the show last night, but we still need to work on, I think, six. Senator Jennings is working on the Dems, and you need to take care of the Republicans."

Com nodded his approval.

"And get this," Kevin continued. "Hailey is working on the bill itself. I told her to follow the money, and she's got some leads."

"Oh, yeah?" Com asked and turned to his political director Hailey Owens, who was seated in a chair opposite his desk.

"Yes," Hailey confirmed as she lifted a seven-hundred-page document onto her knees. "It's been tedious, but I think we've found something. Section seven-ninety-nine 'C' seven contains a provision. It states that, upon passage, the FDIC will acquire the assets of two principle financial firms that have done business within the jurisdiction of Ur since the city's charter was granted."

Com looked at his legislative director. "Really? So, the government is just going to take over these banks?"

"Not really. That wouldn't be very profitable for those involved. Instead, Delano would set up an agency to facilitate and subsidize the takeover of the assets by other bank holding companies—much in the same way as they did during the bank bailouts of 2008 and 2009."

"How much are we talking about?"

"That's the shocking thing. It's not clear exactly how much in assets either firm maintains, but estimates are near twenty-one trillion, U.S., between the both of them."

"Holy shit."

"I know. The next largest U.S. bank barely stacks up with just five trillion in assets. And that's not all," Hailey continued. "What's more, these banks don't participate in the fiat Federal Reserve System—all of their assets are backed with commodities, mainly gold and silver."

Com raised an eyebrow and looked at Kevin for confirmation.

"And that's part of the reason they've gained so much in value. In the last ten years, the dollar has been inflated to half of its value. Gold has doubled in price."

Com nodded. "So that's what this is about? Delano's nothing more than a petty thief," Com said with disgust. "How's he cashing in?"

"Well," Kevin answered. "We don't know that part exactly. And without a clear connection between the bill and the money, we don't have much of a case against him."

Hailey added, "The bill lists about a hundred banking institutions that would benefit. We're not sure how these banks were selected. We're looking into each one to see if there are any glaring connections with Senator Delano."

"Well, nice job, Miss Owens. Keep it up."

She winked at the Senator.

"He shoots! He scores!" a voice projected from just outside Com's office.

Com DeGroot looked over to his office door and saw Senator Roger Thurston burst through, holding a newspaper with Com himself on the cover. Thurston wore an enormous grin, which was matched by some in the small group in Com's office.

"How does it feel to be on the cover of every newspaper in the English-speaking world?" Thurston projected, and then continued, "Hell, if I'd known that making a dern fool out of Thornhill Brooks would mean such good publicity, I'd have done it years ago."

"What can I say?" Com asked rhetorically and stood up to shake Thurston's hand.

Maria interjected, "Well, the story *is* all over the NNC, but they're making Com out to be some criminal."

Thurston threw his hand at Maria. "Oh, bosh. Any press is good press. I tell you what. Looks like the people are really taken by you, son."

"I don't get it. I just gave an interview. What's the big deal?" Com asked Thurston.

"Commie boy, this wasn't just some interview. This was Thornhill Brooks interviewing you on *Face the Facts*, the most watched program on television today. And you made the host look like a bumbling idiot. No one has done that in the thirty years he's been on the air."

Com raised his eyebrow with a shrug. "I just hope that all those people watching paid attention to what I was saying instead of the fact that I just contradicted the host."

Thurston maintained his smile. "Whoa, boy. And wasn't that some brilliant political theater! Way to clean Duane's clock on national television, I tell you what."

Com shook his head but smiled. "Well, I'd like to say it was all political theater, but everything I said was true."

"You shootin' straight, son?" Thurston replied.

"Well, yeah. Delano threatened to ruin me if I went against him."

"And you can guarantee he's not going to lay down on this. He's going to retaliate somehow. We just need to be ready when he hits back."

"Right, and he said there were some powerful interests involved," Com relayed. "Hailey here has discovered a clause in the Delano bill that will make some people very rich if the bill goes through."

"She has, has she?" Thurston said raising an eyebrow at Com's legislative director. Hailey was quiet.

Com continued, "I don't know, but I think Delano might even be taking orders from these people."

"Oh, bosh!" Thurston complained. "That egomaniac doesn't take orders from anyone but himself."

Kevin Donovan turned to Senator Thurston. "Haven't you heard? Delano is working for the devil himself!"

Thurston chuckled. "Well, he sure as hell ain't workin' for the American people, I'll tell you what. Listen," Thurston said, turning back to Com, "you think Delano is dealing with some shady characters?"

Com nodded. "I can almost guarantee it, but, again, I have no proof. It's just a hunch."

Thurston licked his lips. "Well, if you're right—if there's something iffy going on—and we can nail Delano on it, it would mean an enormous boost for the party."

"If we could take the Majority Leader down on this," Kevin Donovan agreed, "this thing could tip. We could put ourselves in a good position to take control of the Senate next year. It'd be all gravy."

"So, what have you got up your sleeve, Com? What's your first move?" Thurston asked.

Com turned to his chief of staff. "Well, that's why I keep this little genius around, right, Chief? Why don't you tell us what our first move is?"

Kevin nodded with a grin. "Well, we have Hailey on the money trail and once we find that connection between who's profiting from the bill and who wrote it, we can expose Delano, and this whole thing will come crashing down. As for you," Kevin said, turning to Com. "You need to meet with Jennings to shore up the nay vote."

"Giddy up," Roger Thurston added.

* * *

Com watched as Freeman Jennings's shaky hands slowly spread butter over a warm English muffin. Com had finished his meal ten minutes before, but the elder senator was still delighting in the sights and aromas in front of him. Mr. Jennings's eyes widened as he looked at the selection of fruit preserves stacked in a plastic container on the side of their table. He smiled and applied the preserves methodically.

"You sure do enjoy your food, sir," Com noted.

Jennings offered a friendly smile. "It's the little things, lad, the little things. That's what makes life worth living." He took a bite and bounced in his seat.

Com smiled at the old man sitting across from him. "So, you think you can pull out four votes from the Dems?"

Jennings nodded. "Oh, yes."

"What are you going to offer? Do you use your big President pro tempore powers to finagle the votes?"

"Oh, heavens, no. I get votes the old fashioned way, through thoughtful dialogue."

"Dialogue? What do you mean?"

"You know, Senator, discussion." Jennings took another bite of bread.

Com shook his head subtly. "I wish it was that easy. Everyone I talk to wants something for their vote. Another vote, earmarks. Some sort of exchange."

"Yes, yes. I know how it's done these days. It's quite a shame."

Com noticed that the elderly senator was finished eating. "Well, let me get this. It's been a pleasure to eat with you." Com put his hand in his pocket and pulled out a small black electronic device that was attached to his keychain.

"That's very nice of you, Senator," Jennings mumbled.

Com waved the electronic device in front of a digital display at the edge of the table that showed the bill for the senators' meal. The display produced an alert that read "Access denied. Please try again." Com waved the electronic device in front of the display and received the same error message.

"Damn it," Com said. "What's wrong with this thing?"

"It's okay, Senator. I'll get it." Jennings pulled a similar device from his pocket and waved it in front of the reader. The machine accepted the new card.

"Thank you, Mr. Jennings. I don't know what's wrong with my card."

"It's quite all right. My pleasure." Jennings blinked and smiled at the younger senator before struggling to stand up.

Thirty-Two

"All right, what do you have?" Com asked as he imitated dribbling a small, orange rubber ball without letting it go.

"I got 'E' man," Senator Wilson said dejectedly. "Wait, how do you spell 'donkey'?"

"'E', 'Y'. You got one more letter, Charles," Thurston coughed.

"All right. Here it is. Blindfold." Com closed his eyes and moved his arms up in a fluid motion, projecting the orange ball up toward a small plastic basketball rim that was secured on the wall of his office. *Swish*.

"Oh!" Com yelled, and he ran around the room. Senator Thurston was sitting back in a chair in the corner, and Com swung by to give him a high five.

"Don't hurt your knee, big guy," Senator Wilson warned as he retrieved the orange ball.

"Ah, my knee's fine," Com said. "Let's see what you got."

Wilson lined up his shot. "Blindfold," he said and shook his head. Charles positioned himself, closed his eyes, and let a shot fly. The ball bounced off the top of the rim and onto the ground.

"And that's 'Y!'" Senator Thurston said. "That's donkey!"

"Man!" Wilson complained. "That's some shit. Get me out on a real court."

Senator Thurston grabbed the ball off the ground and stood up. "Or maybe don't drink three whiskeys before going up against Mr. Pro-Hoops?" Thurston leaned backward in a controlled motion and shot the ball with his left hand, missing badly. "Well, gentlemen, it's nearly midnight. I must get back to the old ball-and-chain."

"You boys having fun in here?" Hailey Owens asked as she walked into the office-turned-recreation-center. She wore a fashionable blouse that covered her shoulders but for some reason revealed the center of her chest and a portion of her smooth abdomen. She was holding a large stack of reports on upcoming legislation.

"Oh, yeah," Com replied enthusiastically.

"Well, how are you, miss?" Senator Thurston asked Hailey as he extended his hand.

"Mr. Leader," the young staffer said with a smile.

"You know this lovely young lady?" Senator Wilson interjected as he moved closer to Thurston and Hailey.

"Just in passing." Thurston winked.

"Uh, weren't you just leaving, Senator?" Charles cleared his throat.

"Ah, yes," Thurston reluctantly confirmed. "A leader's work is never done."

"Well, it was good to see you," Hailey offered with a smile.

"And I'm Senator Charles Wilson," the junior senator said as he extended his hand.

"It's a pleasure."

"The pleasure is all mine."

"Gentlemen," Com announced, making it clear that he wanted them to leave, "it was real. We'll have to make 'Donkey' a regular event."

"Yeah, I want a rematch," Wilson yelled.

"Hey," Com yelled at Wilson before he left the office. "You voting nay on six-sixty-four?"

"Man, you know this. I got ya back brotha."

Com nodded. "Thanks, Charles."

"No sweat, my man." Wilson left the office, and Com turned to his legislative director.

"Hey, let me know when you find something on that Delano bill," Thurston said to Com.

"Will do." Com nodded and Thurston slowly meandered out of the office.

Hailey quietly stepped over to Com's vast mahogany desk and placed the stack of reports on it, then sat down at one of the chairs nearby.

Com turned to Hailey, "Hey, speaking of, did you get any further on that bill?"

Hailey thought for a second, "The Delano bill? No, unfortunately. I'll let you know once I find something."

Com nodded. "Sounds good. Want a drink?"

Hailey looked up and smiled. "Um, okay. Have any cranberry over there?"

"Sure do," Com said. He poured two ounces of vodka over ice in a cocktail glass and topped it off with cranberry juice. He fixed himself another whiskey and brought the drinks over to his legislative director.

"So, what do you have for me?" Com walked around Hailey and leaned against his desk.

Hailey looked at her stack of papers. "We have a butt load of bills. Do you want to get crackin'?"

"Yeah, I'm game. You?"

Hailey lowered her forehead while maintaining her gaze in the direction of her superior. "I will do whatever you want."

Com produced an intoxicated grin and sat down in the chair next to Hailey.

The petite legislative director opened the first folder and scanned the top page. "Okay. First up, the Safe Borders Protection Act, Senator Phillip's bill. You are familiar with this, right?"

"Yes," Com responded, thinking of the bill. "It finishes the border fence and provides a repeat amnesty to all the illegals already here. I'm liking parts, but that first amnesty wasn't a big hit. It absolutely killed the federal health care system. I don't think anyone's going to like this one either."

"So, you're voting no?" Hailey asked.

"Yes. I'm voting no."

"That's yes on a no vote on Safe Borders," Hailey said with a hint of a smile and took another drink before handing the folder to Com. "I just need a signature there." Com grabbed a pen from a jar on his desk and signed his name on a coversheet for the bill.

"Okay, next up," Hailey pressed on, "Senator Foxworthy's Individual Finance Protection Act. This one is going to have a tough time getting through, but you may like some of the aspects. It provides oversight to every corporation within the United States and allows federal intervention in instances of international and domestic sabotage."

"Okay," Com pushed through his lips. "What's the budget hit?"

"Look at you sounding like a real senator!" Hailey said with a grin. "The 'budget hit' is under a billion," Hailey said confidently.

"And how long is the actual bill?" Com inquired.

Hailey chuckled a little and looked at the cover page of the bill, "Uh, it's twelve hundred pages."

"That's long."

"I like long," Hailey smiled.

"Oh, yeah?"

"Yeah, it's my specialty. Not too many analysts know what to do with bills this size." She lifted the bill. "But I have a knack of getting to the core of the bill and extracting all the good stuff."

"That's very attractive in a legislative director, Miss Owens."

"Thank you, Senator DeGroot."

"Well, to be honest, I can't really see such a big bill as being constitutional." Com took another sip and then finished his beverage.

Hailey flipped her hair and gazed into the eyes of the senator. "Well, I certainly see your concern, but as your legislative director, I think that you should at least consider it. I've scrutinized this piece of legislation especially, and I think it's worthy. It protects individual investors from criminal financial moves by multinational corporations."

"So it protects everyday Americans from being robbed?" Com asked honestly.

"In so many words, yes."

"And they need twelve hundred pages to say that stealing is illegal?" Com said sarcastically, then eyed his adamant staff member. "If you think it's a good idea, then I'll consider it."

"Very well . . . ."

As Hailey put the next folder on the pile that was accumulating on the senator's desk, Com leaned over to her. "Here, you're doing it wrong." He stood up and took the pile off Hailey's lap, making sure to brush his fingers over her bare knees, and put the stack on his desk next to the other pile. "These files were going to give you carpel tunnel in those knees of yours." Com shook Hailey's knee before standing.

Hailey looked at him skeptically yet seductively. "Carpel tunnel of the knee, huh?"

"Oh, yeah." Com jumped back up and walked to his bar to fix another drink. "It's a really tragic condition—rare, but very tragic."

Hailey shook her head and pushed air through her nose in amusement. "You're full of shit." She knew that Com didn't take political science very seriously and that he would rather drink and flirt, but that didn't bother her. If he was willing to listen to her, she was happy with that.

Com returned with another pair of drinks and told Hailey to drink up. The senator and his legislative director continued to review upcoming bills and couldn't help but be drawn to each other. Com eyed Hailey's easy femininity every time she crossed her legs and puckered her lips in thought. Every time Hailey shifted in her chair or reached for a new file on the desk, she uncovered an inch more of skin. Cate Heatherton kept flashing through Com's mind, but he could barely keep his eyes off his staffer.

Hailey returned the favor when she could. She glanced at Com's arms, which his rolled-up sleeves revealed, and allowed her eyes to sink into the contours of his muscles. When Com spoke, she watched his lips move more than she listened to what he said. And he left a trace of cologne when he moved closer to her.

After nine bills and four cocktails, Com was ready to call it a night. His legislative director patted herself on her knees before standing up. "Well, Senator, that was a very productive evening."

"Yes, thanks for helping me with all of that." He stood up, acknowledging social etiquette.

Hailey stood up, took a step toward the door, then paused. "Com, do you trust me?" She began to blink repetitively as she questioned the senator. "As your legislative director? Do you trust me?"

Com nodded. "Of course, Hailey."

"All right. I just want you to know that it's fine if you don't understand a piece of legislation. You can be honest with me. I will give you my best judgment on every bill."

Com smiled at Miss Owens. "Thanks. I appreciate that."

"Hey, that's what I'm here for."

The two walked to the door of Com's office, Com following Hailey, and neither spoke. When they arrived at the open door, Hailey spotted Noni at her desk in the front office and abruptly closed the door in front of them. She wrapped Com's arm around her waist, pulling the two together.

"Com," Hailey said breathlessly. Her mind was swimming but she felt more alive than she had ever felt. "I want you. I want you to take me. Right here, tomorrow, I don't care. I want you to have me and do whatever you want with me." She stood still and looked up into his eyes, which were fixed on her.

For a moment, Com was stunned. He had noticed the flirting and sexual tension between his legislative director and him, but was taken off guard by Hailey's advance. The young woman was alluring and attractive and she was making herself completely available to the Senator. Com briefly considered a passionate embrace with Hailey, then he smiled and eased away from his legislative director. "I'm sorry Hailey, but I have someone else on my mind."

Hailey threw her arm around Com's neck and pulled his lips toward hers. She planted a kiss on him, and he let her. "Anytime you want," Hailey whispered in his ear and retreated through the door. Com's eyes followed Hailey as she glided to the front door and out of the office.

Thirty-Three

"United States District Court," Com DeGroot read from the paper in his hand as he walked into Kevin Donovan's office. "District of Columbia. United States of America versus Com DeGroot, warrant arrest. You are hereby commanded to arrest Com DeGroot and bring him or her forthwith to the nearest magistrate to answer a complaint . . . charging him or her with . . . conspired to commit bank fraud in violation of blah blah blah . . . did commit federal income tax evasion and conducted a continuing financial crimes enterprise, in violation of eighteen U.S.C. blah blah blah."

Com looked up to his chief of staff. "Financial crimes enterprise?" He was stunned.

"Holy shit, Com." Kevin Donovan stood up, raced around his desk, and ripped the paper out of his boss's hand. He scanned the paper and mouthed some of the words on the page.

"Yeah," Com agreed. "We now know how Delano is going to retaliate. He's going to try to throw me in jail."

"Wow. This guy's serious," Kevin said, stunned. "They issued a warrant."

"It would appear so, now wouldn't it?"

"You need to get yourself a lawyer," Kevin said as he analyzed the warrant.

"Yeah I do." Com leaned his head back, then pulled his handheld phone out of his pocket and navigated to Cate Heatherton's number. He waited a moment, holding the phone to his ear, then spoke. "Hi, Cate. This is Com. I have a . . . situation I'd like to discuss with you. It's a legal matter. Give me a call when you get a chance. Thanks." Com ended the call and looked at his phone, which displayed Cate Heatherton's image.

"Oh, shit. They didn't," Kevin said, exasperated.

"What?"

"Damn it. Your court date is March fifteenth."

"Yeah?"

"That's when Delano set the vote on six-sixty-four."

Com tilted his head back and moaned.

"Look, we'll see if we can get this date changed or thrown out or something." Kevin waved the warrant in the air. "In the meantime, we have a lot of work to do. We need to get cracking on this Delano bill."

Com observed his chief of staff but did not flinch. "Yeah?"

Kevin looked at his extravagant watch. "Jennings is working on the Dems. You have one undecided on the Republican side to round up," he continued,

"No problem." Com shrugged. "Who do I need to talk to?"

"Senator Foxworthy," Kevin replied. "He's pretty big in the party. He's been around a while."

"Oh, right." Com nodded. "I know Pete. We've worked together before. He's a pretty reasonable guy. I should be able to easily convince him on this bill."

"Look, you got all the ammunition you need. You're on Homeland for God's sake. You have enough earmarks to buy you any vote any time."

Com shook his head and thought for a moment. "Yeah, Kevin? I'm not going to trade earmarks for votes on this. I want to do it the right way."

"And how's that?"

"I'm going to convince Senator Foxworthy that a nay vote is the right thing to do."

Kevin smirked. "Right. Good luck with that."

"Senator Foxworthy, how the hell are you?" Com said, walking up to Senator Foxworthy after the morning Senate session.

"I'm fine, sir, thank you." Pete looked up from his things and said dryly, "How are you?"

"I'm fine, thank you."

"It's been quite a couple weeks for you, Senator," Foxworthy noted.

"Yes it has," Com confirmed. "Listen, about this Delano bill. I noticed you were on the fence, and I was wondering if there was anything I could help you with. Do you have any questions about the bill? Anything I can explain to help you decide?"

"Oh, I don't know, Senator. It's such a complex situation. There are just so many things to consider."

"Yes, sir, there are. But, as you know, I saw the place with my own two eyes, and I can assure you that every concern about the place is unfounded."

Pete Foxworthy raised his eyebrows. "Oh, really?"

"Believe me, you don't want to be on the wrong side of this one."

Foxworthy tilted his head back and peered at Com through squinted eyes. "You do realize you're asking me to vote down a bill with your name on it, right?" Foxworthy smiled.

Com smiled back. "Yes, yes, I know. It seems odd. But I've learned a lot since coming on board as a senator. One of the things I've learned is that a lot of what we do here is not what the Framers intended. It's unconstitutional. Senate bill six-sixty-four is just that, unconstitutional."

Senator Foxworthy rested his hands on his briefcase. "Look, Senator. I'm a pragmatist, and I'm not going to blow smoke up your ass. All that political theory mumbo-jumbo doesn't work with me. It doesn't pay the bills. You know I have a bill out there that will be coming back after the House approves it. Now, I'm going to need some help on that. You voted nay the first time around, I believe."

"Yes, I think I did."

"Well, I think you should take a second look at my bill. If you do that, I will promise to look at the Delano bill from your perspective."

Com nodded. "Look, Senator, I know that's how things are done in this Chamber. I know it's customary to buy your vote with another vote. But I'd like to avoid that if at all possible. My staff is investigating this bill, and it seems there are some shady characters involved. When this comes down, I honestly don't want you on the wrong side."

"What do you mean 'shady characters'?" Foxworthy leaned in to question Com.

"Delano's not in charge. He's being directed by the banks somehow."

Foxworthy stuck out his hand. "You have any proof of impropriety?"

"Not yet. We're getting there."

Pete Foxworthy leaned back and thought for a moment. "Listen, if you find any hard proof, you let me know, and I'll vote nay."

Com nodded. "So, you're on board?"

"Show me the proof," Pete said, gathering his things to leave. "And I'm with you all the way."

"Thanks, sir." Com nodded as Pete Foxworthy walked up the aisle and out of the Senate Chamber.

Com called his chief of staff on his handheld phone. "Kevin, I think we got Foxworthy."

"Oh, yeah?" was the response.

"He wants proof of impropriety by Delano, but I think we got him."

"Excellent!" Kevin nearly yelled.

"And I didn't even need to trade anything for it. It was all legitimate."

Kevin was impressed. "Wow. Look at you. Well, Jennings says he's close to wrapping up the undecideds on the Dems also. We're looking good."

Com let out an exhausted sigh as he entered his office and walked around to his desk. The senator sat in his chair and noticed a newspaper clipping that was placed directly in the middle of a leather desk blotter.

"What do we have here?" Com yawned. He picked up the clipping and rubbed his eyes before reciting the headline, "Questions Abound After Senator's Death."

Com lowered his brow and looked up at his office door, then looked back at the article. The dateline read, "Washington, Feb. 21, 2003." Com continued reading.

"Safety officials looking into the plane crash that killed Senator Paul Wellstone of Minnesota and seven others in a campaign flight have uncovered a trail of oddities in the details of the flight.

"Senator Wellstone, a 58-year-old Democrat seeking election to a third term, displayed clear preflight anxiety before the plane, which was carrying his wife, daughter, three aides, and two pilots, took off. There were no survivors, and the aircraft, a Beech King Air, did not carry a flight data recorder or a cockpit voice recorder.

"In the weeks before the crash, the pilot, Mr. Richard E. Conry, had made numerous in-flight errors such as misidentifying his aircraft type and mistaking a switch that turned on the autopilot for a switch that activated a stabilization system on the plane. Mr. Conry had almost canceled the doomed flight, telling a Federal Aviation Administration official after learning about the weather conditions, 'Okay, ah, you know what, I don't think I'm going to take this flight.' The FAA employee with whom Mr. Conry had spoken told investigators that someone might have pressed Mr. Conry to go ahead.

"No distress calls were made by the pilots, and communication was somehow cut off shortly before the crash, which was investigated by the FBI instead of the usual authority, the National Transportation Safety Board.

"Irregular procedure has fueled a controversial fire in debate about whether there was any foul play involved in the crash.

"Seattle talk-show host Leonard Graves, who has lead the calls for a third-party investigation, said, 'Wellstone was an adamant opponent to the war effort pushed by the [Bush] administration. His opponent in the election was hand-picked by Bush's chief, and conveniently Wellstone dies? That's not a coincidence.'

"No comment has been made by the Bush Administration or Wellstone's office about the matter."

Com flipped the piece of newsprint over to see if the article continued, but found an advertisement. He stood up and walked to the door leading to his front office, where Noni Alvarez was working at her desk.

"Noni," Com announced "who was in my office today?"

Noni looked at Com with wide eyes and replied, "No one."

Com raised the news article in his hand. "You didn't see anyone come in and drop this article off on my desk?"

Noni shook her head slowly. "No. No one has been in here."

Thirty-Four

Sixteen-hundred miles from the District of Columbia, the sun had not yet in the city-state of Ur, Texas. The headquarters of Cate Heatherton's law firm was bustling with activity and Cate office was no exception. Santiago Garza joined Cate in reviewing the eminent domain legislation that had recently been signed into law by President Sullivan and Cate's colleague Hugo Martinez sorted through papers on his knees next to the attorney's desk.

"Oh, this is horrible. How did this ever make it into a bill?" Cate was perturbed as she read over the legislation on her thirty-two inch monitor.

"Not to mention a bill that passed by such a large margin," Santiago agreed.

"And the problem is that we're probably the only people in the country who know this is in this bill. I bet most of Congress doesn't even know it's in here."

"The federal government may acquire any lands or property . . . for any reason deemed beneficial by one half of the Congress . . . ." Santiago said, reading from the electronic document. He looked down. "I am shocked. This is exactly why I fled my country. They say they can just take property away for any reason, and they do it. They took my family refinery business, you know."

Cate breathed in and exhaled. "It's simply unconstitutional, not to mention unethical."

"Oh, come on, Cate," Hugo interrupted. "It's for the general welfare. Remember that clause in the Constitution?"

"I'm not sure if I understand you. How do you mean?" Santiago asked.

"Huh? In Section Eight of the Constitution, it expressly says that Congress shall make laws for the general welfare," Hugo explained.

"Actually, Hugo, Section Eight says that Congress can lay taxes for the general welfare of the United States, not make just any law. Regardless, this bill wouldn't rely on the general welfare clause; it would rely on the ambiguous language in the Fifth Amendment. You see, when the Framers were writing the Bill of Rights, Jefferson wanted to prevent government from taking any land for *any* reason. Hamilton, on the other hand, wanted government to have the authority to take land from anyone for *whatever* reason. The Fifth Amendment is the compromise that resulted. It says the government can take land for the common good but not without just compensation. Up until recently, governments had only used it to buy property for roads, libraries, power lines—for what they called the public good. However, in Kelo versus New London, the Supreme Court ruled that governments could use eminent domain to take land away from homeowners in order to build a shopping mall—arguably a public good, but not everyone's good. It certainly wasn't good for the people who lost their homes in the exchange."

"Remarkable." Santiago shook his head. "The same kind of dictatorship that goes on in my home country."

"Right, but not for the people," Hugo blurted. "Kelo benefitted the corporations."

"Well, they've thrown public good out the window, now, with this bill." Cate pointed at her computer monitor. "And it looks like they've thrown out just compensation as well."

"The government can just take your land," Santiago said in disbelief.

"I say that's completely fine as long as the government doesn't give it to the corporations. As long as they do it for the common good," Hugo responded.

"The question is, what is the common good?" Cate asked. "Is the common good only that which benefits everyone? Or is it just something that benefits a small minority with a lot of influence? Some would say a shopping mall is a public good because more people use it than, say, someone's house. Some would say that a highway is a public good, but I guarantee you the person who owns the house that the highway is being built on top of won't agree. We can't possibly *all* agree on what a public good is, and since that's the case, eminent domain will most certainly be unjust to some party."

"So, it's only just if the government takes it for a public project, not for the corporations."

"Hugo, why does it matter if they give the land to corporations versus some corrupt governmental agency?" Cate wondered.

"Because corporations are the root of all evil."

"Why?"

"Huh? Because their only motive is profit. They will kill the planet and all its inhabitants to earn a buck. That's why."

"But, Hugo, don't you see? Corporations have no legal right to harm people unless the government gives them that right, as was the case in Kelo."

Hugo shook his head. "Sure, it's true that they don't have the legal authority to harm people in the same way that the government does, but if corporations are unregulated, they have the power to manipulate what our choices are—both as customers and as employees—and the information we receive. I don't understand how less regulation can do anything but further disempower the consumer."

Cate thought for a second and replied, "Okay, I see how corporations can manipulate the market as sellers and employers, and that's not ideal. But can they harm us? So what if AT&T was the only cell phone provider and charged a billion dollars a month? We could all just tell them to shine off and go use Morse code. But if they harmed us by breaking contracts or selling us faulty equipment that made us grow a third eye, then that would be a problem. I can't really agree that *manipulation* is a crime, especially if we have the ability to ignore their manipulation by simply not buying their product or service."

"But don't we see examples of corporations harming people all the time? Lucky for us regulations are put into place to abate the harm. I'm thinking about lead paint in toys; the cigarette companies' denial that nicotine was addictive and harmful, and their targeted marketing to children; the insurance companies' collective decision to exclude pre-existing conditions. It is too much of a burden for individuals to bear to have to stay personally informed on the thousands of issues out there. I like that there are government agencies that are ostensibly looking out for our well-being, and I wish they would do more of it. So yes, I do think that corporations are inevitably—if not intrinsically—harmful. They will do all sorts of unethical things to maximize their profit if left to their own devices."

"But do all those regulations work? There are tens of thousands of regulations in the U.S. code, yet people still do bad things. Greedy people still harm the unwitting. Manufacturers still put harmful chemicals in their products. Regulation cannot stop people from harming others. Really the only thing government regulation does is burden the law-abiding companies and citizens, making it impossible for them to produce any good."

"So you would just get rid of all government regulation?" Hugo asked, presuming the opposite.

"Yes. The model they have here in Ur is brilliant—"

Hugo interrupted his colleague. "Ur won't last without stricter regulation. Someone will eventually take advantage of it."

"But how can they? Look at all the consumer advocates that have popped up that effectively do what government has never been able to do: protect the consumer. Charities and non-profits cover every aspect of need here, from legal assistance to food and shelter to counseling services."

Hugo shook his head. "No, I disagree. Voluntary charities aren't the answer. My sister works for a non-profit in New Hampshire, and they have charity drives throughout the year to collect items to benefit the poor people in the community. Last year, they collected eight thousand dollars for aid to battered women leaving a shelter and twenty thousand for holiday gifts to poor people. What this shows to me is that people base their charitable giving not on statistical evidence about human needs, but on whatever speaks to them emotionally. I think we can both agree that shelters for women and children who are at risk of being seriously hurt or killed by an abuser should have priority over Christmas gifts for poor children, but people don't really like to think about domestic violence, and it's certainly not as much of a feel-good charitable contribution as Christmas toys."

Santiago listened in amusement.

Cate raised her eyebrows. "You make a great point. But I don't think it's reasonable or just to say that the problem would go away if a few select people got to determine where all the money goes. For instance, government bureaucracies are subject to the phenomenon just as much as private corporations. The National Institute of Health assigns twenty-nine dollars in research money per victim of cardiovascular disease, but it assigns over three thousand dollars per victim of AIDS. The numbers are more disparate for other diseases. Who decided that? Is that fair? No. Both diseases are horrible, deadly, and, for the most part, preventable, yet AIDS victims get more funding. So it seems that assigning a group of individuals to control where charitable monies are directed is not a perfect solution either. But what's worse in the case of the government is that it is forced irrationality, whereas the irrationality with the charity is voluntary. Government harms people to do their so-called good, but charities do not. I believe you should be able to do whatever you want as long as it doesn't harm anyone else. Unfortunately, the federal government doesn't agree."

"Well, I agree. Do what you want without harming others. But the next obvious question is what constitutes harm? This is where even this ideology contradicts itself. You consider taxation harmful—coerced allocation of one's personal property. I consider it harmful when health insurance companies collectively refuse to cover sick people because it is not profitable. But we must choose one or the other, right?"

Santiago interjected. "I see, Hugo. You want to pit my rights versus yours, but that is not the way it has to be. You say that insurance companies *not* paying for terminal patients is harming them—is that right? I can see how you feel that way, but isn't that like saying that it is my fault that a person shot himself with a gun because I didn't step in front of the muzzle before he pulled the trigger?"

"No, Santiago, I'm not talking about stepping in front of a gun to save a suicidal person—"

"This I know. You are talking about hardworking people donating to health care for an unhealthy person that may or may not deserve their poor health."

"Well, who's to say who deserves poor health?"

Cate frowned. "I can certainly say that a child with leukemia is less deserving of his disease than a life-long smoker with emphysema."

"So you agree that taxing to pay for leukemia victims is okay, then?"

"No. I think the problem with your argument, Hugo, is that the things you see as rights require others to give up their rights. If healthcare is a right, then doctors are forced to care for people whether they want to or not. Is that not harming the doctor?"

"No, Cate, the doctors are paid," Hugo replied.

"And how do you pay for the doctors?"

"Through taxes."

"Hugo, you're just shifting the harm from the doctors to the taxpayer. Now *all* productive people are being harmed to pay for your so-called rights. Harming one's unalienable rights in order to serve justice is injustice. That's simply not sustainable."

"But this is okay," Santiago continued. "Hugo, if you want to live in an economic system in which everyone pays for everyone else's healthcare, then fine, you should be able to do it. But if Cate or I wish to live in a system in which everyone pays for their own care, then we should be able to live in that system, too. But you shouldn't be able to force me to live in your coercive system and pay for someone else's care."

"Huh?" Hugo coughed. "Well we *have* to force people to live in the system. Otherwise, no one would choose the virtuous path. Everyone would choose the greedy, me-first model, and we'd be left with people dying in the gutter because they don't have health insurance."

Cate thought about Hugo's point. "Which model would you choose if you could, Hugo?"

Hugo replied thoughtfully, "Well, I would probably choose the greedy, me-first model for myself."

"So you want to force a system on everyone that you wouldn't even voluntarily participate in yourself?" Cate clarified.

"But if everyone is forced into the system, it works. Otherwise it's broken," Hugo protested.

Santiago shook his head. "Sí, I think there is a name for that. I think it is called fascism."

"No, Santiago, I'm not talking about forced military service or concentration camps, I'm talking about healthcare, for Christ's sake."

"That's an interesting choice of words, Hugo, considering the context," Cate said quietly.

"My friend," Santiago replied, "does it matter what the force benefits? It is still force, is it not? What if the government forces you to pay for a war you don't approve of?"

"Now, that's not okay. War is not a good cause."

"My friend, I think you will find, if you examine your thought process, that all government coercion is wrong. Force for an unjust war is wrong, and force for unjust health care is wrong. What constitutes a 'good cause' is different from person to person. But since you accept the principle that it is okay to take from people in order to support things you think are fine, then you must accept that it is okay for the government to take from people to support things that you think are wrong, including war and unlawful detention and torture."

"Yes, I guess we have to take the bad with the good," Hugo admitted regretfully.

"That is a tragic lie that you have fallen for. The problem," Santiago continued, "is that so many people think like you, Hugo. That's why no one thinks twice about bills like six-sixty-four, which turn unalienable rights completely on their head."

"That is the understatement of the century, Santiago," Cate agreed. "And, from the looks of bills like this one, six-sixty-four is just the tip of the iceberg. We're about to witness a deluge of legislation taking over this city."

Santiago reached in his pocket to produce a vibrating phone. He answered, "This is Garza . . . yes." A stern look came over his face. "I see . . . okay . . . I will be over there as soon as possible."

Santiago ended his call and looked at Cate. "Rioting has broken out in Amaurot. We're going to close off the sector."

Thirty-Five

Cate Heatherton followed Santiago Garza out of her office and toward the elevator. Santiago's stride was controlled yet quick.

"Several residents of Amaurot were denied entrance to a tram to the city center, and they didn't take lightly to it."

"I'm not sure I follow," Cate said as she and Santiago stepped into the elevator. "You're saying the tram operator denied them access?"

"Sí. Evidently, the suspects were on various security watch lists either for criminal activity or known fictitious names. The city center would not accept them, nor would Jefferson Heights, so the tram operator must have rejected their fare."

"So what happened?"

"Well, it seems that the suspects did not like being rejected, so they proceeded to destroy the tram station. That was the report I received."

"My goodness." Cate followed Santiago out of the elevator and through a tunnel to the archon's building.

"They set fire to the tram structure and began pillaging the neighboring land. That is the extent of the report I received."

"Oh, those poor people there. There are innocent people in Amaurot."

"Sí, there are several coordinated attempts at a humanitarian mission beginning immediately."

Cate scrunched her brow. "Santiago, are we safe? Am I safe? I live in Jefferson Heights."

Santiago turned to the worried Cate Heatherton. "My dear, you are perfectly safe. As you know, the security here in Ur is unparalleled. Immediately after damage was done to the tram station in Amaurot, gates to the surrounding sectors were closed. There are security patrols throughout Jefferson Heights day and night. I promise that you are safe."

"Thank you, Santiago."

Cate heard her mobile phone ringing and reached in her purse to retrieve it. She saw who it was and eyed Santiago. "I should take this. You go ahead."

Santiago nodded. "Call me if you have any concern."

"Thanks," Cate said and answered her phone.

"Cate, hi. It's Com," the senator spoke into his handheld phone.

"Hey there, Commodore."

"Hey, I'm glad I finally got a hold of you. Listen, I have kind of a situation."

Cate smiled to herself, "Yeah, it looks like we are all in a kind of situation."

"Seriously," Com agreed. "Look, Cate, I've been called into court for tax evasion."

"What? Com, are you serious?" Cate asked, intrigued.

"Look, I know it sounds bad, but I absolutely know I didn't do anything wrong. This is just Delano's way of getting back at me for bailing on his bill. It's the only thing he can do to stop me."

"Why aren't you talking to your tax attorney now instead of me?"

"Uh, yeah. That's the thing. Evidently my tax attorney is in jail."

Cate couldn't help but laugh. "Oh, Com. This is beginning to sound really bad."

"I know. It doesn't look good, but I promise I didn't do anything wrong."

"I believe you. Has this gone public yet?" Cate wondered.

"Nah. Nothing yet. Kevin seems to think that it will just blow over and that Delano's just using it as a ploy."

"It's possible, Com. But it wouldn't surprise me if they found some technicality that you failed to adhere to—that's tax law for you!"

"What do you mean?"

"Uh," Cate huffed, "the tax code is so complex and convoluted it seems like no one can get it right and everyone is a tax cheat."

"Okay, so you're saying I shouldn't worry about it?"

"Oh, no. I'm saying that *everyone* should worry about it. It seems that at any point, the IRS could come knocking on anyone's door and find them guilty of tax evasion."

"Right, so, I'm like everyone else. There was just a misunderstanding here."

"Com, I'm not a tax attorney. You'll have to talk to someone else about this, but I think you should go to court and fight it."

"Well, I'm going to try."

"Our firm has a really good tax lawyer in D.C. He'll be able to take care of you."

Com smiled a closed-lip smile into his phone. "Where would I be without you?"

Cate ignored the rhetorical question. "So, how's the fight on six-sixty-four going?"

"We're looking good. Jennings is working on the Dems and I've spoken to Senator Foxworthy and I think he's going to join us on the nays."

"What did it take to get Foxworthy to come over?"

"Nothing! I just explained to him that the bill was shady and that he didn't want to be on the wrong side of it and he's on board," Com declared proudly.

"You didn't have to trade votes or earmarks or anything?" Cate asked hopefully.

"No. It was completely on the level. Of course, Cate, this is important to me. I'm willing to do whatever it takes to defeat this bill," Com said with unwaveringly.

Cate hummed. "What do you mean?"

"If I have to trade votes or earmarks to get this thing done, I will do it. My priority is to save Ur."

Cate hesitated before speaking, "Com, are you sure?"

"What are you mean, am I sure? Of course I'm sure. Nothing is going to get in the way of me taking down Delano on this."

"Oh, Com. You can't be serious. That's exactly the type of stuff that got us into this state in the first place!"

"What do you mean, 'state'?"

"This state of corruption where no one cares about the rule of law, just their own political and corporate connections. Please tell me you see all that."

"I do. I do. But what do you want me to do? I want to save your city—Ur—but if the only way I can save it is to trade votes, that's what I'm going to do."

Cate was silent on her end of the call.

"Cate?"

"I'm here." She said softly.

"Look, I gotta go. I'm going to get the job done. You don't have to worry," Com tried to reassure Cate.

"Okay, good luck."

"Thanks. I'll talk to you soon."

"Bye, Com."

"Bye." Com ended the call and took a deep breath of air in.

Thirty-Six

Senator Com DeGroot slapped his alarm clock to shut off its buzzing harangue. Rubbing his eyes, he rolled out of bed and stumbled toward his computer station. After a couple clicks, Com was surveying the news stories from the National News Coalition. Nothing caught his attention, so he spoke the words "Get messages" so that his computer would easily hear the command. The computer brought up a screen full of Com's email, text, and voice messages in list form.

Com yawned. "Let's see. Junk, junk, junk." On the computer's touch screen monitor, Com selected the icons that represented certain messages and flicked them into the computer's trash.

"Junk . . . uh." Com looked at the sender and reconsidered. "Justin Timeus. Oh boy," Com said to himself. The subject of the message read "Warning: high probability of accidental death for Senator Com DeGroot."

Com reflected on the socially awkward young Timeus and smiled at the thought of his inappropriate comments. The senator remembered the claims Timeus had made in their last run-in at the reception at the Arun Kula Museum reception and was compelled to click on the message.

"Well, let's see what little gem of knowledge you have this time, you strange little guy." Com selected the subject and opened the message.

"Hello, Senator Com DeGroot," Justin's message started. "I have cross-referenced the accidental death data with public officials' voting records and have analyzed the data. Please connect with me when you get this message."

Com thought about it for a moment, then looked at his watch. He had nearly two hours before he had to meet with Senator Freeman Jennings, so he shrugged his shoulders and then clicked the chat icon associated with Justin's name on the computer monitor. A small video window opened up and showed a loading icon. Within seconds, Com could see the visage of Justin Timeus in the video window. The young man was leaning toward his computer's camera, and his closeness distorted the video so that he appeared to have a disproportionately large forehead.

"Hello, Senator Com DeGroot," Justin said mathematically.

"Well, hello there, Mr. Justin Timeus. How's it going down there in Ur?"

"It is going well. It is eighty-five degrees Fahrenheit with a humidity of sixty-two percent. Winds are from the west at nine miles per hour. The UV index is eight."

Com laughed out loud. "Justin, you crack me up. Did you just give me a detailed weather report?"

"That is what I remember from the forecast. I cannot be sure if it is one hundred percent accurate."

"That's all right, Justin. You got something for me?"

Justin repeated verbatim his message to the Senator. "Yes, I cross-referenced the accidental death data of public officials with demographics of the public officials and did not find any data with statistical significance."

"Okay," Com said slowly, waiting for more.

"I then cross-referenced the accidental death numbers with the voting records of all historic public officials and then projected it for *current* public officials with their voting history and the projected probable votes and found statistically significant data."

"Something tells me I'm not going to like your findings," Com said hesitatingly.

"Senator Com DeGroot had a correlation of point-seven-two, which was the highest correlation among all active public officials."

Com cracked a smile. "All right, I'm number one, baby!"

"I sense that you are happy about this," Justin mathematically responded, "but I should mention that this is not something you should be happy about. According to the data, you have a higher chance of accidental death based on your voting record."

Com opened his mouth to speak, but did not. He looked up at his ceiling and then back to his computer monitor, where the video of Justin Timeus remained. "I don't get it, Justin. How could my voting record have anything to do with my chance of accidentally dying? I mean, what are you saying, Justin? That I'm going to fall on my toilet and crack my skull open just because of the way I vote?"

"The statistical significance of this data has been accurately represented," Justin said methodically.

"And . . . "

"There is one logical explanation that I can think of, and that is that the cause of death for many of these historical public officials was not accurately reported."

"You're saying they were *intentionally* accidentally killed?" Com said with a sense of aggression.

"That possibility should not be discounted at least for the percentage of accidental deaths for public officials above that of typical citizens."

"All right, all right. Thank you, Justin. I appreciate your help. Wait . . ." Com had an idea. "Does this have anything to do with my bill on the Senate floor?"

"Which is your bill on the Senate floor?"

"'S' six-sixty-four. The Delano-DeGroot bill. How did you project me voting on that bill?"

"Let me check." Justin Timeus was seen in Com's video chat dialogue box typing on his computer and scanning his monitor. "You were projected to vote yea on the bill."

"Oh," Com said hesitantly. "What if you changed my vote to nay on six-sixty-four? Does that lower my chances of getting attacked by goblins in the middle of the night?" Com asked while dangling his fingers in the air in mock fear.

"I'll put the new data in. One moment." Again, Com could see Justin working on his computer. "It went up," he reported.

"What went up?"

"I changed your vote to nay on Senate bill six-sixty-four, and your risk of accidental death went up."

Com shook his head in disbelief. "How much?"

"Twelve-point-five percent."

"Yeah, whatever," Com said. "Are you saying that if I vote against six-sixty-four, someone is going to twelve-point-five percent accidentally kill me? I just don't buy it, Justin."

Justin responded quickly to Com's doubt. "My friend Ahmed has said that people like to experience specific examples with regard to the data that I use in order to better understand the abstract concepts. Would you like to experience a specific example?"

Com subtly shook his head in amusement. "Sure, I'd like to experience that."

Justin was seen working on his computer, and soon another video popped up on Com's message center. Com pushed play. "You didn't send me a virus did you, buddy?"

"No, Senator Com DeGroot."

The video on Com's computer monitor depicted a television program that was clearly over thirty years old. It showed three men in suits having a discussion in an open forum setting. Com didn't recognize the show or its participants, and Justin provided no additional information about the video as he watched it on his computer.

In the video, the man on the left tilted his head and peered at the man in the middle. "Newsweek says this: 'The John Birch Society considers communism only one arm of a master conspiracy in which socialist American insiders are plotting to establish world government.'"

Com pushed his bottom lip down in a frown as he watched.

The talk show host in the video continued. "That kind of silly, asinine statement makes people laugh at the John Birch Society."

The man on the left opened up to a response from the man in the middle. "Well, Tom, I'm sure, being a longstanding member of the Rockefeller—"

"What is this?" Com whispered. Justin did not reply but just pointed at his monitor.

"There is an elitist core," the man in the middle continued, "that has seen value in subsidizing communism, protecting communism—"

"It has?" broke in the man on the left, and all three began talking at once before the man on the right was heard saying, "What are they trying to do?"

"Well, their objective is to try to bring about in our society the dissolving of sovereignty and a steady move to the left on the political spectrum."

"Who?" asked the man on the right.

"You see, Arthur Schlesinger, Jr., writing way back in 1947, says yes, this is the hidden policy of America, but we can't tell the American public because they're too unsophisticated to see the value . . . " The three men all started talking at once again.

Com looked at the young Justin Timeus in his video chat. "Is that what this is all about? Justin, come on. There's no conspiracy. I can attest to that. Okay, the government's not a perfect institution, but I don't understand what you're trying to say . . . dissolve our sovereignty."

Justin replied, "The man the middle of this video is U.S. Representative Larry McDonald from the great state of Georgia. In 1983, he was the chair for the political and philosophical group called the John Birch Society, and he said that there was an elitist core of socialists within the United States that was trying to undermine the sovereignty of the United States."

Com nodded and raised his hand. "Okay, okay. So what? He was wrong. There is no such group."

"On September first, 1983, Congressman McDonald was on a seven-four-seven airliner heading to Seoul, South Korea. A Soviet fighter shot down the airliner he was flying in, and all two-hundred-sixty-nine passengers onboard died. The logical conclusion is that somebody wanted Congressman McDonald dead, and a Soviet pilot used two six-hundred-pound Soviet air missiles to grant that wish. Congressman McDonald's death was officially listed as an accident."

"Oh, yeah? Do you have *his* score from your little accidental death algorithm?"

"Representative Larry McDonald from the great state of Georgia had a correlation of point eight-five before he died."

"And what's mine if I vote down six-sixty-four?"

"Point eight-one," Justin reported.

Com breathed in and straightened his posture. "I don't know, Justin."

Justin's eyes darted around. "There is more information, Senator Com DeGroot. Every elected official with an equivalent correlation to yours has died accidentally."

"Like who?"

"Mel Carnahan died in a plane crash in 2000 while campaigning for a Senate seat, which he posthumously won. United States Secretary of Commerce Ron Brown died in a plane crash in Croatia in 1996. Richard Obenshain died in a plane crash in 1978 after receiving the Republican nomination in the U.S. Senate race in Virginia. Representative Jerry Lon Litton died in a plane crash in 1976 after winning the primary for Missouri. Senator Paul Wellstone of Minnesota died in a plane crash in 2002 while campaigning—"

"Whao, whao. Who did you just say?"

"Senator Paul Wellstone of Minnesota."

Com remembered the name from the news clipping that was placed on his desk days earlier. "What was his correlation?"

Justin looked up the information, then read it to Com. "Senator Paul Wellstone of Minnesota had a correlation of point nine-one."

"Okay, okay. I get the drift," Com said in a defeated tone.

Justin paused for a moment, then continued. "The logical conclusion is that the responsible parties are willing to initiate accidental death on representatives from the House of Representatives and the Senate."

"Who is 'they'? The Soviet Union doesn't even exist anymore," Com protested.

"That is unclear, Senator Com DeGroot, but the people that McDonald was referring to in the video still exist, and they have not relinquished their quest for power—"

Com shook his head. "Well, that's why I'm promoting Homeland Security, so that these supposed perpetrators won't be able to operate here. Borders, intelligence, and Internet security, too. That's why I voted for the Privacy Act."

Justin's eyes continued to dart around, and he began to shift in his seat. "Senator Com DeGroot, the Privacy Act is antithetical to the Constitution of the United States," Justin said, pointing to his display. "The National Security Agency located in Fort Meade in Maryland wants to monitor our homes, our phone conversations, and every other private matter for the sake of protecting us. The Privacy Act grants the National Security Agency located in Fort Meade in Maryland the ability to take control of every citizen's computer or mobile phone device and control what they see or read and keep track of their whereabouts. It nullifies freedom of speech by censoring the Interweb. The National Security Agency will require all citizens to get an implant cellular device in order to track them." Justin again began to shake his head back and forth. "No!" he yelled out. "You want to ensure privacy by infringing on privacy," Justin said in a methodic manner. "You want to ensure privacy by infringing on privacy." Justin continued to repeat himself as he wrapped his arms around his torso and began rocking his body back and forth.

Com's eyes widened. "You all right, buddy?"

Justin blurted out, "No . . . not logical. Not logical. Not logical. You want to ensure privacy by infringing on privacy." He was rocking his body back and forth and stuck out his hand and hit himself on his forehead, then slowed down his rocking. Justin's eyes were closed.

A stunned Com felt uncomfortable and sorry for Justin. Com put his hand in front of the monitor to cover up the embarrassing moment.

Justin was still subtly rocking and whispering, "Not logical. Not logical. Not logical."

"You going to be all right?" Com asked.

"Not logical," Justin whispered.

"Uh, look, I gotta run. You going to be all right?"

Justin had his eyes closed but managed to get out the words, "Yes, I just need to let the hormones pass through my system."

"Okay. Talk to you later," Com said tersely and closed the chat on his computer. Com shook his head and whispered, "Crazy." Then the senator stood up and looked out the window behind his desk to a damp and dreary late winter day.

Thirty-Seven

"Hey Kevin," Com DeGroot yelled at his chief of staff as he walked up the stairs to the Russell Senate Building's entrance. When he got closer, the senator lowered his voice so that passers-by couldn't hear, "What do you know about Larry McDonald?"

Kevin frowned and shook his head, "Don't know the guy."

"He was a representative from the eighties. No?" Com shook his head to search for an answer.

"Nah, never heard of him."

"What about Paul Wellstone?"

"Um, yeah," Kevin said while tilting his head back, "I know that guy. He was a huge lib. He was like the biggest opponent of the wars at the time. Your girlfriend would have probably loved him."

"Yeah, whatever. He died in a plane crash, right?"

"Yeah," Kevin agreed, "I think I remember that."

"And he died really close to the election?"

"Okay?"

"Do you not find that strange? The biggest opponent of the wars in Congress mysteriously dies in a plane crash right before his election and his opponent wins? You think that's completely normal?"

Kevin scrunched his face. "Com, are you serious? You been listening to conspiracy radio dot com again?"

"I don't know, Kevin. It just seems a little odd to me. And it's not just him. Evidently a lot of elected officials have had accidental deaths like that. I got a guy who did the numbers on it."

Kevin dipped his head but looked up to his boss. "Com, we don't have time for this. We have a stack of legislation back at the office, we have meetings all day and one with Senator Jennings in five minutes, and we have Delano's bill to defeat."

Com swallowed and thought about Kevin's words for a moment. "Okay. Fine."

"Can we get to work?"

"Yeah. Sure. So, what's going on with the Delano bill? Do you have anything substantial yet?"

Kevin nodded in relief that Com change the topic of conversation. Then, the chief of staff jumped into his report. "Yeah, so Hailey's been real busy with other stuff, so I took the liberty of jumping on the money trail and I've learned that it's real muddy."

"Okay," Com said almost as a question.

"So, you know about all the banks that are set to profit off of six-sixty-four, right? There are about a hundred."

Com nodded.

"Well, we cross-referenced the board members of all the banks, and it turns out there is a group of six bankers who maintain at least one seat on the majority of the bank boards."

Com raised his eyebrows. "Oh, really?"

Kevin continued as the two entered the building. "But that's not a big deal. Tons of executives have seats on a dozen boards. The kicker here is that these six bankers also have board positions on one specific political action committee, the National Committee for Freedom and Progress—NCFP. It's a big PAC—top twenty of all time and solidly Dem. About ninety-five percent goes to the Dems. Now, this PAC holds various events and fundraisers and it basically got the president elected—but guess who else they helped along the way?"

"Duane D. Delano."

"You guessed it. NCFP was the largest contributor to the Delano campaign by far—over seventy mil."

"No shit?" Com said as he walked through a security checkpoint. "Which office is Jennings' again?"

"End of this hall." Kevin pointed straight and walked in the same direction, then continued with his report, "So the connection is pretty clear. They're going to power grab the coin in Ur and funnel it through the banksters, then into NCFP. We don't have hard evidence yet, but I think any jury would see that the connection."

"Well done, you little Irish bastard."

"It's my pleasure, you big dumb cloggie."

Com and his chief arrived at Senator Jennings' office and noticed the lights were out. Com frowned as he looked around the front office. It was empty, and the open door to Senator Freeman's office on the other side of the front office revealed another dark and vacant space.

"Well, where is the old fart?" Com wondered aloud. He stepped back out to the main hallway and looked down both ends.

"Man, that old guy takes ten minutes to stand. He's probably just taking his time getting here," Kevin said with a smirk.

"It's not like him to be late. You did have the right time?" Com asked, looking at his wristwatch.

"Yeah, nine-thirty."

Com decided they could prepare for the meeting while they waited for Senator Jennings. "So who's Jennings working on?"

Kevin put his hand out. "There are five Dems that are undecided. We need each one of those votes or we're toast on six-sixty-four. Now, Jennings has a good relationship with Blythe and Fitzsimmons, but I'm not sure about the others."

"You think Jennings can come through?"

"No doubt. He's not the most important guy on the Hill, but in this realm, he's unstoppable. He can be pretty persuasive with his old-geezer charm. We don't have much time, but I think it can be done."

"So that's it? Jennings nails the five Dems, and Delano's bill goes down in flames?"

"That's about it. If you're confident about Foxworthy, we're in the money."

"I think all Foxworthy needed was that connection with the NCFP. With that, I think we can count him," Com said.

"Sounds good," Kevin replied. "Now all we need is for Jennings to come through."

"Where is that old fart?" Com asked again, getting impatient. He stepped into the hall and walked down to the next office, which was also occupied by Jennings' staff. That room was dark, too, except for light creeping through some crooked Venetian blinds. The room was empty as well, save for a tiny figure. Jennings' elderly staff assistant was standing in the middle of the office. She looked at Com and Kevin like a deer in headlights.

"Barb?" Com called to her. "Is everything all right? Where's Senator Jennings?"

Barbara's bottom lip quivered, and she began to shake her head.

"Barb?" Kevin said and moved toward her.

Barbara opened her mouth. "The senator's . . . dead."

A cold draft blew through the room. Com looked back to the hall quickly, then walked toward Barbara to console her. "It's okay, Barb." He embraced the elderly lady. "What happened?"

Barb clasped onto Com's arm, then mumbled something inaudible.

"Barb, what happened? How did he die?"

"I walked into my office after breakfast, and the medics were wheeling him out on a stretcher. They said something about an accident."

* * *

Com DeGroot exploded out of the Russell Senate Building and down the front steps. Kevin followed him across Delaware Avenue to the west and into Lower Senate Park, a large wooded field. Com scanned the surroundings and slowed his pace before stopping under a large oak tree. There was no one within hearing distance.

"We're fine, Com," Kevin assured the senator.

"Okay, you're telling me that was completely coincidental?" Com pointed at the Russell Building, referring to the news of Jennings' death.

"Com, what are you saying—that it was a conspiracy?" Kevin shook his head.

The senator looked around. "No, it's too much. First, they try to intimidate me into going along with the bill by putting a warrant out, then the leading Dem—the one that's mounting the fight against the bill—gets bumped?"

"He didn't get bumped, Com. We don't even know how he died."

"Whatever, there's something wrong with this picture."

"Com, this isn't JFK. The man was a hundred and seventy years old," Kevin exaggerated. "People that old die. It's just what they do."

"What did Barb say? That he was the healthiest he had been in years? And all of the sudden, he just ups and dies from too much breakfast? I don't buy it."

Kevin pursed his lips and sternly looked at his boss. "What do you want to do?"

"I don't know." Com looked around and huffed. "Call Reggie Williams. I might need a little heat from here on out."

* * *

"I really appreciate what you've done for me, sir, what with the captain's post and all." Reggie Williams nodded as he stood at attention in front of Com DeGroot's desk.

"Don't even mention it. You have deserved everything I've given you." Com waved his hand at Reggie.

"Very well, sir." He relaxed. "There will be three guards in your vicinity at all times. One will be on your person or within striking distance, and that will most likely be myself or my second in command, Agent Nguyen."

"Well, I know you're capable. How about Nguyen?"

"Agent Nguyen is a second-degree black belt in Hapkido and an excellent marksman."

Com nodded. "Well, I shouldn't expect less from your detail."

Reggie agreed "Yes, sir."

"This is going to be a big commitment on your part, Reggie."

"I understand that, sir."

"You're not going to have much time off."

"That's all right, sir. I don't have a woman. No kids to look after. You've treated me very well, sir, and I'm happy to serve."

Com nodded. "Well, it's certainly appreciated."

Thirty-Eight

Dozens of mourners faced a light mist hanging in the late-winter air at Arlington National Cemetery. The wife of Senator Freeman Jennings began to quietly weep as his casket was lowered into the blackened earth. A younger resemblance threw her arm around the gray woman and held her as the casket became invisible. A bugler wailed *Taps*, and a few elderly service men with whom Jennings had served during the Korean War saluted. When the somber tune ended, there was silence.

Com DeGroot stared into the mist as the crowd slowly dispersed, but he was interrupted by the lispy voice of Senator Duane D. Delano, who walked up beside the junior senator. "The man will be sorely missed."

Com pursed his lips in anger. "Did you do it?"

"Do what?" Delano said, aghast.

Com looked at Delano with a stern face. He began to turn and walk away but halted when the senior senator cleared his throat.

"Uh, Senator?" Delano coughed. "I suggest you take a walk with me."

"Why the hell would I want to take a walk with you?" Com asked, still facing away from Delano.

Delano looked at Com. "Let's take a walk."

Com frowned. He spotted his security captain standing fifty feet away at a black limousine and tilted his head to indicate that he should be followed. Reggie started slowly moving toward Com, who then turned back to Delano.

"What do you want, Delano?" Com asked in a straightforward manner as the two senators began to walk along a gravel path toward the John F. Kennedy Memorial.

"I'm very disappointed in your performance the other night on *Face the Facts*. You confused quite a bit of people with your antics."

"Or did I set them straight?" Com asked defiantly.

Delano sighed. "Ah, so naïve. And so disappointing." Delano looked at the misty setting around the senators. "Do you think all these soldiers knew what they were dying for?" Delano waved his hand out to the thousands of white tombstones aligned in perfect symmetry over the low hills.

"They knew exactly what they were dying for" was Com's reply.

"Oh? Enlighten me." Delano slapped his lips together and looked at Senator DeGroot with a mocking tone.

"Freedom."

Delano burst out laughing. "Well, I guess they got what they were looking for, huh? There's so much freedom there six feet underground."

Com pointed to the graves, "Hey, these people gave up their freedom so that we could enjoy ours. I know 'cause my father was one of them."

"Nice fairy tale if you want to believe it."

Com reflected on his childhood nightmares briefly, then said impatiently, "What do you say we cut the shit?"

"It comes down to this. You're new to Washington, so I'm going to forgive your little brain for not catching on yet. My bill is going to pass, and it will be signed into law, whether you like it or not. You are incapable of altering that fact. There are some very powerful interests involved, and you alone are just not going to stop them. But you've become quite a pain in the ass, Mr. DeGroot. Much of the underground press is buzzing about your erratic behavior, and even some NNC stations are calling into question the validity of my bill."

"Well, it's about time," Com interjected.

"Mr. DeGroot, there are repercussions for your actions. You made a deal to co-sponsor my bill, and I followed through on my end. I placed you on the Homeland Security Committee. Do you realize what I had to do to secure that seat for you? Now, it looks like you want to treat me like a used condom and just toss me out. Well, DeGroot, no one uses Senator Duane D. Delano."

"Well, Mr. Duane D. Delano," Com mocked, "if you wanted me on your side, you should have written a bill that actually makes sense."

Delano brought his hands together under his nose, stopped walking, and paused for dramatic effect. Com followed suit.

"Mr. DeGroot," Delano said, looking up to Com, "you are surely aware of the criminal charges that have been brought on you?"

"Those are bullshit charges and you know it," Com said as if he was catching on to a joke. "I got raped by the government on those paychecks."

"Well, sexual excursions with nonmaterial entities aside, there have been allegations that there were improprieties. The tax code is a wonderfully complex document. It's so very hard to know if you've complied with all of the regulations or not. And it doesn't look good that your attorney at the time of your evasion is in prison currently."

Com's nostrils flared.

Delano continued. "This is such a delicate situation. You would surely be glad to know the federal government is making every effort to bring you into compliance as we speak. You have two investment accounts with the majority of your monies derived from your professional basketball career, both earning around twelve percent—total of approximately thirty-seven million dollars. Not a bad little nest egg."

Com straightened his neck to prepare for Delano's point.

"I have seen to it that those bank accounts have been frozen."

Com's eyes widened and his nostrils flared. "The hell . . . ." Com left his mouth open.

The tall senator dug into his right pocket to bring out his handheld phone. He tapped a few times to bring up information on his bank account and pressed his thumb to the screen to input his biometric information.

"Sure, go ahead and check. You won't be able to access your account," Delano said with confidence.

A warning popped up on Com's handheld device. "Access denied." He tried the procedure again and got the same result.

Com slowly shook his head back and forth. "You can't do this."

"I just did." Delano searched for a reaction in Com's face but found none. "And unless you fall into line quickly, Mr. DeGroot, you can kiss your sweet little nest egg goodbye. And you can expect an indictment and quite possibly a Senate Finance hearing. Of course, the money will eventually be returned to the rightful owner, the fine taxpayers of the United States."

"Don't you mean the government?"

Delano smiled. "Why, yes. That's precisely what I mean."

"This is out of bounds, you fuck."

"Oh, dear, are you really that stupid?"

Com burned a look into Delano.

"Do you think you've ever been *in* bounds?"

Com shook his head. "You're doing this because I'm dumping your stupid bill?"

"I'm doing this because you are out of control. You and your staff need to stop asking questions about powerful people."

Com's pulse picked up. He could hear it thumping in his ear. "What powerful people?"

"You know to whom I'm referring."

Com was breathing heavily.

"It would be a shame to see you end up in jail." Delano produced a wrinkled grin. "Or worse, to end up like our friend, Senator Jennings."

"Are you threatening me?" Com asked. "Was that a threat?" He was livid.

Delano smiled through his thin lips. "Why, not at all. What would have given you that idea?"

Com stood staring at Delano.

"That is all," Delano hummed, and Com walked off.

Thirty-Nine

Com was rubbing his tired eyes with his right hand and attempting to watch a news clip on his mobile device. He sat hunched in a wooden chair with leather upholstery in the sparsely populated but well-appointed dining hall in the basement of the Dirksen Senate Building, waiting for his chief of staff. Beaded raindrops dripped off of Com's raincoat, which he had not removed since the funeral. A cappuccino steamed in front of the senator, but was untouched.

The news reporter in the video clip was a beautiful French woman speaking English with a minor accent. She gazed at the viewer and explained, "The American president spoke at a White House luncheon today and took aim at angry rhetoric coming from those he categorized as 'foes of progress.'"

The video clip transitioned to an image of the president of the United States, a well-dressed, thin, middle-aged man with a full head of hair. The president spoke confidently and firmly as he addressed his audience. "Words like 'socialist,' 'Nazi-styled government takeover,' and 'fascist' do nothing but close the door to real compromise. We must stop this constant antagonism toward government as something inherently bad. Government isn't bad; it's everything that is good in this country. Government is the roads that we drive on and the regulation that keeps your cars from exploding accidentally. Government is the hospitals that save lives and the university research that promotes products that make life worth living in the first place. Government is your local firefighter and teacher. Government is your neighbor, your friend. Government is everywhere. Government is us."

The French commentator returned to the screen and continued. "A small protest was convened outside the White House in opposition.

Racist remarks were reported amongst the crowd, which was waving banners calling the president 'Hitler-esque.'"

A brief shot of angry marching, yelling protesters was shown, and Com closed eyes and shook his head.

"You look like shit," Kevin Donovan said as he approached his employer.

Com looked up and faked a smile. "Yeah, you, too." The senator turned off his news stream.

"Pretty torn up about the funeral, huh?" Kevin asked as he took a seat.

Com lifted his eyebrows. "Yeah."

Kevin observed his boss and lowered his brow.

"Is it worth it?" Com asked.

"Is what worth it?"

"The bill."

Kevin's eyes bulged. "Which bill?"

"The Delano bill." Com put his hands around the cappuccino mug.

"If by 'worth it' you mean should you try to defeat it, then yes. Why?"

"It doesn't stop. It never stops," Com said, staring at the table.

"What are you talking about?"

"Delano. He's not going to give up."

"Well, so what? So, you just give up? Don't give me that crybaby shit. Look, you're hot right now. Your name is on the lips of everyone in the country. This is when we make our move."

A blonde waitress with a tight black skirt and a loose-fitting white blouse walked over and captured Kevin's attention. She asked if the newcomer needed anything, and he replied in the negative. The waitress then walked away but kept Kevin's eyes for a moment.

"I think we're on to something. He told me that my staff and I need to stop asking questions about powerful people."

"He said that?"

Com nodded. "He pretty much threatened that I would end up like Jennings. And that was after he told me he froze my accounts."

"What do you mean? Froze your bank accounts?"

Com's face grew redder as he slowly spoke. "It has to do with the tax evasion charges."

Kevin leaned his face in toward Com. "Come again?"

"I don't know. He got a court order to freeze my bank accounts. He's got connections. You said it yourself—he's got connections."

"Look, he's just trying to distract you, can't you see? This will blow over. Don't worry about it."

Com sighed an obnoxious sigh. "Ah. I need a drink."

Kevin leaned in and tried to get the senator's attention. "Look, you don't need a drink—you need a plan to take that bastard down. What are you doing? You sound pathetic." He produced a squeaky high-pitched voice. "Oh, poor me. Big bad Delano is threatening me." Kevin chuckled.

Com looked up at Kevin and cracked a smile.

"Look, you're going to need to step it up. Now that Jennings is taking a dirt nap, you're going to have to talk to the Dems and convince the undecideds yourself. You're going to have to be the go-to guy."

"I just don't know," Com said and shook his head.

"Man, grab your balls! This is when you hit back. Can't you see? Delano's searching. He needs an ace in the hole and what does he break out? Some lame tax evasion story? You've got to be kidding me. We've got him on the ropes. It's bottom of the ninth . . . he's got four fouls . . . and we're on his one-yard line. Now it's time to shove the hockey stick right up his ass."

Com shook his head and laughed a silent laugh. "I have a feeling he'd probably like that."

"Yeah, no shit."

Com looked back to the table, still somber. "You don't think they're going to try to come after me and accidentally kill me?"

"Look, we'll have Reggie on you like glue. He won't leave your sight. You're going to be all right. We'll nail Delano's corrupt ass on this bill, and you won't have to worry."

Com nodded in approval. He straightened his back, then stood up and stuck his hand in his pocket to pull out a small electronic device. He swiped the device across a small computer affixed to the table, but the computer buzzed in response.

"Hey, uh, Kevin. Can you get this? I'm frozen, remember?"

Kevin nodded and used his card to settle the bill for the cappuccino. The two walked out of the dining hall and up the stairs of the Dirksen Senate Building. Kevin jabbed Com in his side. "Oh, get this. I spoke with Senator Blythe about switching his vote for six-sixty-four. He said he'll consider it if you can get him some good playoffs seats," Kevin said as he opened a door to the southwest corner of the building.

Com chuckled. "You're kidding."

"No, that's what he said."

"That's hilarious. Well, I think I can do that." Com looked down, stopped walking, and huffed. "Kevin, I don't want to do that. I don't want to wheel and deal on this. It's not right."

Kevin rolled his eyes. "Com, it's playoff tickets. It's not a world war."

Com shook his head slowly. "I know. It's just—"

"Com, if you want to win, you're going to have to trade some votes." Kevin let silence hang in the air for a moment. "And, uh, by the way, Foxworthy called. He changed his mind. He wants you to vote on his Individual Finance bill or there's no dice."

"You're shitting me."

"That's what he said."

"Damn it!" Com yelled in frustration. He looked at the various people walking down the sidewalk on Constitution Avenue and shook his head.

"Look, Com," Kevin said with a sigh. "I appreciate what you're trying to do, but sometimes you just gotta bite the bullet. How bad do you want to beat this Delano bill?"

"You have no idea."

The pair stood silent for a moment.

"The hell with it," Com announced. "Let's do it."

The senator pulled out his phone and tapped it a couple times to pull up Senator Foxworthy's personal number. Com held his phone to his ear as he approached a group of pedestrians waiting for a walk signal on First Street. Com looked down the street, saw no cars, and walked across the street, defying the red hand signal. Kevin followed. "Senator Foxworthy. Hi, it's Com DeGroot again. Yes. Yes. You'll have your vote on Individual Finance. Can I count on you to vote no on Delano's bill?"

Kevin awaited Com's reaction.

"Great," Com said excitedly. "I think you're doing the right thing. No, thank you, sir."

Com ended the call and half-grinned at his chief of staff as they reached the stairs to the Russell Building.

"That wasn't so hard, was it?" Kevin asked slyly.

Minutes later, the senator situated himself at his desk in his third-story office. He eyed his chief of staff. "So, who's next?"

Over the course of the next hour, Com DeGroot spoke with four senators. He traded votes on various bills, earmarks, and basketball play-offs tickets for nay votes on Senate bill six-sixty-four.

It was actually pretty easy, Com thought to himself as he ended a call with the last legislator on the list of undecideds.

"Swish!" Kevin commented. "Well done, big boy. Now if everyone goes along as they said, we have a forty-nine to fifty-one lead right now, including your vote. If one of these undecideds switches back, we'll have a tie."

"What happens with a tie?" Com asked uncertainly.

"The vice president gets a vote to break the tie, and we don't want that."

"The veep would side with Delano, I take it?"

"There's no doubt—big time Dem."

"Well, then we'll have to make sure no one switches their vote," Com said confidently.

Forty

"You should be happy, Senator," Hailey Owens said as she rested her hand on Com's arm. "You have the votes. You're going to win tomorrow." She was preparing to leave after discussing various pieces of legislation.

"Then why am I not?" Com looked at his half-empty glass of whiskey, then took a drink.

"I should get back to my papers," Hailey Owens added. She was standing next to Com and placed her index finger on his chest. "If there's anything I can do to help you, just let me know."

Com nodded.

"Anything," Hailey repeated, then left the office.

The senator walked over to his desk and started browsing the Internet. He stumbled upon a collection of his personal event photos and navigated to images that had been taken at the Kula Museum of Art reception in Ur. Com enlarged one of the pictures with a clear shot of Cate Heatherton in it. She was smiling and tilting her head in a natural position.

Com pulled out his phone and stared at Cate's number for a minute, then tapped the call button.

"Hello?" Cate answered.

"Hi. Thanks for peck—picking up."

"Com?"

"Yeah, it's Com."

"It didn't sound like you," Cate said softly.

"Oh."

Cate was silent for a brief moment. "Did you decide what you're going to do about the tax situation? Did you contact our guy in D.C.?"

"Oh, get this. My court date is tomorrow—same as the Delano vote. They want me to miss the vote!" Com explained excitedly.

"Wow. So what are you going to do?"

"Kevin's going to try to get the date changed."

"And if he can't?"

"Uh, I don't know. I can't just give up on the vote. What do you recommend?"

"Well, if you miss a court date, you'll be in contempt of court and they could come down on you. I think you should go to court."

"And what about your—err—Ur?" Com slurred.

"Uh . . . have a little happy juice tonight, did we?"

"Oh, yeah," Com said proudly. "We were celebrating! We got the votes to take Delano down, that dirty scoundrel."

"Well, congratulations. That's good. How did you manage that?" Cate's voice was light, but she did not express much enthusiasm.

"Oh, you know, I threw my weight around a little. I traded a couple votes and—get this—Blythe wanted some playoffs tickets for his vote so I obliged."

"Ah, I see." Cate was not impressed.

"Cate, I thought you'd be ecstatic about this! Now you can drop your lawsuit against the government. We won!"

"Well, Com, defeating six-sixty-four would be great, but that wasn't the only bill threatening the Ur charter. There is still a lot of work to be done."

Cate's words did not register with Com. "Hey, Cate. When I tell the world about this corruption and we beat Delano's bill, that will be that. Once we take Delano down, we have nothing to worry about. I really can't wait to see his fat face when the votes come in. That will be the last time that bastard tries to push me around."

"Hopefully," Cate agreed apprehensively.

"I have some really good dirt on Delano, too, that I'm going to reveal tomorrow in debate. You should tune into the NNC tomorrow to see it unfold. It's going to be a bloodbath!" Com nearly yelled.

"Wow, you're really have it in for Delano, huh?" Cate asked with a worried tone.

"Pretty much."

"So, what is this all about, Com?"

"What do you mean?" Com asked honestly.

"I mean it sounds like you don't know or care what's really going on down here. You're too wrapped up in getting back at Delano—at defeating Delano."

"Damn straight. He's been a constant antagonist since I got here. No one likes the guy, and I'm going take him down. Who does he think he is?" Com slurred.

"Com, really. Is this about trying to protect Ur or something else? Is this about justice or about your pride?"

"Aww, Cate. I'm just trying to do the right thing and save your charter city."

"Are you? Or are you just doing this to feed your ego?"

"Cate, let's not talk about this now. Let's talk about, um, us."

Cate was silent.

"Cate . . . I can't stop thinking of you. I'm—"

"Com, don't."

"No, Cate, I think I'm—"

"Com, I'm engaged."

Com sat silent for a moment and tensed the muscles around his eyes.

"I'm engaged to be married." Cate tried to sound happy despite a sense of awkwardness.

Com couldn't speak for a moment, then bitterly managed, "Wha? I'm sorry, what?"

"I'm sorry to tell you like this."

"When?" Com blurted.

"Yesterday."

"Oh."

"Com . . . "

"Who is it?"

Cate hesitated for a few seconds. "Do you really want to know?"

"Yes, I want to know," Com followed.

"It's Arun—Arun Kula."

"Of course," Com said as if he had already known the answer.

"Com, he's a really amazing man. I want you to meet him."

"Can I just ask you what the hell happened between us? I thought we were doing something."

"I thought we were, too, Com, but we're just too different. It really seems we have two different ideas of how things should be."

"Like how? What are you talking about?"

"Well, like just now. I think people should live by the rule of law, and you—you're talking about trading votes for votes and playoff tickets for votes. You're so consumed with defeating Delano and saving your pride that you've completely forgotten the rule of law or what's right. That's how bad government happens, Com."

"Yeah, but you didn't know about that yesterday. What was it?"

Cate was silent for a moment. "No. Com . . . you're just not . . . not—"

"Not rich enough, huh? Not powerful enough? Not good enough?" Com demanded.

"I didn't say that."

"No, fuck it. You know what? I am the best thing that could ever happen to you. I'm a U.S. fucking senator. Do you know how many women would die to be with me?"

Cate did not answer.

"Um, all right. I have to go now. Have a good life, Cate Heatherton . . . Kula—or whatever the hell." Com ended the call.

The senator stood up, walked over to his wet bar, and poured a tall glass of whiskey. He whispered his angry confusion, then took a large swig from his glass, finishing off the golden liquid with a slight cringe.

He walked to his door and asked his office assistant, "Where's Noni?" Com shook his head violently. "I mean what's her name? Hailey. Where's Hailey?"

"Probably in her office," Noni Alvarez said, pointing out of the office.

"Can you ask her to come back here, please?"

Noni nodded and began to dial on her desk phone.

Minutes later, Com DeGroot sat in one of his guest chairs looking at the lamp light through his whiskey glass.

"You rang?" Hailey Owens said as she appeared at his door.

Com stood, put his glass on his desk, and walked over to Hailey. He closed the door to the front office and gently took his legislative director's hand. Com led Hailey to the front of his desk and stood twelve inches in front of her. He moved his tongue over his lips, and Hailey smiled as she leaned against his desk.

"Can I help you with something, Senator?" Hailey asked coyly.

Without saying a word, Com drew his hand to the buttons that ran along the shoulder of Hailey's blouse and began unfastening them. After undoing six buttons, the front of Hailey's blouse folded over, revealing a nude shoulder and the slope of a breast. Com pinched the other side of the shirt and pulled down, causing the blouse to slightly slip over Hailey's bosom. She folded one arm to catch the fabric from completely falling off and half-heartedly held it up, barely covering her stomach.

Com leaned in to his subject and kissed her lightly on her crimson lips. Hailey eagerly accepted and extended her chin as he retracted. Then Com pressed his lips to hers intensely and kissed her mouth and cheek, then her neck and shoulder. He pushed his frame into hers and secured her waist, then felt her skirted buttocks and thigh. He squeezed and lifted Hailey's slender body onto his desk. His arms involuntarily knocked whatever was on the desk off as he mouthed his subject.

Com gripped Hailey's skirt from the bottom and pushed it up toward her waist, unveiling Hailey's pink thighs from her waist down. She was leaning back with her arms supporting her from behind and offering her breasts to the open air. She breathed heavily and smiled. Hailey then sat up toward Com. Her index finger pressed under Com's chin and directed him to look her in the eye. "Hey," she said breathlessly. "It's about time."

Com grinned and chomped his teeth playfully at Hailey.

Forty-One

"What time is it?" Com mumbled into his phone. The only light that broke through Com's window coverings was from a streetlight outside.

"It's five-thirty," Kevin reported. "I couldn't get your court date changed. No surprise."

Com exhaled. "So ridiculous. Don't they know I have a country to serve today?"

"Yeah. I guess they don't have the same priorities."

Com strained to keep his eyes open and huffed. "What do I do?"

"That's up to you, boss. You can go to court and fight the charges, or you can go to the floor and vote down the Delano bill."

"What happens if I miss my court date?"

"Well, you'd be in contempt of court, and I imagine there would be a slap on the wrist. I don't think it will be too bad."

"And if I miss the vote, we lose, right?"

"Well, we have a fifty-one to forty-nine vote lead. If you are not present, then our lead goes to fifty to forty-nine. But if one of the nays chickens out and abstains, we're toast."

Com huffed. "Unbelievable."

"So what are you going to do?"

Com thought for a moment. "I don't know. I'll give you a ring when I decide."

* * *

Senator Jack Phillips sat next to Duane Delano in the Senate Chamber, and the two often exchanged friendly, erudite banter about legislation or the proceedings on the Senate floor. The morning of March fifteenth was no different.

"Methinks the level of security in the Senate Chamber is higher than usual," Phillips noted as he surveyed a pair of U.S. marshals positioned at the entrance to the large room.

"What dost thou thinketh the cause of such elevated security could be?" Delano replied in a pretentious faux-British accent.

"A wiser man would not assume, but a less sophisticated mind such as mine might guess it had something to do with your renegade senator." Phillips turned toward Delano and cracked a smile.

"That mind may be more sophisticated than one thinks. My renegade senator, as you so aptly put it, seems to have found himself in trouble with the IRS. His presence was requested at the fine U.S. District Court of Delaware today, in fact. His presence here would mean personal time with the U.S. Marshals."

"What a coincidence. To think what role luck plays in these affairs. I guess you'll be winning the vote despite his best efforts, then." Phillips maintained his smile. "Does it make one's mind even less sophisticated to find amusement in such trifles?"

"Not in the least, good sir," Delano confirmed.

"My unsophisticated mind thinks a renegade sighting is unlikely in the Senate Chamber today."

Delano's eyes widened. "Now, would that same mind consider a friendly wager on the subject?"

Phillips' smile widened. "Perhaps."

"I say there will be a renegade senator sighting this very day," Delano pronounced

"Very well," Phillips agreed. "Same ante?"

"The same."

"It's a wager."

United States District Judge Walter P. Errickson reviewed the case brief through his thick spectacles as he sat on the bench of the courtroom. The quiet air allowed the ticking of a clock to be heard, but state attorneys and others present were inaudible.

Judge Errickson grumbled, "All right, facing the charges of conspiring to commit bank fraud, federal income tax evasion, and conducting a financial crimes enterprise. Do we have a Mr. Com DeGroot?" The elder judge raised his head to peer at the defendant's table, which was empty.

No one spoke for a moment, then the prosecution's lead counsel rose and cleared his throat. "Your honor, it appears we have an absent defendant."

"No Com DeGroot?" Judge Errickson asked to confirm.

"That's right."

"No representing counsel?" the judge continued.

"It appears that way."

"All right—"

At that moment, the doors to the courtroom burst open. A tall man with dark, European skin strode into the courtroom.

"Are you Com DeGroot?" Judge Errickson demanded.

The tall man realized the judge was talking to him, and he shook his head in the negative before sitting down in the general public seating.

The judge frowned and hummed. "Well, better draw up a warrant for arrest. The defendant is in contempt."

* * *

"Look," Kevin Donovan reported as he walked Com DeGroot to the Senate Chamber doors, "there are federal agents in there. They said they are going to let you vote on the three bills today and then they're going to take you into custody."

Com twitched his neck. "Damn. Well, if we can nail this vote, it will all be worth it, right?"

"I hope so," Kevin tried to assure his superior. "All right. The first vote up is Foxworthy's Individual Finance Reconciliation," Kevin said, walking Com into the Senate Chamber. "You are a yea on that in exchange for the six-sixty-four vote. Next is Senate bill twenty-one twenty-two. That was the vote you traded with Peterson for. You are a yea for that as well. The last bill is Delano's. And you are obviously a nay."

Com DeGroot and his chief of staff opened the doors to the Chamber and eyed the two U.S. marshals standing at attention just inside. Each stocky marshal wore a dark blue windbreaker with a yellow star badge screen-printed on the left breast. Beneath the badge read "POLICE," and each arm of the jacket read "U.S. MARSHAL" vertically. Com eyed the officers and nodded.

A murmur filled the hall as DeGroot started walking down the aisle toward his desk.

To DeGroot's left, Senator Duane D. Delano reached his hand over to Senator Jack Phillips and smiled a greasy smile. "It was a thrilling wager, my friend, but it appears our little renegade has chosen against reason once again."

"The good senator wins again," Phillips said of Delano with a hint of regret.

Com DeGroot looked down at his chief of staff. "So, what happens after they take me into custody?"

"I'm sure it's just a formality. They're not going throw you in the slammer or anything."

"Shit. Are you going to bail me out?"

"Hey, I got a reservation at the Savoy tonight. You're on your own."

"You're kidding, right?" Com asked disappointedly.

"You'll be fine. I can be your one call if you need it, but I don't think you will."

"You better be right," Com said, shaking his head.

Kevin confidently smiled and, noticing that the clerk was about to begin the legislative session, secured his briefcase in his hand and left the Senate floor. "Adios, amigo," Kevin said and walked up the aisle to exit the Chamber.

The Senate reconvened from the previous session, and the presiding officer went through typical procedure: a call to order, the designation of a presiding officer, a prayer, and the Pledge of Allegiance. Com waited through the Morning Hour and several brief speeches. He nervously tapped his desk and bounced his leg for an hour, periodically looking up at the U.S. marshals standing at the exit of the Chamber.

The presiding officer, Senator Drake from Wisconsin, cleared his throat near the end of the Morning Hour. "Without objection, I have this message from the president." Drake looked down at a piece of paper in front of him and read, "A message from the President of the United States, declaring, pursuant to law, a national emergency with respect to the ongoing riots in the jurisdiction of Ur, Texas."

Com leaned his face in the direction of the presiding officer and squinted. He turned to his neighbor, Senator Michelson. "Did he just say Ur?"

"Yeah, you haven't heard?"

"No, what?"

"There are riots going on down there."

"Oh, for the love!" Com yelled and threw his hands up in disgust. Nearby senators looked at him curiously, but turned back to the presiding officer.

"I don't think the president needed to go and declare a state of emergency, but they are definitely rioting," Michelson added.

Com shook his head and began bouncing his leg again.

Moments later, the first bill, Senator Foxworthy's Individual Finance Reconciliation bill, was introduced for a vote. Senator Foxworthy was the only one who spoke in favor of the Reconciliation bill, and no one was opposed, so the procedure was quick and the clerk called roll in short order. The bill passed, and the presiding officer called the vote after striking the gavel.

Shortly after, Senator Elizabeth Derkins of North Carolina called for a quorum call and a groan was heard throughout the Chamber. Com had remembered Kevin explaining a quorum call. He had mentioned that the Senate could only vote if a quorum—or at least half the Senate—was present. If a senator thought that fewer than half of the Senate was present, he or she could request a quorum call, which consisted of a roll call for each senator. Kevin had mentioned that the purpose of the procedure wasn't really to ensure that there were enough warm bodies in the Senate, but to stall in order to complete unfinished business.

The secretary called roll, and all the senators complied by responding to their names, which took several minutes. After roll, the presiding officer introduced the next bill to be voted on, Senator Peterson's Community Reinvestment Act. A number of senators took turns speaking about the merits and drawbacks of the bill, then the presiding officer called for a vote, which was concluded in short order. The Community Reinvestment Act passed, and the presiding officer called the next order of business, introduction of Senate bill six hundred and sixty-four, Senator Delano's bill to revoke the charter status of Ur, Texas.

Forty-Two

Senator Delano waddled to the podium and presented his bill, repeating everything that had been said before: the charter city was stripping its neighbors of resources, Ur's lack of wage laws had resulted in slave labor, and the land on which Ur rested was saturated with unhealthy levels of fallout radiation.

"What's more," Delano continued. "We hear reports of civil unrest within the city. The citizens there have become disgruntled with the wild, wild west of corporate anarchy there. Isn't it time we stood up for them, too?"

Delano concluded, and the presiding officer opened the floor, which Com DeGroot requested. Com walked past Delano on the way to the podium, and the senior senator muttered, "You can't win, dummy."

Com instantly responded, "Good to see you, too, sweetheart."

Senator DeGroot gathered himself at the podium and thanked the presiding officer for the floor. The entire Chamber was quietly glued to the tall senator. Com surveyed the hall and noticed that every seat was occupied. His eyes darted to the exit guarded by the marshals, who had multiplied into four. One agent was motioning to the balcony seating above the main floor of the Senate Chamber. Com spotted more black-clad federal officers walking along the back row of the gallery seating.

He cleared his throat and looked at his notes.

"You . . . have been had," Senator Com DeGroot began as he stood in front of a scattered collection of legislators in the Senate Chamber. "Well, to be honest, I was fooled myself for some time. I thought Senate bill six-sixty-four was designed to protect citizens from the evils of greedy, harmful, foreign corporations. That's why *I* signed on." Com pointed to himself.

The senator looked around at his fellow legislators. A few were paying attention, others were walking around, and one was sleeping at his desk.

"But let's investigate this bill for a moment. The heart of the legislation is subsection 'A' four, which stipulates that the radiation cleanup upon which the Ur charter was originally based was insufficient, thus the federal government has the authority to nullify the charter and confiscate the assets maintained within that jurisdiction. Sounds like good governance, right? Like justice is being served?"

Com looked around to make sure everyone was following. "Well the EPA report on which this stipulation was based—" Com help up a stack of papers. "I have it right here. The EPA report says—it's hidden way in the middle of the report—says that Ur has an unacceptable level of radiation." Com looked at his report. "Point zero-three microsieverts per hour, to be exact. Now, a microsievert is a level of radiation, some of which happens naturally, some of which does not. Point zero-three microsieverts per hour is the average for a city at sea level. Well, the EPA report claims that the radiation level of Ur is point zero-eight microsieverts per hour, which is more than double that of the EPA standard.

"But, distinguished colleagues, the EPA report must be put into context. While the point zero-three level is a good goal, radiation above that is by no means unsafe. Cities at higher altitudes have higher natural radiation. Mexico City, for instance, has radiation levels of point zero-nine microsieverts per hour, and La Paz, Bolivia gets about point twenty-three microsieverts per hour.

"In addition, we should be skeptical of the accuracy of the EPA report in the first place. When I visited Ur, I saw firsthand a reading on my Geiger counter of point zero-two-five right there over the nuclear meltdown site itself. My personal reading was below the average for a city at sea level. But don't take my word for it. Senator Jennings, may he rest in peace, organized a third-party environmental assessment of the land in question at the same time as my trip to Ur. The results of the study came back just yesterday, and they showed similar findings—a radiation level of point zero-two-seven microsieverts per hour—also under the EPA standard.

"Either way, ladies and gentleman, the EPA standard is arbitrary and shouldn't be used in this case. Why? you ask. Well, it just so happens that many cities on the eastern seaboard of the United States receive radiation levels that are naturally higher than that very EPA standard."

Com pulled a black handheld device out of his coat pocket and placed it on the podium. Ticking noises were heard emanating from the device on the microphone.

"This is a Geiger counter. It reads real-time radiation levels." The senator looked at the Geiger counter. "Right now, it reads point zero-nine microsieverts per hour."

Some in the Chamber gasped as Com let the information sink into his colleagues' heads.

"That means there is more radiation here in the Capitol than in the charter city of Ur. Now, granted, much of that radiation is probably coming from the leftover sandwich in Senator Foxworthy's desk." Com paused while a few of the senators chuckled. "But if you take the EPA report as gospel, then you must consider Washington, D.C.—your home and seat of the federal government—as unlivable as well."

Com's audience made a noticeable commotion.

"The EPA report is truthful, no doubt, but the authors of this bill took that truth and spun it beyond recognition. They used a technicality to support their ridiculous claims about the environment of Ur and to stir up support for this bill. It's just something that we do as politicians to get what we want. We turn attention away from the real matter and rile emotions, knowing full well that very few senators, much less our constituents, are going to read the bill. And no one is going to do the research necessary to make an educated decision on it. It's a sad truth that in Washington, the game is about leverage, and leverage is best gained by emotional force, not intellectual rigor.

"So, it's all sensationalism! Everything you hear about the charter city of Ur, Texas is pure hyperbole and sensationalism. 'They're stealing our water!' Wrong! They make their own water out of the sea. 'They're using slave labor!' Wrong! They're working on their terms, not those of the IRS 'It's a radioactive disaster area!' Wrong again! Ur is safer than Washington, D.C. in that respect.

"So if this bill—Senator Duane D. Delano's bill—is not about protecting the people of Ur, or anyone else for that matter," Com continued, "then what is it about? Well, let's look at who benefits from this bill. If this bill were to pass, section seven-ninety-nine 'C' seven says the federal government can seize the assets of two financial institutions operating in Ur—no doubt for their own good." Com's smile dripped sarcasm. "Now, those monies would be redistributed amongst some one hundred or so banks around the country, but not equally. Four banks based in New York will receive the majority of the assets—worth about twenty-one trillion dollars."

Com noticed a few senators reviewing the statistics on the papers on their desks. Others were whispering to each other and shaking their heads. Still others were giving Com approving looks and nodding.

"Now, there are six individuals who occupy board seats on each of these banks. These people—whom I have nicknamed the Broadway Banksters—also run a nice little political action committee called the National Committee for Freedom and Progress. Among other endeavors, this PAC has consistently donated heavily to political campaigns, most notably that of Senator Duane D. Delano of Vermont, author of Senate bill six-sixty-four.

"Ladies and gentlemen, you have been had. Senate bill six-sixty-four is not designed to protect the people of Ur, it's designed to fill the wallets of already wealthy banksters. Senate bill six-sixty-four is not just another bill of good governance, it is the type of thing we as legislators were voted in to protect against. It's your duty to follow me and vote down this unconstitutional bill that reeks of corruption." Com looked back to the presiding officer. "Thank you. I yield back the remainder of my time."

Com turned in Senator Delano's direction and observed his face. Delano had not been paying attention to Com's speech. He was concentrating on his handheld phone.

After Com spoke, no other senator requested the floor, so the presiding officer asked the secretary to call the vote. The secretary began listing off the senators in alphabetical order, and each official placed his or her vote subsequently.

Small monitors that fit into the corner of each senator's desk displayed C-SPAN coverage of the vote with an image of the Senate floor and a graphic of the number of votes cast. A brief summary of the bill was typed at the top of the screen, and the number of yea and nay votes by both political parties and Independents were tallied.

Com's name was called, and he pressed the nay button on his desk. He turned around to see two federal agents walking down the carpeted aisle toward him.

"You can't be here on the floor," Com said to the straight-faced agents. "Only senators and staffers with official business."

"We were ordered to take you into custody after your third vote, Senator."

"We're still voting." Com pointed to the official Senate clock on the wall.

The marshal nodded, and Com returned to viewing his desk monitor. He watched as the numerals on the C-SPAN graphic changed to reflect additional senators voting. The yeas and nays kept even as they ascended—9, 13, 21, 44, 49 —as the time remaining dwindled down to ten minutes, then five.

The monitor showed 49 for the yeas and 50 for the nays when the secretary called Senator Charles Wilson's name. Com looked up and to his right to see Charles Wilson sitting at his desk. Charles glanced back at Com and nodded. We've got this one in the bag, Com thought.

When Com looked at his monitor again, the vote was 50 to 50.

Forty-Three

Com's stomach sank, and his eyes bulged at the monitor. He stood up and started walking around one of the U.S. marshals.

"Let's go," the officer said and grabbed Com's arm.

Com shook off the agent's grip. "I have four minutes."

"Let's go," the officer repeated.

Com broke loose from the marshal's clutch and ran around the Senate desks, his head flooded with adrenaline.

"What's going on, Charles?" Com's tone was nervous and overly loud as he rushed up the aisle to his friend's desk. Two marshals followed the tall senator, and most of the eyes in the Chamber were fixed on the proceedings. The two marshals stood behind Com but let him talk.

Wilson turned his head up from his handheld phone and proclaimed, "What's up, my brotha from anotha motha?" He noticed the federal agents and returned to Com.

Com was shocked.

"Did you just vote yea on this, Charles?" Com asked.

Wilson shook his head and pushed his lips to the side. "Man, it was a tough vote. That environmental report just wasn't looking good."

"Charles, are you serious?" Com said in a lower voice in an attempt to keep his conversation private. "You know that was my bill, the one I've been busting my ass to defeat." Com looked at the time remaining on the clock. It read 2:13.

Senator Wilson breathed in deeply and looked beyond Com. "I don't know, man. My constituents are getting on board with it, too. They've seen the reports, and they want fairness in the system."

"What are you saying, Charles? I thought you had my back on this. We were going to take Delano down, remember?"

"I do have your back, but it's just not looking very politically advantageous right now."

"Shit, Charles. You can't be serious." Com's words were rushed.

"I am. It's just not lookin' good."

"Charles, you know I am missing a court date to be here today and vote. I'm in contempt of court for this, and you're going to ruin it for me?" Com indicated the agents behind him.

Charles did not answer. Com stared at Wilson and fumed. He thought for a while and left an uncomfortable silence in the air for a moment.

"What did they offer you?" Com demanded.

Wilson tilted his head slightly. "Man, what do you think, they bought me out or something?"

"What did they offer you?" Com yelled.

Senator Wilson looked to the ground to avoid Com's stare.

"Charles?"

"All right, man. They offered me Ways and Means."

Com relaxed his tense stance and rolled his head. "A friggin' committee," Com said, incredulous. "You sold me out for a committee?"

"Not just a committee, Com. Ways and Means."

"Damn it, Charles, you . . . you . . . ." Com let his statement trail off.

Senator Wilson looked at his colleague defiantly. "What? I what?"

Com shook his head and looked around. "I'm not going to say it."

"Say it, dog," Senator Wilson barked. "I what?"

Com looked back at his friend but was silent for a moment.

"You're a damn slave," Com said sternly.

Senator Wilson stood up and grew three inches in his shoes. "Man . . . "

"No, you're a fucking slave."

"Com, don't push me." Wilson was slowly moving his head back and forth.

"I'm a slave. We're all slaves, Charles. We are all scrapping for little crumbs of power. So we do what we're told by the ones who have the power, and we act like we're doing something important in the world. But the game is fixed. You're just playing your role like a good little pawn. And you hope you can get in a position one day to actually do what you want to do. You want enough power to control your own destiny, but by that time you've sold your soul and what you want to do isn't really what you want to do anymore."

Charles was looking away, quietly defiant and grinding his teeth. The outburst by Com left several nearby senators watching with gaping mouths and stunned stares.

"Charles, I know exactly where you are right now. You want to be somebody. You can taste it. I know. But think about it. Does it really make sense to become a slave in order to be a senator?"

Com looked at the clock again. 1:22.

Senator Wilson looked at Com. "We through here?"

"All right, let's go," one federal agent said and gripped the arm of Senator DeGroot. Com stood his ground and kept his stare on Charles. "No! Charles, you can still change your vote. You have one minute."

Charles looked at the marshals securing his friend. The second agent grabbed Com's other arm and pulled it behind the senator, dragging him up the aisle. Charles looked concerned, then turned around to find Duane D. Delano but could not spot him. Most senators had gathered on the floor and were discussing the bills and various other topics as the allotted time for the bill ticked down to seconds.

"Charles, look, I'm going to jail for this. Don't let it be in vain." Com shook his head with a morose stare. "You *know* this bill is busted. You know this bill is unconstitutional. Why are you letting Delano dictate your vote?"

Charles shrugged. "Yeah, I know the bill's unconstitutional." He laughed. "Everything we do here is."

"Charles, then don't let them do this. Take them down with me. This is where we do it. This is where we take a stand." The federal agents had secured both of Com's arms behind his back and applied handcuffs. His arms were bursting out of his suit jacket.

Charles Wilson sat back down, then looked up at Com with uncertainty. Charles shook his head. "Damn it, Com, why you gotta be like that? Ways and Means is just like a field hand moving in as a house slave. You're cleaner and you smell nicer, but you're still a slave. What the hell does more power matter as long as I'm still just using it to do what Delano wants? Damn."

"Right!" Com agreed.

Charles pressed a button on his voting device, and Com looked at the television monitor. The vote changed to 49 yeas and 51 nays. Com yelled out a blast of enthusiasm, and the U.S. marshals tugged on his arms.

"Charles, you did the right thing. You're a good man!" Com yelled out.

The time on the bill expired, and, after a moment's confirmation, the presiding officer announced, "On this vote, the yeas have forty-nine and the nays fifty-one. The bill fails." The officer struck the gavel to put punctuation on the result. Com DeGroot was escorted out of the Senate Chamber by the two arresting agents, and the rest of the hall erupted in conversation.

Forty-Four

Four U.S. marshals escorted Senator Com DeGroot out of the Capitol and to a police van waiting on the sidewalk off of Constitution Avenue. One of the officers uncuffed the prisoner while maintaining a grip on his arm, then opened the van's side door.

Com took the subtle hint to climb into the van, and the federal agent followed.

Another marshal drove the van off the sidewalk and onto the street.

Com took out his handheld device and sent a quick message to Kevin Donovan, "They're taking me in."

He put his phone down and observed the two federal agents with him in the van. The man next to Com was young and wore an emotionless face. A wire fence separated the back of the van from the driver's seat. Com began to feel imprisoned, trapped.

The driver pulled the van around a corner and parked it. Com could see through the fence that the driver was communicating with someone through an implant phone. The driver put his right hand to the area behind his right ear.

"Copy. Will hold until further direction," the driver announced.

Com looked at his neighboring passenger to gather any information about what was going on. "Hey, what's going on here?" The marshal gave Com no response.

Ten minutes later, the driver touched his head again and replied to his caller, "Copy that. We are in transit." The driver immediately stepped on the gas and sped down the street.

Com pulled out his phone again and typed a message: "Find me." He sent it to his security captain Reggie Williams.

Minutes later, the driver pulled the van up to a nondescript door stuck between two buildings. A large man dressed in a black suit stood in front of the door.

Once parked, the marshals jumped into action. The driver flew out of his door and around the van to meet the other officer, who had opened the van's side door.

"Let's go," one marshal demanded Com.

Com hesitated momentarily, then pulled himself across the van's bench seat and stepped out of the vehicle. One marshal took him by the arm and walked him over to the door. The guard patted Com down and hit the senator's cell phone, then took it out of Com's pocket.

"This will have to stay up here with the marshals," the guard explained to Com.

Com did not respond but looked blankly at the guard.

The guard opened the door and bent his arm to welcome Com. Inside the door, there was a small carpeted walkway six feet deep, which led directly to a descending staircase. It was dim inside, and the setting sun behind nearby buildings did little to illuminate the interior.

"You're expected downstairs," the guard said.

Com looked at one of the U.S. marshals. "So I'm not going to jail?"

"Just get down there," the marshal replied.

Com walked through the door and down the staircase. Immediately upon entering, Com could hear live jazz music blaring from the bottom floor, and a whiff of stale cigar smoke accompanied the sounds. Com scrunched his face at the bizarre atmosphere.

When Com landed at the bottom of the stairs, he saw a compact nightclub complete with red-leather booths surrounding semi-circle tables under dim lighting. A scantily clad woman carried a tray of cocktails past Com and winked at the tall legislator.

"Commie boy!" a thick country drawl yelled from behind Com.

Com jumped and turned around. "Thurston." Com put his arms up. "What the hell is this?"

"This, my friend, is the Turf Club."

"The Turf Club?" Com nearly yelled in confusion. "Did you know that federal agents just dropped me off upstairs?" Com pointed up the stairs.

Thurston threw his hand at Com. "Yeah, that was just a little political theater. We need to talk business, son." Thurston threw his arm around the tall shoulders of Senator DeGroot and started walking him through the sparsely populated club.

"So, this is the mystical Turf Club, eh?" Com wondered aloud.

"Yessiree Bob. And they have some magnificent turf." Thurston winked at com and stuck his thumb out toward a dainty cocktail waitress.

Com pushed a breath of air out in a subtle laugh. "What's going on here, Roger?"

Thurston laughed. "You'll see."

The elder senator led the junior legislator to a booth along the side wall to their left. Two people already occupied the booth, and, as Com approached them, their identification became clear.

"Delano?" Com jumped. "What the hell?"

Duane D. Delano was tearing into a slab of barbequed ribs. His sleeves were rolled up, and his hands dripped with dark, reddish-brown sauce. Sitting next to the senior senator was a smiling, stocky man in a red sport jacket. He was not eating but instead held a cocktail glass full of brownish liquid over ice. Com recognized the other man, but could not place his name.

"Shut up, dummy. Have a seat." Delano waved his dirty left hand toward the empty booth opposite the other man.

Com looked at Thurston, who nodded and put his hand out to allow Com to sit down. The younger senator shrugged and sat down at the edge of the booth. Thurston nudged Com to move over, and Com hesitated as he watched Delano voraciously suck rib meat from the bone. After Com reluctantly moved around the booth seat toward the man with the red jacket, Thurston sat down on the other side of Com.

Delano interrupted his chewing briefly to introduce his neighbor. "DeGroot, you know Hank Pierpont, right?"

Com tilted his head backward and opened his mouth. "Yes, I believe you were a major donor to my campaign."

"That's right." Hank smiled a hefty grin.

"What is this about?" Com asked, bewildered.

Delano kept his eyes on his food but mentioned to Hank Pierpont, "What did I tell you? Not the sharpest tool in the shed, this one."

Hank continued his smile aimed at Com. "Aww, that's okay. Not everyone's as brilliant as you are, Duane," Hank said with a hint of sarcasm. "I'll tell you one thing, DeGroot, you've got moxie. I'll give you that!" Hank sipped a drink. "And you've been shrewd in your fight against Delano's bill there."

"Yeah, and I won." Com turned to Delano. "How does that make you feel, fat man?" Com said, ready for a fight.

Delano smiled a mischievous smile and squinted upward from his plate but did not look at any of the other men. "You think you won?"

"Hell, yeah, I won. Your bill failed. I don't know if you saw the vote on the Senate floor or if you were busy stuffing your face at the end there," Com reported with a pompous air about him.

"Mr. DeGroot," Delano enunciated. "My level of acumen far outreaches anything you can possibly comprehend. Thus, you should understand that I am quite aware of the results of the vote on my bill, thank you very much."

"Okay . . . ." Com sought more.

Delano stopped eating and put his rib bones down, then wiped his hands with a cloth napkin and made a loud squeak as he sucked particles of meat through his teeth. "The wheel's spinning, but the hamster's dead, huh, DeGroot?"

Hank Pierpont patted the air in front of Senator Delano. "Come now, Duane." He looked at Com. "Mr. DeGroot, it's time you learned how things work here on the Hill. You see, you defeated Duane's bill, that's certainly true. But while you were working to defeat that particular bill, Duane here and Roger were ensuring that the same exact legislation found its way into other bills. You took down Senate bill six-sixty-four, yes, but the essence of that bill is law right now, thanks to other bills."

Com looked at a quiet Senator Thurston, who was looking at the piece of paper he was twisting in his fingers. "Roger, save me from going crazy right now. Tell me they're just making this up."

"It's okay, Commie boy," Roger Thurston tried to comfort Com.

"Are you telling me that I did all that to defeat six-sixty-four, but it's basically law anyway because of other bills?"

Roger Thurston nodded.

"And you were in on this? Republicans were in on this scam?" Com asked Thurston, unbelieving.

Delano laughed out loud. "You are just quaint, aren't you?"

Thurston added, "Commie boy, there's really no such thing as Republican or Democrat anymore. At this level, we're all working for the same cause."

Com repeated to Thurston, "So you're telling me you were in on this all along?"

Hank Pierpont spoke before Thurston could. "Well, I hate to break it to you, son, but *you* were in on this just as much as anyone."

"What the hell are you talking about?" Com asked the table, too incensed to look at his company.

"Such a little Boy Scout . . . ." Delano shook his head condescendingly.

Com slammed the table.

Delano was unfazed by Com's display. "Tell me, Mr. DeGroot, do you remember the first bill you voted on in the Senate?"

Com shook his head in the negative.

"I'll refresh your memory. Your first vote was the eminent domain bill. You broke the filibuster and you voted to pass the bill. That bill gave us the authority to confiscate any private land for any reason we deem suitable—that includes the entirety of your precious little charter city in

South Texas. Well, then later on you helped pass the Internet Privacy Act, which grants us the authority to monitor and control bank transactions over the Internet. That granted us power over the financial institutions of Ur."

Com's eyes bulged as he listened.

"And you might remember voting on Senator Foxworthy's bill a few hours ago?"

Com looked wide-eyed at Senator Delano and swallowed.

"You'll be happy to know that his bill included the entire banking acquisition clause that was in my bill." Delano grinned.

Com's mouth melted into a disgusted frown. "The Individual Finance bill? What the hell does individual finance have to do with Ur?"

Delano laughed. "Oh, my dear boy, so much to learn. I could have thrown a clause in Foxworthy's bill to give motor homes to every clinically blind person in the country if I wanted. It doesn't matter what the bill is about."

"What gives you the right . . . ." Com shook his head in dismay.

Delano laughed. "Nothing *gives* us the right, we just take it."

"And what about the Constitution? Just throw that out the window?"

"Well, we have techniques and . . . means of circumventing the rules," Thurston answered.

"Legally breaking the law." Com remembered the comment from Cate.

"You're one to talk." Delano smirked. "I won't mention your little tax evasion problem."

"I didn't hurt anyone!" Com declared.

"Maybe not. Still, you wouldn't be here now if *someone* hadn't broken the law." Delano coughed.

"Excuse me?" Com said as he looked down to Delano.

Duane D. Delano turned to Hank Pierpont, and Hank turned to Com and spoke. "You lost your election, Mr. DeGroot."

Com squinted at Hank in confusion.

"That's right. We practically handed that election to you, and you managed to lose quite a substantial lead. Well, I couldn't let my investment go down the drain, so we got help from a little PAC I run."

Com shook his head. "Let me guess. The National Committee for Freedom and Progress."

Hank Pierpont winked. "That's the one. They secured seven hundred and ninety-one votes and got you in."

"What do you mean 'secured'?"

"They bought the votes," Duane Delano blurted out.

Com sat frozen as the information sunk in. He looked around the quiet table filled with eyes fixed on him. Com couldn't help but imagine himself in a wooden box, hidden from the light. The walls around him were closing in. He was mentally suffocating.

"You bought my election?" Com focused on the red-jacketed man.

"That's right. We own you." Delano smirked.

Hank Pierpont chuckled through yellow teeth. "And you can imagine my surprise when one of my code geeks made that announcement to you on election night. Needless to say, he isn't working for me anymore."

"Timeus?"

"Mmm, yes, I believe that was his name."

"This whole thing was fixed?" Com looked at Thurston.

"I'm afraid so, Commie boy."

"And my staff?" Com asked, bewildered.

"Oh, what about them?" Hank asked.

"Are they on the take, too?"

Thurston smiled. "Well, Commie boy, we needed people around you to turn you in the right direction—look," Thurston interrupted himself, "it doesn't matter how you got into the rodeo, it just matters what you do when you're on the bull. Now, we think you got some real potential—there's just something about you, and the people seem to love it. You're enormously popular with the common folks."

"What are you saying?" Com asked the table.

"Senator," Hank Pierpont answered, "we represent an elite core of legislators—Democrats and Republicans—as well as businessmen from around the country. We, in large part, dictate the direction of the economy and the country as a whole toward a better future. We are all working for the common goal of a better, more effective corporate-government alliance."

"What the fuck is that?" Com stared at Pierpont.

"Solutions to the problems of the country through good policy decisions," Hank Pierpont replied.

"Oh, you just mean *more* government?" Com demanded.

"More *good* government," Hank Pierpont corrected.

"I'm learning that there's no such thing," Com replied. Com felt dirt being heaped onto the box he was in. He began to breath rapidly to alleviate his fear.

"Look, you incomparable simpleton," Delano interjected, "there are two classes of people in this world: gods and slaves. We are offering you an invitation to be the former. If you want to remain a slave, well, all I can say is good luck."

"And what if I tell you and your minions to go fuck off?" Com asked defiantly.

"I wouldn't recommend that." Thurston shook his head.

"Let's just say that certain lawmakers in the past have not played along with us." Delano said slowly. "And those lawmakers found untimely ends."

Com nodded and smiled, incredulous. "Unbelievable!" he shouted. "You're threatening to have me killed."

"Look, we don't need to talk like that," Hank Pierpont said.

"Let's just say that there has been precedence for that," Delano said coldly.

"That guy McDonald in the eighties?" Com waved his hand in the air to help him think, then looked at Delano.

"Well, you do your homework, don't you," Delano chuckled. "McDonald had a foolish goal of exposing us to the world."

"And Senator Wellstone?" Com said.

Delano offered a smile and a shrug. "A very stubborn man. He couldn't be persuaded to join us on the war effort."

"And Senator Jennings?" Com said through gritted teeth.

"Became a tad too pushy in his old age." Delano said in a matter-of-fact manner.

"Unbelievable." Com shook his head.

"Isn't it?" Delano smiled. "It's one thing to worry about certain criminals breaking the rule of law. I can't imagine what's racing through your little head now as you realize there is no rule of law."

"You despicable . . . Justin was right," Com whispered to himself. He envisioned a wooden coffin collapsing in on him.

"What are you muttering?" Delano coughed.

Com breathed in and shook his head at the table. "There *is* a conspiracy. *You* are the conspiracy." Delano and Thurston laughed a hearty laugh. "Now, now, Commie boy." Thurston chuckled. "That kind of talk will get you nowhere. People are liable to call you crazy or racist or something. Come now, let's get a twenty-ouncer and talk about your new position as a *god* of Capitol Hill."

"You know, I think I just lost my appetite." Com pushed Thurston away from him, and Thurston reluctantly stood up.

"Now, Commie boy, you don't want to do this."

"You know what? I hate when you call me that." Com thought about it then pointed at Senator Thurston. "Fuck you." Com turned to the others. "And fuck all of you. I'm going to the press. They're going to love how a group of fat old white men are turning the country into their own personal Monopoly game."

Delano erupted in laughter. "What do you think this is, *Mr. Smith Goes to Washington*? Imbecile, we own the press! Sure, go ahead. See if your big speech on the Senate floor made it to the NNC. See if Michelle Torres reported on the *corrupt* bill. You might be disappointed."

Com slowly inched away from Thurston and the table, then jumped back into a cocktail waitress and knocked her tray of drinks down. The collision did not register in Com's swimming mind.

"Where are you going to run, Senator?" Delano yelled at the fleeing Com DeGroot. "Your federal marshals will be waiting for you outside." Delano started to laugh, and Hank Pierpont and Thurston joined in.

Com's face exploded into a red contortion, and the young senator stumbled away from the table and up the stairs.

Gods
of
Ruin

PART 4 :

GÖTTERDÄMMERUNG

Forty-Five

The white accoutrements on the white tablecloths were dimly lit by candles, giving the Savoy restaurant a warm ambiance. A soothing violin quartet played in a far corner, and guests enjoyed wine-drenched conversation throughout the dining room. Marta Saito sipped her glass of Malbec but did not savor it. She was preparing her line of attack on her partisan date sitting across from her at the elegantly adorned table. Kevin Donovan had just brought up the one topic they were not supposed to discuss while on a date, politics, and she was considering whether or not she should call him out.

"You've been watching Fox News way too much. They've brainwashed you," Marta said with a smile.

"Yeah, you would probably have the National News Coalition dump the network altogether."

"Hell, yes, I would. They are just partisan hacks for the right wing and corporations."

"Oh, please. As if CNN isn't just a partisan hack for the Liberals. They make me want to throw up how much they suck up to Sullivan."

"Maybe that's their job. He is the president! Better than sucking up to some unelected, greedy oil company. I mean Kevin, let's be honest. The oil companies are downright evil, and Fox backs them up. The worst disaster this century was caused by the oil companies. Carbon emissions that lead to global warming are caused by the oil companies . . ."

"You're still talking about global warming?" Kevin asked, incredulous.

Marta continued, undaunted. "And three wars and counting—all fought on behalf of the oil companies! Countless people killed and trillions of dollars down the drain. Oil companies are controlling this country, and your Fox News is the mouthpiece."

"Marta, are you kidding me? It's not about oil! Those wars are about people that want to kill us! We need to be over there because if we're not, the terrorists will come here. If it were up to me, I'd nuke the entire place, but you stupid humanitarians might have an issue with that. Since we can't do that, we have to put our guys in the line of fire to protect us. I don't want that, but while that's the only option, I'm going to fully support them."

"Hey, I support the troops, too. I just don't support the war," Marta yelled.

"Bullshit, Marta. How can you support the troops if you don't support what they're doing? That doesn't make any sense."

"What, like killing innocent babies and children? Right, I don't support that."

"See what I mean? You don't support the troops. No one who supports the troops would say something like that."

"Well, it's true. That's what they're doing over there. But you wouldn't know about that because you only watch the Republican propaganda machine, Fox News."

"Look, if innocent people die over there, it's probably their own fault. I mean, they make little girls and women blow themselves up to make their retarded fanatical statements."

"So, it is the child's fault that she lives in such a horrible place that it doesn't matter if she dies?"

"No, I didn't say that. I don't want innocent little girls to die. But it's war. Stuff like that happens in war. If they don't want us over there, they need to stop bombing us."

"I guess you're okay with torture, too?" Marta presumed.

"If it saves American lives to drip some water on some poor sucker's face all day, I don't see anything wrong with it."

"Unbelievable!" Marta said. "They should put you in charge of Guantanamo."

"It's better than the alternative—it saves lives! You would probably rather let terrorists go free than torture them, huh?"

"Never mind torture. We have no right to detain those people indefinitely. In their minds, they are freedom fighters, not terrorists."

"Yeah, freedom fighters that like to blow up public buses and trains."

"Not all of them, Kevin."

"And you probably think the same about prisons here. Just let all the criminals go free, huh?"

"Of course not, but our justice system is completely broken. We should focus on rehabilitation instead of punishment. It's the only way that we're going to progress."

"Right, spend all this money on the criminal and completely forget about the victim. Real genius there, Marta. Real good way to alienate ordinary, law abiding citizens."

"Well, if we weren't at war, we could spend all that wasted money on helping people here at home, not on bombs and bullets."

"Yeah, let's just give all that money to a bunch of evil criminals—or better yet, pathetic slobs who don't deserve it—and reward them for breaking the law."

"Oh, like working single mothers with four kids? Or people who can't find a job because it doesn't fit the oil company's profit model?" Marta asked rhetorically.

"Or the drug addict who can't feed himself because he spends all his cash on meth? Or the perfectly able kid who won't get a job but just wants to suck on the government tit while he lives it up with bottles of Cristal? Or the complete fat ass that uses food stamps for food and buys liquor with her cash?"

"Whatever, Kevin, that doesn't happen."

"Bullshit it doesn't."

Marta yelled out in aggravation, then apologized to the diners sitting at neighboring tables. "I don't know why I put up with you."

Kevin smiled and fully exhaled. "I think you put up with me because you're really a closet Republican."

Marta exploded in laughter. "Yeah, right!"

"Oh, come on. You know you love me."

Marta smiled. "Maybe, but you are such a political idiot. I must be a masochist to want to be with you."

"Or maybe it's just the great sex," Kevin added.

"It's not *that* great," Marta modified and grinned.

Kevin smiled and looked at his phone.

"Why do you keep looking at your phone, Kevin? Is it really that important?"

"Yeah, it's the senator. He was supposed to call at some point. They were going to bring him in to court today after the votes. I haven't heard from him yet."

"Court?"

"Yeah, some technicality or something. Not a big deal, but I was expecting a call."

Marta raised her eyebrows. "Maybe he's busy getting waterboarded." Marta tilted her head and smiled.

"Very funny."

Forty-Six

Com DeGroot kicked open the windowless front door to the Turf Club and saw the two U.S. marshals laughing with the doorman. Reggie Williams was standing behind one of the marshals, laughing along with everyone else.

"Whoa there, tiger!" One of the agents tried to calm the excited DeGroot.

Com turned and tried to walk past the agent but was held up by a sturdy hand. "Where do you think you're going, tough guy? I have strict orders to take you in unless I hear otherwise."

Com said nothing but looked at Reggie, who gave the senator a nearly imperceptible nod. Com turned back to the entrance and whipped back to the marshal, unleashing the most forceful punch he could muster.

In an instant, Reggie cracked the neck of the other marshal, kicked the doorman in the stomach, and rapped Com's target on the skull, shocking his autonomic nervous system and rendering him unconscious. Reggie then repeated the technique on the security guard.

Com's entire body was tense as he observed Reggie. "What the hell was that?"

"Dim Mak. They should come to in about ten minutes after the nervous system figures out what the hell just happened." Reggie checked the vitals on his victims. "Now that we have officially picked a fight with the U.S. Marshals, you want to tell me what the hell is going on?"

"Where's the car? I'll tell you on the way." Com reached down and quickly searched one of the federal agent's pockets, revealing his handheld phone. "Thanks, big guy."

Minutes later, Reggie tore around the corner in the Lincoln Town Car with Com in the passenger seat. They were headed south toward the interstate.

"Reggie, you got my back, right?" Com asked. "You're not going to sell me out?"

"Sir, I think my actions back there proved what sort of allegiance I have."

"Look, here's the deal. Delano and Thurston are working together with the banks in this elite power circle or something, and I think I just declared war with them. They set me up with the phony tax charges, and they pretty much threatened to kill me if I didn't play along with their little political game. Now, I don't expect you to come with me, but I have to get the hell out of here."

Reggie looked sternly at his passenger. "Sir, are you talking a conspiracy?"

"I don't know about a conspiracy, Reggie. All I know is that it looks like those pricks are calling the shots around here, and I'm not welcome."

Reggie thought about it for a moment, and then turned to Com, nodding. "All right, sir. I'm with you."

"Are you?"

"Sir, I told you my situation. I ain't got nothing else. I'm prepared to do my duty to protect you."

"All right, then," Com said with a nod. "Let's get the hell out of Dodge."

"Yes, sir," Reggie confirmed and turned his eyes back to the road.

Com noticed a showy building to his right and what looked like a restaurant through the first floor glass. Above the entrance was a sign that read "SAVOY."

"Shit, stop," Com blurted out.

"Sir?"

"Stop here. I need to make one last pit stop."

Reggie drove the Town Car directly up to a red carpet entrance to the glimmering Savoy Hotel restaurant. The red carpet aisle was covered by a long awning and flanked by a smattering of photographers.

Com DeGroot jumped out of the nearly-stopped vehicle, and the photographers bolted into action. A valet showed interest in helping Com out of the car, but the senator ignored him and instead brushed past. Com walked up to the Savoy's glass doors, which were opened by a doorman.

"Can I help you?" a friendly young man asked in a soft voice.

Com ignored the maître d' and looked around the elegant dining area. Com scanned the patrons on the left side of the maître d', then the right. Finally he spotted Kevin Donovan sitting across from a brunette in the middle of the dining room. He was hunched over the table, deep in conversation, when he noticed his boss walking toward him out of the corner of his eye.

Kevin jumped in his seat, then stood up slowly and stepped toward Com. The taller man looked furious, and Kevin was wide-eyed as Com approached. "There you are, man!"

Com dragged his right arm back, and then fired it toward his chief of staff, landing his large fist on Kevin's cheekbone. Kevin's head ricocheted backwards and pulled his body with it. The entire weight of Kevin's body flew away from Com into Kevin's table, knocking over glasses, a flower vase, and a half-empty wine bottle.

The nicely dressed Marta Saito had been staring at her date, confused. She screamed when he landed on the table in front of her. Restaurant patrons turned wide-eyed as they stared at the altercation.

"You're fired!" Com yelled. He turned around, fuming, and stomped out of the restaurant.

In front of the restaurant, Reggie was nowhere to be found so Com impatiently asked the valet where his car was. The photographers were milling about but gained interest in the commotion in front of them.

"We asked him to move," the valet responded nervously.

"What the hell?"

The valet shrugged his shoulders.

"You are nothing!" Com yelled at the valet.

"What the hell was all that about?" Kevin demanded as he flung the door open.

Com ignored his former chief of staff and looked for Reggie down the street. Com spotted the security captain walking toward the restaurant from down the street, so he rushed toward him.

"Are you going to tell me what's going on?" Kevin repeated as he followed Com.

The second question warranted a response from the senator. "I spoke with Delano and Thurston. The game is up. I know everything."

"What game, Com? What do you mean?"

"The conspiracy between Delano and Thurston. They told me you're on the take."

"I'm what?" Kevin yelled. "What conspiracy?"

"Don't act dumb, Kevin. They told me everything. Oh, it was so perfect. Get the big dumb jock into the Senate and feed him a bunch of whiskey and cheap women and he'll vote however you want him to—just like a damn puppet. And I fell for it."

"Com, you're crazy. What are you talking about?"

Com stopped just short of Reggie Williams and turned to Kevin. "You're going to try and tell me that you didn't know about the little partnership between Delano and Thurston and that you're not working for them? I bet the entire staff is on the take, too, huh? Noni? Hailey?"

"Partnership?" Kevin said with a distorted frown. "Com, I would never work for . . . " Kevin let his words trail off.

Com huffed and looked at Kevin, "Yeah, the partnership. And it worked because we lost Ur."

"What do you mean 'we lost Ur'? We won. You won the vote!"

Com raised his head and returned to Kevin, "You really don't know?"

Kevin looked stunned and shook his head no.

"Everything in Delano's bill was hidden in some other bill at some point, including Foxworthy's bill today—the eminent domain, the bank assets—and I voted for it all—everything."

Kevin released his tense neck and opened his mouth. "Oh, shit. It was a decoy."

"A what?"

"A decoy. They put out six-sixty-four to get all the headlines, then snuck the entire legislation through in other bills. They do it every once in a while when they want to ensure a bill's passage."

"They worked it, Kevin. They worked me bad." Com shook his head.

"Thurston, too?" Kevin looked down in shock. "I mean, he had talked to me about directing you on certain bills, but I thought that was just showing me the ropes. I never knew he was working with Delano. Oh, Jesus, it makes me want to puke."

"And now the fucking U.S. Marshals are after me."

Kevin realized the gravity. "Shit, Com. You're on the lam? What happened?"

"Kevin, they threatened to kill me back there. I didn't know what to do. We broke out of there." Com walked toward the Town Car.

"Com . . . " Kevin followed his boss. "Com, listen to me, you need to get the hell out of here."

"No shit."

"Look, do you have your phone?"

"Why?"

"Do you?"

"Yeah," Com said, looking curiously at Kevin.

"Give it to me."

Com looked warily, then handed his phone to his chief of staff, who immediately threw it on the concrete sidewalk and stomped on it.

"What the hell?" Com involuntarily reached for his destroyed electronics.

"These things have electronic identifiers. They can track your phone," Kevin said with authority. "You have one?" Kevin asked Reggie.

Reggie nodded and pulled it out, then reluctantly tossed it to Kevin, who threw it to the ground and stepped on it as well.

"They'll be tracking the car, too." Kevin looked down then pulled out a keychain from his pocket. "Here, take these." Kevin nodded at a car across the street. "It's Marta's. They won't know to track it. I'll let her use mine this week."

Com gave Kevin a smile of gratitude.

"Oh, and here." Kevin pulled out a roll of cash. "Since you have no cash now either."

"Thanks," Com said plainly.

"Get out of here," Kevin demanded.

Com and Reggie ran across the poorly lighted street, and Kevin watched as the car pulled out and reversed direction. Kevin returned to the restaurant with a worried look. When he got back to the red carpet, Marta was looking around for him and screamed at him when he presented himself. "What was that all about?"

Kevin put his arm around her. "Oh, that was a high school friend. We like to play practical jokes like that on each other."

"Don't give me that shit, it was your boss!" Marta screeched.

"Nah, you're imagining things," Kevin said calmly. "Hey, how would you like to drive a brand-new Beemer this week?"

Forty-Seven

Com DeGroot put down the pocket-sized book with a surprised shrug. "It says that 'The powers not delegated to the United States by the Constitution, nor prohibited by it to the States, are reserved to the States respectively, or to the people.' That means that the Constitution has to allow for it or it shouldn't be law."

Reggie nodded to acknowledge that he had heard Com. He was paying more attention to the unfamiliar road as he pulled into a gas station outside of Harrisonburg, Virginia.

"It's all corruption and deceit. There is no justice. There is no law." Com thought about his words for a moment. "No, it's worse. We live in a place where crime has *become* the law."

Reggie placed the car in park and looked at his friend with a stern look of empathy.

"What am I going to do, Reggie?"

"I don't know, but we need to get out of the area as soon as possible. Them marshals probably have an APB out right now."

"I got nothing, Reggie. No job, no money, no woman. I used to have everything. . . ." Com waved his hand in the air to represent everything.

"Yessir," Reggie said.

"If I go back to Washington, they're going to kill me." Com looked earnestly into his companion's face. "Did you hear that? They're going to kill me. I know they are. I'll be just another one in the list of political assassinations, like that Congressman McDonald, or Kennedy."

"Yes, sir," Reggie repeated with a less certain tone.

"So, it's Mexico, then?" Com raised his eyebrow at Reggie.

"Mexico." Reggie nodded.

"Thanks for doing this, Reggie. I owe you my life."

Reggie nodded but said nothing, then opened the door and walked into the gas station store, still heavily lighted in contrast to the pitch-black night. Com pinched the bridge of his nose under his sunglasses and groaned. He reached for the on button to the passenger-side video display and navigated to the news channel.

"... the flooding is the worst it has been in over five years," a reporter in the video said. "President Sullivan has promised immediate relief for those in affected areas."

A beautiful young news anchor was seen in the video.

"In other news, riots continue in the charter city of Ur, Texas." Video images of fire billowing from a mountain of debris were shown. People danced around the fire in the video and threw nondescript items into the blaze. "Officials close to the story have told NNC that the riots are in response to inequitable treatment by the private corporations in charge of the transportation system there. State and federal aid agencies have offered assistance to the beleaguered city, but have been turned away by the city council. U.S. President Horace Sullivan has declared a state of emergency and says he's prepared to enter the city by force if necessary."

Com blurted, "Of course he is!"

"Back in Washington, a United States senator is on the loose tonight after escaping the custody of two U.S. marshals on the way to a district court. Senator Com DeGroot of Delaware, wanted on tax evasion charges, failed to show for his arraignment earlier today, putting him in contempt of court, a spokesman for the federal court said. It was reported that the senator had an altercation at a local D.C. restaurant after he escaped custody. The whereabouts of Senator DeGroot are still unknown at this hour, and several federal agencies are conducting extensive searches."

Com switched off the news and looked around the empty gas station. His pulse quickened briefly and released a deep breath after he spotted Reggie walking back toward the car.

"What the hell do you mean, you don't know where he is?" Duane D. Delano barked at the prestigious company in his Senate office.

The recipient of Delano's words was Bobby Mariotti, the Assistant Director of the Investigative Operations Division of the U.S. Marshals Service. Mr. Mariotti was not used to being barked at—he usually did the barking in his circles—but that day was not usual. Mariotti's department had failed to contain the transportation of a very important prisoner, Senator Com DeGroot, and interested parties, such as the Senate Majority Leader and Chairman of the Homeland Security Committee, were furious.

"I'm telling you that we don't know where he is," Mariotti repeated himself in an impatient tone. The director acknowledged his organization's failure but noted that it came during a substantially irregular procedure. "Let me be clear, our men are extremely capable at what they do. They are some of the best crime fighters in the world with numerous safeties and redundancies in procedure that prevent instances like these. But when they are ordered to do something out of typical protocol—as was the case last evening—risks are presented, risks that do not normally exist."

Delano shook off the excuse. "Don't give me that crap. You were told to do a job, and you failed."

Mariotti added quickly, "We have reason to believe that there was an elaborate plot to break the prisoner. It could have involved five agents or more. My men were helpless without the redundancies typically in place."

"Again, you may kindly desist with the excuse-making. I want DeGroot's ass. You have any number of assets at your discretion: FBI, NSA, whatever." Delano's thought was interrupted by a visitor in his office.

A young analyst from the National Security Agency, who had been temporarily stationed in Delano's front office, knocked on the doorframe. "Senator, I think we may have something."

Delano smirked and looked at Mariotti with contempt. "Well?" Delano barked impatiently at the analyst.

The young man walked over to Delano's desk. "We have no sign of DeGroot, but one of our automated drones has captured the visage of this man." The analyst dropped a folder on the senator's desk. The folder had a black-and-white headshot of Reggie Williams fastened to the front.

"Who is he?" Delano coughed.

"His name is Reginald P. Williams. Hired for Senator DeGroot's security team during his campaign, it appears he is now the security captain—"

"One of ours?" Delano wondered.

"No. We believe that DeGroot promoted him internally."

Delano slowly nodded his head. "Where is he?"

"The drone spotted him first in Virginia at twenty-one hundred, then in Arkansas at oh-five-thirty."

"Oh, how I love modern surveillance." Delano smiled.

"He's making a run for it—Mexico," Mariotti exclaimed.

Delano gave Mariotti a short stare then laughed. "Mexico, huh? What a weasel that big ape is turning out to be."

"What do you want to do, sir?" the analyst inquired of his superior officer. Director Mariotti turned to Delano to deflect the question to him.

Delano thought for a moment, then spoke slowly while looking at the image of Reggie Williams. "Try to head off the fugitive. But secure every border crossing." Delano pointed at Mariotti. "That man will not cross into Mexico, is that clear?"

"Crystal," Mariotti replied.

Kevin Donovan stood as tall as his five-foot-six frame could manage in front of the entire senatorial staff of Com DeGroot. He wanted to address everyone together to allay fears or concerns about the bizarre situation regarding the senator.

"I'm sure you have all heard rumors about the senator. That he's on the run from the law, that he's in trouble, that he's a criminal." Kevin let his statement sink in for a moment. "All of that is complete speculation. The truth of the matter is that we don't know what has happened or who is involved. The only thing we can be sure of is that the senator will not be coming in to work today."

Noni Alvarez's face expressed concern, while Hailey Owens produced a sardonic grin. The entire staff listened intently to the chief's words.

"But that should not prevent you from acting in a strictly professional manner. As far as we are concerned in this office, nothing has changed. I want you to continue your duties as you normally would until we learn of anything officially. Does everyone understand?"

Most of the staff nodded and voiced their agreement.

"All right, then. Let's get to work. We have a Senate office to run!"

Forty-Eight

Com DeGroot hid from the blazing sun pouring through the driver's side window and the windshield. He turned to his driver, Reggie Williams. "Did we get into an accident last night? I feel like a Mack truck slammed into my cerebellum."

Reggie smiled. "You did."

Com moaned. "Where are we?"

"Right outside a place called Kingsville."

"What state?"

"Texas. We just passed Corpus."

Com tried to keep his eyes open as he rubbed his forehead with his right hand. "Damn. We're really doing this?"

"I don't know what you're doing, sir, but I'm dropping you off at the border to Mexico."

Com shook his head and squeezed his eyes shut. "I can't believe this is happening."

Reggie was quiet.

"I'm going to be a fugitive of justice. What am I saying? Everyone's a fugitive from justice. There is no justice." He looked at his driver for an answer. None was provided. "Mexico? I can't go to Mexico? Why are we going to Mexico?"

"You seemed to think it was a good idea last night, sir," Reggie reported.

"I can't go to Mexico. What would I do? Sell Chicklets on the street to foreigners?"

Reggie grinned. "I bet you could corner the market. You're a lot bigger than them kids they got doing that."

Com laughed. "Yeah, I would take those little kids down!" Com put out his hands and imitated a small beggar child. "Chicklet? Chicklet?" The senator looked around for his sunglasses but couldn't find them. He put his arm on his stomach and grimaced. "I think I'm going to get sick."

Minutes later, the tall figure stumbled up the embankment to the shoulder of the four-lane highway and maneuvered his way back into the car.

Reggie sat patiently with his hands on the steering wheel. "So what you gonna do?"

Com shook his head and voiced no answer.

"You know what's up there about fifty miles, don't you?" Reggie asked.

Com looked at the flat, featureless land in front of him. "Yup."

"We can be there in about a half hour."

"I don't have anything left for me there."

Reggie looked at his passenger. "That's more than you have anywhere else, isn't it?"

Com returned the look.

* * *

"I don't get it," Com said impatiently. "Why do I need to tell you who I am? Why do you need my handprint? I'm not going to be driving." Com waved his hand at a letter-sized, clear, plastic tablet that a young man was holding.

The young man was clearly an entry-level employee for the car rental company but was dressed in a fashionable suit and spoke with clarity. "Certainly you can understand our predicament with the riots going on now. And you must appreciate that the highway has a responsibility to ensure that only law-abiding citizens enter the city, and we have a responsibility to the highway corporation to only lease vehicles to those parties. If we let an unidentified person lease a car and that person went on to break the law, we would be held responsible and would probably lose our license. This company would go out of business, and I would lose my job. I'm sorry, sir, but there's no way around it. I must ask you to provide your biometric information."

The young man stared at Com DeGroot and extended the plastic tablet computer to the tall man.

Com looked at Reggie, who shrugged then leaned toward Com to whisper something. "Maybe they don't know about your little incident."

Com huffed. He put his hand on the tablet computer. The computer produced a pleasant chime sound, and the young attendant smiled. "Thank you. I'll be right back." He walked around a corner of the light blue plastic interior room.

"What's the worse they can do?" Reggie asked in a low voice.

"I don't know. But it's too late to go back now."

Com looked out the clear doors of the rental agency to a bright, scorching day.

"Mr. DeGroot?" a bulky man in a black suit asked calmly. He walked around the same corner that the employee had disappeared behind and was accompanied by two others dressed in an identical manner. Com looked away from the newcomers.

It was useless, Com thought as his head sunk. "Oh, come on. You've got to be kidding me."

"Will you come with us, sir?" one of the men in the black suits asked calmly.

Reggie Williams inched to the side of one of the black-suited men, and Com nodded at Reggie subtly.

"If you would just come with—"

In a split second, Reggie flashed in front of Com, struck one of the three guards on the neck with his right hand and flung his left hand toward a pressure point on another guard's forehead. The two men collapsed. The third flinched backward, and Com flew at him, throwing his fist. The guard stumbled away from the attackers and pulled out a flat metal object from his suit jacket. He pointed it at Reggie, who was swinging his arm to knock the device out of the guard's hand, but the guard pressed the device before Reggie could reach him and the object projected a clear ripple of energy consisting of nine hundred and fifty thousand volts of electricity toward the abdomens of Com and Reggie. The wave incapacitated the combatants, and they fell to the ground, unconscious.

* * *

Reggie Williams flinched and slid off of the brushed metal chair that had been supporting him in the stark white room. He looked around and found an unconscious Com DeGroot, who was sprawled over three similar chairs next to him. Reggie jumped to his feet and lunged at Com to check his pulse. He pulled the senator up and pressed his knuckle in Com's back, just below his shoulder blade. Com's eyes widened and he gasped for air.

Com started swinging his head around in an attempt to assess the situation. He spotted a closed door in front of him and acknowledged Reggie next to him.

"What the hell happened?" Com spilled.

"They got us, sir. It was some sort of wireless stun gun. Knocked us out." Reggie looked up and surveyed the white walls. "Sir, it was a bad idea to come here. I apologize for even mentioning it."

Com shook it off and blinked, trying to come to his senses. "Don't worry about it, Reggie. It was my idea to come here. I should have known they were going to find me—security here is so tight. What was I thinking?" Com yelled in frustration.

Reggie walked over to the door and found it locked. He then followed the ceiling panels from one end of the room to the other. For a short while, Reggie punched the walls and otherwise inspected the room as Com sat dejectedly in one of the chairs.

"You trying to find an escape route?" Com asked with amusement.

"I can't just sit here, sir," Reggie replied.

Reggie walked to the line of chairs opposite the door and stood on one in order to push up a ceiling panel. "Come over here," Reggie demanded. "Lift me up."

Com obliged and walked over to Reggie. He cupped his hands to offer Reggie a step up, which he took. Reggie stood on Com's supported hands and the top of the chair and pushed aside a ceiling tile. Reggie peeked his head above the ceiling but saw only darkness.

The door to the room flung open.

"Dios mío!" Santiago Garza exclaimed at the sight. "This is quite embarrassing."

Com released his hands and Reggie fell suddenly but landed on the floor deftly. Both men looked at Santiago and smiled awkwardly.

Forty-Nine

Santiago Garza walked Com DeGroot and Reggie Williams through a stylish hall in the archon building of Ur, Texas. "I truly apologize for all of that confusion this morning," Santiago said through his thick accent. "None of this should have happened. But you see, security has been extremely tight recently due to the riots going on in one of our sectors—I'm sure you are aware."

"Yeah, I heard." Com nodded.

"Anyway, I learned about your plight in Washington, and I instructed my contacts at the border checkpoints that if a person by the name of Com DeGroot showed up to one of these checkpoints, they were to bring him immediately to me. These men were under explicit instructions to explain the situation and to not harm you."

Com laughed. "Well, I think we may have provoked them a bit." Com gave a nod to his security chief.

"Yes. But I am just regretful that any of this happened."

"Don't worry about it, Santiago. I'm just glad they weren't the feds." Com looked at Santiago and stopped walking. "By the way, does this mean that you're not going to turn me in?" Com wondered skeptically.

"To whom? The same government that has their greedy lusting eyes fixed on this city?" Santiago asked rhetorically.

"Right." Com shook his head.

"Let me assure you, señor, you are perfectly safe here in Ur. You can relax here." Santiago looked at Com intently to get the message across. "Please, you are my guests. Take some time for rest. You both must be exhausted from a long day. Please be my guest at the hotel next door. I will arrange rooms for you both and . . . ," Santiago looked at Com's mud-stained clothes, "a refreshed wardrobe?" Santiago smiled. "I would be glad for you to meet me for dinner after you are refreshed."

* * *

"You don't have those creepy robot humanoids running around the room, do you?" Com DeGroot smiled at the friendly young lady behind the hotel's front desk.

The clerk returned the amusement. "Yes, we do. But I can I have them deactivated for you if you'd like."

Com nodded. "That would be fantastic. Those things tripped me out last time."

The young lady smiled and made some adjustments on her computer. "Okay, you're all set." The clerk reached over the counter with a thick-stock envelope containing a key card. "Here are your keys. You're in rooms five-ten and five-fifty-five." The clerk opened the envelope to reveal a yellow note attached to the inside. "And Mr. Garza thought you might need this number." She smiled at Com and nodded.

Com looked at the note. It read, "Miss Heatherton's # 77-534-0087." Com nodded and thanked the clerk.

After a hot shower in his suite, a robed Com DeGroot walked to the window side of his king-sized bed and sat down. He looked at the note with Cate Heatherton's number and picked up the handset of the hotel phone.

"Seven seven?" Com questioned as he looked at the number.

He began dialing seven seven and the phone produced a beeping tone indicating that the phone number was invalid. Com frowned, then tried dialing seven seven again with the same result. Com hung up and dialed nine and waited. There was no dial tone or beeping, so he proceeded with dialing a one then seven and another seven, and the phone started beeping at him again.

"Ah, for the love!" Com yelled in frustration.

He hung up and picked up again. The caller dialed nine then pound and heard nothing, so he proceeded dialing seven, seven, five. The phone started beeping again, and Com slammed the receiver down on the phone base. Then he knocked the phone off the nightstand and onto the floor. "The hell with it." The senator turned around and spotted a stationary humanoid robot standing in a recess in the wall. "Well, what the hell are you looking at?"

* * *

"That was excellent, Santiago," Com said, wiping his mouth with a fine cloth napkin.

"Yes, thank you, Mr. Garza," Reggie added.

Com smiled. "You sure know how to treat fugitives of justice."

"My friend," Santiago replied. "You are no more a fugitive of justice than anyone here attempting to live outside of the coercion of the federal government."

Com nodded, and there was a momentary comfortable silence until the senator broke it. "So, tell me about these riots. The first I heard of them was when the president declared it a national emergency in session."

"Sí. Well, I believe it is a bit overblown," Santiago mentioned. "But it is true that there is rioting in one of the sectors here in Ur. I am going to the security center after dinner to assess the situation."

"Oh, really? May I go with you?" Com asked, eager to learn about the situation.

"You are very welcome to, señor."

The group finished their meals and left the fine dining room. Minutes later, Com and Reggie followed Santiago to a door in the archon building blocked by a security guard and a biometric scanner. The guard nodded at Santiago, and all three passed through the biometric scan and into the security center.

Inside, three large screens positioned near the top of the twenty-foot wall opposite the entrance showed footage of different aspects of unrest. The first screen depicted a small group of scruffy looking hood-lums throwing random objects into a bonfire near a graffiti-ridden gray wall. The second screen showed what appeared to be a satellite image of the entire area. Large swaths of land were charcoal black and bordered with a red glow of flame. The third screen played video from a National News Coalition broadcast of the disorder.

Santiago examined the room and the destruction on the large screens. "Not a good day for liberty, my friend." Garza gave some instruc-tion to an operator at one of the computer stations and returned his attention to the senator.

"So, what happened?" Com asked Santiago.

"We have been piecing it together for the last two days, but it appears that some of the residents of Amaurot were denied—"

"Amaurot?" Com asked.

"Sí, it is the socialist sector of Ur. I believe we visited it in my wonderful tour of the city. Do you remember?"

"Oh, yes. So tell me. I thought the security in Ur was top notch. How did all these hoodlums get in?" Com inquired.

"Well, the council of Amaurot tracks who enters and leaves the sector, but that is about it. Their admission requirements are significantly less strict than other sectors in Ur."

"I guess we chose the strict sector this morning," Com added.

"Sí, that was Washington Heights. They are very strict about who enters. At any rate, some of the residents of Amaurot were denied access to other areas of Ur, notably the neighboring sectors of Washington Heights and Jefferson Heights. They were denied access to the tram-cars leaving Amaurot. Well, those residents did not take that too nicely, so they proceeded to destroy the tram station in Amaurot. At that, the surrounding sectors closed their gates to the area. Hours later, we received reports of crop fires throughout Amaurot and rioting at the gates of Jefferson Heights. It is an ugly scene, as you can see." Santiago pointed at the screen depicting the rioters. "Our only comfort is that Amaurot does not permit guns, so the rioters are left with makeshift arms—knives, pitchforks, ethanol bombs."

"Bastards," Com spewed. "Can I ask why you don't just take them out?"

Santiago shook his head rapidly. "We do have technology to incapacitate these people without harming them, but the NNC is watching us like a hawk. If they see one false move by the security forces in Ur, the feds will move in."

"So you can't protect yourselves from these punks?" Com interrogated Santiago.

"I have a feeling that if we move on them, the federales will use it as an excuse to move on *us*," Santiago said regretfully.

Com breathed in heavily. "Do you know who these people are?"

Santiago nodded and asked an analyst at a nearby computer station to bring up a video on the middle large wall monitor.

"This footage was taken last evening," Santiago said and looked up at the large middle screen. It was a close-up video of rioters huddled in small groups around scattered fires. The video showed one of the rioters throwing a brick in the direction of the camera that was capturing the unrest.

"This man," Santiago said, pointing to the screen as it froze. "The man at the top of the screen is the recently elected premiere council member of Amaurot. His name is Ilarion Yoan. Bulgarian by birth. He has been in Ur for years, and he has a clean record, but it appears from the video that he is organizing the riot, if that can be said." Santiago told the computer operator to continue the video.

The video showed Ilarion Yoan in a dark green military jacket and black jeans conversing with another rioter. Out of the corner of the video, a glass jar was seen flying into the camera area. It exploded into flames, and the video turned completely black.

"As you can see, my friend," Santiago explained, "we don't have much to go on."

"Wait, can you rewind that last part?" Com directed his request to the computer operator.

Santiago nodded, and the operator rewound the video, then played it. Ilarion Yoan was seen again, as was the jar being flung into the camera.

"This guy," Com blurted out and pointed at the screen. "The guy who threw the Molotov cocktail. Can you zoom in on him?"

The video operator maneuvered his mouse and pressed some keys on his keyboard to enlarge the man who threw the bottle at the camera. The enlarged image was not clear, but it showed the culprit to be a bald, light-skinned man wrapped in black fatigues.

"Can you clean this image up at all?" Com asked, looking at the large screen.

The operator did not respond but typed on his keyboard and applied a filter to the image on the screen. Santiago looked at Com with uncertainty. The filter sharpened the edges of the image, seemingly making the image clearer.

"Zoom into his forehead?" Com suggested.

The operator zoomed into the perpetrator's forehead. He advanced a couple of frames in the video, and the subject turned his head to reveal what looked like a tattoo of barbed wire on his forehead.

"Son of a bitch," Com announced.

Everyone looked at the senator.

"I've seen this guy in D.C. He was working for Delano. Son of a bitch!"

Fifty

Com DeGroot and Reggie Williams sat opposite each other on chairs in a stylish lounge area adjacent to the archon building lobby. Com leaned forward with his elbows resting on his knees, and Reggie reclined in a drowsy pose. Santiago Garza walked slowly toward the two, looking at his tablet computer.

"His name is Andrei Nicolayevich Volkov," Santiago reported as he approached Com and Reggie. He served time in a Soviet labor camp outside of Moscow in the eighties for his involvement in the murder of a high-ranking party member. He was released after the revolution in ninety-one and spent time drifting around the capitol."

"So what the hell is he doing in the South of Texas?" Com asked with an aggressive tone.

Santiago looked up from his tablet. "Well, it appears that Señor Volkov arrived here just days ago. He is part of a major influx of citizens that we've seen here in Ur in recent months."

"What do you mean 'major influx'?" Com interrogated.

"Just that, my friend. We have seen a one-hundred-percent increase in the population of some of the sectors of the city."

"Let me guess," Com said expectantly. "They're all ex-convicts like this guy Volkov?"

Santiago shook his head. "No, no, señor. I do not think they are all ex-convicts. As you know, there is no universal control of security here in Ur. Each sector is responsible for its own safety measures." The tall, well-dressed man looked back to his tablet computer. "It appears that Señor Volkov was rejected entry to Washington Heights on March the fourteenth, but Amaurot accepted him the next day. *They* accept everyone."

"Did you find any connection to Delano?" Com raised an eyebrow.

"No. It is possible that if he were working with the senator, he could have used fake identification or been, how do you say, off the books?"

"It's a setup," Com said, making a realization.

"How do you mean?" Reggie asked. He was tired but curious.

"They sent these bastards here to do exactly this. They sent them to cause a riot."

"Who's 'they'?" Reggie asked.

"Those sons of bitches in D.C. Delano and Thurston and Hank Pierpont—the *gods* of the Hill," he mocked.

Santiago nodded. "Sí, I have thought of this."

"You said yourself," Com continued to Santiago, "that they've all come recently. They probably all planned to convene in the same place and unleash hell. This is a concerted setup."

Santiago nodded. "And they will use this as an excuse to enter the city and perhaps revoke the charter despite the fact that the bill was defeated."

"Of course," Com said, confirming.

"Well," Santiago said, breaking a tense stare, "I will need to discuss—"

An assistant to the archon walked up to Mr. Garza and interrupted him with a hurried message. "Sir, the feds have bypassed security on the north gate. They are headed here—to the archon building."

Santiago's eyes bulged, and he fumed silently.

"They're making their move," Reggie exclaimed.

At that moment, several men with black riot gear poured into the archon building through the front doors. Santiago turned to Com. "Go! There is a café across the office park," Santiago said while going over several thoughts in his mind at once. "You will be safe there. I will retrieve you when I know more."

A loud crash was heard at the front doors. Com and Santiago looked to see a dozen U.S. marshals lined up on the opposite side of the glass doors, destroying one of the biometric scanners. Com's nostrils flared as he watched the federal agents destroy the security features and stomp into the lobby. He inched toward the men who were fifty feet away and grinded his teeth, but was held back by Santiago.

"Go, my friend. Take the side exit," Santiago said and pointed the tall man to a set of side doors.

* * *

"I can't stand just waiting here!" Com let out in frustration. He paced back and forth in front of the café window and looked up at the entrance to the archon building a hundred yards away. In the late dusk lighting, the senator was able to make out a group of men with blue U.S. Marshal uniforms as they stood outside the entrance, talking to each other and pointing.

"Here comes Mr. Garza," Reggie noted.

The tall man walked across the office park to the café and, within seconds, walked through the front door.

"What's going on? We're dying over here," Com blurted out.

"It is a catastrophe, my friend. The federales have declared marshal law in Ur," Santiago said in disgust.

"What?" Com yelled.

"On authority of the president of the United States, the U.S. Marshals have entered Ur to protect the city in this time of civil unrest." Santiago relayed the message he had received.

"It's exactly what we were talking about. They're using the riots as an excuse to take over," Com claimed.

"And in order to secure this area, they've made the incredible move to disable all of the security features in the city. They are working on disabling the security around Amaurot now." Santiago looked back at the marshals grouped around the archon building entrance.

"What are they thinking?" Com yelled.

"They have disabled the biometric scanners at most buildings in the city center, and most of the automated trams have been disabled as well."

"This is madness!" a female customer at the café said after overhearing the conversation.

Com remembered what his legislative director had told him. "They want the gold reserves. The banks. . . ."

"Sí. They said that they are in the process of *protecting* the banks." Santiago stressed the word protecting. "They have surrounded the two headquarters of Ur Bank and Royalty Swiss Bank, where the majority of the reserves are. I can only imagine that they are now attempting to break past their security systems."

"It's outright theft," Com protested.

"Sí."

"And that big shot Kula or whatever his name is couldn't stop this?" Com asked skeptically.

"Señor Kula is presently on a plane flying back from Hong Kong, unfortunately."

"Figures," Com said.

"So what do we do?" Reggie asked level-headedly.

"We flee. We evacuate," Santiago said flatly.

"What?" Com demanded. "What are you talking about?"

"Señor, the federales have taken over. They have won. Fairly soon, they will figure out the way to shut off the security perimeter to Amaurot, and the rioters will be able to enter the other sectors of the city. It will be mass hysteria. Chaos."

"So you just give up? Run?"

"My friend, this is not new. My family has a long history of removing themselves from this type of oppression. This will be no different. There is always another place that will welcome freedom-seeking people."

"But where?"

"Singapore, Liechtenstein, the Caymans," Santiago said hopefully.

"But not here. Not in America," Com was dismayed.

"No, unfortunately. Ur was the last hope for this country," Santiago said in a low tone.

"Doesn't that infuriate you? How can you just give up? This is America!" Com nearly yelled.

"My friend, it is not the location that matters, it is the spirit of the people within that matters. And right now, that spirit—the Constitution—has nearly vanished from this nation," Santiago said.

Com shook his head in confusion.

"You see, living on this soil does not make me American. Believing what I believe—that's what makes me American." Santiago pointed to his head. "I'm American because I believe in liberty. And that can exist anywhere that is free tyranny."

Com shook his head again. "No. We can't just leave, Santiago. We have to fight them!" Com said.

"My friend, you are a fugitive according to those gentlemen in blue suits over there. I am merely a doctor and administrator. It is useless. What do you suggest we do?"

"I don't know. We have to do something. Don't you have a security force or something? What about those guys that took us out this morning at the checkpoint?"

"Sí, but what shall we do?" Santiago asked honestly. "Shall we attack the U.S. Marshals? Shall we declare war on the United States of America?"

"We wouldn't be declaring war, we would be defending ourselves. They're attacking us!"

"There are no suitable outcomes to that solution, my friend."

At that moment, a chirping sound began to pulse in the café and throughout the surrounding office park. It was accompanied by a flash from fire alarms placed throughout the hall.

Santiago shook his head. "It's done. They have ruined us."

"They cut off the security?" Com said impatiently.

"Sí. I'm afraid so," Santiago replied.

"Pretty soon, those rioters are going to be pouring through here. No one will be safe," Reggie warned.

A thought struck Com. "Santiago, where is Cate Heatherton?"

"She's in . . . Jefferson Heights—next to Amaurot. Dios mío."

Com jumped toward the door. "Where, Santiago? How can I get to Cate?"

Santiago reached in his pockets and produced a small rectangular electronic device. "Here, you can take my Ana V. Just say the name of the person you want to drive to, and the car will do the rest. I'm parked in the garage below this building."

Fifty-One

Cate Heatherton sat in a stool at the bar surrounding her pristine modern kitchen. Reflected light gave the room a warm glow and compensated for the retreating sun. She breathed in heavily and took at bite of the garden wrap she had just made. She chewed, but the usually tasty recipe produced a slight frown on Cate's face. She shrugged and put the wrap down as she finished chewing, then looked at her mobile phone, which was resting on the bar.

"Why aren't you texting?" Cate nearly yelled at the device.

She navigated to a news application on her computer, then navigated back to her inbox, which showed no new messages.

She placed her free hand at the base of a glass of red wine and methodically tapped each finger on the glass, then looked back at her phone. Cate jumped in her seat, startled as the phone erupted in vibration and an audible ring. Cate placed her hand over her heart as she read the caller's name—"Santiago"—and picked up the device.

"Hi, Santiago."

"Señorita Heatherton! Is your door locked?"

Her bottom lip began instantly quivering. "Yes, Santiago. Why?" She did not want her question to be answered.

"The federales have taken control of Ur. They shut down the perimeter around Amaurot, and the rioters are loose in the city."

"Oh, Santiago," Cate said with a low tone. "What are they thinking?"

"They are not thinking, señorita."

Cate looked around her apartment. "What do I do?"

"You must stay where you are. Señor DeGroot is on his way—"

"Com?" Cate asked, confused but hopeful. "He's here?"

"Sí, señorita. He was awfully concerned over you."

Cate smiled and tilted her head.

"I'm afraid," Santiago said on the other line. "I'm afraid it's as if we have been living wonderfully in our little Camelot, but unaware of the dragon that slept just outside. Now it looks like that dragon has awoken and is hungry for blood. Please, for me, can you make sure that your doors are locked?"

"Thank you, Santiago, they are."

"Señoriata Cate, do you need anything?"

"No." Cate heard a knock at the door and smiled. "Oh, I think Com is here now."

"That was fast. Señorita, you know he cares for you very much," Santiago said warmly.

Cate smiled as she walked to the door. "I know."

"He is a great man, the senator."

Cate held her phone between her ear and shoulder and slid over the chain lock, then unlocked the deadbolt on her door.

A violent crack of the door hit Cate in the forehead and knocked her toward the cold ground. Cate's phone flew from her grasp and careened along the floor several feet. She was half aware as she looked up to see a mountain of a greasy, soot-stained man stomp through her door to tower over her.

"Jackpot." The word slithered through several rotten teeth and the crusted lips of the intruder.

Cate scrunched her face and pulled herself up on her elbows. She slowly began to crawl backwards, away from the filthy intruder. She rotated around to her stomach and struggled to shake off the concussion she had just received. Cate spotted her pocket computer and clambered toward it.

The hefty intruder leaned down and grabbed Cate's ankle, producing a shriek by the victim. The man grumbled, "Where you going, little missy?" Sturdy on one knee, the man's grip crushed Cate's ankle, and he yanked the victim back toward him. She collapsed on a bent leg and her extended arms. Cate yelled again as the dirt-soaked man flipped her over so that she was lying on her back. The man held Cate's legs securely as she squirmed, pushing the cement floor away from her.

"I have friends coming. Just leave. Just take whatever you want," Cate said, trying to be calm.

"Oh, I'm gonna take exactly what I want," the stinking criminal said. He pulled Cate toward him by her legs and started breathing heavily.

A rush of adrenaline overcame Cate and she screamed loudly while thrusting herself up to the beastly mound in front of her. She slapped, swiped, and hit whatever she could, but the thick man just laughed as he attempted to secure her arms. He gave up trying to grab her hands and let his heavy arm fly across Cate's face.

Still conscious, Cate fell to the concrete floor and convulsed. Blood began to form on her cheek, and she felt something wet on the back of her head.

"Now, where were we?" The brutal man cackled and sat on Cate's legs, inching up toward her torso.

Cate was wearing a sheer black dress with a V-neck. The criminal grabbed both sides of the V-neck and ripped the dress down the middle. The chapped face of the criminal grew a grin as he viewed the nude breasts of a young woman under his total control. He ripped more of the dress, revealing the woman's stomach, and grunted.

Cate slowly put her arms over her bare body and tilted her head up and away from the beast imprisoning her. "Please don't hurt me," Cate whispered, her lips quivering.

The man threw Cate's arms to the side and held them down with his hands. Like an animal, the man lunged down on the young woman and licked her stomach and breasts. "You taste like a candy." He moved his way up to her neck and cheek. Cate's neck was arched and she avoided looking at the stinking man.

The intruder moved down the woman's body and pulled up her dress. He ripped off Cate's underwear and grunted again.

A tear fell from the closed right eye of Cate Heatherton as she leaned back and whispered, "God, help . . . me."

The beast snickered. "Ain't no god here, bitch."

The room dimmed, and Cate felt as if she were falling through the concrete floor. She imagined the beastly intruder floating off of her and away into the darkness. The helpless young woman began to lose all sensation and finally saw nothing but black.

* * *

Com DeGroot instantly knew something was wrong when he spotted the door to Cate's townhome angled open. He picked up his pace, inviting Reggie Williams to do so as well, and finally started running through the thick night air to Cate's door.

Once Com charged across the threshold, he was a machine. He marked two pale legs trapped under a hulking mass of barbarism ten feet in front of him.

Adrenaline exploded through Com's body like lightning. He lunged toward the thug. Mindless, he tore the two-hundred-fifty-pound mass off of its victim and projected him toward a cabinet full of ceramics. The cabinet came crashing down, and Com attacked the stunned beast.

Com swung at his face, then his gut. He landed blow after blow on the mound of a man.

The dazed criminal swung his thick arm in the tall assailant's direction, but Com was too quick, and the strike missed. Com took the opportunity to push the criminal's face with one hand, then the next, and to knock him down over his extended leg.

Reggie approached the ruckus and kneeled down next to the criminal, ready to detain him, but Com was too active to allow Reggie to get close.

Com's arms swung alternative strikes on the criminal's stubborn head and, when the man brought his arms up to protect his face, Com pounded the man's arms.

Com was possessed. "I'm gonna kill you fuck . . . I'm gonna kill—"

"Whoa, Senator!" Reggie yelled in an attempt to wake Com out of his violent trance. "That's enough. I can handle it from here."

Com kept going, obliterating his opponent. After a number of blows, the criminal gave no fight and lay dormant. Reggie gently secured Com's arms and led him away from the pile of waste on the floor.

Com was breathing heavily and looked at the criminal with disgust, then kicked him.

The tall senator sat with his legs extended on the concrete floor and turned to Cate Heatherton, lying five feet away, motionless. He rushed to her, delicately put his hand under her head, and scanned her face for signs of life. Cate's eyes were closed, and her forehead wrinkled as if she was having a bad dream.

"Oh God, Cate."

She was unconscious but she was alive.

Fifty-Two

The rounded British-American, Peter Westings, cupped a pint of beer in front of him and mumbled to himself as much as to his companion, his tall Nigerian-American friend, George Aboyami. "Soon, we will all need to take a stand and fight or be forced into a life of servitude."

George Aboyami opened his mouth to speak but was interrupted by a man bursting through the pub door. "We're being invaded!" the cracking voice declared.

Peter Westings stood up from his bar stool at the news. He looked at the messenger in stunned silence, then spoke. "Preposterous."

"No," the messenger proclaimed. "They are clearing the streets. They are imposing marshal law! The rioters have sacked the city center and destroyed several buildings already." He pointed out the door to the north. "The National Guard is combing the streets and sending everyone home."

Peter's face, already red from several beers, became even redder. "This is . . . this is tyranny!" His neck muscles tensed and he breathed heavily. "Not on my watch they don't!" Peter exclaimed in a thick British accent.

A worried bartender dried a glass with a stained white towel. "Peetie, what do you think you are you going to do about it?"

"I'm going to stop them. That's what!" He was fidgeting.

"Aww, stay and finish your beer, Peter," George Aboyami said, tilting his head and showing his brilliant white teeth in contrast to his dark skin.

"No, sir! This is what I was referring to. This is where we take a stand. I will not sit idly by. Thousands of people died defeating my home country for the cause of freedom. I'm not going to stand by now and let the tyrannical sons of freedom fighters destroy that for which those heroes fought!" Peter Westings walked around a table and out the door into the dimly lit street. George Aboyami and a number of bar patrons followed the sturdy man.

"Return to your homes . . . Do not leave your place of residence . . . You are under marshal law," a federal deputy shouted through a megaphone. He trailed a line of riot police in black military fatigues carrying body-length black shields. The clank of boots on the pavement sounded mechanical, reverberating off the buildings as the police slowly walked down the street toward the bar and Peter Westings. Peter defiantly walked into the middle of the street and stood with his hands calmly folded behind him.

Immediately, the voice of the riot police directed his megaphone toward Peter. "Please clear the road. For your own safety, please return to your home. There are dangerous people on the loose."

The line of riot police stepped closer, and Peter boldly stood in their way with his chin up. "Under what authority do you conduct your business?" Peter asked firmly.

"Please, clear the area." The deputy ignored Peter's question.

"Peter, get out of their way. Come inside!" an onlooker in the pub yelled.

"We have God-given rights, my friends," Peter Westings proclaimed. "Woe to those who try to take them from us."

The row of police officers held short of Peter just ten feet away. "Please remove from this location or you will be removed."

"Under what authority do you operate?" Peter repeated.

"Under the authority of the federal government of the United States" was the answer.

"You have no right to be here. I would kindly ask that you turn around and leave this city. We were perfectly fine before you came, and we don't want your protection," Peter yelled at none of the police officers in particular.

"I am warning you, sir," the megaphone produced.

"No, sir. I am warning *you*!" Peter yelled back.

Two riot policemen lowered their shields and extended their arms toward Peter. They each held a large spray can.

"Sir, remove from this quadrant or you will be removed. This is the last warning," the man behind the megaphone yelled.

Peter relaxed his arms and lowered his head. "Now let me show you something." Peter opened his suit jacket with his left hand and reached his right hand into the breast pocket. "I have something that might change your mind."

"Don't, Peter!" George yelled.

"He's got a gun!"

"Fire!"

"No!" a shrill voice screamed.

A single shot was fired from a federal agent's SIG-Sauer P225 handgun.

Without passage of time, Peter Westings was lying on his back, draining blood onto the street.

"Peter!" George yelled and ran to the victim. George looked over his friend's body, then up at the riot police officers.

Peter Westings was dead. His hand fell out of his jacket and brought with it a small, bloodstained book with a blue cover. The cover read, "The Constitution of the United States of America."

* * *

A faint cacophony of sirens and distant yelling filled the quiet void in Cate Heatherton's apartment as Com DeGroot held the fair woman's head in his hand.

"He's alive," Reggie Williams reported unenthusiastically to Com after checking the criminal's pulse. He had found duct tape and was taping the criminal's feet together.

Com did not respond as he attempted to cover Cate Heatherton with her torn dress. Reggie continued. "Okay, I'm going to get rid of this guy. You take care of her."

Com looked over to his security captain and nodded.

Reggie stood up and adjusted his belt before dragging the mound of flesh across the floor with one of the criminal's arms. When Reggie got to the door, he was blocked by Santiago Garza standing in the doorway.

Santiago crossed himself as he observed the activity.

"Santiago!" Com yelled. "You're a doctor, right? Cate needs help."

Santiago rushed past Reggie pulling the criminal, kneeled down to Cate, and began to check her vital signs. Reggie finished pulling the criminal out of Cate's apartment into the night.

"Can you find a first-aid kit?" Santiago looked at Com, who nodded and rushed to the kitchen. He found an elaborate first-aid kit under the kitchen sink and brought it back to Santiago.

"Excellent," Santiago said and opened the kit. Santiago cleaned and dressed a gash on the back of Cate's head, then cleaned the bruise on her cheek. Santiago then visually inspected the rest of Cate's body without displaying concern. "She will be fine. She has probably had a concussion, but will recover."

Com observed Santiago's survey. "Did that bastard do anything to her?" Com tilted his head to Cate's midsection.

"No. Gracias a Dios. It appears she was not violated."

Com sat back in relief, then shook his head in fury.

"Sí. Now can you. . . ." Santiago held out a gauze pad and a bottle of alcohol. "She will need to be washed, and we need to find her a bed."

"Should we take her to the hospital?" Com asked.

"They have closed St. Vincent's, mi amigo. The federales have closed the hospital and are directing people to the FEMA triage center in Raymondville. I do not recommend this." Santiago shook his head, but Com was too busy tending to Cate to notice.

* * *

"Despite efforts by the National Guard, rioting has spread in the beleaguered charter city of Ur, Texas," Michelle Torres reported on a late news segment while video clips of looters and rioters were shown. "Massive fires have engulfed entire city blocks, and dozens of square miles of residential and retail space have been ransacked by citizens of the controversial municipality. It is believed that the rioters were lashing out against the controlling corporate interests responsible for unfair labor practices and potentially hazardous environmental conditions. Rioters had numerous clashes with the National Guard today and other peace-keeping forces in recent hours."

Video showed young men with bandanas running toward a column of riot police and throwing rocks and other objects. The riot police wore helmets and carried black, body-length shields. Some shot rounds of tear gas toward the rioters while small fires shot up smoke from scattered combustibles throughout the street.

Michelle Torres continued her report. "Senator Duane D. Delano of Vermont held a press conference earlier this evening in response to the unrest."

A clip of the Senate Majority Leader standing in front of the Senate Press Gallery was shown. "This simply goes to show that the type of lawless environment in places like Ur is unsustainable. I've been saying it for months now. This type of lackadaisical, laissez-faire style of governance simply does not work, and recent problems down there are evidence of this. We need stricter control over the jurisdictions throughout this great land if we want to prevent tragedies like this.

"I will continue to do everything in my power to prevent catastrophic situations like this from arising in the future. But we must also call to account defenders of anarchy like the fugitive of justice Com DeGroot. So, tonight I am calling for that man, wherever he is, to come back and account for the injustices he has aided."

Michelle Torres returned to the screen. "At this hour, a national manhunt continues for Senator DeGroot. If you or anyone you know has any information regarding the whereabouts of Senator DeGroot, please contact your local law enforcement agency."

Fifty-Three

The first thing Cate noticed was a pounding headache. She heard talking, and her entire body was sore, but all she could concentrate on was the intense throbbing in her skull. She was wrapped in a warm comforter and laying sideways on her pillow-top bed. She slowly opened her eyes to faintly make out a well-dressed man moving toward her.

"Ah, she is awake. Now, then, just relax," the kind Venezuelan accent offered.

Cate scrunched her face.

Santiago continued. "You suffered a grade-three concussion, and you lost consciousness. You'll be fine. You just need to take it slow to fully recover, señorita."

Cate smiled and managed to gaze up to her friend. "Santiago."

"That's a good sign." Santiago grinned. "At least you remember my name. Do you know where you are?"

"I'm in my bed."

"Good, señorita Heatherton. Now, your body needs fluids, so please drink up." Santiago handed Cate a glass of water. She drank a sip then engulfed half the glass before smiling and handing it back to Santiago.

"What—what happened?" Cate asked hesitantly.

"Cate, you were physically assaulted," Santiago said regretfully.

She nodded into her pillow in remembrance.

"Assaulted?"

"Sí, there was an intruder here. We think he was one of the rioters. You're safe now though. It appears you have a guardian angel. He saved you before that animal could do anything to you."

"You, Santiago?" Cate said, relieved.

"No, no." Mr. Garza turned to his left, and Com DeGroot appeared in Cate's field of vision. "Señor DeGroot."

Cate looked longingly at Com and smiled. The tall figure walked over to Cate and maintained a serious statuesque façade.

"I am so sorry," Com said grimly.

Cate smiled but wrinkled her forehead at the memory of being attacked.

Com's face became stern. "I should have gotten here sooner."

"It's okay. I'll be okay." Cate nodded.

"Well," Santiago interrupted, "you should get your rest." He turned to leave Cate's bedroom, as did Com.

Cate put up her frail hand toward the two. "Com?"

"Yes?"

"Would you do a favor for me?" Cate asked softly.

"Anything," Com said reassuringly.

"Can you find some Tylenol for me?" She smiled and squinted her eyes through pain.

Com nodded and walked over to the nightstand a foot away from the bed. He handed her a small pill and the glass of water.

Cate gulped and gave the glass back to Com. "Thank you," she gasped.

Com stepped back toward the door.

"Com?"

He turned around again. "Yes?"

"Will you do another favor for me?"

Com nodded.

"Will you stay with me until I fall asleep?"

Com let a firm smile out. He looked to Santiago and nodded.

"I will be outside with señor Williams," Santiago informed the two. "Just yell if you need anything at all."

Com casually walked over to Cate's bed and sat down on the floor with his back against the nightstand. His head was on the same level as

Cate's, and she peered at him silently for a moment, then crackled, "Did you save my life, Com?"

The worn man's face turned toward Cate's and produced a warm smile. He turned his head back down to the floor, "I was going to kill him Cate. I didn't care."

Cate swallowed and gave Com a worried look, "Can we not talk about it?"

"Of course." Com shook his head, then gave Cate a comforting smile.

The two sat calmly in a comfortable silence for a moment.

Cate scratched an itch on her cheek by rubbing her face against her pillow, then looked at Com. "So, what are you going to do?"

Com was looking into space but turned to the prostrate woman. "I don't know, Cate. We've got to fight this. I just can't let those bastards do this to this city." Com thought about his, then shook his head in frustration. "But I can't go back to Washington—it's not what you think it is. There is no law there. Delano and Thurston own that place. They're in this collusion with the bankers. It's a conspiracy."

Cate wrinkled her forehead at Com's explanation but said nothing.

"I wanted to play by the rules to change things, but there are no rules. I wanted to work within the system to fix the problems, but the system turned out to be the problem. Now I wish there was something I could do, but I am absolutely powerless. I am nothing, and if I fight this, they will finish me off. I have no doubt about that."

"So leave."

"And give up? To Delano? No, thanks." Com shook his head and looked down.

Cate frowned. "That doesn't leave many options."

"No, it doesn't."

After a brief silence, Cate raised her head a few inches and opened her mouth. "I think I may know someone who will have a solution."

Com tilted his head back on the nightstand and looked at the ceiling. "Your fiancé?"

"If there's anyone in the world that can help us, it's Arun."

Com frowned and glanced at Cate's left hand tucked under her cheek. "Nice ring, by the way." His face belied the compliment.

Cate smiled and extended her hand to observe the two-carat gem. "Thank you."

Com huffed in disbelief. "Awesome." He looked at Cate. "Do you love him?"

Cate smiled. "Hey, weren't we talking about saving Ur?"

"Seriously. Do you?"

"Com, he is the most amazing person I have ever met. Powerful, yet generous. Hard-working and kind. And absolutely brilliant."

"You didn't answer the question. Do you love him?"

Cate looked down, then nodded at Com. "Yes."

Com turned his head away. After a short silence, Com told the wall opposite him, "I feel like I would do anything for you."

Cate frowned and focused on Com's eyes, which she could see were watering.

"I know I screwed up, Cate. I'm not. . . ."

"Yes?" was the soft reply.

"I did stuff, bad stuff—"

She shook her head, "Com, don't."

Com waved off Cate's concern. "No, it's okay. Look, do you think that this Kula guy can help us?"

Cate nodded silently into her pillow. "Yes. He should be returning sometime tonight. We can meet up with him tomorrow . . . if we're all still alive in the morning," she joked.

Com stood up and leaned in over Cate, who didn't move. He kissed her forehead and moved his face down to her bruised cheekbone. Her skin was soft as he pressed his lips down. He thought for a moment, and Cate was motionless.

"Good night," Com said as he stood up, walked out of Cate's room, and quietly closed the door.

In the living room, Reggie approached Com with a piece of paper in his hand.

"This was in that son of a bitch's pocket," Reggie reported. "He knew exactly where he was going."

Com looked at the piece of paper. It contained the address of Cate's apartment. Com grew furious as he looked at Reggie and Santiago, who returned his livid stare.

Fifty-Four

A warm, orange aura was breaking the dark in the still, predawn morning of a northern sector of the city of Ur, Texas. A huddled group of people ran briskly down a sidewalk lined up next to a two-story brick building. Santiago Garza held up his hand to hold up the group as he inched his head around the corner of the building to observe the street. The crowd stopped silently behind Santiago.

There was a riot policeman walking away from the group on the street. He was equipped with full body armor and a heavy semi-automatic weapon. The policeman slowly walked another fifteen feet and turned the corner up another street.

Santiago inched out into the street and, after a brief pause, waved everyone in the group across the street and down a natural embankment toward a row of wooden boat docks. Com DeGroot helped Cate Heatherton onto a thirty-five-foot motor yacht tied to the furthest dock, and Reggie Williams helped Santiago Garza unhitch the mooring lines from horned metal cleats. Reggie pushed off from the dock as Garza jumped onboard to start the motor. Reggie took a look at the sky and made out a storm cloud building to the southwest. He noticed the warm morning breeze blowing from the same direction.

Com scanned the street just above the embankment and spotted a man in a black suit standing one hundred feet away from the docks. He was smoking a cigarette and staring at the activity on the boat. Com squinted at the man and saw that he was pale and bald. He imagined seeing a tattoo on the man's forehead but doubted himself. He reached out his hand and pulled Santiago away from his launch preparation.

Santiago looked at the man and shook his head. "If he does not have an AK-forty-seven, he is of no concern to us."

The small motor yacht floated away from the docks in silence, and within minutes, the docks were a faint outline on the horizon. The ship's captain, Santiago, explained to his passengers that they had to motor out over twenty-four nautical miles. There, Arun Kula awaited them on his personal yacht in what was, for all intents and purposes, international water.

Santiago steered the boat in and out of islands and manmade channels through Laguna Madre, directly east of Ur, and finally through Packery Channel, which opened up to the Gulf of Mexico. By the time the boat was moving at thirty knots in the open water, dawn had broken over the water, but storm clouds had caught up to the watercraft and were spitting large pellets of rain onto the roof and decks.

Sixty minutes later, Santiago was coasting toward a massive white power yacht floating stationary in the open water. Its five levels seemed to stretch forever across the horizon. Several armed men walked along the decks, and a security watercraft floated just off the stern. On the bow, a small helicopter tender rested on a landing pad. Just below the helipad on the hull of the massive ship, a script font read "Ayn."

Santiago smoothly motored toward the stern, but Com, Cate, and Reggie all stared at the gigantic vessel with awe.

"Who *is* this guy?" Com asked.

After boarding, the guests were directed through a galley in which recessed lighting illuminated chrome walls and flooring. The guests walked up a flight of stairs to a similarly designed lounge. The room was stylishly cold with angular furniture. This place is ugly, Com thought to himself, but expensive.

The guests explored the lounge quietly until they heard voices approaching. Com bristled and turned in the direction of the voices. A short man with dark European skin led a taller East Indian gentleman through a tight passageway into the lounge. They were deep in conversation, but the thirty-five-year-old Indian man immediately spotted Cate Heatherton wrapped in a shawl, standing in the middle of the lounge.

"My dear, I am so terribly sorry for what happened." The Indian spoke with an Oxford-influenced accent as he walked across the lounge with his hands extended.

"Hello, Arun," Cate said, shaking her head to allow her hair to fall down naturally.

Arun Kula framed Cate's face with his hands and placed a light kiss on her cheek. "You must be exhausted." He brushed Cate's bruised cheek with the back of his soft fingers and frowned. "You poor creature."

"I'm feeling okay."

"I take it Santiago here has been taking care of you," Arun said, looking at the Venezuelan-American.

"Yes," Cate agreed, "along with my friend." She turned to Com and held out her hand. "Arun, this is Com DeGroot. Com, Arun Kula."

Com stepped toward Arun and held out his hand.

"Of course," Arun said, shaking Com's hand. "The fugitive senator. I've heard about you from the news wire."

"Is that right?" Com asked skeptically.

"You're a wanted man. An entire country is searching for you," Arun said in a straightforward manner.

"Are they?"

"Yes. They've declared you an enemy of the state." Kula produced a crisp yet subtle smile then continued. "That's quite all right. Any enemy of a corrupt slave state is a friend of mine."

"We need your help, sir," Com said flatly.

"Of course. Let the us convene in the conference room." Arun turned to walk toward the proposed destination, then saw Cate begin to follow. "My dear," Kula said to Cate and then to Santiago and Reggie as well, "make yourselves at home. Armando here will help you with anything you may need."

Cate looked down in disappointment, which Com noticed. He gave Cate a nod, put his hand to her arm, then followed Kula out of the room.

* * *

"So, how is it that I can help you, sir?" Arun asked as he stirred sugar into a cup of tea. He was seated at the end of a cold gray conference table in a stark room with brushed chrome walls found elsewhere throughout the modern ship's interior.

Com was standing at the window looking at the whitecaps caused by heavy winds. A smattering of rain hit the window periodically. He turned around to Arun Kula. "We're in a real fix here."

"Yes."

"Well, you're a pretty cosmopolitan guy. You probably know what's going on in the federal government. These bankers and legislators are all working together to control the whole thing. They are the ones that planned the whole takeover of Ur. And it's all legal evidently. I beat Delano's bill, but these guys are so entrenched, the language for that bill was in a hundred other bills. Now they can legally take whatever land, property, or whatever they want in Ur for whatever reason. They can trace and restrict any form of communication. And they can criminalize any person that acts against them."

Arun sat still and listened.

"Anyway, I want to fight them. I want to save your city. I want to save my country. But I'm completely worthless. I have no power to do anything in this situation. I have no money, no connections, and dozens of federal agents are trying to hunt me down. I come to you with complete humility to ask for your help. You're the only person in the world that has enough power to stop these people. I need your help. American needs your help."

Arun Kula nodded subtly then spoke. "What should you have me do?"

"I don't know. Pay off the legislators? Use your security forces to defend your city? Hire mercenaries to invade D.C.? I don't know. Something!" Com's voice elevated.

"And what good would that do?" Arun inquired.

"Maybe it would save your city and cause such a controversy that people know it's worth fighting for? I mean, aren't you the least bit concerned about your city being destroyed?"

Arun Kula looked at Com firmly. "I am not. The city of Ur was nothing more than an experiment. An experiment which happened to fail. It was an investment, yes, but it was a poor investment."

"So you're not going to do anything about the federal takeover?"

"I should expect not."

"Mr. Kula, with all due respect, you can't do this. You can't just wipe your hands clean and leave the country. Ur was a model for the rest of the country. If we can save Ur, we can save the country."

Kula faced Com stoically. "I'm not sure that I can help you, sir."

"Or you *won't* help me?" Com wondered aloud.

"Sir, there would be no benefit to me if I were to fight the bureaucratic juggernaut of the federal government."

Com shook his head. "No benefit? Well, can you at least help me? Please, Mr. Kula, I am at my wit's end. I don't know what to do. I want to fight these bastards, but they're just too strong. It's beyond me. I need help. Please, Mr. Kula, help me out and I will help you out. I'll do anything."

"Anything?" Arun said with a raised eyebrow.

"Yes, anything," Com confirmed. "Just help me take these bastards down."

Arun sipped from his teacup and replaced it on a coaster in front of him. Com had seated himself opposite Arun at the conference table and was leaning into the polished aristocrat.

"All right, I'll help you," Arun Kula said as he looked into Com's eyes. Com gave the man a smile of gratitude. "I will help you depose the power structure in place right now. And I will even help you keep your position as senator, and your antagonists will be rendered impotent."

"Okay." Com's voice indicated he expected a catch. "And?"

Kula ignored the question. "I can do all of that. If I help shut down the current political system and help position you into that power structure, I should require that you become an agent of mine and work solely for me within that structure. I should need to ask favors of you."

"Name it."

"Would you be willing to promote legislation and earmarks that directly benefit my companies worldwide?"

"Absolutely."

"If required, would you be willing to introduce legislation that inhibits competition to my companies?"

"Not a problem." Com pushed his bottom lip up.

"And if I help you, you may be required to do tasks of a more clandestine nature."

"Okay," Com said hesitatingly.

"Are you prepared to acquire certain confidential information and intelligence from other legislators if the opportunity arises?"

Com nodded. "Sure."

"Additionally, you may also be required to assist in the termination of certain legislators."

"What do you mean—termination?" Com lowered his eyebrow.

"Assassinate. Are you prepared to assist in the assassination of certain legislators?"

"Are you serious?" Com scrunched his face.

"Good sir, we live in a state of grave existence. Many believe that extreme situations like we have call for extreme measures."

Com breathed in heavily as his pulse began to quicken. "Are we talking about Delano or Thurston?"

"Perhaps," Arun Kula replied.

Com shook his head. "I don't know."

"I assure you, sir, it would be nothing of a gory nature. Most assassinations nowadays are done by poisoning."

"Oh, that's nice to know." Com nodded.

"Well? I require an answer," Kula persisted.

"We're at war, right?" Com shook his head. "I suppose I could do something like that if it was absolutely necessary."

"Good," Kula said coldly. "Finally, would you be willing to provide false information to your constituents for their own good?"

"Shit, what's that compared to knocking off a senator?" Com laughed.

"Sir?" Kula was not laughing.

Com looked at the table and shook his head. "Yeah, I guess I can do that." Com reflected on the situation for a moment. "Just . . . can you do something about this? Can you help us out?"

"Unfortunately, sir, it appears that I cannot."

Com flinched. "What? What do you mean? I told you I would do whatever you want me to."

"Sir, if you are willing to lie, cheat, steal, and even kill in order to escape your desperate status, why on Earth should I consider working with you or helping you out?"

Com leaned back in his chair and pursed his lips while staring at the calm Arun Kula. He had been trapped, and he knew it.

Kula continued. "Sir, I operate under the strict principle that there are no necessary evils. In order to do good, one is not required to do evil, no matter how insignificant the evil may seem. I positively believe this with all of my being, and I live by it absolutely. What you agreed to just now is evil, plain and simple. Granted, you may rightly think that the lying, cheating, and murder would be for a good cause, namely to save your country and to provide you with personal security. But that doesn't change the fact that such behavior is nonetheless evil. It is the type of behavior that I expend all of my energy fighting and exactly the behavior you are attempting to overcome in the federal government—the corruption, the threats, the vice. The assumption that necessary evils exist is what got your country into this corrupt mess of national fascism in the first place. I simply cannot promote more of it by endorsing you, a man who still seems confused about what you are fighting for."

"I'm fighting for my country—for America," Com defended himself.

"Yes, but what does America stand for? Does it stand for freedom and production, creativity and charity? Or does it stand for authority, corruption, and abuse of power? Lying to save your hide? Cheating for principles? Killing to save lives? I would say that America used to stand for all that was good in the world, but now it stands for all of those nasty ideas. America as we remember it and love it is gone. It has been replaced by an insatiably menacing bureaucracy—the United States federal government. I will not fight to keep that beastly juggernaut alive. On the contrary, it is tragic but correct to say that the United States must die for America to live."

Com's eyes widened at the thought. "What are you saying?"

"The truth," Kula said coolly.

"I don't buy it, Mr. Kula."

Kula turned his eyes down, then spoke. "Sir, how do you fancy your history?"

"I don't really."

"That is a shame, sir. I will attempt to enlighten you, then." Kula sipped from his tea and began. "Ever since the first humans learned they could get others to do something by threat of force, fascism has been a force in life. The original coercive powers were the largest, most powerful males of primitive tribes throughout the world, then specific tribes themselves, then entire races or classes. For the majority of history, various small groups of people have controlled entire populations with the threat of force or death. Leaders of those groups were called different names throughout history: a chieftain, a king, a czar, or a führer. But, regardless of the nomenclature, all of these people had one thing in common, absolute control over their population.

"An alternative concept to this coercive power was born in Ancient Greece, however, and got its legs, as it were, in the philosophy of the Enlightenment, which spawned its first-born child, the United States of America, the greatest experiment in the history of the world. The hypothesis? A people left to rule themselves will be the most prosperous on Earth.

"For a while, the experiment was a smashing success. Most of the population lived in a productive, self-governing manner for one hundred and forty years, despite some glaring initial flaws such as African slavery and incomplete suffrage. But the coercive powers would not just let well enough alone. They challenged the liberal ideas of the Founders throughout the history of the country, albeit with little success, until the early twentieth century when, ironically, the autarchical ideal of America was finally being realized by every American. In the fateful year of 1913, Congress ratified the Sixteenth Amendment to the Constitution, which granted the federal government the authority to tax income, and Congress passed the Federal Reserve Act, which put into place a central bank with unprecedented power to control the economy."

Rain smacked the window to the ship's conference room in sheets. Com looked behind him to see beads of water covering the Plexiglas pane.

The Indian man continued in his proper British accent. "The coercive powers in America were clever as well. Whereas similar leaders in Europe and Asia were overt about their displays of power, using bright red armbands, American fascists preferred to infuse their red into more fashionable accessories such as neckties. And their policies were more covert as well. They knew that the American public was not going to accept a heavy-handed coercive power dictating their lives. So they started a diabolical campaign. Sir, can you imagine how the coercive powers in America managed to introduce ever-increasing taxation and control over a decidedly liberty-minded population?"

Arun Kula looked for an answer from Com but received a shrug instead. "I don't know. Enlighten me."

"The coercive powers introduced their brand of fascism by making the people *want* it. They seized crisis after crisis in order to scare people into welcoming the controlling security of the federal government, and they did so in every aspect of life: financial markets, welfare, housing, healthcare, and every other realm that the government has invaded since 1913. In each instance, the daft governmental programs—some good-natured, others not—led to massive unintended problems and hardship. The resulting crises inevitably led to the citizenry asking for a more controlling government and, consequently, less individual freedom.

"Case in point is the Great Depression. Most independent economists point to the Federal Reserve's inflation of the U.S. dollar during the 1920s and the lack of subsequent deflation as one of the central causes of the stock market crash of 1929, which contributed to the Great Depression. No doubt this flaw in economic logic was not intentional, but it was government action that created the problem, and those in power seized the opportunity of the crisis to expand the size and breadth of government even more, this time in an unprecedented manner.

"Likewise, government programs designed to eliminate poverty through direct assistance to the poor only encouraged abuse of the system and exacerbated the problem. Programs developed to increase homeownership simply drove up the cost of housing, making it more difficult to own a home—that was until the housing bubble burst and caused a tsunami throughout the economy.

"Similarities can be seen in the healthcare system, in which government forced insurance companies to provide coverage for everyone despite their need. These mandates, accompanied with restrictions on competition between health insurance companies and removal of individual choice throughout the system, drove up the costs of health care in the United States to outrageous levels, forcing some people to lose their coverage altogether. Government intervention simply does not work. As history has clearly shown us time and time again, government has forced good intentions on the people, which have continually led to unintended negative results. It is shocking, but people haven't realized the point that making universal prosperity a right is the surest way to universal poverty.

"When crises like financial depressions, widespread poverty, or runaway costs shock the system, the people start to panic. And who is always there to fix the problems? Why it is government, of course—the same organization that caused the problems. What's more is that they offer the same irrational solutions in order to fix the problems that produced the problems in the first place. Out of the frying pan and into the fire. The result is an endless spiral of government intrusion into the daily lives of individuals and the exact opposite of what the government intrusion was intended to solve. Only in government can an organization completely and utterly fail at what they were tasked to do and then get a raise.

"And if an intrusive, controlling program isn't universally accepted to fix a problem, the coercive powers pit Republican versus Democrat, Left versus Right in fabricated political theater in order to convince the people that what the government is doing is legitimate. Sure, on the whole, Democrats stand for some good—namely, protection of civil liberties— and Republicans stand for some good—namely, economic freedom—but when these two forces combine, the result is a dirty compromise that reduces liberty on both fronts. It has been seen consistently throughout history that fiscal conservatives go mute when a Republican spends the country into unprecedented debt, and civil libertarian Democrats turn a blind eye when a Democrat is in the White House. This double standard is ubiquitous. Republicans were vehemently against healthcare reform when the Democrats were pushing it, but they shrugged their shoulders at an unprecedented prescription drug bill that Republican leaders passed. Democrats were vehemently anti-war when it was Bush's war, but didn't mind when it became Obama's war. Leaders in both political parties want to wrap people up in tribal furor on either side of the political divide to obscure the real question of whether or not it is just for any of their coercion to take place at all.

"They fight the opposition in order to get a bigger slice of the pie, but are ignorant of the arsenic strewn throughout that pie. A brilliant French historian on tour in America in the nineteenth century—Alexis de Tocqueville—wrote, '*Democracy will fail* when *people realize* they can vote themselves money from the public purse.' Well, the people have sussed out that they can vote themselves money from the public purse all right, but they have failed to realize that handcuffs come with that bribe. Sure, the handcuffs allow thirty-percent mobility, but seventy-percent slavery is still slavery.

"It is all very disturbing, but the single most ghastly aspect of this history is that the people are asking for the fascism *themselves.* I maintain that nothing is more tragic than a population volunteering itself into slavery. And that's exactly what your country is becoming, sir, a land of slaves. Those who operate under the dictate of a central power without any autonomy are slaves, pure and simple.

"And all the while, the architects of this modern thralldom sit perched on their hill, dictating to the masses. Their lust for power over others can only be quenched at the end of gun. Oh, yes, they have their power now. They are giants. They are gods." Arun Kula nodded. "But their kingdom is nothing more than an ant heap of totalitarianism where one party gains only at the expense of the other, where justice is a quaint concept and where crime has become the law. They have produced an interdependent population in which no one can live together. They have created an unsustainable land of contradiction. These architects are gods, all right—they are gods of ruin.

"It all comes down to one question. Is it acceptable to force someone or a group of people to do something against their will, whether it is for their own good or even for the common good? I believe it is not acceptable to force someone against their will. Some will disagree, but we must be honest about who these people are. They are not governors or senators or presidents, they are slavers. And the majority of the people within their jurisdiction who submit to their will are slaves.

"The rub is, the slavers are nothing without their slaves. They depend upon the slaves for everything—their luxuries, their wealth, and their power—and would crumble without them. All it would take to overcome is for the slaves to realize their plight and to simply reject it—to deny the slavers their control. When enough people realize that they are slaves but don't have to be, revolutions happen. But either the slaves in America are too blissfully ignorant of their condition or they are too afraid of taking responsibility for themselves that they do not act.

"Ur was the last hope for America. It was the lone opportunity to allow people to opt out of the juggernaut of the federal government. We wanted to create a place where residents could say no to irrational government spending and regulation and stop paying into a corrupt imperial leviathan, and so thousands of productive people from all over the world came to participate and contribute to the greatest city on Earth. But of course the United States government couldn't stand to have such competition. They wouldn't allow people to opt out of their non sequitur policies because, without the productive people to fuel them, the leeches—the moochers—were faced with collapse. So they did everything they could to capture the creativity and wealth that Ur represented, first legally, then by whatever illegal means they could think of. And now that the juggernaut has succeeded in engulfing Ur, there is very little likelihood that another charter city will arise in a similar manner.

"This is why I have already initiated development with The Green Group on a fully sovereign, floating city-state completely outside of the jurisdiction of any world government. Hundreds of the world's brightest and most motivated will join me. Unfortunately, I cannot help everyone. The rest of the mindless horde throughout the world will be left to wallow in this lawless, self-destructive cavity that they have allowed to grow.

"Eventually, there will come a time when these gods of ruin have coerced the last ounce of production out of the mindless horde, their empire will teeter on the brink of implosion, and they will turn to us, the producers. When we reject their pleas for assistance, they will do what any other scoundrel race does. They will fight, cheat, and kill to survive. They will go to war with each other and everything else in a clash between gods." Kula sipped his tea. "Wagner wrote a moving epic about such a clash, which was modeled after the Norse myth Ragnarök. In the myth, natural disasters plague the world, the entire planet is flooded, and several prominent gods meet their fate. My friend, we will have our götterdämmerung soon enough."

"And in the meantime you're going to run off to your floating paradise and everyone else will be trapped under the thumb of those bureaucratic bastards."

"Yes." Kula nodded.

"And you don't care?"

"Sir, the people to whom you refer have done this thing to themselves. They have created their own state of enslavement and have done nothing to escape. It is a lost cause."

Com breathed in heavily and exhaled. "Kula, you're making me want to jump off your boat and drown myself in the fucking Gulf of Mexico. What's the point of telling me all of this if I can't do anything about it? What's the point if you're not going to help me?"

Kula thought for a moment as he peered at Com. "Well, sir, there may be a solution after all. Ur has lost in the court of law or whatever is left of it in the United States. But I believe that Ur still has a chance in the court of public opinion. If the general public were to see this situation for what it is—if they were to see beyond the media smoke screen and the endless propaganda from the political elites about Ur, there is a chance that they would call off the dogs and force the federal government to leave Ur. The power structure could not stand against such a large population. But for the people to stand up for Ur, they would need to understand that Ur represents the Founder's America and that the current federal government is nothing more than a mass slaver. They should need to forsake the benefits they receive from the government in exchange for liberty. They should need to see liberty as the best way—nay, the only way—to achieve lasting prosperity. They should need to stop identifying themselves as Republican or Democrat and start identifying themselves as American. And they should have to see their government for the corrupt, bipartisan regime that it is. It is not a two-party system you have here in the United States; it is a unified beast designed to keep the power where it is."

"But how do you teach an entire population all of that?"

"Well, sir, there may be something you specifically can do to convey this message. Would you care to know my thoughts?"

Com nodded begrudgingly.

"At this moment, a sizeable portion of the American population is wondering one thing: where is the rogue senator Com DeGroot? That question is on the news, in the tabloids, and on the lips of most socially aware people."

"And?"

"What does that mean to you?"

"Uh, it means that those people don't have lives."

Arun Kula missed Com's humor. "Perhaps, but, let me just say this. The citizens of America are, broadly speaking, the most creative, intelligent, and productive population in the world. The general populace also vastly outnumbers the elitist government bureaucrats. If they were to say enough is enough, then there would be no stopping them. It just so happens that they are also asleep to the tyranny raining down on them. But you, sir, have their attention. I recommend that you capitalize on that attention." Kula paused to let his next statement sink in to Com. "I recommend that you wake them up."

"Wake them up?"

"Ring the bell, sir. Sound the trumpet. Wake them up. If anyone is capable of revealing the state of affairs as they truly are to the masses right now, it is you. Someone from whom everyone is eager to hear and who has experienced the federal government firsthand—someone who has looked the devil in the face and lived to tell about it."

Com smiled at the thought of having an entire country listen to him, then looked down in disappointment. "But I can't talk to the people," he whined. "I can only get to the people through the media, and like you said, Delano and them control the media. That's why I've never been able to get my message out."

Arun Kula nodded. "Yes, it's true." He paused. "But I think you are clever enough to figure out a way to get your message out."

Com faked a smile. "Thanks."

"I can have you flown to Houston in my helicopter this afternoon. From there, all I can do is wish you luck."

Fifty-five

Com DeGroot sat in a passageway leading to the bow of the ship and the helicopter pad. He bit the thumb of his right hand and stared at the ground. How? he thought. "How am I going to do this?"

"Do what?" The soft voice of Cate Heatherton startled Com as she appeared in the doorway at the end of the passage.

He flinched and watched her walk toward him through the passageway. "How am I going to wake up the people? If I could somehow show everyone what is really going on in their government, they would force the feds out of Ur. And if Ur survives, there's hope for the country. At least that's what Kula thinks." Com returned to his pensive pose, and Cate sat down next to him.

"Right."

"He said that I had an opportunity to wake up the people—make them aware of what they've been sucked into—but I can't. The media won't listen to me, and once I get back to D.C., they're going to throw me in jail. I'm useless."

"You don't know that for sure, Com. Everything will be all right." She looked at him hopefully. "I have confidence in you. You'll figure something out."

Com raised his eyebrows in mocking protest. "He's not going to help though—your boyfriend. He's running off to some boat in the South Pacific."

"Com, he did everything he could, and he had more at stake than anyone. You saw Ur. He put everything into that city, and now it's all but obliterated."

"I know, so why doesn't he stay and fight?"

Gods of Ruin

"He believes that the best course of action is to get out and let the corrupt system implode on itself."

Com nodded while looking at the ground. "Yeah. So what are *you* going to do?"

Cate smiled. "Well, I'm going to the South Pacific. I can't imagine a more perfect situation."

Com frowned, then looked up to see a newcomer turn into the passageway. It was Reggie Williams.

"You ready to do this, sir?" Reggie asked.

"I guess."

"Mr. Kula said he would have a car waiting for us in Houston. I'll be driving you back to D.C. from there."

"And somewhere in between, I'm going to come up with a brilliant plan to take down the evil empire and set this country straight."

"There's always a chance for a miracle, sir," Reggie confirmed.

A man in a beige flight suit ran to the door from the windy deck and pulled it open. A warm gust blew misty rain into the passageway, and Com and Cate stood up. Reggie walked through the door and out onto the deck.

Com embraced Cate as the flight crewman held open the door. "I hate leaving you."

Cate smiled and put her head down on the tall man's shoulder.

Com broke the embrace and walked through the door and onto the helicopter tender. The rotor was already moving and kicking up wind around the helipad. The pilot made his final onboard maintenance checks and accelerated the rotor.

Com looked out the window of the helicopter and noticed Arun Kula walking toward the vehicle, so Com opened the door.

Arun handed Com a small black phone and yelled over the noise of the engines. "You can use this phone. It's untraceable. It's encoded so that the NSA won't understand anything you are sending or receiving. There will be a car for you in Houston. I wish you luck." Com nodded, and Arun

Com looked at his driver briefly. "It's the Russian." Com turned his head back to the Mercedes, but it was gone. Com flinched and looked to the highway behind them—all around. No cars could be seen.

"What the hell?" Com breathed. Com searched for the car he was absolutely sure he had just seen, but to no avail.

"Sir?"

Com's face became flush. "Uh, never mind, Reg. I think I'm flippin' out over here."

Reggie lifted his foot off the gas and the car slowed to a reasonable highway speed.

* * *

"What? Are you crazy? You're coming back here?" Kevin Donovan screamed through Com's phone. "Man, why aren't you on a beach in some exotic country with two women on each arm? I thought you'd be long gone by now!"

Com was seated on a reclining doctor's chair. "I *was* long gone until my employer," Com cleared his throat, "my employer came down and completely destroyed my little hideaway."

"Right. You're talking about Ur?" Kevin was eager.

"Yeah."

"Com, where are you?"

"We're about a half hour outside D.C. Look, Kevin, I need you to do something for me."

"Sure."

"I need you to get Maria and call the press—call everyone. I want the media there as witnesses."

"Media where, Com? What are you talking about?"

"The Turf Club. Have them meet me there at five. I need to take care of something right now, but I want the media at the Turf Club at five."

"Tonight? What's going on?" Kevin asked impatiently.

Com smiled to himself. "I'm going to pick a fight." The senator ended his call with Kevin without another word and navigated to another number on the phone, then put the device to his ear.

"Senator Duane D. Delano's office, this is Terry," the office assistant answered his phone.

"Well, hello there, Terry. This is Com D. DeGroot," Com replied in a patronizing tone.

In Senator Delano's front office, Terry jumped in his seat and waved at a NSA analyst who was in his office. The federal agent typed into his laptop computer, which was connected through an Ethernet cable to the secured phone of Delano's front office. The federal agent watched as a graphic display on the computer's monitor indicated an analysis of the telephone call.

"Oh, hello, Mr. DeGroot!" Terry tried unsuccessfully to contain his excitement. "How can I help you?"

"Can you patch me into your boss there, Terry?"

"One moment please," Terry said and placed the call on hold. He looked at the NSA agent, who shook his head. The software program on the agent's computer had been unable to trace the location of Com's call. Terry asked, "Can I redirect him to the senator?"

The federal agent nodded in the affirmative, so Terry buzzed Duane D. Delano, who was in his office next door. "Senator, it's DeGroot on one."

Delano picked up the phone immediately and selected line one on the base of his phone.

"Well, if it isn't our big dumb fugitive lawmaker," Delano lisped condescendingly.

"Shut the hell up, asshole," Com barked. "I'm going to come in and give myself up. But I want a word with you and Thurston first. You might as well bring Hank Pierpont, too. You think you can arrange that, you corrupt sack of shit?"

"Well, why on Earth would you want to meet with me and Senator Thurston and Hank Pierpont, of all people?"

"I want to set the record straight between us—mano a mano . . . a mano a mano. And no funny business. I don't want any cops or security there. You man enough for that, asswipe?"

Delano was silent for a moment while he thought about Com's proposition. The federal intelligence agent who had been stationed at the laptop in Delano's front office leaned through the doorframe with his hands up, shaking his head. He made a circle with his left hand and mouthed the word 'stall.' Delano slowly started speaking into his phone. "Okay . . . you can have your little powwow with us. Shall I schedule something for you next week some time?"

"Five o'clock tonight. Turf Club." Com abruptly pulled the phone away from his ear and ended the call.

Com leaned back in the doctor's chair and gave the ceiling of the white office a determined stare. "Okay, I'm ready."

The middle-aged, graying doctor was resting on a nearby table but stood erect at Com's direction. He selected a scalpel from the instrument table and turned toward the patient. "Now you will need to be very still. Patients are usually under anesthesia during this procedure."

Com did not reply but closed his eyes.

Fifty-Six

Com DeGroot peered at the entrance to the Turf Club through sunglasses and a windshield. He sat in the passenger seat of the car Arun Kula had lent him and was speaking on the phone with his chief of staff, Kevin Donovan. Reggie Williams sat in the driver's seat and rested his forehead on his fist in a display of exhaustion.

"No, I'm about half a mile down from you. I see the entrance now. There are a bunch of people standing outside, and it looks like they have cameras. I just want you to confirm that Delano and Thurston are down there."

Kevin responded. "Yes, I've been here all afternoon. I saw them go in a half hour ago. But Com, they're not letting anyone else in."

"That's fine. I just want to make sure Delano and Thurston are down there."

"Oh, they're down there, all right," Kevin confirmed.

Com ended the call and looked at Reggie, who looked back with cracked open, puffy eyes.

"You need me to do anything?" Reggie wondered.

"Nope. This I have to do on my own."

Reggie nodded and bobbed his head. "Good, because I don't think the caffeine is working."

Com smiled and looked up the street again for a minute, trying to make out the situation. Com's phone beeped, and he glanced down at it. A message came in from Justin Timeus: Ready.

"All right, I'm going in," Com said with a tilt of his head. He looked over to Reggie, who had leaned his head back and let sleep overcome him. Com smiled, then opened his car door and stood up on the nearby sidewalk. The tall figure quietly closed his car door and walked toward the crowd of people two city blocks down the street. A shot of adrenaline burst through his body from his gut, and his breathing picked up.

Abruptly, Com was tackled by two bulky men in suits and projected into an alleyway off the street.

"What the fuck?" Com let out as he hit the ground of the grimy alley. The two men towered over Com as the victim surveyed his attackers. The one on the right was a thick Samoan-looking gentleman who wore a wicked grin. The one on the left was a thicker, fair-skinned Russian gentleman. Com noticed a half-done tattoo of barbed wire on the Russian's forehead. "Oh, shit. . . ."

The two abductors collapsed on Com and shoved him through the alley into a pile of cardboard boxes and next to a large, dilapidated dumpster. There was no exit to the alleyway besides the way they had come in.

Com regained his balance and stood up as the criminals slowed their pace toward their victim. "Talk about to-your-door service," Com said with a smile as he attempted to climb into the nearby dumpster. "You guys are great. This is exactly where I had wanted to get dropped off."

The Samoan reached for Com and threw him back onto the pavement. "Cut the shit, funny guy. You're about to have an accident."

"What are you, Miss Cleo? You gonna read my palm and tell my future?" Com quipped as he stood back up.

The Samoan looked at the Russian and nodded toward Com. The Russian stepped toward Com and slugged him in the stomach. There was nothing Com could do but buckle down in agony. He couldn't breathe and vomited a small amount of bile. His head was spinning, and he looked around on the ground for something to use as a weapon.

"Do you know who I am?" he asked while staring at the polluted ground. "I'm a U.S. senator."

"We know exactly who you are, Senator. That's why we're here." The Samoan leaned down over Com, who was on all fours. He spotted a piece of broken bottle nearby and secured it in his hand. The Samoan whispered in his ear, "And there's nothing you can do about it."

Com jumped up and punched the broken glass into the Samoan's face, causing the man's cheek to split and spew blood. The Russian stepped over and grabbed Com's hand with the glass. Com retaliated by swinging his other hand toward the Russian, but two fingers got caught in the Russian's suit sleeve and twisted out of their socket. Com blurted something out in terror. The Samoan regained his presence and immediately lunged at Com, landing the entire eight hundred pounds of pressure from a fist blow squarely on Com's cheek. Com felt as if he had been knocked off the ground and thrown back to Earth in a violent collision.

The tall man lay stationary on the wet, grungy alleyway, and the Samoan crept over him, dripping blood from his cheek. "Now where were we? Oh, yes. You were about to have an accident."

"Oh, boy," Com mocked, barely audible. "I've always wanted one of those."

Com breathed in, trying to muster the energy to defend himself from the brooding figure above him, when the mass of a man was suddenly ejected from Com's periphery. Still lightheaded from the blow Com took to his head, he rolled over to see that Reggie Williams had tackled the Samoan and struck him on his neck, rendering him unconscious.

The Russian pulled out a revolver and took aim at Com's security captain. Com DeGroot lunged at the Russian's hand and deflected the gun toward the brick wall that lined the alley. The pistol went off, and a round ricocheted off a metal pipe with a crack.

The Russian struggled to pull the gun free of Com's grasp but was unsuccessful. Reggie regained his footing and struck quickly on the Russian's forearm, causing his grip to falter. The gun dropped to the alley floor, and Reggie kicked it to the side but received a stunning blow to the head from the Russian. Com retaliated by swinging his arm at the Russian's head. His elbow knocked into the Russian's forehead, causing the Russian to smile at Com and grab him by his suit collar. The Russian threw Com to the ground and prepared as a retaliating Reggie stepped toward him.

Reggie crouched into a fighter's stance and danced around the Russian. The pale Russian stood calmly then, after assessing the situation briefly, threw his arms out and plowed his entire body into Reggie. Reggie turned around and attempted a bunkai escape from his attacker but failed. The Russian suffocated Reggie with a grip on his throat and smashed him into the steel trash bin just behind the defendant.

Reggie couldn't breath. He tried swinging his arms and kneeing his opponent but could muster no clean blows. The Russian opened his mouth and bit into Reggie's cheekbone, resulting in a loud scream from the victim.

"Enough!" Com yelled.

The Russian slowly turned to the tall man on his left. Com was holding the pistol and directing it at the massive Russian.

The Russian grinned and turned back to the pinned Reggie. He threw his head into Reggie's nose bridge, which exploded with red fluid. The Russian then pulled his right arm back and slugged Reggie in the stomach.

Com gritted his teeth and scrunched his face, then pulled the trigger of the pistol. The round found the Russian's right shoulder and expelled flesh and blood from the recipient, but the Russian was not fazed. He turned toward Com and let a demolished Reggie collapse to the ground.

Com stepped toward the Russian and aimed the gun at the Russian's midsection. He fired, and the bullet landed directly in the middle of the Russian's chest. The bulky man took a step back but did not falter. There was no blood, and it appeared that the Russian wore a bulletproof vest. Com fired again and again. The Russian took the hits and staggered. He swung his fist in a drunken manner at the air in front of him, then fell to the ground.

Reggie stepped up behind the Russian and slammed a fist into the corner of the Russian's neck, shocking his nervous system. The Russian fell backwards, unconscious.

Reggie limped around the Russian and held his hand out for Com to give him the gun. "Go!" Reggie yelled. "I'll take care of them."

Com handed the gun to Reggie and staggered away from the bloody scene.

Fifty-Seven

Com DeGroot tried to swallow, but his mouth was too parched as he looked up at the crowd in front of him. He licked his bleeding lip instead. Twenty feet away from the door, the crowd realized who the ragged newcomer was and turned toward Com with a flurry of questions and camera flashes. Com was silent, moving through the crowd of journalists until he was standing in front of the door to the Turf Club. He spotted Kevin Donovan and nodded.

"What the hell happened to you?" Kevin was able to project above the cacophony of questions from the crowd of journalists.

"I almost just had an accident," Com mocked. His cheek was flushed with a bruise, and the fingers on his left hand dangled in impotence. The rest of his body shook with the effects of adrenaline as he turned toward the journalists.

"What do you mean? What's the plan, Com? What are you going to do?" Kevin asked eagerly.

Com smiled at his chief. "I'm going to do nothing."

"What?" Kevin was confused.

"You heard me."

"Can you account for your disappearance the last three days?" a journalist was able to yell.

"Ladies and gentlemen of the press, I just got my ass kicked," Com started as some of the journalists gasped. "Someone wanted very badly to prevent me from getting here. In fact, many people have tried very hard to prevent much of what I've done since becoming a U.S. senator. It is my hope that I can reveal exactly who those people are to you today."

All eyes and cameras were focused on the disheveled senator as he continued. "I invited you here to report on the most important story of our generation. You are about to witness the true state of American government—a small group of elite bankers and politicians in collusion to control the entire economy of the United States and even the world."

Com pointed to the wooden entrance to his left. "Behind that door is the cause of every major catastrophe in this country right now. It's the cause of the banking collapse, the healthcare crisis, and, of course, the siege of Ur, Texas." Com reached for the handle on the door and opened it while still looking at the group of journalists. They directed their video cameras toward the tall senator.

Com slowly opened the door, and the scene exploded into action. Two U.S. marshals burst through the door and secured Com. A police van screeched around the corner and stopped just in front of the gathering. Six additional officers launched out of the van and surrounded the area. The journalists started reporting the incidents into their microphones or cameras.

"Com DeGroot, you are under arrest on suspicion of resisting arrest, assaulting an officer of the peace . . . " one of the U.S. marshals said as others knocked Com to the ground and began frisking him. One agent produced Com's cell phone and handed it to another agent. The marshal secured Com's hands behind his back. "You have the right to remain silent. Anything you say can and will be used against you in a court of law. . . ." Com's face was pushed against the concrete, crushing his cheekbone. Metal restraints were applied to Com's wrists and ankles.

"Get the hell off!" Kevin Donovan yelled in helpless frustration as he watched the scene unfold in front of him.

As one U.S. marshal read Com's Miranda rights, another leaned in to Com's head and whispered, "We got you now, asshole."

Assistant Director of the U.S. Marshals Bobby Mariotti walked out of the dark Turf Club hallway and into the dusk light. Some of the reporters directed their attention to the aged bureaucrat dressed in a finely-pressed, blue suit, and others kept their focus on the silent, fuming Com DeGroot.

"Ladies and gentleman," Mariotti proclaimed, "it is a pleasure to announce the arrest of the fugitive, Mr. DeGroot. In a coordinated effort with District and federal law enforcement agencies, we were able to lure in the man wanted on several federal criminal charges."

The marshals pulled Com up on his feet and walked him to the police van on the street. Com stepped into the van and muttered, "It's like déjà vu all over again."

"We will be making an official statement shortly," Mariotti announced to the journalists.

The police van, along with its unwitting passenger, sped away from the group standing outside of the Turf Club. After a sharp right turn, the driver took another right into the alley behind the Turf Club building. Com DeGroot had his head resting on the van window but noticed the unexpected turns.

"We going back to the Turf Club, chief?" Com asked his neighboring marshal.

"Shut the fuck up," the marshal replied. He opened the van door and exited the vehicle, waving the prisoner to move out as well. Com lowered his head and groaned, then moved along the van's bench, using his cuffed hands as leverage. Once out of the van, two marshals secured the senator and opened a gray metal door, which led into the brick building to the right of the van.

Inside, the marshals directed Com down a flight of stairs and into the Turf Club. The place was familiar to Com, but now the lights were up, there was no live music, and no pretty cocktail waitresses. Com expected the marshals to bring him to a booth where Duane D. Delano and Roger Thurston were sitting, but instead they brought him to a side room. The room was empty except for one chair in the middle of the bare concrete floor.

One marshal sat Com on the chair and secured Com's handcuffs to a bottom rung.

Seconds later, Senators Delano and Thurston walked through the door.

Delano looked Com up and down, noticed the bruised cheek, and coughed. "Well, I see you had a run in with our friends. But no terminal accident. It's a shame."

At Delano's comment, Com produced an obnoxious and out-of-place grin.

Delano stopped in his tracks and viewed the grinning Com but spoke to Roger Thurston. "Oh, would you look at the tragically ignorant monkey? He smiles, unaware that he is utterly finished."

Com maintained his defiant smile.

Delano walked closer to the captive and lisped, "What did you think you could do? Did you think you could outwit us? Did you think you could really come here with a crew of journalists and unveil our little group to the world? Didn't I tell you we own the media?"

Com just smiled and nodded at Delano for an uncomfortable pause.

"Make sure to frisk him, boys," Roger Thurston commanded to the U.S. marshals.

One of the agents extended his arm with Com's cell phone, which contained a blinking green light. "We already searched him, sir. We found this."

"Well, search him again!" Thurston said. "You can't be too sure." Thurston took the cell phone, chuckled, and dropped it on the concrete floor front of him. He stomped on the phone and watched it die.

Com laughed out loud.

Thurston looked at Com with confusion. "What in tarnation is so damned funny, boy?" Com gave no response but smiled at the elder senator.

The federal agents frisked Com again and turned to the senators with nothing new.

"You can go," Delano commanded the marshals. "And make sure no one gets in or out this time." He pointed to the left and right, indicating the exits. "Do you understand? No one! For any reason."

The marshals nodded, and both federal agents exited the way they had entered.

Duane D. Delano started walking around the seated Com DeGroot. "Look at you. You're going to lose your seat in the Senate. You're about to go to jail. You're broke. You're handcuffed to a fucking chair." Delano finished a walk around Com and looked at the prisoner with a huff. He was stunned. "And you're smiling? What is going through your little pea brain?"

Com did not reply but maintained a smile directed at Duane D. Delano.

"Well, you wanted to meet. What did you want to meet about?" Delano observed Com. "Here's your opportunity to let it all out. Let us have it."

Com stared at Delano but said nothing.

"No? Not going to talk?" Delano slowly walked around Com again. "I must say, you threw it all away. You had everything. You had popularity, you had political capital, and you had wealth. You were going to be the most powerful senator on the Hill."

"Hell," Thurston interjected, "Hank Pierpont even wanted you in the Group, Commie boy. Do you know what kind of elite company you would have kept in the Group?"

Delano extended his hand and slapped Com on the back of the head. "But you just couldn't play ball, could you?"

At first, Com was stunned at the slap, but he regained his composure and his smile. Delano looked for the reaction on Com's face and was frustrated.

"Well," Delano continued. "When we made our offer to you a few days ago, you weren't a criminal. You weren't a fugitive of justice. You weren't a lunatic. You were just stupid. Now, it appears all of that has changed—except for the stupid part."

Com couldn't help the eruption of a laugh that hit the back of his mouth, but he restrained himself as if he were a child in the principle's office.

Roger Thurston continued. "Yeah, we don't make deals with stupid, fugitive lunatics. I hate to say it, Commie boy, but you are useless to us now."

Com then winced and opened and shut his jaw repetitively and flexed his shoulders. Delano scrunched his face and squinted at Senator DeGroot, who was evidently experiencing some pain.

"Damn, boy. What the hell's wrong with you?" Thurston looked on in confusion.

Com gave no response but regained a smile with a few blinks.

Delano then turned back to Com, squinting. "In any event, we need you to keep your mouth shut about all this—though that doesn't appear to be a problem right now, you contemptible, deaf mute. But it would be an annoyance for you to start spouting off about our little arrangement. So, we are offering to keep you out of jail in exchange for you keeping your big mouth shut. No press." Delano snorted a laugh. "And no book deals." Thurston chuckled at Delano's joke. Delano continued. "The deal is that you don't disclose any of this to anyone. Otherwise, we'll have you rung up so fast, you'll be bunking up with Harry the serial rapist before they can read you your Miranda rights."

Com did not nod. He did not respond with any auditory confirmation. He just stared at the speaker.

Delano huffed. "Well?"

"Boy, you gonna answer the man?" Thurston inquired.

Com did not answer.

Delano threw his hands in the air. "Absolutely useless! What are you holding out for? You want something from us? Is that it?"

Com's expression didn't change.

"Or do you need a little more inspiration to start singing?" Delano stepped closer to Com and placed his hand on Com's face, his thumb on one cheek and the rest of his fingers on the other. Delano squeezed the flesh of Com's face. Com maintained his gaze on Delano and smiled. "Talk, you little prick!" Delano yelled.

Com noticed faint yells and noise from outside of the Turf Club. There was something stirring.

Thurston turned to Delano. "Maybe he's just waiting to get into the justice system and be handled by the law."

"Is that what it is, you clumsy ogre?" Delano said and leaned into Com.

Com kept the smile on his face but squinted in a defiant manner.

When Delano spoke, he ejected bits of saliva toward Com. "Are you hoping for the law to protect you? Well, I've got news. There is no law. I make the laws, you son of a bitch. Me!" Delano let go of his grip and turned away from the defiant Com DeGroot. "Fuck the law!"

"This is useless, Duane. Let's go," Thurston said and turned toward the door.

Delano slowly turned around to follow Thurston, but before he reached the door, he turned and ran at Com, yelling, "Why don't you speak, you obstinate moron?"

Com smiled.

Thurston looked at the two from the door. "What do we tell Hank?"

"Fuck Hank!" Delano said, looking halfway back to Thurston. "This is my show."

At that, Com burst into laughter.

Delano turned red and tensed. "What is so fucking funny?"

Com stared at Delano and smiled.

"This is my show! I control what goes on. Not Pierpont." Delano talked down to the captive. "Oh, you think you're so cute in your little deaf mute act. Meanwhile, you are absolutely helpless to do anything as your precious charter city in Texas burns to the ground." Delano's lispy voice turned condescending, as if he were speaking to a child. "Oh, did you cry a little when they let the rioters out?"

The smile slowly vanished from Com's face.

"That's right. Who do you think ordered the riots? That incapable louse Ilarion Yoan?" Delano shook his head. "Hank Pierpont? That man doesn't have the guts to order a pizza." Delano pointed to his chest and stared at Com. "No, I ordered those riots."

Com's eyes bulged.

Thurston walked back to Delano. "Duane, be careful."

Delano rejected Thurston's caution and leaned into Com's face. "And I ordered the security shutdown."

Com pursed his lips but did not say anything.

"Oh, does that bother you?" Delano tilted his head in counterfeit empathy. Com looked past Delano and silently fumed. Delano cracked a smile at the thought that he was getting under Com's skin.

Delano looked back to Thurston to see where he was, then inched closer to Com. He moved in to Com's ear and whispered, "And I was the one who had your little girlfriend raped, too. What do you think about that?"

Com exploded. He flexed his arms and pulled the cuffs, clanking them on the chair. Com fumed and let his face boil up into a rage. He fidgeted in his chair trying to break loose.

"Oh! That wakes you up huh? What are you going to do? Are you going to cry?" Delano smirked.

Suddenly, noise from the club's entrance exploded. Two pairs of footsteps pounded down the stairs.

Delano stepped out of the side room and turned to the staircase to shriek, "I said no one gets in!"

Two U.S. marshals stopped at the bottom of the stairs and looked stunned at the senior senator.

"Well?" Delano demanded.

One of the marshals pointed to Com. "He taped the whole thing. He's broadcasting it to everyone. It's on every phone out there." The marshal handed Delano a video player, which displayed a video of Com's view.

In Com DeGroot's struggle, he had broken the bar on the chair to which his cuffs were chained and was able to stand. He elevated himself above the other men and looked down on them with furious anger. Duane D. Delano stared at the video player, stunned.

Com spoke sternly and clearly. "You were saying, Mr. Delano?"

Roger Thurston slowly stepped backward and looked at the destroyed phone on the ground, then looked at the marshal. "What do you mean, boy—he taped the whole thing?"

"He must have an implant," the marshal responded.

"But how . . ." Thurston grumbled.

Com DeGroot took the rhetorical question, "In my right eye, I have a contact lens that operates as a video camera. You may not have heard about these because there's too much regulation for the company to sell them anywhere but Ur. It sent the video to a cell phone that I had surgically implanted into my jaw." Com pointed to his jaw and stared at the two senators in front of him. "That's sending the signal to every cell tower in the area and then on to local Internet service providers.

"You see, a friend of mine is sitting at his massive computer workstation, ensuring that the signal from my phone and video camera made it on to the Internet Security Network, which you all tricked me into voting for. You know the bill!" Com exclaimed. "I think we approved the bill a couple weeks ago and now every electronic device in America capable of audio or video display is connected to the network. Everyone on that network saw what just happened."

Outside of the Turf Club entrance, a dozen journalists watched the happenings in the basement of the club on their handheld devices and phones. At the end of the block, a young man sat on a mountain bike and watched the video on his mobile phone. In the living room of a house in Alexandria, Virginia, a family watched the events on a desktop computer with opened jaws. At a convenience store in Columbus, Ohio, patrons gathered around an old flat-screen television and viewed the incident. Every computer, every television, every phone, and every other electronic in the country displayed the video of Duane D. Delano and Roger Thurston's interaction with Com DeGroot.

Com continued, "For those of you who can hear this, these are the people who you've entrusted to lead you." He directed his video camera contact lens to Delano and then to Thurston. "A group of corrupt con artists, who create crisis after crisis and mask them with good intentions, then solve the problems they created with an iron fist of ever-increasing confiscation of your freedom."

"Shut up!" Delano yelled. "Stop it!"

Com continued and walked toward the men. "You trust them with the authority to protect your God-given, unalienable rights, but they use that authority to strip you of your property, take away your freedom, and, as is often the case, take away your life."

"Shut up. Shut him up!" Delano directed the U.S. marshals. But the marshals stood, skeptical of Delano, and let Com speak.

"To everyone out there who respects life and liberty—wake up! You are being lulled into a wicked state of slavery by these men—these men? Ha! These animals. Rise up! Opt out of this corrupt feudal system. See this two-party sham for what it is. Get past the partisanship and kill this beast of statism before it kills you! Stop fighting each other and start fighting the government! Stop suing each other and sue the government! Create a charter city. Nullify unconstitutional acts! Tell the federal government that you don't want to participate in their corrupt welfare-warfare state anymore. Tell your Congressmen to just stop! And if they don't listen, elect someone who will adhere to the Constitution, not someone who will throw political candy at you in exchange for shackles. Stand up for life! Stand up for liberty! Believe this, when enough of you out there realize that you are slaves but don't have to be, a revolution will happen!"

"Oh, the hell with this." Delano waved his hand at Com and walked toward the stairs. He waddled up the stairs and out the front door. Delano threw open the door and found a dozen journalists sitting on the sidewalk or leaning against the brick building. They were all listening to or watching their phones or handheld computers. "Aren't you going to join him, Thurston?" Com's voice was heard from a number of different sources in the group. When the reporters recognized Delano, they jumped into action and focused their cameras on the perspiring senator.

"Was that you on the video?"

"Who is Ilarion Yoan?"

"Who was that on the broadcast?"

"Who is Hank Pierpont?"

Delano was bombarded by questions as he waved his hands down and searched on the sidewalk for something to say. "No, no. That was clearly a practical joke." Delano smiled. "An early April Fool's gag."

No one in the crowd was laughing.

Fifty-Eight

"Tonight, *Politics Behind Closed Doors*—the undercover video that has taken America by storm. Was it staged? Was it manipulated? And what does it mean for you?" Michelle Torres' voice announced the headline for the evening news as a video showed a blurry Duane D. Delano approaching the camera and muttering something into it. "Plus, *Sex, Lies, and Big Oil*—the dirty little secretes behind corporate America." A video showed titillating images of a woman dancing.

"Oh, turn that crap off," Com DeGroot, dressed in an orange jump suit, said to his chief of staff Kevin Donovan through a solid Plexiglas window. Black telephone receivers allowed the prisoner to communicate to his visitor on the other side.

Kevin put down the handheld computer that was playing the newscast. "Yeah, it's pretty ridiculous."

"What's this shit about 'was it staged?' And why aren't they talking about the corruption? Delano laid it all out there in that video." Com shook his head.

"Com, what do you expect? It's the National News Coalition. They get all of their funding through the federal government."

"Right. So what about the underground wire?"

"Oh, they are lovin' it. Every outlet is blasting the video. The NNC is trying to say that because you used the Internet Security Act pipeline to broadcast the video, the video itself is property of the U.S. government and can only be used with authorization from the FCC. And who has authorization from the FCC? The NNC, of course."

"So ludicrous. Nothing's going to change, is it, Kevin?"

Kevin pushed up his lips and shook his head. "Well, there have been calls for Delano and Thurston to step down from their leadership roles. And there have been charges brought against Delano for his possible role in the riots."

"That's it?" Com nearly yelled. Com looked down and let the idea sink in. "And I get to rot away in prison?"

"Yeah, and that's the point. We have to focus on getting you out of here."

Com nodded. "Right. So, any progress on the bail money?"

Kevin's face turned sour. "Unfortunately, no. Your bank accounts are still frozen, and ten mil is not easy to come by. I mean, really? Ten million bail for a former U.S. senator?"

Com started laughing. "I did punch a U.S. marshal in the face."

Kevin laughed. "Yeah. They say you're a flight risk, too."

"They haven't charged Reggie with anything, have they?"

Kevin shook his head. "Nothing yet."

"Good."

"Hey, you heard about the raid in Ur, right?" Kevin asked excitedly, and Com shook his head. "Oh, this is great. All right, so you knew the plan for the feds was to go in and secure the banks in Ur. It was a total money-grab, right? So, the feds surround Royalty Swiss Bank, and the president comes out of the bank and explains that they have no assets on the premises, that they moved everything to Ur Bank, so the feds moved to Ur bank down the street. The place was completely locked down. No security guards, no personnel, just layers and layers of locks and automated security features. So the feds spend days breaking through and disabling these locks, one after another, until they get to the reserve vault with all the gold—twenty-percent of all the world's mined gold in this vault. It's a pretty big undertaking, right? But when the feds get in there finally, they find the vault completely empty."

"What?" Com yelled.

"The vault was completely empty except for a small note in the middle of the room. It said, 'You owe us a door.'"

Com broke out in laughter. "What?" he repeated.

"I know, isn't it hilarious? They must have gotten rid of the reserves somehow before the takeover if they ever even had them. Who knows?"

"That's the funniest thing I've ever heard."

A buzzer sounded and a prison guard yelled out, "Com DeGroot."

Com held his phone away from his head. "What, already? I just got here."

The guard yelled back, "Let's go, your bail was posted."

Com pushed his head back in surprise, then looked at Kevin. Kevin lifted his left hand and shrugged.

Com replaced the telephone receiver on the wall and stood up, looking at the guard. He raised his eyebrows and walked toward the guard and out of the room.

* * *

A guard pulled a barred gate across the hallway, and Com DeGroot, dressed in the suit he had been arrested in, walked through it and down the hall to the exit of the prison.

Com took a moment to adjust his eyes to the bright spring morning and finally acclimated himself to the open air. His eyes came to rest on two people talking at the bottom of the concrete stairs leading to the prison entrance.

Cate Heatherton pulled down a few strands of her hair that had been loosened by the wind as she nodded at Kevin Donovan, who was speaking to her. Once Com started to walk down the stairs, Cate looked up and smiled at the tall figure. Kevin turned around to see the subject of Cate's gaze.

Cate yelled at Com, "Hiya, jailbird!"

Com shook his head in amusement as he walked toward his two friends. He stretched out his arms. "Thus ends the short and eventful senatorial career of Com DeGroot."

Cate smiled. "You sure about that?"

"Yeah, I'm pretty sure about that." Com looked at Cate. "So, did *you* post my bail, Miss Heatherton?"

Cate laughed. "Yeah, I took it out of my billion-dollar trust fund. No, The Green Group did."

"Kula?"

Cate nodded affirmation. "He considered you a wise investment."

"God help him," Kevin quipped.

Com let his mouth open involuntarily. "Right, so what does he want me to do in return?"

Cate laughed. "Nothing. He sees it as payment for work you've already done."

"Well," Kevin said, "I should let you two catch up." Kevin hit Com on his arm. "Good to see you in street clothes, brother."

Com thanked his chief of staff, and Kevin walked away toward the parking lot.

Cate Heatherton reached out her arm toward Com but hesitated. "Can I—can I give you a hug?"

Com nodded and embraced Cate. When they released their hold on each other, Com looked into Cate's eyes. "Are you all right after what happened?"

Cate pursed her lips and nodded slowly. "I try not to think about it much. I went to a shrink."

"Yeah?"

"She said it's just going to take time."

"I can imagine." Com shook his head.

"But, can we not talk about it?"

"Sure. I'm here, though, whenever you want to talk."

"Thanks." Cate looked down in thought, then changed the subject. "Arun also has offered to fund your defense in court. He believes you have a good chance at getting off."

"Wow. Really? I'm starting to like this boyfriend of yours." Com smiled.

"And he also wants you to come work for him on the floating city he's building."

"Ah! A catch!"

"No, there's no catch. You're free to do whatever you want. But it really is a good opportunity. This place he's building is the first of its kind—a completely autonomous floating city. He wants you to work there. I want you to work there."

Com nodded. "Is Santiago going?"

Cate smiled. "Yes, as a matter of fact."

"And, of course, you're going to be living down there?"

Cate shrugged and hummed confirmation.

Com stretched his lips and bounced his head. "Well, that is very considerate of Mr. Kula, but unfortunately, I don't really see myself enjoying tea every afternoon and watching you two traipse around on the Love Boat for the rest of my life."

Cate bowed her head in reflection. "Com, the engagement is off. We're not getting married."

Com dropped his jaw and stared at Cate for a moment. "What? What happened?"

"Arun is a brilliant and amazing person. He is successful and motivated. But he is rational to a fault. He leaves absolutely no room for the spirit. He leaves no room for love." Cate smiled. "He never loved me, Com. He just thought it was a fitting, rational partnership."

"And you never loved him, I take it?"

"No, I never loved him. Respect him? Yes. Admire him? Of course. But love him? No."

"So you turned him down?"

Cate moved her head up and down and smiled.

"And he isn't mad?"

Cate shook her head. "No, he was very analytical about it. He was more worried about the opportunity costs of being engaged to me for the few weeks." Cate let out an exaggerated sigh. "I want someone who is full of passion—who can feel what I feel. I want someone . . . who will do anything for me."

Com smiled. "Hey, I know someone like that."

"You do?" Cate asked hopefully, and Com nodded.

"But he sometimes screws up."

Cate pushed her lips out. "Well, as long as he isn't proud about screwing up."

Com shook his head. "No way."

The two started walking toward the parking lot.

"Cate, listen. I have some time off before my court date. What do you say we take some time? I have a cabin in the mountains—how does that sound? It's real peaceful. No contact with the real world. What do you say?"

Cate let a grin creep over her face. "I don't know, Com. It's all so sudden."

Com looked at the ground. "Right. I understand."

The two walked silently for a moment.

"Okay, Com. I'll go," Cate said through a smile. "But only as friends."

Com laughed. "Okay."

They arrived at Cate's car, and she handed Com the keys, which he accepted naturally.

"Thanks for breaking me out of the big house, Cate."

"Anytime. Just call me your Bonnie. Wait, was she a criminal?"

Com chuckled. "Yeah, Bonnie and Clyde? They were criminals."

"Okay, then never mind," Cate said with a smile as she opened her door and maneuvered into the car seat.

Com got in as well, started the car, and drove out of the parking lot.

Fifty-Nine

Roger Thurston looked down at his notes before looking at the throng of journalists in the Senate Press Gallery. He clicked his mouth as he opened it to speak. "I have been extremely irresponsible."

Photographers clicked and reporters held out their recording devices as Thurston surveyed the room.

"I have let my undying love of country and the great people that live here get in the way of my clear duty as a representative in the United State Senate. That love drove me to abandon my party and to collude with the likes of Senator Majority Leader Delano. It was my deep, heartfelt desire to see America prosper that led me to my actions. Perhaps I overstepped my bounds. Maybe I tried too hard.

"I've overcome a lot to get where I am—a lot of adversity and tribulations—but I made it through. I'm proud of who I am and what I've done. And while the bad guys may have gotten the best of me this time, they won't change my character, and they will never—I repeat, never—stop me from loving this country."

Thurston's bottom lip began to quiver, and a tear dropped from his left eye. "I love my family. I love my wife, more than anything. And I am so sorry if any of this controversy has reflected poorly on them. It just kills me inside to know that my passion for this country and the freedom and well-being of each and every American has led to such an unfortunate end.

"As that is the case, however, I offer my resignation as Senator of the United States of America, effective immediately."

Roger Thurston pulled a sheet of paper with his notes off of the podium and turned to his left to exit the stage. The reporters exploded in questions as camera flashes lit up the entire press gallery.

"What is your response to the charges of infidelity?"

"How involved were you in the Ur controversy?"

"Did you collude with Duane Delano on the riots in Ur?" a reporter blurted out, but couldn't capture Thurston's attention and he slowly walked off stage ignoring the questions.

* * *

Duane D. Delano threw the unfinished leg of fried chicken down onto a mound of bones and wrapper in disgust. The office was dim and quiet as the entire staff was gone. Delano had eaten the equivalent of three whole chickens—legs, wings, and breasts—but his appetite was not satisfied. Grease saturated the senator's hands and mouth and Delano snarled at the leftovers. Delano closed his eyes and shook his head in discontent.

When he opened his eyes, Delano saw a stern Hank Pierpont walk through his office door.

"What the hell do you want?" Delano threw at his surprise company.

Hank walked to the front of Delano's desk and stood silent for a moment. "You're out."

"Well no shit." Delano replied.

"Our employer has cut all ties with you and declared you a distinct liability. You have put in danger the entire organization—"

"I have put the organization in danger? What about DeGroot? He was the one that caused all this. It was his fault we were caught—not mine."

Hank Pierpont moved saliva around in his mouth before speaking, "DeGroot is on a no-touch list right now. He's far too popular. Besides, he's resigned his position. He's got no power now."

Delano protested. "What about Roger? What about Pete? Those sons of bitches were in this as much as me."

Hank grumbled, "Roger has resigned. Anyway, *they* stuck to the plan, Duane. They didn't break the law."

"The law?" Delano struck back. "You're bringing up the law? Hank, I make the law. Anything I say is law. I did everything you were planning on doing down there—grab the land, the reserves, flush out The Green Group. I was just able to expedite the process. It worked didn't it?"

"Yes, but you just can't go acting like a vigilante. Hiring ex-convicts to start a riot, Duane? Getting a hit man to rape and murder? If you hadn't done any of that, we would still have reached our objectives and there would be nothing anyone could do about it. But it's a complete mess right now—a disaster."

"I see, your method was just as corrupt. Mine was just quicker!" Delano barked.

Hank Pierpont shook his head, "Do you even know who that young woman was you had attacked down there?"

"Oh, this is what this is all about?" Delano coughed. "I could have had any bimbo raped and murdered, just not her. Is that it?"

Hank ignored the question, "I'm sorry Duane. You went over the deep end. You need to take responsibility for your actions—for the sake of our cause. You need to resign and disappear."

"What if I don't want to?" Delano asked resentfully.

"You know what can happen if you resist us here."

"You contemptible asshole."

"Do the right thing, Duane." Hank Pierpont turned and walked through the door, leaving the Senator alone in his office.

Sixty

Com DeGroot was lying on his leather sofa, struggling to stay awake in the mid-afternoon warmth of his Georgetown condominium, when Cate Heatherton brought over a slice of blackberry pie.

"You are absolutely amazing, you know that?" Com said as he sat upright, accepting the plate full of pie and ice cream. "The first thing you do when we get back is bake the most amazing pie ever."

"Well, wait 'til you taste it." She stood and watched Com portion out a large area of pie and ice cream with his fork and place it in his mouth.

Com moaned in ecstasy and bulged his eyes. "Oh, my God, this is unbelievable."

Cate smiled. "Do you like it?"

"It's like heaven in my mouth. I love it." Com went in for another bite. "We need to get Reggie up here to get a slice."

Cate rubbed her fingers to remove some stickiness. "Way ahead of you. I baked him an entire pie, along with this."

"Absolutely amazing." Com shook his head and placed another bite into his mouth.

"Well, I'm glad you liked it because you get to do the dishes," Cate said as she sat down next to an engrossed eater.

"My pleasure."

Cate looked at Com. "You know, I've been thinking. I'm going to take Arun up on his offer."

"What, and move to the floating city?" Com asked before licking his fork.

"Well, I hate to say it, but there's nothing left for me here."

"What about me?"

"You should come, too."

"So that's it? We just go and leave this country behind?"

Cate shrugged. "Com, I don't think we're leaving this country as much as it's leaving us—or rather, left us. It's one thing to try to change what's going on in Washington, but it's quite another thing to try to change the minds of an entire country. It seems like, for the most part, people want it this way. Your video showed them the true nature of the corruption here, and no one is asking any questions or doing anything about it. We can't force people to want to be free."

"No, we can't," Com said dejectedly.

"It kills me to say it, but if America wants slavery, they can have it. I will politely decline."

Com nodded in reflection. "Do you think Kula will let me open up a microdistillery on his island?"

Cate smiled. "I'm sure you will be able to do whatever you want on the island."

"Will I be able to play a little one on one with you?" Com leaned into Cate's neck and playfully bit it. Cate screamed a laugh and slapped Com's knee.

From outside of Com's townhome, the couple heard a voice yelling, "Hello?" They heard pounding on the door, causing them to look at each other and scrunched their faces in confusion.

Com handed his plate to Cate. "Don't even think about taking any of this."

Cate smiled. "Of course not." She proceeded to take a bite for herself as Com stood up to walk to the door. He looked through the peephole and looked back at Cate with a frown.

"Where the hell have you been?" Kevin Donovan yelled after Com opened the door.

Com walked back over to the couch. "We were in the mountains for a week. We decided to take some time off."

Kevin was stunned. "Well, don't they have satellite or ham radio in the mountains? Haven't you heard?"

Com shook his head. "No, what?"

Kevin pointed back toward the door. "They are marching on the Capitol. There are millions. The National News Coalition is reporting just sixty thousand, but Com, you have to see this. It's the biggest protest I've ever seen."

"What the hell?"

"It was all underground. They say they want an end to the corruption or they're opting out. Over five thousand municipalities across the country have applied for charter status. There have been hundreds of lawsuits filed on the federal government in the last few days alone. There are people all over Texas talking about secession. They want out of the system. And it's all because of you Com, your video."

Com was speechless.

* * *

Com DeGroot jumped out of the car when it became evident that they weren't moving. The traffic jam had backed up several blocks, and Pennsylvania Avenue was a parking lot.

He leaned back into the car. "Kevin, can you take care of the car? Reggie, you want to come with us?"

Kevin nodded, and Reggie and Cate got out. They followed Com southeast toward the National Mall.

"I've never seen it like this," Cate said as they hurried along the sidewalk.

The three moved past countless cars idling on the street and several other people standing around observing the complete stoppage of traffic on Pennsylvania Avenue and then on its cross street, Constitution Avenue.

As the three moved closer to the Mall, they saw increasingly more people waving signs and chanting. Signs read, "KING GEORGE DIDN'T LISTEN EITHER," "NULLIFY!" "WE OPT OUT!" and "GOVERNMENT = SLAVER." Some protestors had noisemakers and drums and created a festival atmosphere. They waved American flags and yellow ones with a coiled snake that declared, "DON'T TREAD ON ME." There were overweight truck drivers with faded, undersized T-shirts, and young students with shaggy hair and neckties. There were moms with young children perched on their hips and grandmothers with walkers. There were Africans, Asians, Europeans, Arabs, Israelis, Iroquois, Shawnee, and Havasupai, but all were undeniably American.

Com held Cate's hand and pushed through the crowd. He saw that the grass fields around the Capitol Reflecting Pool were packed. Protesters had filled the entire area west of the Capitol and were blocking traffic in every direction. Police were attempting to move people, but their effort was futile. Com led Cate and Reggie along the Reflecting Pool to the middle so that they stood directly in front of the Capitol. He turned around and gazed upon a mass of humanity stretching beyond what he could see. The entire Mall was packed with people—beyond the Washington Monument and in all directions.

Cate nudged Com and pointed to a nearby sign. It read, "DEGROOT FOR PRESIDENT!" Another sign read, "FIRE THE DICTATOR, HIRE DEGROOT!" Com smiled and shook his head at Cate.

An overweight lady dressed in a comfortable red shirt stood next to the newcomers and smiled. "I have to ask, you're Com DeGroot, right?" She spoke with a friendly country drawl.

Com nodded and smiled in affirmation.

"Oh, I just think you are amazin'." She started into a rapid monologue. "I love the way you speak your mind and how you just stand up against those corrupt monsters in the Capitol and, oh, when I heard your story about going down to Texas—my cousin's in Texas—and when you went down there and saved your sweetheart from those rioters, oh, it just about made me cry." The lady wiped her right eye, which had begun to water. "I'm sorry, I just get worked up about what they're trying to do here in Washington—they're trying to tell us all how to live our lives—I just don't' think it's right, but tell me, is this your sweetheart right here?" She looked at Cate.

"Yes, Miss Cate Heatherton," Com introduced Cate.

"I'm Patrice Abernathy. It is such an honor. Oh, aren't you just the sweetest little thing."

"It's a pleasure," Cate said.

"And this is my friend, Reggie Williams," Com held his hand out to Reggie.

"Oh, my, is this the man that helped you down there in Texas?"

Com nodded again.

"Oh, bless your heart. You are a good man for doing what you done," Patrice said. "Oh, bless you all. Oh, I think this could be the best day of my life!" she sang.

Com sensed a tug on his suit pants and looked down. A young boy was pulling on the knee of Com's pants. "Hey there, little fella," he said.

"Excuse me, mistuh."

"Oh, I'm sorry, that's my boy," Patrice gave the disclaimer. "Don't mind him."

"You're tall," the little boy said.

"That's right," Com replied.

"Can I ride on your shoulders, mistuh?" the boy asked.

"Oh, don't bother the man," Patrice scolded the boy.

Com smiled. "That's quite all right ma'am." He bent down. "What's your name?"

"My name is Tucker Abernaffy."

"Well, Tucker Abernathy, it's good to meet you. Here we go!" Com took the young boy under his arms and raised him up over his shoulders.

"Wow!" the young boy exclaimed. "This is awesome!"

"It's a pretty good view up there, huh?" Com asked Tucker.

"Mommy, there's a billion gazillion people here!"

"Thank you so much," Patrice said and shook her head and looked up at her boy proudly as he held on to Com's head.

Com smiled at the woman and turned his gaze toward the vast crowd in front of him.

Com walked Cate into the Capitol Rotunda well after dark. The place was dimly lit and empty except for a small man mopping the floors in a nearby hallway.

"Are we going to climb to the top again?" Cate asked, almost joking.

"I'm way too tired for that," Com replied. "Here, I want to show you my favorite statue."

They strolled to the bronze statue of Washington standing under the Rotunda.

"It's beautiful," Cate marveled.

"Yeah, they say it is the closest likeness to the actual man."

"I believe it."

The janitor softly walked up behind the couple. "You know," he said, getting their attention. "They repeat his entire farewell address every year in the Senate. Washington's, I mean."

Com smiled and turned back to view the balding old janitor. "I didn't know that."

"Oh, yes," the janitor said. "It's kinda like his wish of how government should continue to operate after he was gone from service."

Cate smiled at the idea.

The janitor rested his hands on his mop. "He ended with a nice phrase. He said, 'I anticipate with pleasing expectation that retreat in which I promise myself to realize, without alloy, the sweetest enjoyment of partaking, in the midst of my fellow-citizens, the benign influence of good laws under a free government, the ever-favorite object of my heart, and the happy regard, as I trust, of our mutual cares, labors, and dangers.'" The old janitor reflected on the statement for a moment. "It's just really nice, I think." He then gripped his mop and resumed his cleaning.

Com and Cate smiled and returned their gaze upward to the statue of George Washington.

"A throng of protestors filled the west lawn of the Capitol Building in Washington D.C. earlier today, stopping traffic and causing delays throughout the city," Michelle Torres reported into the television camera. "The rally, which organizers said was held to protest President Sullivan and the federal government in general, was the largest in months. Handwritten signs were seen throughout the crowd criticizing the size and scope of government and its various services. As protestors sang verse after verse of traditional American hymns, however, combative words of profane nature could be heard throughout the crowd.

"The demonstrators numbered well into the thousands, though the police declined to estimate the official size of the crowd.

"In other news, Senate leaders applauded a bi-partisan bill aimed at reigning in corruption on Wall Street. The bill, spearheaded by Senator Foxworthy of Arizona consolidates various financial oversight agencies and bureaus into one central authority in charge of regulation of all consumer products like mortgages and credit cards. Proponents say that the new agency will have sweeping power to clean up the corruption that has continued to plague the financial sector since the mortgage meltdown over one decade ago. Foxworthy's bill has already passed the House of Representatives and President Sullivan is likely to sign the bill into law early next week.

"Questions over who will take over the role of Economic Czar at the head of Financial Oversight Agency were answered today as President Sullivan tapped banking industry leader Hank Pierpont. Mr. Pierpont declined to comment on the new post."

End

Acknowledgements

Upon reflection, it almost seems laughable for me to take credit for this project. Whatever success I've accomplished has been entirely supported and influenced by the strong network of friends and family I have been fortunate enough to maintain.

First and foremost, I have been constantly graced with opportunity and a will to take advantage of that opportunity by the Creator of which our Founders spoke so eloquently. It is Nature's God, which embodies all that is good (life, liberty, love) and is in sharp contrast with the false gods of the state, to which I am forever indebted.

I also owe infinite gratitude to my brother, Eric Morse, whose ideas about story, positive support, and inspiring writings made this book possible. Without Eric, this book would have the ineffective title, *The Senator*, and the story would be inconsequential. If you are interested in the craft of storytelling, Eric's book *The 90-minute Effect* is a must-read and if you are interested in anything at all, you must read his game-changer, *Juggernaut*. I also owe a debt to my friend Matthew Fischer, whose expert perspective into character and story were invaluable throughout the editing process. Also, a great thanks is owed to my editor and friend Kristen Depken, whose input on the characters was insightful and whose efficient and thorough editing brought the prose up to the lofty goal set by the title.

Many thanks are owed to my mom, Stephanie for everything; my sister, Aly for helping in the editing process; and to my grandpa, Bob, whose good-natured humanity is more inspirational than he may know.

I am grateful.

The Declaration of Independence

IN CONGRESS, July 4, 1776.

The unanimous Declaration of the thirteen united States of America,

When in the Course of human events, it becomes necessary for one people to dissolve the political bands which have connected them with another, and to assume among the powers of the earth, the separate and equal station to which the Laws of Nature and of Nature's God entitle them, a decent respect to the opinions of mankind requires that they should declare the causes which impel them to the separation.

We hold these truths to be self-evident, that all men are created equal, that they are endowed by their Creator with certain unalienable Rights, that among these are Life, Liberty and the pursuit of Happiness.--That to secure these rights, Governments are instituted among Men, deriving their just powers from the consent of the governed, --That whenever any Form of Government becomes destructive of these ends, it is the Right of the People to alter or to abolish it, and to institute new Government, laying its foundation on such principles and organizing its powers in such form, as to them shall seem most likely to effect their Safety and Happiness. Prudence, indeed, will dictate that Governments long established should not be changed for light and transient causes; and accordingly all experience hath shewn, that mankind are more disposed to suffer, while evils are sufferable, than to right themselves by abolishing the forms to which they are accustomed. But when a long train of abuses and usurpations, pursuing invariably the same Object evinces a design to reduce them under absolute Despotism, it is their right, it is their duty, to throw off such Government, and to provide new Guards for their future security.--Such has been the patient sufferance of these Colonies; and such is now the necessity which constrains them to alter their former Systems of Government. The history of the present King of Great Britain is a history of repeated injuries and usurpations, all having in direct object the establishment of an absolute Tyranny over these States. To prove this, let Facts be submitted to a candid world.

He has refused his Assent to Laws, the most wholesome and necessary for the public good.

He has forbidden his Governors to pass Laws of immediate and pressing importance, unless suspended in their operation till his Assent should be obtained; and when so suspended, he has utterly neglected to attend to them.

He has refused to pass other Laws for the accommodation of large districts of people, unless those people would relinquish the right of Representation in the Legislature, a right inestimable to them and formidable to tyrants only.

He has called together legislative bodies at places unusual, uncomfortable, and distant from the depository of their public Records, for the sole purpose of fatiguing them into compliance with his measures.

He has dissolved Representative Houses repeatedly, for opposing with manly firmness his invasions on the rights of the people.

He has refused for a long time, after such dissolutions, to cause others to be elected; whereby the Legislative powers, incapable of Annihilation, have returned to the People at large for their exercise; the State remaining in the mean time exposed to all the dangers of invasion from without, and convulsions within.

He has endeavoured to prevent the population of these States; for that purpose obstructing the Laws for Naturalization of Foreigners; refusing to pass others to encourage their migrations hither, and raising the conditions of new Appropriations of Lands.

He has obstructed the Administration of Justice, by refusing his Assent to Laws for establishing Judiciary powers.

He has made Judges dependent on his Will alone, for the tenure of their offices, and the amount and payment of their salaries.

He has erected a multitude of New Offices, and sent hither swarms of Officers to harrass our people, and eat out their substance.

He has kept among us, in times of peace, Standing Armies without the Consent of our legislatures.

He has affected to render the Military independent of and superior to the Civil power.

He has combined with others to subject us to a jurisdiction foreign to our constitution, and unacknowledged by our laws; giving his Assent to their Acts of pretended Legislation:

For Quartering large bodies of armed troops among us:

For protecting them, by a mock Trial, from punishment for any Murders which they should commit on the Inhabitants of these States:

For cutting off our Trade with all parts of the world:

For imposing Taxes on us without our Consent:

For depriving us in many cases, of the benefits of Trial by Jury:

For transporting us beyond Seas to be tried for pretended offences

For abolishing the free System of English Laws in a neighbouring Province, establishing therein an Arbitrary government, and enlarging its Boundaries so as to render it at once an example and fit instrument for introducing the same absolute rule into these Colonies:

For taking away our Charters, abolishing our most valuable Laws, and altering fundamentally the Forms of our Governments:

For suspending our own Legislatures, and declaring themselves invested with power to legislate for us in all cases whatsoever.

He has abdicated Government here, by declaring us out of his Protection and waging War against us.

He has plundered our seas, ravaged our Coasts, burnt our towns, and destroyed the lives of our people.

He is at this time transporting large Armies of foreign Mercenaries to compleat the works of death, desolation and tyranny, already begun with circumstances of Cruelty & perfidy scarcely paralleled in the most barbarous ages, and totally unworthy the Head of a civilized nation.

He has constrained our fellow Citizens taken Captive on the high Seas to bear Arms against their Country, to become the executioners of their friends and Brethren, or to fall themselves by their Hands.

He has excited domestic insurrections amongst us, and has endeavoured to bring on the inhabitants of our frontiers, the merciless Indian Savages, whose known rule of warfare, is an undistinguished destruction of all ages, sexes and conditions.

In every stage of these Oppressions We have Petitioned for Redress in the most humble terms: Our repeated Petitions have been answered only by repeated injury. A Prince whose character is thus marked by every act which may define a Tyrant, is unfit to be the ruler of a free people.

Nor have We been wanting in attentions to our Brittish brethren. We have warned them from time to time of attempts by their legislature to extend an unwarrantable jurisdiction over us. We have reminded them of the circumstances of our emigration and settlement here. We have appealed to their native justice and magnanimity, and we have conjured them by the ties of our common kindred to disavow these usurpations, which, would inevitably interrupt our connections and correspondence. They too have been deaf to the voice of justice and of consanguinity. We must, therefore, acquiesce in the necessity, which denounces our Separation, and hold them, as we hold the rest of mankind, Enemies in War, in Peace Friends.

We, therefore, the Representatives of the united States of America, in General Congress, Assembled, appealing to the Supreme Judge of the world for the rectitude of our intentions, do, in the Name, and by Authority of the good People of these Colonies, solemnly publish and declare, That these United Colonies are, and of Right ought to be Free and Independent States; that they are Absolved from all Allegiance to the British Crown, and that all political connection between them and the State of Great Britain, is and ought to be totally dissolved; and that as Free and Independent States, they have full Power to levy War, conclude Peace, contract Alliances, establish Commerce, and to do all other Acts and Things which Independent States may of right do. And for the support of this Declaration, with a firm reliance on the protection of divine Providence, we mutually pledge to each other our Lives, our Fortunes and our sacred Honor.

Resources

Article I, Section 8 of the Constitution of the United States

The Congress shall have Power To lay and collect Taxes, Duties, Imposts and Excises, to pay the Debts and provide for the common Defence and general Welfare of the United States; but all Duties, Imposts and Excises shall be uniform throughout the United States;

To borrow money on the credit of the United States;

To regulate Commerce with foreign Nations, and among the several States, and with the Indian Tribes;

To establish an uniform Rule of Naturalization, and uniform Laws on the subject of Bankruptcies throughout the United States;

To coin Money, regulate the Value thereof, and of foreign Coin, and fix the Standard of Weights and Measures;

To provide for the Punishment of counterfeiting the Securities and current Coin of the United States;

To establish Post Offices and Post Roads;

To promote the Progress of Science and useful Arts, by securing for limited Times to Authors and Inventors the exclusive Right to their respective Writings and Discoveries;

To constitute Tribunals inferior to the supreme Court;

To define and punish Piracies and Felonies committed on the high Seas, and Offenses against the Law of Nations;

To declare War, grant Letters of Marque and Reprisal, and make Rules concerning Captures on Land and Water;

To raise and support Armies, but no Appropriation of Money to that Use shall be for a longer Term than two Years;

To provide and maintain a Navy;

To make Rules for the Government and Regulation of the land and naval Forces;

To provide for calling forth the Militia to execute the Laws of the Union, suppress Insurrections and repel Invasions;

To provide for organizing, arming, and disciplining, the Militia, and for governing such Part of them as may be employed in the Service of the United States, reserving to the States respectively, the Appointment of the Officers, and the Authority of training the Militia according to the discipline prescribed by Congress;

To exercise exclusive Legislation in all Cases whatsoever, over such District (not exceeding ten Miles square) as may, by Cession of particular States, and the acceptance of Congress, become the Seat of the Government of the United States, and to exercise like Authority over all Places purchased by the Consent of the Legislature of the State in which the Same shall be, for the Erection of Forts, Magazines, Arsenals, dock-Yards, and other needful Buildings; And

To make all Laws which shall be necessary and proper for carrying into Execution the foregoing Powers, and all other Powers vested by this Constitution in the Government of the United States, or in any Department or Officer thereof.

The Bill of Rights

Amendment 1
Congress shall make no law respecting an establishment of religion, or prohibiting the free exercise thereof; or abridging the freedom of speech, or of the press; or the right of the people peaceably to assemble, and to petition the Government for a redress of grievances.

Amendment 2
A well regulated Militia, being necessary to the security of a free State, the right of the people to keep and bear Arms, shall not be infringed.

Amendment 3
No Soldier shall, in time of peace be quartered in any house, without the consent of the Owner, nor in time of war, but in a manner to be prescribed by law.

Amendment 4
The right of the people to be secure in their persons, houses, papers, and effects, against unreasonable searches and seizures, shall not be violated, and no Warrants shall issue, but upon probable cause, supported by Oath or affirmation, and particularly describing the place to be searched, and the persons or things to be seized.

Amendment 5
No person shall be held to answer for a capital, or otherwise infamous crime, unless on a presentment or indictment of a Grand Jury, except in cases arising in the land or naval forces, or in the Militia, when in actual service in time of War or public danger; nor shall any person be subject for the same offense to be twice put in jeopardy of life or limb; nor shall be compelled in any criminal case to be a witness against himself, nor be deprived of life,

liberty, or property, without due process of law; nor shall private property be taken for public use, without just compensation.

Amendment 6
In all criminal prosecutions, the accused shall enjoy the right to a speedy and public trial, by an impartial jury of the State and district wherein the crime shall have been committed, which district shall have been previously ascertained by law, and to be informed of the nature and cause of the accusation; to be confronted with the witnesses against him; to have compulsory process for obtaining witnesses in his favor, and to have the Assistance of Counsel for his defence.

Amendment 7
In Suits at common law, where the value in controversy shall exceed twenty dollars, the right of trial by jury shall be preserved, and no fact tried by a jury, shall be otherwise re-examined in any Court of the United States, than according to the rules of the common law.

Amendment 8
Excessive bail shall not be required, nor excessive fines imposed, nor cruel and unusual punishments inflicted.

Amendment 9
The enumeration in the Constitution, of certain rights, shall not be construed to deny or disparage others retained by the people.

Amendment 10
The powers not delegated to the United States by the Constitution, nor prohibited by it to the States, are reserved to the States respectively, or to the people.

Map of Ur

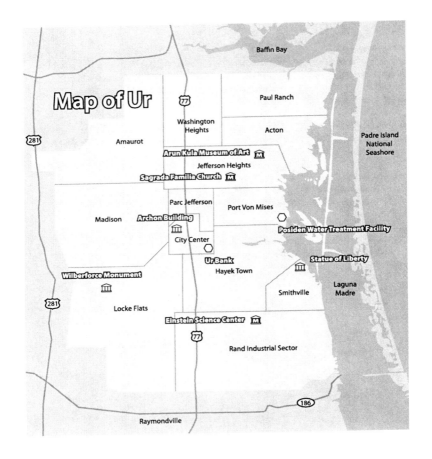

9 781600 200489

"The God who gave us life gave us liberty at the same time; the hand of force may destroy, but cannot disjoin them."
- Thomas Jefferson

"When men yield up the privilege of thinking, the last shadow of liberty quits the horizon."
- Thomas Paine